Truck Stop
Jesus

by
Buck Storm

HERITAGE BEACON
FICTION

TRUCK STOP JESUS BY BUCK STORM
Published by Heritage Beacon Fiction
an imprint of Lighthouse Publishing of the Carolinas
2333 Barton Oaks Dr., Raleigh, NC, 27614

ISBN: 978-1-938499-51-7
Copyright © 2016 by Buck Storm
Cover design by Elaina Lee
Interior design by AtriTeX Technologies P Ltd

Available in print from your local bookstore, online, or from the publisher at:
www.lighthousepublishingofthecarolinas.com

For more information on this book and the author visit: buckstorm.com

Brought to you by the creative team at Lighthouse Publishing of the Carolinas:
Eddie Jones, Ann Tatlock, Shonda Savage, Brian Cross, Paige Boggs

Library of Congress Cataloging-in-Publication Data
Storm, Buck.
Truck Stop Jesus / Buck Storm 1st ed.

Printed in the United States of America

Praise for *Truck Stop Jesus*

Truck Stop Jesus is a winner in every sense of the word. The skillfully written suspense, quirky characters (including a plastic bobble-head Jesus who's quite a conversationalist), a centuries-old mystery, and an unlikely romance keep the reader turning pages—chapter after chapter after chapter to the very satisfying conclusion. Rarely do I recommend that my wife put a book I've just read at the top of her TBR list, but I did that with *Truck Stop Jesus*. It's that good.

~ **Roger E. Bruner**
Author of *The Devil and Pastor Gus, Found in Translation,* and *Lost in Dreams*

Truck Stop Jesus is witty, fast-paced, and highly intriguing. Buck Storm holds a unique voice that makes his storytelling lovable.

~ **Alice J. Wisler**
Award-winning author of *Rain Song* and *How Sweet It Is*

Authenticity is louder than a Marshall Amp stack.... Buck Storm is an authentic singer/songwriter and friend. His heart is loud and has great tone.

~ **Paul Clark**
Singer, songwriter and recording artist

This guy just keeps getting better! His characters spring to life with rich compelling imagery, and he effortlessly ushers the reader into the world of the story, so you never want to leave!

~ **Randy Stonehill**
National Recording Artist, Christian Music Hall of Fame

Truck Stop Jesus is a delightful smorgasbord of twists, turns and unexpected surprises. A literary adventure! I loved it!

~ **Bruce Carroll**
American CCM singer and multi Grammy and
Dove Award-winning recording artist

I predict you'll love *Truck Stop Jesus* as much as I did. And it solidly confirms that Buck's first book, *The Miracle Man*, was certainly no fluke or beginner's luck. Again, the storytelling is top-notch and his eye for detail is in full evidence. In short, you'll have a fine adventure!

~ Bob Bennett
International Award-winning CCM Recording Artist

As a songwriter and as one who loves to read, I was drawn to Buck Storm's beautiful and vivid descriptions. Buck's ability to tell an enthralling story and his wonderful character development kept me turning the pages. With his clever plot twists, I found myself spellbound as to what would happen next. *Truck Stop Jesus!* Hip hip hooray!

~ Mitch McVicker
Dove Award-winning singer/songwriter

ACKNOWLEDGMENTS

The journey to publication is a lot like life—valleys and mountaintops. Here are the people who have stuck with me no matter the altitude…

My family. You are everything, always, forever.

Jim Hart, Hartline Literary Agency.

Ann Tatlock, Managing Editor – Heritage Beacon.

All my friends out there in America-ville and beyond. So many miles and years—you've shown me there is still love and hope in this world. Thanks for the songs.

See you on the road, amigos,

Buck

For Michelle.

It's been a heck of a road-trip. I love you.

Looking forward to many, many miles to come.

PROLOGUE

Dos Escudos

NEW SPAIN (SOUTHERN ARIZONA), 1726

Pregnant with rain, dark clouds hid the moon and held the dawn at bay. No matter. The light would come eventually and with it the Apaches. Too late now. No escape. No way to make it to the relative safety of the mission. Joaquin de Montejo gripped his sword. It would be his last sunrise, of that there was no doubt. Of one other thing, there could be no doubt—he would die fighting. He was a conquistador. A Spaniard. But of even more importance, Montejo blood ran through his veins.

"They'll come soon, brother." Joaquin kept his voice low—a hoarse whisper. "We came into this world together. So shall we enter the next."

Lucas met his gaze through bloodshot eyes. Joaquin's twin, identical except for their attire. Priest and soldier, they must look an odd pair. When had either of them last slept? Lucas' black robe blended into the pre-dawn ink, giving him the ghostly appearance of a disembodied head.

"No," Lucas said. "We split up. We can't let them take us in one place. If Ojeda gets both coins, he may piece it together. It can't happen. For the sake of Spain—for the sake of God."

Joaquin punched his fist into the soft bank of the *arroyo*. "We would have had everything, Lucas!"

Lucas shook his head. "It isn't God's will. Perhaps it never was."

"How do you know Ojeda is behind the Apaches?"

"They've been quiet until now. They never bother the mission. We've traded with them. I hear Ojeda makes promises. Weapons. Whatever they want. He's lying, of course. He gives them only trinkets, but he has a convincing way about him. You know him. No, brother, it wasn't for us to have it."

"Better us than that filthy heathen traitor Ojeda. He followed me here. He's the only other that knew of the coins."

Lucas' face went tight. "Maybe. But stories have a way of traveling. Joaquin, he *can't* get both coins. I'm going to try to make it to the mission. Perhaps they'll follow me. You go the opposite direction, down the arroyo. We may have a chance."

Grasping at straws, and they both knew it.

Joaquin shook his head, his helmet heavy. "No. You'll be killed. At least, here we have my sword. I can hold them off."

"I don't think they'll attack a priest. The Apaches are superstitious about such things. And you have armor their arrows won't penetrate. Besides, you have a good chance if their attention is on me. If I can get to the mission, I can hide one of the coins there. I know places. Good places. You take the other. Escape. Then, when you can, come back. Maybe Ojeda will tire of the chase."

"Ojeda will never tire. Not when the smell of profit is on the wind."

"Then kill him, Joaquin. Make your escape and kill him."

Lucas' face reflected the gathering light. No more time. It was now or never. The two men clasped hands.

"*Vaya con Dios*, Lucas de Montejo, my brother. I'll see you again—if not in this world then in the next."

"*Vaya con Dios*, Joaquin."

Joaquin slipped a dagger from his belt and pressed it into Lucas' hand. "Take this, priest. If God is late to the fight, a good piece of Toledo steel can be a welcome friend."

Lucas hesitated, and then nodded and took the knife. He stood and walked in the direction of the mission, his robe flapping in the wind of the gathering storm. He made it a long stone's throw from the arroyo before a man stepped out of the brush in front of him. Even in the low light, Joaquin recognized the form.

Ojedo.

Words were passed between the men, too low to be heard from Joaquin's position. Lucas walked on, pushing his way past Ojedo. As he did, Ojedo drew his blade.

Joaquin rose from hiding. "Lucas!"

At the sound of his name, Lucas spun, the Toledo dagger in his hand. The move came too late. Ojedo's blade plunged through the priest's mid-section, and Lucas went down.

"Lucas!" Joaquin called again, a sob of rage catching in his throat.

Ojedo turned toward Joaquin, then stumbled and fell himself, the Toledo dagger stuck into his neck to the hilt.

They came then, the Apaches. Out of nowhere and from every direction. How many fell beneath Joaquin's blade and burning anger he didn't know. An eternity of blood, pain, and exhaustion. Finally the moment came that he could raise his arm no more. The clouds opened, and the rain fell with a roar.

Still the Apaches came, and Joaquin cursed them with his dying breath.

After all, he was a Montejo.

CHAPTER ONE

East of the Sun, West of the Moon

SILVERLAKE, CALIFORNIA
AUGUST 3, 2015

Paradise Jones groaned through a mouth stuffed with bitter cotton. "Shut up, bees."

The bees didn't.

She tipped up her sleep mask and squinted an eye against the morning glare, looking around the room for the swarm.

It must have been a dream.

Then why did she still hear them?

Reality, in no particular hurry, wormed its way into her sleep-addled brain. Not bees—her cell phone vibrating. She pulled the mask off. A glance told her the phone wasn't on the nightstand. *Where is the stupid thing?*

It stopped.

Peaceful silence filled the room. She flopped back onto her pillow and pulled the sheet over her head.

Bee-free bliss.

The bees kicked in again. *Ugh.* The cell had to be under the blankets somewhere. It took four vibrations, but she peeled back layers until she found it. She tapped the screen with her thumb and pushed a tangle of blonde hair out of her face. "Ash, this better be good. It's the middle of the night. I'm asleep."

The Boston-soaked accent on the other end of the line shot back with unapologetic directness. "It's almost noon," said Ashleigh Abrams. "Why can't you wake up in the morning like normal people?"

"We went to Jack's Grotto last night. Arnie had me out with some of the studio people. That swing band from the Valley played. I didn't get home till after three."

11

"I'm sure it was the band and not the fact that the studio people were there that kept you, right? You know you're gonna be the next Scarlett. They must like you for the part."

"I don't want to get my hopes up. I'm trying not to think about it."

"Uh huh. Good luck with that."

"I danced with Colin Prince. They took pictures. You think that means anything?"

"Shut up! You danced with Colin Prince?"

"Well, he's playing Rhett, and he was there with the producer. His breath smelled like he ate a dead rat sandwich."

"Colin Prince has halitosis? I'm calling the *National Enquirer*."

"Go ahead. There's no such thing as bad press."

"Scarlett and Rhett, together again. I'm proud of you, you know that? A remake of *Gone with the Wind* is about as big as it gets. You're not gonna forget us little people, right?"

"Oh, give me a break. I don't have the part yet." Paradise pulled the sheet back over her head and the world shrunk to a manageable pink cocoon. A steady drone of street noise shoved its way through the bedroom window. On the other side of the wall, Silverlake—up-and-coming arts pocket of Los Angeles, California— went about its business.

Silverlake. Los Angeles. California. United States. Planet Earth.

And Paradise Jones, an ant in a hole under a pink sheet. How could any living person be so small?

Her friend's voice pushed through the tiny speaker again. "Look, Paradise, you know the scene. Retro's kind of dying. And your whole '40s starlet vibe is pretty out there anyway. This movie happening right now is like winning the Hollywood lottery for you. You were born for it. You're getting cast in the lead role of the biggest remake of the century."

"Please, don't jinx it. Just stop talking about it."

"What does the manager to the stars say?"

"Arnie swears I'm a shoo-in."

"See?"

"You know how many times I've heard that from him?"

"Yeah, well, get over it. Fame's gonna look good on you. And if nothing else, you got to dance with Colin Prince. That's not what I called to talk to you about, though."

"Wait, what do you mean my '40s starlet thing isn't happening?"

"Truth hurts."

"Uh huh. It actually does."

"You know you're my pal. I love your starlet thing. Live in the '40s, who cares? You are who you are, you know?"

"I know."

"So, Paradise," Ashleigh's voice was hesitant, "you're still lying down?"

"I haven't moved. Why? What's wrong with you?" Paradise sat up. "Are you sick or something?"

"I'm your friend, right? I need to tell you something. You need to hear this from a friend. I'm not sure how you'll take it."

"You're scaring me. What's going on? Oh, never mind anyway. Tell me something happy. It's too early in the morning for bad news."

There was a long pause. "It's not happy. You've been asleep, right? You haven't seen the news or anything?"

"I slept like a baby till you woke me. And you know I haven't. I never look at the news. What's going on? What are you afraid to say?" Now the thumping in her chest competed with the traffic noise.

"It's your dad. You always say you're not close, right?"

"I hardly know the guy. Why?"

"I'm not sure how to say this, but at least, that makes it easier."

"Say what?"

"I'm really not good at this sort of thing, you know?"

"What sort of thing?"

"He's dead, Paradise. He's ... been killed."

The world went silent. *Silverlake. Los Angeles. California. United States. Planet Earth. Universe ...* All quiet.

Killed? Her father? Paradise searched deep inside for emotion, for some feeling, but came up blank. Only numbness. "Does my mom know?" *A stupid thing to ask.*

"I don't know," Ashleigh said. "I just heard myself. On the TV at work. I knew you'd still be in bed. I didn't want you to hear it on the news or from some stranger or something."

"Okay. Thanks. I appreciate it. How's life in the exciting world of movie-biz catering?" Paradise dropped her feet to the floor.

"Getting ready for a hardware store commercial shoot tomorrow. And don't change the subject. Why do you sound chipper? What are you doing?"

"Thanks for calling. It's sad, I suppose, but people die, right?"

"Are you okay?"

"Of course."

"Paradise … "

"Oh, I don't know, Ash. What am I supposed to say? I hardly knew him. Am I a bad person if I'm not broken up?"

"Yeah, I know. But he was still your dad."

Her dad. Was that true? She supposed it was. "How? How did he get killed?"

"T-boned. Driving that old Fiat Spider of his. They said he went through a light, and a truck hit him right in the driver-side door. There were pictures on the news. It's all over the Internet."

"Was he drinking?" Paradise set the phone on the nightstand and pressed the speaker button.

"I don't know. Probably. Wasn't he always? Does it matter?"

"Where did it happen?"

"It's crazy. You're not gonna believe it. Hollywood and Vine."

Hollywood and Vine? So the great Gregory Jones cashed in his chips not a hundred yards from the Walk of Fame star he'd always dreamed of. Like something out of one of his screenplays.

"Hey, Ash. Thanks for calling. I'm going to ring off, okay? I have a busy day." Paradise picked up the phone and carried it with her as she headed for the bathroom.

"Ring off? Why do I always feel like I'm talking to Audrey Hepburn with you? What movie did you get 'ring off' from? And no, you don't—you never have a busy day. You're not okay. I'm coming over. I can get the afternoon off."

"You think I sound like Audrey Hepburn?"

"That's all you got from that? Yeah, if Doris Day and Audrey Hepburn had a weird, raspy kid, it'd be you."

"What do you mean raspy?"

"Here we go. Everybody hang on while the world spins around Paradise Jones. You get raspy sometimes. Relax. It's adorable. And you're only talking about it because your dad just died. Stop deflecting. I'm coming over."

"No, please … Seriously, I'm fine. I'll see you later. Don't worry about me. Like I said, I hardly knew him."

Ashleigh sighed. "Okay, call me if you need me. Anytime. Seriously, I can come."

"Thanks, Ash. Bye." She hung up before her friend could reply.

In the bathroom, Paradise leaned her hands on the sink and studied herself in the mirror. Bright, blonde hair a mess. Last night's makeup didn't work this morning. She'd been too tired to deal with it when she got home. Red lipstick slightly smeared like some twisted Andy Warhol painting. At least her gray eyes were wide and clear. No bloodshot remnants of last night's Jack's Grotto adventure. Thank goodness she wasn't a drinker.

Drinker ... Her father came into focus, a wraith tugging on her sleeve. Could it be true? He was really dead? Larger-than-life Gregory Jones? Again, she ran through a quick emotional inventory. *I should feel something, right?* He'd been her father, after all. At least as much of a father as she'd ever known. But, nothing. Nothing at all.

She was a blank. An empty pocket.

The face in the mirror stared at her, hollow as a ghost. The smattering of freckles across her nose stood out stark against her pale skin. *How could a person not feel?*

She dropped her head to the sink and vomited.

Okay, maybe she *did* feel something.

Pulling up the story on the Internet was a mistake. The mangled Fiat, the sheet-covered body being wheeled into the back of the ambulance. The reporter relaying the event in that ridiculous lilted reporter-eeze. "Gregory Jones, actor and '70s heartthrob, was killed today in an automobile accident in Hollywood. Jones starred in a handful of big-budget thrillers but was best known for his role as Detective Matt Gunn in NBC's hit crime drama *After Sunset*. The award-winning show ran an impressive nine years, first airing in 1973 and continuing until 1982."

Paradise counted 1973 to 1982, ticking the years off on her fingers. *What are you doing? Get a grip ...*

Big smile on the bubbly reporter's perfect face ... In other news ...

Paradise closed her laptop. So that's it. Gregory Jones' last hurrah. A giant, invisible fist squeezed her insides, and nausea threatened again.

Billie Holiday began singing "East of the Sun." New ringtone. Paradise didn't recognize the number.

"Hello?"

"Paradise Jones?" A man's voice, warm but unfamiliar.

She hesitated. "Yes?"

"Hi, Miss Jones. Richard Ferguson from the *Los Angeles Times*. Listen, sorry for your loss. I was hoping you'd have a moment to answer just a few questions about your father?"

The nausea pushed harder. Her head spun. "I'm sorry. Who is this? How did you get this number?"

"Richard Ferguson. *LA Times*. Just a few questions, Miss Jones. I won't impose on your time."

"I'm sorry. You *are* imposing on my time. Listen, I didn't know my dad, okay? I met him a few times, and that's it. He's dead. End of story. Please don't call back."

She terminated the call with a tap of her thumb.

The apartment walls closed in. She should go somewhere, do something. In the kitchen, she used a bottle opener to pop the top off a Coke bottle. She looked at it, then set it on the counter without taking a sip.

Billie started to sing again. Anger surged. Something else, too. Grief? She grabbed for the phone. Her hand shook so badly she almost dropped it. "I asked you not to call back."

A woman's voice this time. Cultured and every bit as cool as the reporter's had been warm. "Paradise. It's Eve."

Eve. Her mother. That hadn't taken long.

"Where are you calling from, Mom?"

Her mother hated being called Mom.

"New York. I'm shopping. You've heard, I suppose."

"Yes, Mom. I've heard."

"Well, it's no surprise to me."

"Uh huh. You don't sound very upset."

"Don't judge me, Paradise. The man was a trial."

Paradise picked up the Coke and took a sip, then poured the rest into the sink. "He was your husband once. *And* your meal ticket. Doesn't that count for anything?"

"We were married for five minutes. He was about as much a husband as he was a father, don't you think? And if I were you, I wouldn't be making any cracks about meal tickets."

Her mother had a point. Say what you might about the psychological trauma of Eve's erratic, on again-off again parenting, she never failed to send money in

Paradise's direction. Even now, and Paradise was twenty-four, the checks came. Larger on birthdays and at Christmas in lieu of presents.

The urge to crawl back under the pink sheet overwhelmed. "Yes, Mom. I'm not complaining. I appreciate all your help. But maybe I'll be able to stand on my own two feet soon. I'm up for a part. It looks pretty good."

"Paradise, you're always up for a part."

"I'm tired, Mom. Why are you calling? When will you be back in LA?"

"That's what I wanted to tell you. I won't make it to any funeral. Burt and I have plans to go to Cabo, and I can't break them. I'm shopping for the trip now."

Burt—therapist to the stars. Benevolent stepfather with wandering hands. Eve's meal ticket number-two.

Her mother went on. "I talked to your father's attorney ten minutes ago. Gregory left everything to you. Not that I'd expect much."

"Well, Mom. Don't trouble yourself. I'm sure things will work out on this end."

"Paradise … Are you going to be all right?"

Motherly Eve? That stranger didn't rear her head very often.

"Yes, Mom, I think so."

"Come to the house when we get back, all right?"

"Sure."

"You can tell me all about the new part then. I have to run. Burt's waiting. You know how he gets."

"Uh huh. I know how he gets." *Understatement of the year.*

"I'll be in touch soon. You'll be fine, I'm sure."

The line went dead before Paradise could respond.

She'd be fine … Eve was sure. *Okay.*

Her father had left everything to her? Why? What everything? Gregory Jones hadn't worked in years, and he certainly wasn't one to save. Maybe she should call the man from the *Times* back. At least she could get some publicity out of it.

Billie Holiday sang again and Arnie, her agent, offered a television-preacher smile from the glowing cell phone screen.

She let Billie sing half a verse before she picked it up. "Hey, Arnie."

"So, I know you weren't close to your old man, but you need anything? You know, I mean I'm sorry for your loss and all."

Arnie had grown up in Orange County but never failed to bring his best Brooklyn wiseguy accent to any conversation. He said it gave him an edge.

"No. I'm okay. Just tired after last night."

"Yeah, well, get used to it. We're just getting started. Now you've got six weeks or so before the reading and rehearsals. Man, you should see the sets they're building down on the lot. What do you have going this afternoon? I'll run you over there. Kinda get your mind off this other deal, ya know?"

Other deal? Was that what you called it when your dad got crushed in an Italian tin can?

"I don't think so, Arnie. I don't even have the part. I'm tired. I think I'll just stay here today. Maybe watch a movie or something."

"*Yet*. You don't have the part *yet*. I'm telling you, your name is the one that keeps coming up. Let me ask you something—you're a razor's edge away from scoring the role of a lifetime. You know how hard I worked to get you this shot? You know how many big-name stars wanted it? Not to mention the legion of no-names—you included. Know what I'm saying? I'm a miracle worker; that's what *I* am. I'm turning water into wine here. Why aren't you excited?"

"Are you kidding? Excited? Of course, I'm excited. If I don't get this part, I'm going to bang my head against the wall until I bleed out of my ears. And I'm not exactly a no-name. I've been in things."

"B horror flicks and pet shampoo commercials don't count. Every Midwest wannabe and their grandma's done that. Look, kid, you been dreaming about this your whole life. You were made for this movie. You *are* a classic actress. Don't let this Gregory Jones thing pull your eyes off the prize. We need this."

Paradise rubbed her temple with her free hand. "Arnie, he just died. Please. I appreciate all you've done for me. And I *am* happy. *Really* I am. I'm dying for the part. I don't know what's wrong with me. Maybe I just don't want to get my hopes up."

"Paradise, cut it out. I can tell when you're feeling sorry for yourself. First, you hardly knew the guy. Second, you're right there—on the cusp. Keep focused on what's important here. You're special. You're a rare breed. One in a million and all that. You belong on the red carpet. And you'll be there, I promise."

What the world needed—another Arnie pep talk.

Am I happy? How could a person be surrounded by people all the time and still feel lonely? Like watching herself in a movie—an outside spectator to her own life. Maybe she was going crazy.

Focus ... "You really think I'm going to get the part?"

"I know it. I'm an old dog. I get how this town works, and I feel this one in my bones. So how about it? Let's go see the set."

"Thanks, Arnie. I really need to be alone for a while. I'll get out there, I promise."

"Okay, kid, whatever. Tomorrow, though, Beverly Hills Hotel. I want you to meet some people. Real players. Colin Prince will be there, too. I gather you made quite an impression on him last night. He wants to see you again. I'll pick you up about eleven, sound good?"

"Tell him to brush his teeth."

"What?"

"Nothing. Okay. I'll be ready. Thanks for watching out for me."

"Hey, sorry again about your old man. That's a hard deal. But remember, focus on what's important. Focus on *right now*."

"See you tomorrow, Arnie."

Makeup gone, back under the sheet, the world turned pink again. Billie sang Ashleigh's face onto the phone screen, but Paradise didn't answer. Gregory Jones was dead. Eve was somewhere between LA and Cabo via New York or Paris or wherever the wind blew her.

Paradise Jones, hidden safely away in some '40s movie. Feet sore from dancing with one of the biggest leading men on the planet. Everything she'd ever dreamed of very possibly within her reach.

Pink cocoon. Silverlake. Los Angeles. USA. Planet Earth. Universe.

Paradise Jones … Alone.

Chapter Two

The Green Monster

Paradise, Arizona
August 6, 2015

Small towns tend to rest beneath the biggest skies. Vast expanses of blue that stretch away on every side, horizon to horizon. The sky holds clouds, suns, planets, and stars. Galaxies nestle in its depths. But no sky is big enough to hold dreams. Especially small-town dreams.

At thirty-eight hundred feet above sea level, Paradise, Arizona, didn't suffer the regular triple-digit temperatures of Phoenix or Tucson, but ninety-six came close enough. The cloudless sky hung above. A deep blue inverted ocean stuffed full of dreams.

A perfect day for baseball.

Doc Morales stretched, then swung the bat in a lazy arc. Bending at the waist, he let his knuckles brush the dust. Hey, twenty-six years old, three years out of the game, and he could still find the ground. Not bad, considering. Upright again, he studied the red-dirt field. A sad sight by any standard. No fence marked the perimeter. Deep ruts grooved the unmarked base lines leading out from the rusty chain link—a sorry excuse for a backstop. The players on the field weren't much better. A rag-tag bunch ranging in age from about thirteen to thirty. A couple of them wore mismatched uniforms. Others, just shorts and T-shirts.

"Let's go, little brother." Doc's brother played third base and stood out like the proverbial sore thumb. His black cassock covered his cleats, at odds with the sweat-stained cowboy hat—a holdout from his rodeo days—that shaded his eyes from the bright Arizona sun. Father Jake, as everyone except Doc called him, smacked a hand into his glove and spat into the dust.

Micky Granger's scratchy taunt pulled Doc back to the plate. "You gonna hit today, superstar? No rush or anything."

Micky's catcher's gear bore the green and white colors of Yavapai College.

"Yavapai know you stole their stuff, Mickey?" Doc stepped into the batter's box. No white chalk marked it, just a rectangle scraped into the dust with somebody's cleat.

"They'll survive. I'll take it back in the fall. Besides, they can't live without me. I own that place."

"Uh huh. Sure you do. What'd you hit last year, one twenty-seven?" Doc stepped back out of the box. He leaned and grabbed a handful of dust and rubbed it on his hands.

"I was in a slump. Happens to everybody," Mickey said. "C'mon, man. What're you doing? Waiting for the groundskeeper to mow the dirt?"

"Doc, it's hot out here," Jake called from third.

"Relax. You're a priest. Isn't patience supposed to be one of your virtues? Maybe they ought to think about making those dresses in something besides black." Doc stepped back into the box and kicked his cleats into the soft earth, tapping the plate with the end of the bat.

Jake spat again. "Just hit the ball, little brother!"

"I hate it when he calls me that," Doc grumbled.

"Yeah, well, that's why he does it." Mickey lifted his catcher's mask, spat, then shouted to the pitcher, a giant kid with acne-pocked cheeks. "Let's go, Trevor. Sit this clown down."

Doc air-swung over the plate. "So this guy drove all the way up here from Phoenix just to pitch against me?"

"What can I say?" Mickey said. "You're a legend. Get over yourself."

All business, Trevor kicked at the dirt in front of the rubber. A cloud of dust rose up to his knees. He bent forward, ball behind his back, and stared Doc down from under his hat brim.

"Looks like he's got your number, Morales. What'd you do, insult his mom?" Mickey asked.

Doc eyed the pitcher. "Who is this guy? Satan? I think his eyes are glowing red. Nope, never met him. How tall is he? Six-five? Six-six? Looks like he could hand the ball to you without leaving the mound."

"He's starting for ASU this year. As a freshman, if you can believe it."

Trevor shook off a sign with a quick jerk of his head.

"Didn't like that one, huh?" Doc said. "What'd you call? Fastball?"

Mickey leaned forward and brushed dirt from the plate. "Don't laugh, superstar. Kid's got a filthy splitter. You won't touch him."

Trevor shook off another sign.

"You calling pitches or just suggesting 'em today, Mickey?" Doc let the bat fall onto his shoulder and straightened. "This is getting boring."

"He worked out with the Diamondbacks last spring. Going to the bigs for sure. But he thinks he knows it all. Throws what he wants. I'm just a lowly Junior College guy. What do I know, right?"

Trevor finally nodded at one of Mickey's signs and went into his wind-up.

"Fastball outside corner," Doc said.

The ball popped Mickey's glove like a cannon shot.

"How'd you know that?" Mickey asked.

"What can I say? I'm a baseball prophet."

"Strike!" Mickey shouted.

Doc turned and looked down at the catcher. "Strike?"

"You heard me."

"It was six inches outside."

"Strike!" Mickey called again.

Doc shook his head. "I wanna see the replay. Kid's bringing some heat, though."

"Every bit of ninety-six, ninety-seven, I bet," Mickey said. "Just ask my hand."

Doc stepped out of the batter's box and rolled his head back. The sun warmed his shoulder muscles. Good and loose.

"C'mon, Morales. Let's go. Between you and Trevor, it'll be dark before this is over." Mickey tossed the ball back to the pitcher.

Doc stepped back in the box.

Trevor caught the ball and walked off the back of the mound, rubbing it hard with his palm. When he finally stepped back on the rubber, he shook off four consecutive signs before he nodded.

"It's like a million degrees out here. I'm gonna kill him," Mickey mumbled.

"This guy's got what you call a million-dollar arm and a ten-cent head," Doc said.

Trevor came set and gave a very Major-League-looking glance at first.

"Why's he looking at first? He does know there's nobody on base, right?" Doc said.

Mickey sighed. "Too much ESPN. Unbelievable, man. The guy's probably gonna make more money his first year in the show than I'll see in my lifetime."

Trevor rocked back for his delivery.

"Fastball inside," Doc said. He leaned back as the ball came in hard, brushing the front of his T-shirt.

"That's getting annoying, you calling 'em like that." Mickey threw the ball back. "Strike!"

Doc shook his head. "You're the worst catcher-slash-ump I've ever seen, you know that?"

"You get what you pay for. Let's go."

"Why? I've got five minutes of watching Nolan Ryan Jr. shake off signs before he throws the ball again."

"Not this time, superstar. Get in the box."

Doc looked out over the field and took a deep breath, savoring the moment. He loved this game. Sure, the Arizona air was dry, not humid like Florida spring training. And the red dirt was a far cry from the manicured grass of any real ballpark, but baseball was baseball. And baseball was life.

Don't go there.

He shoved uninvited memories to the back of his brain and pointed his bat out to left. "Hey, Mickey, what do you see out there?"

"Dirt, scrub oak, and a bunch of nothing. Why?"

"C'mon, man. Use your imagination. You don't see it?" Doc dug his cleats into the batter's box one at a time, lifting his left hand to hold off the pitch.

On the mound, Trevor leaned over, his eyes invisible in the shade of his Diamondbacks hat brim.

Mickey pounded a fist into his glove. "See what?"

"The Green Monster, man. The left field wall at Fenway."

Mickey snorted a laugh. "I know what the Green Monster is. This is Paradise, Arizona, genius. Not Boston. This ain't no Fenway Park."

On the mound, Trevor nodded and came set, then rocked back for his delivery.

Doc grinned. "It's always Fenway, Mick."

Trevor released, his arm flashing in the sun.

"Splitter," Doc said, and swung.

The sound of the bat hitting the ball cracked through the clear afternoon air. "Man!" Mickey stood, cleats scraping. "Say goodbye to that one. You teed off on his splitter. Unbelievable. I woulda said it was impossible."

"Yeah, well, he left it up." Doc watched the ball go for a full three seconds before he dropped the bat and headed to first. "Green Monster, Mickey. Right over the Green Monster, man."

On the mound, Trevor shook his head and spat at the dust.

As Doc rounded third, Jake smacked him on the back with his glove. "Last ball. You hit it, you find it."

Doc finished his lap with a one-legged jump onto home plate, favoring his good knee, then turned and walked back down the third base line toward Jake. "Hey, Cade! Get on the ball-search, kid!"

Cade, the left fielder, threw his glove down. "C'mon, Doc! You hit it! Why do I got to find it?"

"Because you're the kid out here! You want to play, you got to pay."

Cade shook his head and trotted out toward the low trees and brush that ringed the outfield. Doc and Jake found the shade of a *palos verde* tree just off the third base line. The rest of the players walked off the field, talking and laughing. They headed for an assortment of cars, trucks and bikes that had been parked a distance away to avoid foul balls. Several commented to Doc about the homer.

Trevor threw Doc a wave as he passed. "You got every bit of that one, Morales. Next time."

"Sure. You'll knock 'em dead at ASU, Trevor. See ya. And try to leave that splitter down," Doc said.

"Yeah."

Mickey approached, his catcher's glove propped on top of his backward hat, arms full of gear. "How'd you know he'd bring the splitter?"

Doc shrugged. "Two strikes. Gotta be the money pitch. He's gonna have to learn to mix it up."

"I guess so. Well, see you guys." Mickey tossed his gear into the back of his ancient Nissan pickup.

"Adios, Mick," Jake said.

Mickey's tires kicked gravel and dust as he pulled away.

Doc glanced at his brother. Jake had always been the handsome one, although he'd heard people say the same about him. At six feet two, Jake had Doc by three years and three inches. Unruly, black hair curled its way out from under the battered, straw cowboy hat. Dark eyes smiled above an aquiline nose. Father Jake the priest. The invincible. Nearly a year since his brother had taken the holy orders, and Doc still couldn't get used to it.

Jake bent and fished a couple of water bottles out of a dented Coleman ice chest. He shot one at Doc, and it thumped off his chest. Doc caught it on the bounce, unscrewed the lid and took a long drink.

"So, little brother." Jake's crow's feet deepened. "Dreaming about Fenway? That was a long-hit ball."

"Fenway." Doc sighed. "I wish. I hit that thing four-fifty at least, but practically limped around the bases. No Fenway for me."

"You'll get your shot."

"Won't be at Boston. With this knee, it won't be in the Majors at all. That ship sailed three years ago."

Jake took a pull from his water and his Adam's apple dipped. He tipped the top of the bottle toward Doc. "You put the uniform on. Stood on the grass. That's more than most can say." Relaxed. Quiet, but strong. The same voice that had calmed Doc for as long as he could remember.

Doc pulled a dead twig off the tree and flicked it away, following it with his eyes. "A year in Double-A, another in Triple. I worked my butt off, man. One at bat, that's it. One at bat in the Majors. That God of yours has a twisted sense of humor."

"Your God too, Doc. Don't forget that. And it wasn't funny."

Doc shoved his glove into a duffle bag. "I guess it wasn't."

"There's more to life than baseball, Doc."

"So you keep telling me."

"And so I'll *keep* telling you till you get it through that fat head of yours." Jake hiked up his black robe and examined a bloody shin.

"More to life than baseball ... Don't you know the Pope is a Red Sox fan?"

"Nah. Cardinals."

"You didn't just say that." Doc rubbed the water bottle across his forehead and let the condensation drip down his face.

"Father Jake! Hey, Doc! You guys gotta see this!" Cade's adolescent voice cracked through the still afternoon. He waved his ball glove over his head from the edge of the brush behind left field. "Seriously! C'mon!"

Jake took off his hat and wiped sweat from his brow with the back of his sleeve. He squinted toward the junior left fielder. "What do ya suppose he wants?"

"Probably found a lizard. Kid's excitable," Doc said.

Neither of the men moved.

"I'm serious! C'mon!" Cade pressed.

"What's up, Cade?" Doc called. "It's hot, man!"

"C'mon, Doc! You guys gotta see this! I found a dead guy!"

Chapter Three

Devils, Dust, and a Serious Lack of Pockets

"Four hundred and fifty feet at least. Don't you think?" Doc stood at the bottom of a shallow wash, looking back toward the ball field.

"What?" Jake said.

Doc bent down and grabbed the baseball out of the sand. "Four-fifty at least. I knocked the cover off this ball."

"Still has a cover."

"Four-fifty ... At least."

"Hey, Earth to Doc. That's a skull lying there. These are human bones. Why are you talking about baseball?"

Doc shifted his gaze back to the subject at hand. "Yeah. The kid knows his dead guys. Got to give him that."

"We need to call the police." Jake squatted on his heels and poked at the skull with his finger. "You got your cell on you, Doc?"

"No. Where's yours? No pockets in the robe?"

"At the mission."

"Mine's in the truck. Joke's on us—you never know when you're gonna stumble across bones. Always be prepared. Boy Scout motto, right, Cade?"

"I'm not a Boy Scout." Cade's face was pale.

"Yeah, apparently neither were we. You all right, kid?" Doc asked.

"I never saw anybody dead before that wasn't on TV. That's a real skull, man. You want me to run back and get your phone?"

"Nah. I don't think there's any hurry," Doc said. "This guy's not going anywhere. He hasn't for a while."

Jake looked up at him. "What d'you mean?"

Doc kicked at what looked like an old can sticking out of the earth. His cleat clanked on metal. Dropping to one knee, he pulled a rusted helmet from the sand. He brushed it off and held it up in the light. "Conquistador. Spanish. This guy's

been here a long, long time. The storm last week must have undercut the bank."
He pointed at the edge of the wash. "When the sand collapsed above the cut, our
boy here probably saw the light of day for the first time in a few hundred years."

Jake took the helmet and examined it, turning it over in his hands.
"Conquistador. No doubt. You're right."

Color began to return to Cade's cheeks. "So that helmet used to protect that
skull? That's crazy."

"Looks like it," Jake said. "He must have been connected to the mission
somehow."

"Seriously?" Cade said. "How long has the mission been here?"

Doc picked up a stick and began scraping the sand around the bones. "Don't
they teach history in school anymore?"

"The mission was established in 1692." Jake stood and handed the helmet to
Doc.

Doc tossed it up and caught it again. "Spoken like a tried-and-true tour
guide."

"Somebody has to do it," Jake said.

"Uh huh. For the three and a half visitors that get lost off I-10 and wind up
in Paradise every year."

"Sixteen ninety-two?" Cade said. "Wasn't that before America was even here?"

"It was," Jake said. "But the Spanish explored this country as early as the fifteen
hundreds. Cabeza de Vaca came through here in 1536. And Native Americans
had been here for thousands of years before the Spanish showed up."

Cade nudged a bone with his toe. "So this guy was born in Spain?"

Jake pushed his hat back and crossed his arms, studying the bones. "Good
chance of it. If he was, he died a long way from home."

A dust devil danced across the wash and peppered them with sand. Jake's
cassock rippled and snapped in the sudden gust. The spinning tower of dirt,
sand, and pieces of trash whipped away across a landscape dotted with scrub oak
and occasional pine. It slowed and dissipated when it reached the baseball field.
Restlessness put a hand on Doc's shoulder, an unwelcome visitor that showed up
more and more frequently of late.

Some distance beyond the field, Jardin de Dios Mission stood white against
the deep blue of the Arizona sky, its bell tower high and domed. Just outside the
adobe rear wall, Doc's old Airstream trailer shone—a tiny silver bullet reflecting
the light of the late afternoon sun.

The mission itself made up one of the buildings that ringed downtown Paradise. Doc loved this community. The mom-and-pop storefronts that edged the old town square centered by its massive oak tree. The neighborhoods that stretched up into the hills and down the wide valley toward the low-lying ranches. This was home. He had no real desire to leave, but every once in a while, the feeling came. The restlessness. A small voice deep inside, inviting and urging him on to new things. Unexplored Fenway Parks with their own Green Monsters whispering his name from left field.

"We need to tell someone," Jake said. "This could be historically important. Doc, quit scratching around with that stick."

"It's not a crime scene, Jake. You've been watching too much TV."

Doc's stick bumped something just below the surface of the loose sand. He tapped down a couple of times and received a dull metallic thump. He grinned at Jake. "Now tell me you're not curious about that, Father Jake the Priest."

The inward battle with his conscience played in living color across Jake's face.

Doc thumped again. "C'mon, Jakey boy. You know you want to dig it up."

Jake caved with a shake of his head. "All right. Do it."

"Yes!" Cade said.

Doc began scraping the sand and clay away with his stick. Cade dropped and used his hands. The outline of what appeared to be a large metal turtle shell materialized.

Cade leaned back on his heels. "Whoa!"

"It's a breastplate." Doc brushed more sand. Digging his fingers in deep around what he thought might be the edge of the piece of armor, he found a lip and pulled. The shell lifted. "Looks like it's in good shape. I wonder what one of these things is worth?"

"Nothing to us." Jake squatted next to him, tracing his finger along the metal. "This'll go in a museum."

Cade dropped to his hands and knees. "Oh, man. Look underneath."

Doc lifted the breastplate a little more, revealing an intact human ribcage.

"Okay, Doc." Jake stood. "That's enough. Time to call in someone who knows this kind of thing."

"That's you. You're in charge of the museum, right?"

"Yeah, but not digging up bodies."

"It's bones, not a body."

"Just the same …" Jake said.

"Huh." Doc held the armor propped with one hand and bent low to the ground, studying the new bones. "Check this out." He reached into the cavity and pulled a worn but intact leather pouch from the sand between the ribs.

"How could that have lasted all this time?" Cade asked.

"Got me. But it did," Doc said.

"They've found leather a whole lot older than the conquistadors in canyons north of here," Jake said. "Couple thousand years even. I've read about it. The dry climate can preserve things for a long, long time."

Doc worked the leather strip that tied the top of the pouch. "He must have kept this shoved under his armor for safekeeping. I wonder what's in it."

"Money?" Cade crowded close to Doc's side.

The strip came free. Doc angled the pouch, trying to make use of the sunlight. He peered inside. "This is actually creepy. The last guy to open this thing is a pile of bones right now."

"What's in it, Doc? C'mon." Cade stretched to his tiptoes, trying to see into the pouch.

Something glinted at the bottom of the sack. Doc very carefully inserted his index and middle fingers into the stiff leather. Something hard. Slowly he pulled out a large gold coin.

"Whoa. It *is* money. Let me see it, Doc." Cade reached for the coin.

"Easy, Junior." Doc turned the coin over in his palm. "Hey, Jake. I think this is gold."

"Looks like gold. Is it heavy?"

Doc hefted it, considering. "Yeah. Pretty heavy."

Jake leaned in for a closer look. "It's an eight *escudos* coin—Spanish currency—definitely gold. We have one at the museum."

Doc held the coin up in the light. "No kidding? You mean like a doubloon? Or pieces-of-eight? As in pirates?"

Jake nodded. "Kind of. But a doubloon was a two escudos coin. One-fourth the size and weight of this one. Pieces-of-eight were silver. Our man here got his hands on an eight escudos."

Doc held the coin close to his face. "Good for him, except for the dying in a ditch part. But I think you got this one wrong. It says dos escudos right on it. I can read it clear as day."

"No, a dos escudos would be a lot smaller. That one's more like silver-dollar size. Even a little bigger. Let me see it."

Doc passed the coin to his brother.

Jake held it up. "Look, right here above the cross. See that number eight? That means eight escudos."

"Yeah, but look at the other side. Dos Escudos," Doc said.

Jake flipped it. "It would be impossible to ... Huh ..."

"What?" Doc said.

Jake stared at the coin. "This couldn't be ..."

"Couldn't be what?" Doc said.

Jake glanced at Doc. "There's this story ..."

Doc took the coin back and looked at it again. "What story? What are you talking about?"

Jake climbed the bank of the wash and headed toward the falling sun. Fresh wind whipped his robe. Jake the Priest—like some minor god in a Hollywood production. "C'mon, Doc. I want to show that coin to Paco."

Chapter Four

LA Normal

Three days after the news of her father's death, Paradise found herself standing in his shabby Van Nuys apartment. A dingy-curtain-shrouded cave of a place. Gregory Jones had lived here? She'd never known. *What kind of daughter doesn't know where her father lives?*

One whose father never showed his face. Never told her he loved her. Never called. One whose father left her life a long time ago.

He was nobody to her. She was nobody to him.

Then why does it hurt so badly?

It had been a couple of years since she'd seen him. She'd been singing then, or trying to, filling in between acting auditions and bit parts. But nobody wanted to hear big-band jazz—at least in the fickle LA club scene. The aging star, still handsome, had waltzed into The Mint nightclub during one of her sets like Sinatra stepping into the Vegas Sands. All heads turned.

They'd chatted a bit. Just small talk. She'd felt uncomfortable and tongue-tied. People took pictures. He'd posed with the band. It had been nice enough but hardly a father-daughter moment. It hadn't struck her until later that he'd somehow known where she would be singing. He must have kept *some* sort of tabs on her. Tears, familiar pests these last three days, welled and she brushed them away with a hard palm.

Just get the thing over with.

She glanced at Ashleigh, who was thankfully too busy rummaging through a desk drawer to notice Paradise's tears. Paradise took a deep breath and went on looking around this place that had been her father's home. The apartment presented like something from a '70s sitcom. Or maybe one of the sets from *After Sunset*. Right down to the worn, orange shag carpet and avocado appliances. Pictures hung here and there with no particular theme or order, as if there had been very little or no planning involved. She should take them, she supposed. Gregory

Jones with various stars and dignitaries. A shot of him receiving an Emmy—wide lapels and feathered hair. There was a picture of him and a younger Eve, as well as one of the three of them together. *Too young to remember that one.* And most surprising—a framed article from the *LA Independent* about Paradise's acting and singing. The headline read *PARADISE JONES, Eccentric Talent or Just Eccentric?* She scanned the article though she'd seen it a hundred times. The familiar lines about halfway down drew her eyes. "What's it like to wake up every morning to 1945? Ask Paradise Jones! Yes, retro's in, but this wannabe starlet marches to the enchanted beat of her own drummer—or sousaphone player. Let's just say hers is no act, brother. Say hello to the happy little voices in your head for us, Miss Jones."

She'd leave that one alone.

Ashleigh pushed open a sliding glass door at the back of the living room and pulled back the heavy drape. "Ugh, it smells like a barroom on Sunday morning in here."

California light flooded the room, and Paradise shielded her eyes. "Except it's Thursday."

"I know I'm not supposed to speak ill of the dead and all that, but this place is really depressing."

"I can't argue with you. It's strange I've never been here before."

The two of them moved through the apartment, emptying drawers and cabinets, sorting and boxing.

Everything of value, pictures included, could just about fit into a couple large boxes. At least, the items Paradise cared to take. She'd agreed to leave the furniture and clothing for the landlord to help cover back rent. The closet held three decades of moth-balled clothes and shoes but little else. The dresser, in turn, offered up no surprises.

The hall closet sported a vacuum and Paradise surprised herself by using it. She'd never been much of a housekeeper—must have taken after her father. After a quick once-over of the hallway and bedroom, she put it back and found Ash dragging a wet mop across the Saltillo tile kitchen floor.

Ash's bright pink rubber gloves with plastic daisies hot-glued to them brought a smile to Paradise's lips. Webster's Dictionary could have had a picture of Ashleigh next to its entry for *color*. A staple in LA's vintage scene, today her friend wore capris, a madras blouse, and pink, cat-eye glasses with fake diamonds on the frames. Her black hair stood at sprayed attention in a mile-high beehive. A cartoon of a '50s housewife, if it weren't for the full-sleeve tattoos.

While Ashleigh worked hard at retro, Paradise had tumbled in by default. The glamour of Hollywood's Golden Age had drawn her for as long as she could remember. Ava Gardner, Irene Dunn, Esther Williams—they'd had it all. And could anyone ever have been happier than Doris Day? Paradise never forgot that fateful night in fourth grade—just a year after Eve had married Burt—when Audrey Hepburn stepped through the TV screen into her bedroom and dazzled with glamour and style. Saturday morning she'd skipped cartoons and insisted Eve take her shopping. No argument there. Eve raised spending to an art form. At first, her mother laughed off Paradise's obsession with all things vintage Tinsel Town, dismissing it as a fad. Fifteen years later, nobody laughed anymore.

The hardcore retro purists down on Melrose Avenue talked a big game about giving up all things modern. Paradise never thought like that. She never really thought about it at all. She just *was*. Besides, Audrey and Doris would have reveled in the convenience of smartphones and quick access to the Internet. Paradise was simply Paradise, able to transform to vintage starlet of her choice with the change of an outfit. Maybe born a few decades too late, but why let that stop her? Her closet was stuffed to overflowing with outfits, dresses, and shoes in profusion from that more glamorous time.

Lights, fame, Rodeo Drive—she'd attempted acting. Her lineage and natural beauty gave her a leg up on the competition, but no one made great movies anymore. She dreamed of Lauren Bacall in *Key Largo* and wound up with some bit part in *Scream One Hundred and Six*. Singing seemed a good choice. She could hold a tune. Just the classics—quirky enough to work in a town like Los Angeles. She'd scrapped it out in the clubs for a while. Who was she kidding? Forever, in LA years. Jack's Grotto, The Viper Room, The Mint, anywhere her band could land a gig; she'd played them all. Now, though, thanks to Arnie's tenacity, the role of a lifetime—Scarlett in the remake of *Gone with the Wind*—looked like a very real possibility. She might actually be part of the highest budgeted and most talked-about film of the year, maybe of the decade.

"So let me get this straight." Ashleigh pushed her glasses up with a gloved index finger. "Your inheritance from your television-star dad is getting to clean his weird, depressing apartment?"

Paradise held up a cardboard box of things worth taking. "That's the size of it. Not a lot here besides dirt, I'm afraid."

"Didn't he win an Emmy or something like that? Seems like one of those things would be worth a buck or six. Or at least, worth keeping."

"I didn't see anything like that. If he had some awards, he must have pawned them or sold them."

Ashleigh set the mop down, then picked up a dishrag and started wiping off the orange Formica counters. "Do people do that? Sell Emmys?"

"I guess they'll do anything if they're broke enough. And want a drink. From the look of this place, he was … and did. Want a drink, that is."

With a last swipe, Ashleigh threw the dishrag into the sink. "That's about it, chickie. I say we bounce. Too many dark colors in here for me. It's depressing. I don't know what they were thinking in the '70s. Avocado green makes my eye twitch."

Paradise set a big cardboard box by the front door. "Okay. One more quick check, then we'll go."

But instead she sat down on the worn leather couch. Grief welled again.

Ashleigh sat next to her and put her arm across her shoulders. "You okay?"

Paradise blinked, tired of fighting the tears. "I don't know what's wrong with me. I hardly knew him, you know? Maybe they're right. Maybe I *am* crazy."

Ash pulled a handkerchief from her purse and dabbed Paradise's eyes. "Crazy's relative. Be who you are, in all your starlet glory. Yeah, you'd stand out in Omaha, but this is LA. Here you're just pretty much normal. Depends on your neighborhood. Oh, *and* you're a movie star."

"Not yet. I could use a Coke."

"Then again, this is LA, and you don't drink or smoke. Maybe you *are* crazy."

"I watch him sometimes."

"And now you've lost me. As usual."

"My dad. I have the complete DVD set of *After Sunset*. I bought it on Amazon a long time ago, but I never told anyone. I know all his lines by heart."

Ash gave her a squeeze.

"You think it's going to work?" Paradise said.

"Memorizing your dad's lines? Work for what?"

"No, the movie. Getting the part. I can't imagine it really happening."

"Listen. Paradise Jones' dreams are finally coming true. You're gonna have a zillion fans. They'll all love my quirky pal."

"And if I have a zillion fans who love me, will I feel normal?"

"It's worth a shot."

"I should be excited. I *was* excited. Why did he have to die right now?"

"Should he have checked with you first? Maybe he did you a favor. One last fatherly hurrah got you some extra attention. People are talking about you. That's a plus in this town any way you look at it." Ash dug through her purse, fished out a small compact, and began to doctor her already perfect makeup. She pointed a long nail at a small end table next to the couch. "Did you check that drawer in the end table?"

"No. I didn't even see it." Paradise pulled it open. "*TV Guide.*" She picked up the magazine. "August, 1975. Guess who's on the cover?"

"Ah, the legendary Gregory Jones, I presume. Same year he bought the rabbit ears on the TV, I'll bet"

"You can have them. Very retro. Right up your alley."

"Thanks, buddy."

Paradise dropped the magazine into her purse and then felt the back of the drawer just to be sure she wasn't missing anything. Her hand bumped something hard. "Ash, look at this."

A small wooden box darkened with age and handling.

Ashleigh's eyebrows rose. "Jewelry?"

Using her nails, Paradise worked the small clasp that held the lid. After a few seconds, it snapped back with a click. Inside, she found a worn gold coin about the size of a silver dollar.

Ashleigh let out a long whistle. "Wow. Good thing you double-checked. What is it?"

"Maybe a collector's edition coin or something? I don't know. It has writing on it."

"He sold an Emmy but not a coin? That doesn't make sense. Let me see it. What does it say?"

"I think it's Spanish. Dos Escudos? What does that mean?"

Chapter Five

Gato Negro

The coolness and silence of the mission paired like an old, married couple as Doc followed Jake into the vestibule. Doc took off his cleats so they wouldn't scratch the polished stone floor. How many generations of feet would it take to make stone shine like that? Ahead of them, through a high, arched entryway, the narrow chapel stretched into the dim interior of the building, consistent with early Spanish Colonial architecture. To the right, the entrance to the mission's museum welcomed visitors with a carved pine sign over a wooden door—Jake's domain. Well, more a passion than a domain. How many times had his brother regaled him with stories and history of mission life? Then again, given Jake's natural calm, maybe *regaled* was the wrong word.

Opposite the door to the museum stood another archway and a thick, unmarked wooden door leading up to the staff offices. Doc shut it behind them as they passed through. Up a stone stair and down a series of hallways, the brothers found Pastor Paco Hollis behind his desk in an office that smelled like leather and old books. A well-worn Stetson *Open Road* hung on a hat rack behind him.

Doc smiled at the sight. Not one to stand on formality, the pastor insisted the brothers call him by his first name and skip the title. A thin man, constructed of rawhide and aged wood, his strong hands presented like those of a rancher or a longshoreman. In actuality, they belonged to a guy looking in the rearview mirror at a long career as Paradise Chief of Police. Now, ten years into retirement from law enforcement, Paco filled his hours with pastoral work, something that had been relegated to a part-time profession in his younger days.

His eyes warmed as Jake and Doc walked in. "Butch and Sundance. Game over already?"

"Got something for you to see, Paco," Jake said, handing the pastor the coin. "You're not going to believe it. Doc found this escudos along with—get this—the remains of a conquistador, out past the ball field."

Paco's eyes widened a bit. His slight Mexican accent flowed soft as warm molasses as he turned the coin over in his fingers. "A conquistador? As in an actual body?"

"Yup. Well, sort of. At least the bones of one," Jake said. "In the wash. Looked like storm runoff dug in under the bank and collapsed it. The bones and armor were half buried in the sand. That," he pointed at the coin, "was under a breastplate in this." He tossed the small leather sack onto the desk.

"Next to a ball I hit," Doc added. "Four-fifty if it was an inch."

Paco rasped a soft laugh. "Of course, it was. Couldn't leave that important detail out, could we, Red Sox?"

Jake leaned forward, resting his palms on Paco's desk. "It's an eight escudos; I'm fairly sure. But look at the markings—dos escudos."

Paco pulled a pair of bent wire reading glasses from his desk drawer and propped them on the end of his nose, though Doc had a strong suspicion they weren't necessary. Deep into his seventies, age and gray somehow had a tough time getting a grip on the energetic pastor. In fact, people marveled at the old man's youthfulness. Black eyebrows furrowed beneath thick, black hair combed back from his face.

"You got a picture aging for you in an attic somewhere, Paco?" Doc said.

"Hmm. *Dorian Gray*. Not bad for a jock. You read the book or see the movie? And by book, I don't mean comic," Paco said.

"Both. I'm well-rounded."

"I'm sure you are. But about your coin … Says dos escudos, sure enough. Although it's certainly an eight escudos coin. You're right, Jake. This side," he pointed to the stamped imprint, "is not original. At least not like any eight escudos I've ever seen. It was probably Spanish currency, but it's been altered. Dos Escudos followed by *Gato Negro*—Black Cat. I'm betting it's a key to the cipher."

Jake leaned forward. "So you think the story is real? This is one of the coins?"

"Sure, it's real. At least as far as the cipher goes. Who knows if it actually means anything? Everybody guesses, but nobody really knows."

Doc crossed one leg over the other. A toe showed through a hole in his sock, and he covered it with his hand. "A cipher? As in a code? What story are you talking about?"

Jake turned toward Doc. "There's this story in one of the old diaries here. We have it in the museum archives. It's well known to collectors and historians. Something told to one of the priests by a local Apache. He talked about two coins.

Called them the Dos Escudos. And two brothers, the Montejos. Each brother kept a coin. One had a cipher, or a code, on it and the other one had a keyword. One coin was supposed to decode the other."

Doc raised his eyebrows. "An Apache told him this? I thought they were hostile back then. Come to think of it, some still are. Jack Harjo over at the Texaco's a real piece of work. Then again, I dated his sister. Can't blame him."

Paco placed the coin carefully on the desk and removed the reading glasses, his face alive with amateur historian zeal—a passion that had long pulled Jake into its whirling vortex. "Not all were hostile. Some welcomed the missionaries. Even traded with them. And don't forget, it was mostly Indian labor that built this place. Some even converted to Catholicism."

"So what was coded?" Doc said. "Military secrets? Map to Coronado's gold?"

Paco shrugged. "No one knows. Historians have debated it for years. One theory is that the coins hold a clue to the location of the Fountain of Youth. Juan Ponce de León thought he'd found it in Florida at one time. León is rumored to have been a distant cousin of the brothers. There are other theories, of course. Religious artifacts. The tomb of some saint. *El Dorado.* There's always gold. That's the most popular. Lots of pilfered Incan gold floating around back then. The Spanish melted and minted constantly."

Jake leaned back in his chair and linked his hands behind his head. "I figured it was just a tall tale. Maybe had some basis in real people—like the brothers—but exaggerated. But I wonder, now that I've seen this coin."

"Not just a story," Paco said. "It's true. Both coins are real, code and key, although I have no idea what they might lead to, if anything."

Jake leaned forward again, hands on his knees. "You think the other coin's out there? Buried somewhere? You think it exists?"

"It exists, sure enough," Paco said. "But it's not buried. At least, I don't think it is. It wasn't last time I saw it."

"The last time you saw it?" Jake said. "You're saying you've seen the other dos escudos?"

Paco picked up the coin again. "I'm almost sure of it. It's been a long time. Lots of years. Before you both were even born, in fact. A young man found it out there on your ball field. Kicked it right up out of the center field dirt. Eight escudos coin. Gold. But it had Dos Escudos stamped on one side exactly like this one. That one had a lot more writing on it, though. I'm thinking that coin held the cipher, and this one's got the key—the key being *Gato Negro*."

"Wait," Jake said. "So the coin was here? Where is it? I've never seen it in the museum or the archives. Not even a mention."

"No, you wouldn't. It wasn't here long. Since it was found on mission land, it was considered the property of the church. Father Montgomery was still alive then. He put it in a drawer behind one of the glass cases in the museum so he could archive it and make it public the next day. But when he went to get it, it was gone. I remember because I was the officer that responded to the theft complaint."

Doc's toe popped through the hole in his sock. He let it be. "Theft? Gone, as in stolen? Didn't he lock it up in a safe or something?"

"Why would he?" Paco said. "Nobody felt the need for any real security back then. Father Montgomery was here all the time. Calvary Christian shared the building like we do now, and one of our people was usually around. Church, small town, who would steal from the mission building? There was a lock on the door to the museum like now, but nobody could remember if anyone locked it. Probably not."

"So you think someone just walked in and took it?" Doc said. "Did anyone look? You didn't find out who it was?"

"I asked around, but I had a pretty good idea who took it. Greg Jones, the kid who kicked it up in the first place—he wasn't very happy about having to hand it over to the church. And I didn't want to press too hard. The poor kid had a rough home life. His father was abusive. His mom hid in a bottle. I felt like he needed something to help him along. Father Montgomery agreed with me, and we let the whole thing go. We didn't pursue it."

Doc flipped his ball cap around backward. "So the question of the hour is what happened to Greg? Is he still around? It seems like he'd be curious to find out what happens when you put the coins together. It's been a long time now. He might be willing to talk to us."

Paco shook his head. "No, Greg eventually headed to California to become an actor. He did well, too. Local boy makes good. Like you, Doc."

"Wait a minute," Jake said. "Greg? As in Gregory Jones? He's the only actor from Paradise I know of. He's the guy that found the other coin?"

"One and only," Paco said. "He found it, and I'm almost sure he took it."

"No kidding," Doc said. "How do you go about contacting a famous actor about a coin he may or may not have stolen fifty years ago? Do they have people for that?"

"Interesting you ask." Paco held the coin up to the light. "You *don't* talk to him. Greg Jones was killed in a car accident a few days ago. Not front-page news, but it seems like you would have seen something about it."

"You know Doc doesn't read the paper past the sports page," Jake said. "Not much for the Internet either. Just his old movies and books."

"Like *Dorian Gray*." Doc walked across the office and looked out the small window. He could see the ball field through the dusty glass. "Man, that's a crazy coincidence. The one guy who may have the other coin dies within days of someone finding the second one. Unbelievable."

Paco stood up from his desk and tossed Doc the coin, then joined him at the window. "Can I tell you something, Doc? As a friend and a pastor? I have a feeling … You know, you and Jake have been sons to me. Especially after your parents died. I've watched you play on that baseball field about as long as you've been able to walk. Even as a kid, you were a standout. Destined for big things, and we all knew it. I was proud. Followed you through high school, Legion ball, college, and right into the Minors. When you got your shot at the Major Leagues, I thought you'd finally found a home. I was watching, like everyone else around here, the night you got your first at bat. Man, we held our breath. I can still see it. Fenway Park. Second pitch. Fastball down the middle and you lined it to left. I couldn't have been prouder if you'd been my own flesh and blood. None of us could. Then after that first baseman smacked into you, I watched them carry you off. Our hearts were broken. For you and for ourselves. Now listen to what I'm saying here, okay? You might have thought that was the end of your story, but I knew better. Even when they were carrying you off. Destined for big things doesn't mean one at bat with the Red Sox. Or even a Hall of Fame career in baseball. And it *definitely* doesn't mean hiding out in a trailer behind the mission, watching old black-and-white movies and feeling sorry for yourself. There are a lot of innings left."

Doc looked at the coin in his hand. "Jake says the same thing. It's like seeing the same horse keep coming back around on a merry-go-round. So what do I do? Become a priest? I don't think black's my color."

"Wasn't too long ago that I tried to talk your brother out of that very thing."

"You were banging your head against generations of good Catholics," Jake said.

Paco laughed. "You ever heard of Martin Luther, Jake?" He took the coin back and held it up. "Doc, what you do with your life, that's your call. And nobody can hear that call but you. But Gregory Jones meeting his Maker and you finding this coin within a few days of each other is no coincidence. I can feel it. It's part of your story. You need to start reading."

Chapter Six

Esther Dash Williams Dot Com

The Santa Ana winds picked up heat over the Mohave Desert and furnace-blasted it across the Los Angeles basin before continuing out to sea. The city wilted and sagged under the late afternoon sun. Paradise considered putting the top up as she drove through Santa Monica but decided against it as she turned right onto Highway 1 toward Malibu. Her brand-new-used Oldsmobile Eighty-Eight came complete with after-market air conditioning, but she ignored it. Something about the scorching afternoon fit her mood. She pulled the scarf off her head and let the wind demolish her hair.

Very Marilyn.

The road to Eve and Burt's Malibu home curved and climbed through the typical brown and yellow scrub of Southern California. Oak trees dotted the landscape. The closer Paradise got to the faux-Mediterranean mansion, the slower she drove. It always happened that way.

Eve and Burt—cocktails at five. *Wake me when it's safe again.*

Her stomach knotted as she pulled the car into the huge circular drive. A fountain bubbled and splashed in its center. The house itself rose up against the ocean blue of the Southern California sky. A cozy glass and stucco castle built for two. The place didn't say new money; it shouted it from its earth-tone turrets. Beyond the house and the steep downward slope that backed it, the diamond-studded Pacific winked and sparkled.

Eve appeared in the doorway, martini glass in hand. Tall, thin and one part Cabo San Lucas, two parts tanning-bed tan. Her short, white shag lay stark and stylish against her dark skin. Casual, cocktail Eve. She wore slacks and a tank, both white—clearly an effort to accentuate her chemically enhanced, sun-kissed skin.

Paradise slammed the car door and started for the house. "Meeting me at the door, Mom? Very un-Malibu, you know. Don't you have somebody for that?"

The skin around Eve's eyes tightened. Not that it could get much tighter. The last round of plastic surgery stretched it like a drum. "Don't be peevish, Paradise. I've been worried sick about you."

"Right. I could tell by the frequency of your phone calls. How was Cabo?" she asked, referring to her mother's recent trip to Baja California.

Eve shooed both the statement and question away with a wave of her hand. "Cabo is Cabo. You know how it is. At least the weather was nice. What happened to your hair and what are you wearing?"

Paradise pointed to the car. "It's California, Mom. I bought a convertible. And it's a sarong dress. Vintage Hawaiian, 1945."

"It looks like you bought it at a thrift store." Eve's nose wrinkled. "Where and why did you get that car? Please explain."

Paradise glanced behind her. "Where? I bought it from a man in Venice Beach. Why? Because I like it. It's a 1949 Olds Eighty-Eight. Convertible, very hard to find."

"What color is it supposed to be?" Eve's eyes flicked to the road and back.

"Don't worry, Mom. The neighbors can't see from where they are." Paradise turned to the car. "Blue. Well, mostly blue, at least, I think blue. Blue-*ish* ... I suppose it needs paint. Can we please go inside? It's hot out here."

Eve crossed her arms as if considering.

"How do you do that?" Paradise asked.

"Do what?"

"Cross you arms like that without spilling your drink."

"I don't remember offering to buy you a car. Not that we wouldn't have. But we could have gotten you something new. Reliable. Where did you get the money?"

"I don't want a new car. I want an Olds Eighty-Eight. It wasn't expensive. Not like a new one. I save, you know."

"I thought maybe Gregory left you something. Although I'd be stunned."

"Not much. Some pictures. I found an old coin in his apartment. That's about it."

"That Spanish thing? You mean he still had it after all these years? I'm surprised he didn't blow that on booze and women long ago."

"He's dead, Mom. Don't you think it's time to drop the bitterness?"

"I'm just saying I'm surprised he still had the thing, that's all."

"And I'm surprised you remember it. It must have meant something to him."

"I suppose. He found it when he was a boy. Back in that town in Arizona. He always had a soft spot for that place. I've no idea why. Godforsaken hole, if you ask me. One visit was enough."

"Thank you. I was named after that hole," Paradise said.

Eve waved a hand. "That's not what I meant. Now, let us buy you a car. A *real* car. Something sporty, like a BMW."

"You mean something you won't be embarrassed to have parked in your driveway?"

"I mean something worthy of a Simmons."

"I'm not a Simmons. I'm a Jones. Can we please go inside?"

With a resigned sigh, Eve turned on a heel and led the way through the massive teak double doors.

The coolness of the foyer washed over Paradise like water. Another fountain bubbled. Her heels clacked on the flagstone floor as Eve, graceful and silent as a ghost, led the way through the interior of the house to the football field-sized great room. Floor to ceiling glass made up the entire back wall, offering a view of the infinity pool and the ocean far below.

"So, Mom, I'm up for the part of Scarlett in the new *Gone with the Wind*. Arnie says I have a great shot," Paradise said.

Eve ghost-floated left and curved around the bar. A massive mahogany piece, rescued from a hotel in Santa Barbara. One of the few actual antiques in the place. She refreshed her martini. Gin and a new olive, no vermouth. "Arnie ... " The name came out like a curse word. "Well, fabulous. Little Paradise, the movie star. I hope they do better with this version than the first. I never could stand that movie. *So* melodramatic. Ashley this, Rhett that. Blah blah blah. What are you drinking these days? We're fully stocked."

"You know I don't drink, Mom. But I'll take some iced tea, if you have it. And I don't have the part yet. I'm trying not to get my hopes up."

"Ugh ... Why can't you call me Eve? You were so much easier when you were little."

No iced tea appeared.

"Because you're my mother, like it or not. I hated calling you Eve, by the way."

"Of course, I'm your mother. But Mom sounds so ... I don't know ... old. Why don't you drink? I always forget. I don't know any movie stars that don't drink."

"Do I need a reason for not drinking? And Mom's better than Grandma, not that you are one. Or likely to be soon. Where's Burt?"

Eve shuddered and downed half her gin in one long gulp. Whether a reaction to the word Grandma or Burt, who could tell? "This is Malibu. Of course you need a reason for not drinking. And Burt Simmons, international man of mystery, is running late as usual. He should be here any minute."

Paradise dropped onto a leather sofa—much harder than its plush appearance led one to believe. "Do you have tea or not, Mom?"

Eve shuffled under the bar and came up with a jar of olives and a half-full bottle of gin. "I ordered Geoffrey's for dinner. It won't be here for a while. Why don't you take a swim? Then maybe you could do something about that hair. You know how Burt hates you to look messy."

Swimming. The one thing Paradise liked about coming to the house. Eve seemed preoccupied with the olive jar, so Paradise didn't bother answering. Tea was an obvious lost cause, so she grabbed her bag and headed for the pool. Infinity, they called it. A chlorinated oasis giving the illusion of a shared border with the Pacific Ocean. In the pool house—four times the size of her apartment— she changed into her suit. Two-piece classic sheath recently purchased from the official Esther Williams Swimwear website. *Who says the Internet's not handy?*

Black and white stripes. Eve would hate it.

Perfect.

Paradise paused in front of the mirror. Okay, yes, the hair was out of control. Loose, blonde curls exploded everywhere. But the suit and the body it covered would have made Esther Williams proud. She tried to envision Scarlett O'Hara in the reflected image, but couldn't. Oh well, that's what the makeup trailer was for. Besides, Colin Prince was no Gable. What would *that* have been like? To play opposite Gable? Then again she'd heard *his* breath wasn't so hot either.

What was wrong with her? Half the women in the world would give an eyetooth to even be in the same room as Colin Prince. She could hear Ash now.

The sun on her back in contrast to the cool water rushing over her body eased her tension. She swam hard for half an hour. How long could she go like this? An hour? A week? A year? Esther Williams crossing the English Channel.

Dangerous When Wet.

No time. Her hair would take awhile, and she had no desire to hear Eve harp about it all night. At the edge of the pool, she rested her arms on the side and stared out at the endless Pacific.

Paradise Jones. Malibu. California. Pacific Ocean. Planet Earth. Universe.

She felt small again. An atom in the endlessness of physical space. And atoms never felt pressure to be known or important. Sweet oblivion. If only for this moment, free from the thing down inside that drove her with unsympathetic resolution. Why was that thing still there, here on the cusp of dreams come true? Or maybe it intensified as dreams approached? When everything important hovered within grasp?

Far below, the ocean swelled and breathed. *"What do you want, Paradise?"* it said.

Good question. What did she want? *Gone with the Wind?* Money? Fame? Definitely fame. She needed it like air. Like a farmer's field needs rain. Someone had to notice. To take her seriously.

To love her.

And there it was. The place she always returned to, no matter how far she ran. Love.

She wanted love. As badly as Scarlett wanted Rhett back as he walked off into the mist.

"I want to be famous," she spoke out to the infinite horizon.

The ocean swelled, shimmering. *"Be famous to me."*

Was she losing it? Allowing her arms to slide off the slick tile, she sank under the surface. Weightless. Nothing. An atom lost in infinity.

She floated like that till she couldn't hold her breath any longer.

"Be famous to me ... "

In the pool house, she showered and changed. With a blow dryer and several bobby pins, she managed a very passable up-do. It wouldn't work for publicity photos or a night on the town with Colin Prince, but fine for dinner at home with Eve and Burt. Anyway, looking a little off couldn't hurt. Maybe it would help keep Burt's eyes from wandering where they shouldn't.

Fat chance.

A tap sounded at the door, and it swung open almost simultaneously.

Speak of the devil.

Burt Simmons was still a handsome man at sixty. Broad shoulders filled out his white dress shirt.

Two buttons unbuttoned. Must have been casual Friday in the Beverly Hills psychiatry world.

He pushed his steel-gray hair back from his face and flashed white, capped teeth at her. His smile shone brightly against his tan. "There you are! My favorite girl! It's been way too long."

A coldness touched her inside. "Hello, Burt."

"Where've you been keeping yourself, Pare? We've missed you. You should have come down to Cabo. We would've had a blast."

"Please don't call me that."

The sarong clung to her damp body, and she crossed her arms in front of her, feeling the blood come to her face. True to form, he made no attempt at subtlety. His eyes wandered down, then up again.

"Be friendly, Paradise. We always got along when you were younger. No reason we can't now."

"Where's Eve? Is dinner here yet? We should go in."

"Asleep on the couch. We have some time."

Paradise glanced at the door. "Time for what? I'm hungry."

He stepped closer and Paradise smelled alcohol on his breath. "You've been avoiding me, Pare. It hurts my feelings."

"You're drunk. And I'm not avoiding you. I don't think about you at all. You're crossing a line, and you need to stop."

"So, Paradise Jones … The next big thing, I hear. Had a guy on the couch talking about it just today. Studio exec. You'd know his name if I told you. Man, that guy's a freak behind closed doors. Congratulations. I always knew my Paradise was something special."

"They haven't given me the part yet. And I'm not yours. I'm not anybody's. Please leave me alone so I can get ready for dinner."

"So get ready. Don't let me stop you." He reached out and toyed with her dress strap. "Paradise Jones … I always said you lived up to your name, remember?"

She moved his hand away. "Please, Burt. Don't."

A flush made his tanned cheeks even darker. His words slurred, and a drop of spit formed at the corner of his mouth. "Let's lay our cards out, Pare. You live on my dime. The apartment, the clothes, all of it—I pay for it."

"I don't want your help anymore, Burt. And besides, I never asked you for anything. I can stand on my own."

"That's true. You're not a kid anymore, are you, movie star? Hard not to notice. In fact, you're an attractive woman. I like attractive women. I like *you*. Always have."

"And Eve? My mom? The person you're married to? Do you like her?"

He swayed on his feet. "Leave her out of it. It's not like I'm a hundred. You and I could have something, Paradise. Something special. This is LA. Nothing is surprising here. Nothing new under the sun and all that. Nobody cares about propriety. Trust me, I hear the crazies talk all day long. And I think you know how I feel about you."

Paradise tried to swallow but couldn't. "Stop, please. I want to go inside. I want to leave."

"I love you, Paradise … I *need* you … " He'd never taken it this far before.

Paradise fought rising nausea. "Stop."

Burt's face hardened. He shoved her and her back thumped into the mirror. "You spoiled brat. I ought to take you over my knee and spank you. I gave you your life. I still do. You know I pulled strings with clients, big ones, to help you get that audition? You're a freak show. Everybody knows it. They all think you're nuts. I could yank the opportunity away just as fast as I made it happen. You eat and breathe and act and wear your dresses … You sing your stupid golden moldies because *I* allow it. And I'm not asking anymore. I'm telling. We've both wanted this for a long time." He wobbled and caught himself on the wall.

Drunker than she'd thought.

"We? And if I say no? If I don't want to … how did you put it? Get along? What then?"

"Then you're done, you little tramp. Cut off. I'll even make a few calls to the studio. You know how many of those millionaire poser movie execs I see in my office every week? But that's not going to happen, is it? You need me. You *want* me."

He grabbed her then, gripping her shoulders with strong hands. Paradise shoved against his chest, but it might as well have been a brick wall. His mouth smashed against hers, and she gagged. He let up and stepped back, victory shining in his eyes.

"I've been waiting years to do that," he said.

Tears flooded her eyes. "I know."

Concern came to his face. "Hey, Pare. It's gonna be okay. We'll get through this together."

"What's the matter with you? Are you crazy?"

He turned to the mirror and watched himself as he started to unbutton his shirt. "Don't talk like that, Paradise. I might change my mind and cut you off anyway. Regardless of how special what we have here is."

The lamp smashing against the back of his head surprised her as much as it did him. When had she picked it up? How? She was small—an atom floating in infinity. Too inconsequential to hit a man with a lamp, but there it was, broken on the floor.

He stumbled to an overstuffed chair and sank into it. Not like in the movies. Had she killed him? A loud snore sent a flood of relief through her body. More alcohol than smashed lamp, hopefully. She grabbed her bag and ran.

Sure enough, Eve lay curled up on the couch.

Welcome to dinner with Eve and Burt. Why didn't she drink? Really?

She paused in the drive and leaned against Burt's car to catch her breath and slow her heart that threatened to pound through her chest. The sun hung low. Red and angry in the leftover Santa Ana heat.

Her stepfather had flirted and gawked at her most of her life while Eve turned a blind eye, but he'd never gone this far. Paradise's insides twisted with a surge of anger and residual fear. She wiped her palms on the front of her sarong and willed her legs not to buckle. Who did he think he was?

Past the drive and across a narrow strip of manicured grass the steep hill fell away and the ocean burned yellow beneath the dying sun, peaceful blue now gone.

"What do you want, Paradise?" Its voice more insistent now.

Strength began to return to her legs.

A garden rake leaned against a replica of the Venus de Milo. Poor Venus. No arms. Helpless.

Join the club, sister.

"What do you want, Paradise?" the ocean called again.

"I don't know! Leave me alone."

No way to tell when the idea sparked, but there it was and wouldn't be deterred. Years of Burt's wandering eyes and *oh sorry, that was an accident* touches, overwhelmed her. The rake came to her hand with a mind of its own.

Burt's car practically glowed in the evening light. Panamera. Porsche's most expensive model—just ask him. Burt's pride and joy. The kind of car you wouldn't be embarrassed to have parked in your Malibu driveway. Keys still in it. He must have been eager to see her.

Easy. Just like in the movies. Start the engine, loop the seat belt through the steering wheel to keep it straight, wedge the rake handle against the gas pedal, pop it in gear and …

There it went.

Some things really did work like they did in the movies.

"What do you think of that? Just like *Thelma and Louise*," Paradise said.

Venus de Milo remained silent on the issue.

Poor Burt. Couldn't happen to a nicer guy.

The Olds was fast, the original muscle car and Paradise took the turns hard, feeling good for the first time in days. Burt would explode. He'd kill her.

Goodbye, Burt.

Hello, life. Hello, fame. Hello, money. Hello, independence. She didn't need Burt or Eve or anyone anymore. She was Scarlett O'Hara.

"After all, tomorrow *is* another day … " she said to the wind.

Then again, what if Burt made good on his threat? What if he really did have connections with the studio?

What had she done?

Stars poked through the Malibu sky above. They sang to her, perfect voices in beautiful harmony. "*What do you want, Paradise?*"

"Sorry, Paradise Jones can't come to the phone right now. Please leave a message and she'll get back to you … later … maybe."

She braked hard into a turn, then hit the gas as the road straightened.

Chapter Seven

Jesus is My Copilot

Paradise rolled up the windows but left the top down. A kaleidoscope of neon and florescent glow played across the Olds as Los Angeles hugged her like an old friend. The sun, having recited the day's lines, had long since exited the stage, but the night still held a healthy remnant of the desert heat.

She drove for a while, reluctant to return to her empty apartment. She contemplated calling Ash but opted against it. Her friend would probably be busy bouncing through the Melrose club scene with the latest man in her life.

And like they said, whoever *they* were, three's a crowd.

Daytime and nighttime Los Angeles. Two very different cities simultaneously occupying the same 469 square miles of coastal Southern California desert. One a sun-drenched wonderland of tourism and industry. A bright-sky, Rose Parade kind of place with a smog-alert where Midwesterners stood in line at Universal Studios and crowded the streets of Hollywood, snapping cell-phone pictures of the stars on the Walk of Fame.

But past the red carpet and the paparazzi's flashbulbs, nighttime Los Angeles read from a whole different script. With Gidget safely holed up in her bedroom doing homework, it became Marlowe's turn. Unlike Malibu, no stars graced the night sky here. The city's domed ceiling glowed a perpetual twilight of brown and orange. Beneath it, pale-faced musicians haunted the club scene and bragged about the big break right around the corner, never dreaming that in twenty years most of them would be working the counter at Guitar Center, telling and retelling tales of the glory days to clones of their former selves. Waiters and waitresses, temp workers and Radio Shack sales clerks shed their polyester and became actors, huddled around micro-brews and skinny lattes. Drug dealers and con men moved in and out of the streetlight glow, looking to cull the weakest of the herd while the invisible homeless army shuffled the shadows on silent feet.

Day or night, Paradise loved the city. She drove the streets for an hour, waiting for her heart to slow. Finally, back in her narrow apartment driveway, she turned off the engine and let her forehead thump against the steering wheel. The anger wasn't gone, but it had at least moved to the backseat.

Good night, Los Angeles. You've been a great audience.

What had she been thinking?

Would Burt call the police? Of course, he would. He knew how to spin things. She'd be arrested. Go to jail. He'd be the respected innocent victim of his crazy stepdaughter. She'd lose everything.

What could she do? Go to the police and tell them her side of the story? His word against hers, and even if they believed her, there was still the pesky little fact that she'd sent his hundred-thousand-dollar car off a cliff. No denying that one.

Now you've done it, Paradise Jones. How's the weather in Costa Rica this time of year?

And what about *Gone with the Wind*? It might become the working title of her life story—or at least, her acting career.

Think about that later.

She'd bought the huge red suitcase at an estate sale in Brentwood. The amount of clothes she was able to shove into it surprised her, and she managed to snap it shut by sitting on it. She left her cell phone on the kitchen counter because she'd seen a crime drama where the police were able to track them.

Lady sings the blues. Goodbye, Billie Holiday.

Thirty minutes in and out.

The heavy suitcase thumped on each stair on the way down to the car.

Now, where to go? Where could she hide? Big Bear, maybe? Santa Barbara? Too close. Lake Tahoe might be good. It looked nice in *North by Northwest*, and there wouldn't be any snow this time of year. Mexico? Too scary. Plus they might be looking for her at the border. They did that, didn't they?

In the end, the Olds found its way onto Interstate 10 and headed east, the whole thing feeling like a dream. What would Eve say? Nothing. When had she said anything before? And how about Ash? And Arnie? She didn't even want to think about Arnie. He'd blow a gasket.

Her stomach growled, reminding her that she'd never gotten around to eating dinner. At a 7-Eleven in Ontario, she bought a banana, a Snickers Bar, bottled water, cherry cola, and a prepaid cell phone. The kind they called a burner phone on the crime shows.

They hadn't had that technology in *After Sunset*.

She forced herself to keep to the speed limit, imagining police cruisers behind every pair of headlights.

Her eyes began to get heavy. She needed sleep. At a motel on the backside of Banning, the Chinese woman behind the check-in desk hardly gave her a glance. Paradise registered as Veronica Lake and paid with cash. Thanks to her carefully hoarded savings, she wasn't short of it, at least, for the moment. She had enough to run or hide on. At least until she figured something out—or went to prison. She shuddered at the thought of a wardrobe limited to one orange jumpsuit.

The television didn't work, but the room was clean. Under the covers, tired as she was, sleep eluded her. Frustrated, she turned on the bedside light. No television, no smartphone, nothing to read except a list of local restaurants. All pizza and sub shops. Life on the go.

In a drawer, she found a Gideon Bible. She'd heard of one in "Rocky Raccoon." She liked that song, even if she wasn't a Beatles fan.

No thanks, Gideon. Whoever you are.

She crawled back into bed and tried counting sheep but kept thinking of Burt. How could he have done it? The feel of his lips . . .

More sheep, but every time one passed, it tried to bite her, gnashing out with nasty little teeth.

Mercifully, when sleep finally came, it brought no dreams.

Sun in her eyes woke her. Nine-thirty. When was the last time she'd been up at nine-thirty in the morning? She showered and dressed. Sailor theme—navy and white. *Put on a happy face.* Doris Day does summer.

The silence of the room wrapped itself around her. For a bit, the temptation to crawl back into bed and fade back into sleep overwhelmed her. What went on outside? Were they looking for her? She had to keep moving. She left without returning the key to the front desk.

Whatever will be, will be, right? *Que sera, sera . . .*

WWDD—what would Doris do?

West of Palm Springs she parked in the shade of the larger of two massive concrete dinosaurs. Top up and AC running, she dialed Ash from her pre-paid phone.

Her friend answered on the second ring. Boston with extra Boston sauce. "Yeah?"

"It's me."

"Chickie! Where are you? The police are looking for you. They came to my apartment asking if I knew where you were."

So her fears were confirmed.

"What did they say?"

"That you made a pass at Burt and got mad and pushed his Porsche over a cliff when he turned you down. Which I told them was ridiculous, of course."

"Leave it to Burt to turn things around. He made a pass at *me*. I mean a *real* pass. I can't believe I did it."

"You're kidding. He came on to you?"

"It was disgusting. I hit him with a lamp."

"What? I wish I could have seen *that!*"

"And I did sort of push his Porsche over the cliff."

"Wait—that's true? You really did that?"

Paradise couldn't help smiling at her friend's enthusiasm. "Actually, I didn't push it, I started it and shoved a rake handle against the gas pedal. You should have seen it. It was like *Thelma and Louise*. The thing practically sprouted wings."

"Oh man! Burt must be livid."

"I don't even want to think about it. I just need to figure out how to set things right so I can get back there. The producers aren't going to wait around for me to clear up my personal life. Besides, Burt might try to ruin things with them. He knows *everybody*. I don't know what to do."

"Yeah, I understand. Speaking of that, Arnie called to see if I knew where you were. He's freaking out."

"Tell him what happened. I need some time to think."

"He already heard. Word travels fast. We're talking Hollywood, you know. Hey, you'll be okay. You need to get back here. We can go talk to the cops. Tell them what happened."

Sure. Except for the fist twisting her insides into knots. How could this be happening? The memory of Burt's thick, wet lips came without invitation. She fought it off by replaying the sight of his Porsche heading over the cliff.

"They'll never take my word over his. I'm crazy Paradise Jones, remember? I'm stuck. I have to disappear for a while. But you're a good friend. Tell Arnie I'm okay, and I'll be there as soon as I can. I'll try to call him."

"Disappear? This isn't a movie, Paradise. Come home."

"Can't, buddy. Too much heat."

"Oh, brother. So where are you?"

"Let's just say I've left town. It's better if I don't tell you. That way, if they ask, you don't have to lie. Plausible deniability and all that." Paradise sunk a couple of inches as a Highway Patrol car cruised by. The scarf and sunglasses wouldn't fool anyone. Not to mention the less-than-low-profile of the Olds.

"Why are you whispering? I'm worried about you."

"Don't be. I'll call you in a few days, okay?"

"Paradise, listen to me. I always shoot straight with you, right? You live in a fantasy world. It's not actually 1949. I'm worried about you out there. It's the real world we're talking about, not LA. It's like somebody dropping Sandra Dee in the middle of *Nightmare on Elm Street*. Come back where it's safe."

"Los Angeles is safe?"

"Yeah. *Safer*. For people like you and me. Out there you're a fish out of water. You won't be able to breathe."

"I don't think fish breathe."

"You know what I mean. Don't change the subject."

"You don't think I know I'm different? I like who I am. It makes me happy."

"This is not a movie, Chickie. Let me paint you a picture. You're probably sitting by the side of the road in some one-horse town, right? What are you wearing?"

"Two dinosaur town, actually. Sailor. Montgomery Wards."

"Year?"

"Fifty-one."

"Hair?"

"Veronica Lake. It's how I registered at the motel."

"And that makes sense because ... never mind. Are you driving the Oldsmobile?"

"Of course. It's comfortable." Paradise stretched out on the seat and put her feet against the passenger-side window.

"You see what I mean? That's *America* out there. Not Silverlake. Not Hollywood."

"That doesn't make sense."

"For you and me it does. Look, if it were anyone else, I wouldn't be saying this, but you're ... I don't know, innocent. Different, you know?"

"Not innocent in the eyes of the law, buddy. Or in the eyes of Dr. Burt Simmons, bloodshot as they may be." Paradise wiggled her toes as the sun caught her nail polish. When she dropped her feet to the seat, two perfect steamy footprints remained on the car window.

"The police aren't coming back here. Tell me where you are," Ash said.

"I'm parked beneath a dinosaur."

"See? You worry me. Where are you going?"

"Were they really that big?"

"Were what that big?"

"Dinosaurs."

"Where are you going?"

"I'll call you when I get there."

"Will you?"

"I promise."

"What about *Gone with the Wind*?"

The movie *was* a problem. "I don't even have the part, and like I said, Burt will crush my chances anyway. He told me."

"He was bluffing."

"I don't think so. I have to go. I'll call you later, okay?"

"Just promise you'll be careful."

"Bye, Ash. Thanks for being you. Call you soon. I have to ring off."

"You're killing me."

"I know." Paradise pushed the end button. She dropped her Greta Garbo circa 1955 sunglasses to the end of her nose and took a slow look around, adjusting her scarf as she did so. Nobody paid her much mind. The concrete dinosaur dozed in the morning sun. She started the Olds and dropped it into drive.

The truck stop on I-10 sprawled like its own sovereign nation made up of several small caliphate states. A line for the air pumps, truck wash, Linda's Diner, gas and diesel—separate lanes for cars and trucks.

She filled the Olds with regular.

In the station mini-mart, Paradise headed past the greasy food-on-a-stick section and the hot dogs spinning on metal rollers toward the "Restrooms for Customers Only" sign. Once inside, she checked herself in the mirror and decided to keep the sunglasses and scarf on for safety. *No need to tempt fate.* In no hurry—and not yet decided on where she was going anyway—she roamed the aisles. The air conditioner hummed. In fact, the whole place hummed. Bleary-eyed from the road, travelers wandered, grabbing up trail mix, candy bars, and huge sodas. The line for coffee stood five truckers and one soccer mom deep. Paradise side-stepped as a traveling baseball team—their flat brimmed hats having something to do with sharks—swam by. One of them gave her an acne-faced smile as he passed. *What would that be like? To belong to someone? To be part of a team?*

She picked a few things up. Coke in a bottle, a Greek yogurt, and an apple. In the back of the store, from the top shelf of an aisle that sported religious paraphernalia, a bobble-head Jesus smiled down at her with a benevolently mellow, all's-right-with-the-world surfer grin. *Perfect for the Olds.* She picked him up and added him to her take.

A stand next to the cash register held a stack of the latest Rand McNally road atlases. She picked one up and dropped it on the counter between Jesus and the yogurt.

Veronica Lake with Greta Garbo sunglasses and a Doris Day attitude.

The man ringing her up wore camouflage cargo shorts that hung past his knees. His red polyester shirt wasn't buttoned, and the tobacco stain that stopped at the end of his beard picked up again on the front of his used-to-be-white V-neck undershirt. He looked Paradise up and down with Burt eyes. Her skin crawled as she dropped cash on the counter. Not waiting for change, she scooped up her booty and headed out. The acne-faced ballplayer held the door for her, blushing bright pink when she smiled at him.

Back in the Olds, she stuck Jesus on the dash with the supplied Velcro strip and gave his head a wiggle. A thought came to her. She opened the Rand McNally and scanned the index. It took awhile to find the town, but when she did, she placed a finger on it and looked up.

"What do you think?"

Jesus smiled and gave her a thumbs-up.

She smiled back.

"All righty, then." She removed her finger and circled the town with a red pen. Paradise, Arizona.

Chapter Eight

A Little Long in the Tooth for the Cage

Hollister Finch lifted a hand to fend off the sudden blinding stab of light that attacked him like a pit bull. Forty-five minutes in the dim interior waiting room had ill-prepared him for the California sun filling Dr. Burt Simmons' third-story, glass-walled corner office. Psychiatrists had sure come a long way since Bob Newhart's day. At least, these Beverly Hills yahoos.

Dr. Simmons didn't rise but indicated a chair in front of an ebony desk that could have had its own zip code. Hollister sunk into the soft leather—a position that forced him to look up at the doctor.

I guess the yahoo knows his stuff.

Simmons clasped his hands on the desk in front of him and leaned forward with a practiced I'm-a-doctor look. "So good to see you, Hollister. It's been too long. Tell me, how is Crystal?"

Hollister crossed and uncrossed his legs, searching for a comfortable position. A spasm of pain shot across his lower back and through his right hip and thigh. "Fine. What can I do for you, Dr. Simmons?"

"She still fighting? MMA and all that?"

Really? We can't dump the small talk?

"Yeah … I don't know … kind of. More sparring than actual fights. She's getting a little long in the tooth for the cage."

"Aren't we all?"

Hollister tried to focus, but his mind wandered to the bottle of Demerol in the glove box of his Camaro. Man, this chair killed. "I'm in a little bit of a rush today, Dr. Simmons. Why did you need to see me? What's so important?"

Burt Simmons leaned back and looked at the ceiling, lacing his fingers behind his head.

Open body language. Must teach that in medical school—or on YouTube.

"I'd like to think I've been helpful to you, Hollister. To both you *and* Crystal. I hope our counseling sessions together were beneficial. We all need a little push in the communication department now and then."

"Uh huh." *Get to the point.*

The counseling had been Crystal's idea, and she'd dragged Hollister along kicking and screaming, sometimes literally.

"So you're sharing your feelings more, and the fights have settled down?"

"Sure. I guess."

True enough. At least a little power had gone out of Crystal's right hook, although that might be the Xanax. Miracles of modern medicine.

"Hollister, I'm going to level with you. I need help. In particular, I need someone with your … uh … shall we say … *special* skills. Yours and Crystal's."

"You making a movie? Need a stunt man? I'm retired. Young man's game."

Dr. Simmons spoke with slow deliberation as if to a child. "No, your other work. As a—how do you put it—investigator?"

Hollister clenched and unclenched his fists, fighting with effort the urge to toss Dr. Burt Simmons through the glass wall of his office and let him drop three stories to the Beverly Hills street below.

"You okay, Hollister?" Simmons asked.

Hollister's temper, never shy to show itself, threatened to breach the dam.

"At the moment, Dr. Simmons, I'm practicing my anger management. You taught me that, remember? I'm not an idiot, so stop talking to me like one. My back feels like it's got a shovel stuck in it, and I just spent forty-five minutes reading *Golf Digest* in your waiting room. Know what? I hate golf. You get the picture? Get on with it. What do you want?"

Dr. Simmons' eyes widened, and he put his hands up, palms forward. More body language skills at work. "Hey now, Hollister. We're old friends here. I didn't mean to offend. I simply need a little help, and I thought you'd be the man to talk to. Like I said, I need an investigator."

"I'm not an investigator. I'm a solver. I don't investigate. I solve. I don't hunt. I find."

"Even better."

An odd pair, the two of them. Simmons impeccable in his designer suit and Hollister with his shaved and tattooed head and muscles bulging through his black T-shirt. A young man's body at forty-nine. *Why do I feel so old?*

"Let's hear it," Hollister said.

"My stinking tramp of a stepdaughter ... You might have seen it on the news. Channel six did a big story."

"Don't watch it."

"Paper?"

"Nope."

"Anyway, she made a pass at me. In my own pool house. Can you imagine? My wife was asleep on the couch. Right inside! I mean the girl was all over me. It was crazy. I shut her down, of course. She got angry—she's always struggled with anger. You'd understand that. Classic delusional disorder too. She thinks she lives in the '40s. Clothes, hair, the whole *enchilada*. But hey, she's my wife's daughter. I've always tried to do the right thing. I'm a patient man."

"So she got mad and left. So what?"

"Oh, she didn't just leave. First, the little lunatic launched my Porsche off a cliff, *then* she left."

Now here was a bright spot. Hollister struggled not to smile. Not for a minute did he believe the daughter had been the one to make the sexual advance, but hey, didn't hurt to listen. A job's a job.

"And now she's running, and you need someone to bring her back to the party," Hollister said.

Something shone in the doctor's eyes. Not just anger. Hate? Lust, maybe?

"Yes. I want her back. I *own* her, do you understand? I pay for everything she does and everything she has. The police aren't any help. At least, not the kind of help I need. So I called you. I want you and Crystal to find her and bring her back."

"Dead or alive?"

"Oh no. Very much alive."

Definitely lust.

"I was joking," Hollister said.

Simmons grinned. "Hollister, I know what side of the law you dance on. You're no Boy Scout. You've hurt people ... Maybe even killed people?"

"No comment. But I don't touch women."

"Crystal does, though. That's why you make such a good team."

"But you don't want the girl hurt, right?"

"I didn't say that. I said I want her alive. If she's got a few bruises upon delivery, I promise not to complain about damaged goods."

Hollister clenched and unclenched again. *Feel him out.* "So you want her, but you want it under the radar? That can be expensive."

"What's expensive?"

Hollister really didn't feel like chasing down Simmons' dirty little secrets. He wanted a Demerol, a cold beer, and his chair in front of his big flat screen.

Shoot high, discourage the guy. "Forty thousand now and another forty when we deliver her," he said.

"Done."

Had he heard right?

Simmons pulled out a checkbook and wrote a check. He slid it across the desk along with a picture of a girl. "Her name is Paradise Jones. She's hard to miss. Could be the easiest eighty thousand dollars you've ever made."

She was pretty in an un-Hollywood-Boulevard-club-dancer sort of way. She had class, this one.

"She looks like one of those stars from the classic movie channel."

"Like I mentioned previously, she's delusional," Simmons said.

Hollister went fishing. "Pretty. I can see why you want her back."

Simmons didn't bite. "It was an expensive car. Worth more than your fee, as a matter of fact. A lot more."

"Should've asked for more dough."

"Yes, but you didn't."

"No, I don't guess I did." Hollister stood. He couldn't mask the grimace as pain shot down his sciatic nerve all the way to his foot.

Simmons scribbled on a piece of paper, wadded it up and tossed it to Hollister. "A little gift from me to you, my friend. Consider it a bonus."

Hollister smoothed it. A prescription for Demerol. He stuffed it into the pocket of his jeans and turned to leave.

"Hollister?" Simmons called.

"Yeah?"

"Be sure to take Crystal."

"That's the plan."

"And tell her not to worry about a few bruises."

"I heard you the first time." Hollister made no effort to keep the door from slamming as he left.

CHAPTER NINE

Coke in a Bottle and Loud Vampires

Hollister watched Crystal rummage through Paradise Jones' dresser. Her biceps rippled as she pulled drawers, dumping them on the floor after she molested them. MMA cage-fighting days behind her, Crystal filled the gap by focusing on her semi-professional bodybuilding career. Pie-in-the-sky stuff, if you asked Hollister. No money in it. Total waste of time.

Plus she always smelled like a gym locker.

"So you couldn't find it in your heart to take a shower?" Hollister said.

Crystal straightened and checked herself in the mirror. "Shut up. I was in a hurry."

Always quick with the witty comeback.

"You always in a hurry? 'Cause I'm wracking my brain, and I can't remember the last one you took."

"I said, shut up. Eighty grand is eighty grand." She raised her tattooed-on eyebrows at her reflection then turned her face up and examined the inside of her nose. The head tilt gave her voice a strained sound. "And all we gotta do is chase down Dr. Simmons' little princess. Do I have a booger?"

"Who cares?" Hollister considered his wife. Sixteen years since they'd stood in front of the judge for the piece of paper making it legal. Seemed like a good idea at the time. *Was I drinking?* Nah. It had been blind love—the worst kind. Crystal's tie-dye tank stretched across her muscular back above her salt-crusted, spandex workout shorts. A tattoo on the back of her neck showed itself beneath her black Mohawk. GAME OVER in green block letters. Scribbled with all the artistic talent of an average third grader. *Hey, you get what you pay for.* Crystal was into ink. Quality was an afterthought. Or no thought at all.

"I never liked Simmons. Another cocky rich guy," Hollister said.

"You'll like his money."

"Whatever. His story's bogus, too. The girl never came on to him. Simmons rubs me the wrong way. Got perv written all over him."

Crystal drilled him with a stare. Her eyes were too close together. Way too close. Practically in the same socket. Funny how it had never bothered him until recently.

"I don't care if he's Ted Bundy," she said. "Or Al Bundy. We're talking eighty grand. Know what, Hollister? You're getting old. When did that happen? You used to be tough."

Hollister shrugged. "Maybe I am. You're no spring chicken, either."

"I'm thirty-seven."

"Forty."

"Moron."

"I'm just saying it ain't young."

Crystal continued to stare. Did the woman ever blink? Then she showed him her shark-toothed grin. "I thought I told you to shut up, sweetie."

He sighed and walked into the living room. His back ached, and now his head throbbed, thanks to Crystal. He rubbed a knot in his neck, then shook a Demerol out of the bottle from his pocket. He swallowed it without water and grimaced.

"Look at all this pink," Crystal called from the bedroom. She sounded almost happy. "It's gonna be fun slapping little Miss Princess around."

Hollister sighed. He squinted at the bottle and thought about taking another, then stuck it back in his jeans. "No violence. Dr. Simmons wants her back unharmed. He was very clear about that."

He took in the apartment. Not fancy but not a slum either. Not too neat but not messy.

Normal.

Lots of old stuff. Forties and fifties. Matched the clothes in the closet. Pictures of movie stars all over the walls. Simmons said she was into that. Retro chick. LA was full of them these days. Hollister made a mental note. You never knew what might help during a missing-person search.

Except Paradise Jones wasn't really missing. She was a runner, and most likely running for good reason. The thought of the good doctor's Porsche sailing over a cliff made Hollister chuckle. Loud in the quiet room. Good for her. Still, Crystal was right, no matter what she smelled like. Eighty grand was eighty grand.

A tiled counter separated the living room from the kitchen.

Open floor plan. Good for entertaining. Man, he *was* getting old.

Hollister opened the refrigerator. Yogurt, eggs, cheese. In the meat drawer, he found some sliced deli chicken. She ate healthy. He pulled out the chicken and cheese. Why let it go to waste? Lots of Cokes, too. Old school. The kind in a glass bottle. No cans or plastic. He grabbed one, then looked around for a bottle opener.

Nothing visible.

He shrugged and pried the cap off with his teeth. Once he'd known a Russian who could pop one off with his eye socket. Great bar trick.

Hollister wrapped some cheese in a slice of chicken and took a bite, washing it down with a swig of Coke. He'd skipped lunch. He pulled open a drawer. Plastic wrap, aluminum foil, sandwich bags, a couple dishtowels—pink, of course. The next drawer held cooking utensils, the one after that, silverware. Fourth—the inevitable junk drawer.

Bingo.

Pens, paperclips, movie ticket stubs, a Swiss Army knife. Piles of receipts— these he stuffed in his pocket—and a small notepad. The top page displayed a scribbled note.

R and S Coins—15 to 25.

Fifteen to twenty-five what? Minutes? Dollars? Hundred dollars? Thousand? On a hunch, he pulled the receipts from his pocket and rifled through them. On a yellow sheet folded in quarters, he found what he was looking for.

Dated last week. R and S Coins. Written Estimate, eight escudos gold coin. Rare. Altered. $32,000.

Thirty-two thousand? Looks like they had underestimated over the phone. Or Paradise Jones drove a hard bargain. Either way, it meant the girl made out. If she'd sold it, she wouldn't be short of cash. It made the job that much harder.

"What's that?" Crystal said.

"Geez, Crystal … Let me peel myself off the ceiling. What're you, a vampire? Why do you have to sneak up on me like that?"

Crystal blinked her too-close-together eyes. "Ghosts are quiet, not vampires."

Hollister stared at her, then said, "I think vampires are pretty quiet, too."

"They have loud shoes. Like boots with heels or something."

"Who cares? The point is they sneak up on people. Suck their blood and all that."

"You're an idiot. That's only in the movies."

"What are you talking about? As opposed to the vampires *not* in the movies? Just quit sneaking up on me." Hollister started to say more but fought his temper down. His head throbbed already and getting clocked by his crazy wife was the last thing he needed.

Crystal jerked her chin at the paper in Hollister's hand. "I asked what you had."

"Nothing. Just a receipt." He started to stick it in his pocket, but Crystal grabbed it.

"Thirty-two thousand? You call this nothing?"

"C'mon. We were hired to do a job. Let's just get on with it—get it over with."

Crystal's lips curled up, but her eyes didn't shed the hard edge. She scrolled her smartphone. "This little miss is running with either a gold coin or over thirty grand. That sounds to me like a nice little bonus we can rattle out of her. I say we make a stop at R and S Coins and get some details. Here it is, in the Valley. Thirty minutes, tops."

Hollister leaned back against the counter and took a long drink from the Coke bottle. Simmons … Hollister remembered his own stepdad. "You know what? Let's just bag this one. We're not hurting for cash. Let the girl run. Maybe she'll get lucky and get clear of Dr. Freak Show for good."

"Uh-huh. And say what to him?"

"I'd be happy to bounce his head off the curb. How 'bout I say that?"

"Hey, he helped *us*, didn't he?" Crystal showed her shark teeth again. Her twisted version of a smile. "Look how well we get along now, sweetie. And it's an easy eighty grand."

Hollister shook his head. Insanity. It was all crazy. *Helped us? The stuntman bounty-hunter and his psychotic sidekick wife?* How did he get here?

"Yeah, Ozzie and Harriet, that's us."

"Get in the car, Hollister. Just shut up and let's go. You're a pathetic old man, you know that?"

Hollister rubbed his temples. "And you're still no spring chicken." He took another drink of the Coke.

Crystal raised a fist, and he flinched. She laughed and headed for the door, receipt still in hand. "And leave the Coke. That stuff'll kill ya."

He downed the remainder and followed. "Not soon enough."

The trip to the Valley took an hour and ten, and the traffic did nothing to help Hollister's aching head. Thankfully, Crystal kept quiet, marking time by staring out the window. Every once in a while, she cackled her abrasive laugh at nothing in particular. Who knew what went on in the woman's head? Hollister definitely didn't, and didn't want to.

R and S Coins proved unimpressive from the outside. It occupied the end unit of a graffiti-covered, stucco strip mall—one of a thousand like it in the San Fernando Valley. Mariachi music blared through the open door of a burrito joint adjoining the coin shop. The smell of grilling meat made Hollister's stomach growl. The deli meat and cheese hadn't done much for him.

Crystal looked up at the plastic R and S COINS sign above the place. Or, rather, R and S COI since the N and S were both bashed in.

"What a dump," she said.

"Can't argue with that."

Crisscrossed bars covered the plate-glass window. A neon OPEN sign hung dark. Great, all that way and the place was closed. Hollister tried the glass door anyway. It opened, surprising him. A cowbell on the handle thunked as they entered. Hollister expected the usual cool blast of California air-conditioning but was met instead with thick, muggy heat. Glass cases covered by about a decade's worth of dust lined the walls, each one filled with coins of every size and shape. A cobweb-draped ceiling fan hung above.

"What the ...?" Crystal said, coming in behind Hollister. "It's like a sauna in here. Your AC broke or something?" This last statement she directed toward a slight man perched on a stool behind a book-piled glass counter. He wore a balled turtleneck sweater—the Irish Fisherman kind—and a Dodgers baseball cap.

The man blinked at her, his eyes buggy like something off the nature channel. "No, why?"

"Are you kidding me?" Crystal said.

Hollister approached the counter, pulling the estimate from the pocket of his jeans. "What's the R and S stand for?"

"Ronald and Sylvia." Another blink.

The little man wore a gold, plastic name tag. Hollister had to squint to read it. It said MATT.

"So, Matt, you a Dodgers fan?" he asked.

"My name's Ronald. Ronald and Sylvia. Remember?"

"Huh," Hollister grunted, then laid the estimate in front of the man. "You write this?"

Ronald scratched his cheek. "You guys cops? You don't look like cops."

"Private investigator," Hollister said.

"I'm a cop," Crystal added.

"You don't look like a cop," Ronald said.

"She's not a cop," Hollister said.

Crystal shrugged and wrote H + C in the dust on a glass case. "I'd be a good one if I was, though."

"Could you please just answer the question?" Hollister said, trying to keep things on point.

"See, I don't have to answer since you're not cops. Estimates are private."

Crystal approached the counter. "Since we're not cops, how 'bout I pick you up by your size-six Hush Puppies and drop you through this glass?"

The man blinked, then looked at Hollister. "Would she do that?"

Hollister's eye began to twitch. "Yeah. She'd definitely do that, Ronald."

The man took the paper and studied it. "Yeah, I wrote it. Hard to forget this one."

"Yeah? Why is that?" Hollister said.

"First of all, the girl that brought the coin in was strange. A knockout, Marilyn Monroe-type, but strange. Talked like she was in an old movie or something."

"Keep going," Hollister prodded.

"The coin, though. The Dos Escudos. That was the thing, man, I wish she'd have sold it."

"She kept it?" Crystal said.

"Yeah. Wouldn't part with it. I would've given her top dollar too. More than she could get on Ebay or anywhere else."

The little man hesitated. Crystal cracked her knuckles, and the bug eyes blinked several times. "See, it was an Escudos. Valuable enough as is. Gold, you know? They're around, but this one wasn't your standard find. It was special," he said.

Hollister leaned forward, hands on the glass counter. "Special in what way?"

"Altered on one side. I knew the coin. I mean that *particular* coin. Stories have circulated about them for years."

"Them?" Hollister said.

"Yeah. Two of them. The Dos Escudos. They're really eight escudos coins, but they say *dos*—two—'cause they're a pair. They work together. One's a cipher and the other one's a key to decode it. They're supposed to lead to some big treasure. Gold or something—nobody actually knows what. There was a rumor one of the coins had been found years ago." He pointed to the estimate. "I never believed it, but I'm sure the girl's was one of them."

"But it's no good without the other coin," Hollister said. "At least, as far as the treasure's concerned, right? Why'd you want to buy it so bad?"

The bug eyes darted toward Crystal. "The thing is, I saw on the Internet—hot news for collectors ... Some guys found the other coin. They published it on an archeology forum. Weird that the escudos would turn up at the same time, huh? So both of them are out there now."

"Both? Key and cipher? You tell the girl this?" Hollister said.

"Yeah. I figured what's the point in keeping it secret? She didn't want to sell anyway."

"Where's the other coin? Where was it found?"

"Paradise, Arizona. It's in a museum there. At an old mission."

"Yeah, well, thanks." Hollister scooped up the estimate and headed for the door.

"Thanks for supporting local law enforcement, Matt," Crystal said.

"Go Dodgers," he replied.

"I never heard of Paradise, Arizona," Crystal said, once they were back outside.

"I heard of Paradise Jones, though. And something tells me that it ain't no coincidence. I'm getting a burrito."

"Those things'll kill ya."

"Keeping my fingers crossed. One can only hope."

"Get it to go then. It's a long way to Arizona. We can drive through the night."

"Whatever."

Crystal shark-grinned him. "And I'm driving."

The tick in Hollister's eye moved down to his cheek.

Chapter Ten

The African Queen and Yesterdays Special

The air conditioner on top of the old Airstream rattled and shook like a high school kid's hand-me-down pickup truck. On the flat screen, Katharine Hepburn dumped bottles of booze over the side of the *African Queen* while Bogey snored chainsaws. Doc gave them an occasional glance as he lay on his leather couch, enjoying the breeze from the AC. He'd had to completely disassemble the couch to get it through the undersized trailer door, but the effort had been worth it. Most nights he even slept there. He tossed a baseball up for the hundredth time and caught it just before it hit his face.

He tossed the ball again.

Trevor struck him out today. Doc's homer had brought him up from Phoenix for another go.

Not that Doc considered himself invincible. And sure, the kid was a heck of a pitcher, but the thing rankled and multiplied his restlessness times a thousand. Doc had taped his knee, braced up, and pushed himself through a six-mile run after the game, but it hadn't helped.

What was he doing? Paco was right, there had to be more to life out there somewhere.

Bogey held his aching head while Katharine, prim, proper, and perfect in the African heat, continued to dump his hooch into the river.

Doc picked up the Spanish coin and rubbed his thumb across it.

Gato Negro. What do you open? What were those brothers trying to hide? The answer, lost in the misty recesses of time, taunted him. He'd never know. The whole thing would simply go down as a dusty story about a four-hundred-fifty—maybe sixty—foot home run and some old bones.

The coin had value. At least fifteen or twenty thousand dollars, from what information he could gather on the Internet. Maybe a lot more, but he had no desire to sell it. Things weren't that bad. At least not yet. Besides, it really belonged in Jake's museum.

Doc's old rotary dial phone rattled out its fire-alarm ring. A quick visual hunt showed the phone cord terminating under a couch pillow on the floor. He ignored it.

Bogey started gathering his wits and the phone stopped ringing.

Doc's cell lit up. Gregorian chant. Jake's ring tone.

"What's up, oh holy one?" Doc said.

"You at home? I never know which phone to call. Why do you keep both?" Jake said.

"Yeah, I'm here. Because we had this landline number forever, man. Mom and Dad had it."

"Yeah. Let me guess. You're on the couch. Old movie. Feeling sorry for yourself." Jake's slight cowboy drawl always comforted Doc.

"Yes, yes, and no."

"Liar. He struck you out, get over it. What are you doing tonight?"

A click of the remote ended Katharine's righteous rant. "Found a copy of *Vertigo*. Hanging with Hitchcock."

"DVD?"

"VCR."

"At the *Jesus is Coming Soon Thrift Store?*"

"Yup."

Jake sighed. "I bought you a DVD player for Christmas."

"And I love it."

"It's still in the box, right?"

"But the box is now by the TV. We're making progress."

"You eaten?"

"Yeah, but I'll eat again. Nothing going in the kingdom of God tonight?"

"Meet me out front. We'll go to Shorty's," Jake said.

"Can't argue with a priest."

"No, you can't."

The line went dead.

Like the mission, Shorty's Café and Restaurant faced the town square and the massive oak tree that stood in its center. Pictures lined the café's walls showing the place much the same fifty and even a hundred years ago as it was today. In 1998, the National Registry of Historic Places officially listed Shorty's as an Arizona landmark.

None of that mattered to Doc. Shorty's was simply his second home. It'd been in the Morales family for generations, and he'd grown up there.

The bell above the door rang as the brothers entered. Mostly empty. Still too early for the dinner crowd. Doc took a booth by the window while Jake grabbed a chess set from behind the counter.

The kitchen door swung open, and Katie Morales poked her head through. "*Mijos*, you here to eat?"

Doc waved. "Hey, Aunt Katie. If you're cooking, we're here to eat. Where's Uncle Lou?"

"He ran to the store. We're out of milk. I'll make you the special. *Tacos Guadalajara*." Katie's head disappeared.

Jake dropped his cowboy hat onto the seat next to him and let out a soft grunt. "Wasn't that the special yesterday?"

"Don't complain. Price is right."

"True."

The kitchen door swung again. Honey Hicks emerged and came toward them, navigating empty tables. She tucked a loose strand of sandy blonde hair behind her ear. An order pad protruded from the pocket of her sunshine-yellow uniform, but she didn't pull it out. "Hey, Doc. Hey, Jake. Don't want the counter?"

Jake indicated the chess set with a nod. "No, thanks. Need the space."

Honey nodded. "You want something to drink?"

Jake ordered a *Dos Equis*, Doc, a grapefruit juice. Honey returned with the drinks thirty seconds later.

"How's your grandma, Honey?" Jake asked.

"Fine. Over at the bingo hall tonight. Woman never fades."

"Good for her."

As Honey sauntered off, Jake laid out the board with a lopsided grin. "I think it's my night, little brother."

"Could be. You did beat me that one time when I was in fourth grade and had that high fever."

"Keep talking. Pride cometh before a fall. I've been studying moves."

"I like playing with you. I always know you won't cheat. Catholic guilt and all that."

"Maybe that's my problem."

"Nah. You just need to learn to look ahead. Read people. That's why baseball's such a great game. It's like chess on grass and dirt."

"So you always say." They played for a few minutes before Jake picked the conversation back up. "Speaking of looking ahead, what are you gonna do, Doc? Live in that trailer the rest of your life? You're too smart for that."

"And here it comes, the stern yet loving priestly advice. Can we have a night that we just play chess, please? Check."

"Check? That was only six or seven moves."

"Six. What can I say? You're distracted with worry over my future. Pay attention."

Jake studied the board, then sighed and made his move. "How do you do that? You're the only one who beats me."

"Checkmate."

"Do you actually have to say it?"

"Trevor struck me out today. Toss me a bone."

The kitchen door banged, and Honey appeared with the food. "Tacos for the Morales boys. Game over already?"

Doc grinned. "Want to know who won?"

"No, she doesn't," Jake said.

"Plates are hot. Doc won. Doc always wins. You guys never change," Honey said. Jake slid the board aside as Honey set down the plates.

"How hot?" Doc asked.

Honey crossed her arms. "Go ahead then."

Doc touched the plate. His hand jerked back of its own volition. "Yeah. Really hot."

Honey shook her head and headed back to the kitchen. "Shout if you need anything."

Jake forked some refried beans and blew on them to cool them down. "You been doing that since you were a kid, you know that? Hot means hot."

Doc leaned back in the booth. "Is it weird? You and Honey?"

"Why would it be weird?"

"You know. You were together for so long. Now you're a priest. It must be weird."

"Things change, Doc."

"Yeah, but why a priest? Why not a pastor, like Paco? Pastors can get married, have a family. I never thought you bought into the whole liturgy and Eucharist thing."

"We each walk our own path. I have to walk mine. And now who's giving the advice?"

"I guess. I thought you'd marry Honey and give me a yard full of nieces and nephews. Everybody did."

"Like I said …"

"Yeah. Things change. But I notice Honey never calls you *Father* Jake."

"Can we please change the subject?" Jake said.

Doc wiped guacamole from his face with a napkin. "Back to my wasted life?"

"What else? I'm getting worried about you. Taking a breather is one thing, but you just checked out. It's been too long."

Across the street, shadows gathered beneath the big oak. Lights began to come on. The bell above the door rang, and a family came in. Ranchers by the look of them—Mom, Dad, and four kids.

"Listen, Doc," Jake said around a forkful of beans. "God gives us things. Talents. Gifts that we're supposed to use." He swallowed. "*Need* to use. You're one of the most gifted people I've ever known. And I don't just say that because you're my brother. Problem is, you've left all those gifts sitting in a box like that DVD player. It's time to live. You need to see that."

"About that DVD player, you know you can watch movies on the computer now? Stream them right to the TV?"

"C'mon, Doc."

Doc kept his eyes on the window. "I *opened* the box, man. I had my shot. It was God's idea to bench me, not mine."

"We all know you're a great ballplayer, Doc. C'mon, though. There's more to life. Calling baseball your only gift is like opening a pair of pajamas from Aunt Katie on Christmas Eve, then skipping Christmas morning altogether. Baseball's baseball, but you've got a whole world in front of you."

"So what should I do? Become a priest? Like you?"

Jake frowned. "Give me a break."

Doc shrugged. "I've thought about it. It worked for you. Except when you see Honey."

"Service to the church isn't a place to hide, Doc. It's not like that. It's a calling. You can't run from baseball to the priesthood. Besides, we're talking about years, and that's just to get started."

"I can't be called?"

Jake put his fork down. "I didn't say that. I'm just saying, don't make knee-jerk decisions that will affect the rest of your life."

Doc shot a glance at the kitchen door. "Didn't you?"

Jake hesitated. "No ... I didn't."

"Three years, Jake. I've been back here for three years, man. Living in Dad's old trailer. Maybe it's not a knee-jerk decision. Maybe it's the right thing to do."

"I don't see it, Doc. I don't want to discourage you. I really don't. But I know you."

"You sure you're not trying to discourage me from making a mistake because you think you made one?"

"Leave it alone now, Doc."

Neither spoke for a while. Food gone, Honey brought coffee. The café started to rattle with activity as the dinner crowd trickled in. Tables filled. Laughter and conversation shoved the evening quiet out the door. Honey handled all of it with practiced ease, everywhere at once.

Jake started to sip his coffee, then blew on it instead and set the cup down. "Paco contacted Gregory Jones' lawyer. He said he'd never heard of the coin. If Jones *did* have it—and there's no evidence he did—he could've sold it or even lost it years ago. No way to know."

"And so dies the great mystery of the Dos Escudos."

"Looks like it. I wish I could have taken a crack at figuring out what it was all about."

"If wishes were horses, right?"

The bell rang again as the front door opened. Doc's coffee cup stopped halfway between the table and his mouth as Lana Turner walked in.

Right off the set of *Two Girls on Broadway.*

A scarf held her blonde hair back. She wore a white cotton blouse and red shorts. Just like the movie poster. Even the shoes were right.

Only it wasn't Lana Turner. It was a girl. A girl like Doc had never seen.

"Hey, Jake."

"What?"

"I just changed my mind. I don't want to be a priest after all."

CHAPTER ELEVEN

Louisville Slugger

In younger days, Doc often tagged along while Jake bounced from rodeo to rodeo, dragging their dad's old Airstream behind Jake's Chevy truck. There had been plenty of time to talk. The kind of talk only brothers know. Jokes and jabs until far past midnight, when the Big Gulps and jerky were long gone and the desert sky swirled with satellites and mystery. The time of night when things get serious. When thoughts turn to dreams and love and girls and God. Sometimes Doc imagined the bodiless spirits of his parents storming and swirling along beside the pickup, smiling and protecting, free from cumbersome flesh and blood, but every bit as real as the inevitable truck-stop sign on the horizon.

One time—Doc never forgot it—somewhere between Lubbock and Abilene, Jake broke character and waxed eloquent on what it was like to have your guts pounded out of you while perched on the hurricane deck of a saddle-bronc. How everything comes into focus and time stands still. Eight seconds stretches out in front of you like a lifetime. When the chute opens and a day is like a thousand years and a thousand years is like a day. Doc tried hard to imagine the sensation but hadn't been able to pull it off. Not even during his own rodeo, standing chest-to-chest with the Green Monster in Fenway Park.

He understood now, sitting in a booth at Shorty's. He understood with perfect clarity as God jerked the rug out from under him with a mighty fist. The calm in the eye of a typhoon and an NFL defensive line smashing every bone in your body all at once.

Everything, just like Jake described—and in living Technicolor.

The girl took a stool at the counter.

"You all right?" Jake talked loud to make himself heard over the dinner crowd.

"If you call not being able to breathe all right."

Jake turned and glanced at the counter and gave a low whistle. "And how the mighty fall. You gonna talk to her?"

"Just a second, I'm deciding. Look at her. What do you say to a girl like that?"

"You're the smart one. Play chess, it's like baseball."

Doc tapped his knife on the table. "She's not from here."

"Brilliant. Hey, you were a Major League ballplayer. Any lady would want to talk to you."

Doc nodded toward the girl. "That one's different. She's no spring-training groupie. She doesn't look like the type that watches ESPN."

"Yeah? Neither did Marilyn. And Joltin' Joe DiMaggio didn't do too bad."

"Why are you pushing me?"

"Because you need a distraction. Something to drag yourself away from your pity party and old movies." Jake nodded toward the girl. "She looks like she just stepped out of one. Might be just the ticket."

Honey stopped in front of the girl and pulled out her order pad. They spoke and Honey jotted down the order.

"So go talk to her," Jake said.

"She just ordered. It'd be awkward now."

Jake sipped his coffee, eyes amused.

"What?" Doc said when he couldn't take it anymore.

"Just enjoying the moment. What happened to Mr. Three Moves Ahead?"

"Sometimes the board gets knocked over. You have to take a breather to reassess."

Honey walked over to the table. "You guys done or do you want something else?"

"Not in a hurry. How about some more chips and salsa?" Jake said.

"And a warm-up on the coffee?" Doc added. "Do you know the girl at the counter?"

Honey raised an eyebrow. "What? The golden boy is interested in something besides baseball?"

Jake grinned.

"Nope," Honey said. "She didn't introduce herself, just ordered. Seems quiet."

While Honey and Jake carried on their usual, easy conversation, Doc watched the girl. Seated at the counter, her back was to him now. Blonde hair fell past perfect shoulders. She snuck a furtive glance toward the door—the third one in the last minute—and he caught the smattering of freckles across her nose and cheeks.

Why keep looking at the door? Afraid of something?

Her style and look drew him, made him curious, but there was something else. She had softness. Grace out of place in this day and age—or at least rare. She had sadness too. Maybe loneliness. A thousand questions crowded Doc's mind. He wondered what her voice sounded like. Lana Turner?

A tortilla chip bounced off Doc's chest.

"Earth to Doc," Jake said, pulling him from his thoughts.

Doc picked the chip up off the table, scooped salsa on it and crunched. "What?"

"Don't talk with your mouth full. What are you doing?"

"You're the king of talking with your mouth full. Trying to figure out her story. What do you think it is?"

Jake shook his head. "Nope. I know you. You have a working theory already anyway. If you want to know, go ask her. She doesn't look scary."

"You don't think so? Why are my palms sweating?"

"Because she looks like she's from 1950, and you have a thing for old movie stars."

Doc laughed. "A thing for old movie stars? Like Cloris Leachman? Or the lady from *Driving Miss Daisy*?"

"You know what I mean. Besides, Cloris seems cool."

Doc glanced again toward the counter. "Look at her, Jake. It's more than that. You see it, right?"

"Nope. I'm a priest, remember? Made of stone."

"Give me a break. I'm not just talking about what she looks like."

"Uh huh."

"All right, sure, there's that. But I mean *look* at her. She's graceful."

Jake didn't respond right away. When he finally did he said, "Sometimes God pokes you with a stick and says, 'Listen up.' If God's poking you, pay attention."

"Does God ever use a Louisville Slugger?"

Jake leaned forward. "Your move, Doc. What do you want to do?"

"I don't know. Don't rush me."

Jake glanced up, then back at Doc. "Don't have to. Here she comes."

CHAPTER TWELVE

Two Girls on Broadway ... Hypothetically

The priest looked surprised but not unhappy to see her coming, giving Paradise the impression she'd been a topic of conversation. The other man watched her come as well, his face a bright question. His sun-bleached blond hair threatened to curl should length allow, in contrast to dark brown eyes that held a touch of both uncertainty and trouble. Still, not bad looking. Confident. Not shy, this one.

But it was the priest who drew her. She'd been watching him in the mirrored pie cabinet since she sat down—well, watching both men, really. But it was the priest who had the kind eyes and easy smile. Very solid. Grounded to the earth in a Gregory Peck sort of way. He had a calmness she could almost physically feel. Could she talk to him? That's what priests did, right? Listen to people? She knew nothing about religion except what she'd seen in movies. She thought of Peck's portrayal of Father O'Flaherty in *The Scarlet and the Black*—he was nice. And he'd known what to do, too.

Yes. The man in the white collar eating chips and salsa was a young, slightly darker, Gregory Peck.

Pull it together, girl.

Ash would have a field day if she could hear the scattered thoughts ricocheting around Paradise's skull. Questions pressed and flitted like moths around a light bulb. What was she doing? Why had she come to this little town? What did she think she'd find, some kind of history? Roots? Then again, where could she go? Here was as good a place as any, but how long could she run? What started as an adventure now felt ominous. If the whole thing were a movie, the orchestra would be building tension while the villain closed in.

But this wasn't a movie. No promised happy ending just before the credits. Paradise hated the thought. Worse than anything, loneliness enveloped her. And it had grown with every mile she put between the Olds and Los Angeles. Once, she'd even come close to calling Eve--she really was losing it.

Butterflies swirled in her stomach. Why? The priest didn't look scary.

Shoot for the stars, kid. Here goes nothing.

Paradise addressed the priest and ignored the blond man. "Hello."

"Hello," he said.

So, off to a swimming start.

"I, um ..."

"Would you like to sit?" The priest leaned, and reached a long arm out for a chair at a neighboring table. He pulled it over for her.

"Thanks," she said. "You're a priest, right?"

"I am. Can I help you with something? Are you okay?"

"*Two Girls on Broadway,*" the other man said.

Paradise glanced at him. "Excuse me?"

His eyes had sun lines at the edges. "Lana Turner. *Two Girls on Broadway*—the outfit, the look, the whole package. It's perfect."

"You know the movie?" she said.

"Sure." He started to continue, but the priest interrupted.

"I'm Father Jake. This is my brother, Doc."

She liked his voice. Slow, like a cowboy, and smooth. Yes—very Gregory.

"Nineteen-forty. Directed by S. Sylvan Simon. Lana played Pat Mahoney," Blond Hair said.

"Wow," Paradise said. "And did you like it?"

He turned his coffee cup in increments on the table with short little moves of his fingers. Strong fingers she couldn't help noticing.

"Not a lot," he said.

"Me either. It was horrible. Except for the clothes. I loved the clothes," Paradise said.

He smiled, lifting an eyebrow.

"What?" she said.

"Your voice. It's perfect."

"Thank you, I think." She turned her attention back to young Gregory.

"Was there something I could help you with?" Father Jake said. He did have *very* kind eyes.

Paradise hesitated, then took a slow breath. Fear rose with a rush. "I don't know. I don't know why I came over. I should probably go. I'm sorry for bothering you."

Father Jake stopped her with a gentle hand on her arm. "It's okay. Tell you what, why don't you just sit and have a cup of coffee? We'll talk. All right?"

Such nice eyes. So brown. They calmed her. The fear eased, and she nodded her head. He called to the waitress and asked for another coffee. The front door opened and she jumped. No police, just a man in a John Deere trucker hat talking on a cell phone. Not looking for her or anybody else. Didn't even know she existed. Just like a billion people in China. Or the whole world, except for creepy Burt and the police. And Ash and Arnie, maybe. The brother's eyes shifted to the John Deere man, then back to her, but he didn't comment. A cup of coffee appeared in front of her.

What do you want, Paradise ...

"Excuse me?' Paradise said, turning.

The waitress smiled down at her, "I didn't say anything."

"Oh ... I'm sorry. Thank you for the coffee."

"You bet," she said over her shoulder, heading for another table.

Neither Father Jake nor his brother pressed Paradise to speak. She added sugar and cream to her cup and stirred. The coffee continued to swirl for long seconds after she pulled the spoon out.

"Thank you for the coffee," she said finally.

"Thanks for not leaving," Father Jake said.

Paradise searched his eyes, but said nothing.

"Have you come a long way?" Father Jake asked.

"Yes. LA ... Um ... Los Angeles."

Father Jake laughed. "I know what LA stands for. Are you an actress?"

Paradise tasted the coffee. "It's strange, isn't it? They all call themselves actors now. Both men *and* women, I mean."

"Oh. Right. I think I knew that," Father Jake said.

"It's ridiculous. Actor this, actor that. Why not an actress? What are they trying to prove? *Actress* has more glamour, don't you think?"

Father Jake glanced at his brother, then back. "I suppose it does ... So you are? An actress?"

"Yes. No. Well, not really. I mean I've *been* in a few things ... Nothing good. There's this part I'm up for, and Arnie thinks I'll get it."

"Who's Arnie?"

"Oh … Arnie's my manager. Do you know he talks like he's from New York, but he's really from Orange County?"

Father Jake nodded with either gravity or confusion.

"Ah. Well … good for you, about the part." He left it at that, which made her feel grateful, though she didn't know why.

"Is someone looking for you? Are you in trouble?" Doc asked.

"Doc …" Father Jake said.

"No. It's okay," Paradise said. "Why is your name Doc?"

She meant to throw him off guard, but he only smiled. He had nice teeth. "'Cause it's better than Grumpy or Bashful. You didn't tell us your name, by the way."

"No, I didn't," she answered. The reply sounded good. Firm. Very Hepburn. Katharine, not Audrey.

"Ignore him," Father Jake said. "I know it's easier said than done. Listen, I'd really like to help, whatever the problem is."

Paradise dismissed Doc with a purposeful turn of her shoulder. Again, very Hepburn. Audrey this time, not Katharine. "My father died."

Father Jake nodded. "I'm sorry. Was it recently?"

"Yes. Not long ago." Why was she telling him this?

"Did he live in Paradise? Is that why you're here?"

"No. Well, yes. I mean he *did*. A long time ago. And, sort of … sort of that's why I'm here, I mean. Actually, I didn't know him very well at all."

"It's still hard. Losing your dad. Whether you knew him or not."

"Have you ever lost someone? Like a parent? Someone close?" she asked.

The men glanced at each other.

"I'm sorry," she said. "I shouldn't pry. It's none of my business."

"No, it's okay," Father Jake said. "Yes. Our parents died when we were young. Car accident."

"Oh. How young?"

"I was fifteen and Doc was eleven."

"So who raised you?"

When Father Jake shrugged, the corners of his mouth turned down. "Everyone. It's a small town. And we come from a big family. Some of them own this place. The Moraleses. Our last name is Morales, too."

Paradise looked around. "It's nice." It wasn't really a lie, was it? Visions of *Gregory's of Malibu* flashed through her mind. Come to think of it, she liked this place better. "My father was in a car accident, too."

"In Los Angeles?" Doc asked.

"Yes."

"How about your mother?" Father Jake said.

"She lives in Malibu. They haven't been together for years. Since I was a little girl."

"So you came here to see where your father grew up?" Doc said.

Paradise surveyed him. He had eyes the same brown as his brother's, with deep crow's feet. But instead of the priest's calming kindness, this one's gaze spoke something else altogether.

He *was* handsome.

Not now, Paradise Jones...

"Why don't you look like brothers?" she said.

Doc shrugged and grinned. "Maybe God likes me better. But probably because our dad was Mexican and our mom was Welsh."

"Well, your brother's much more handsome. Like a young Gregory Peck."

Doc laughed, surprising her—a nice sound. "That's true."

"How did you know?" she said.

"How did I know you thought Jake was handsome?"

"Of course not—pay attention. About Lana Turner and *Two Girls on Broadway*. Are you really that into old films?"

Doc leaned back in the booth, still smiling. "Do you always answer questions with questions?"

Paradise considered this, then said, "Paradise Jones."

"What?"

"Paradise. You asked me what my name was. Remember? Which means I just answered a question with an answer. So, no."

"I thought I asked you about coming to see where your dad grew up?"

"You really need to learn to focus." She turned back to Father Jake. "If I talk to you, is there confidentiality? Like doctor-patient?"

Father Jake scratched his Gregory chin. "Did you break the law?"

"Technically, yes, I suppose. But I wouldn't take it back. At least, I don't think I would."

"Technically? It's a yes-or-no question."

Honey stopped at the table and refilled the coffee cups. The waitress's pretty eyes lingered on Father Jake a little longer than Paradise or Doc. A customer called for a check and she moved off.

"Do you like being a priest?" Paradise asked.

"Why do you ask?"

She glanced at Honey, totaling a bill on her waitress-pad. "No reason. All right. Yes, I black-and-white broke the law. Technically and every other way. Yes, there's someone looking for me. And yes, I'm in trouble. Does that cover it?"

"I'd like to help you," Father Jake said, his voice still slow and calm.

"You won't turn me in?"

"Why don't you tell me what happened. We're just talking, remember? When I say I want to help, I mean it."

"That's not an answer. How did you put it? It's a yes-or-no question."

"This isn't a confessional, so I'm obligated to report something I hear if it's illegal, just like anyone else. That being said, I still want to help. I promise you can trust me to do the right thing, whatever it is."

"Jake, what if you heard about a hypothetical situation?" Doc said. "You know, just in a passing conversation at a diner?"

"C'mon, Doc, I already said I wanted to help."

Doc turned toward Paradise. "Nobody's going to turn you in. Hypothetically, what happened?"

The front door opened again, but this time Paradise didn't look up. She felt safe sitting with the two men.

"Okay. Let's just say there was a hypothetical stepfather who couldn't keep his very real and very creepy hands to himself. And what if he tried to force himself on his stepdaughter when she was changing in a pool house? Wouldn't she be justified, for instance—hypothetically—if she whacked him over the head with a lamp and then sent his very expensive Porsche over a cliff? Hypothetically, I mean?"

"You're serious?" Doc looked surprised but not at all unhappy.

"Hypothetically serious."

"What model?" Doc said.

"Lamp?"

"Porsche."

"Panamera. Brand new."

Doc whistled between his teeth.

A wrinkle of concern formed between Father Jake's eyes. "Did you report him? For the assault?"

"No. He's a big, hypothetical psychiatrist in Beverly Hills, and he beat me to the police. He told them it was all me. That *I* made a pass at *him,* if you can believe it. And that I got mad and wrecked his car when he turned me down."

"You could tell them the truth," Father Jake said. "That's always a good place to start."

"It's his word against mine. And Beverly Hills justice tends to land on the side of the stepfather with the fattest wallet."

"So you're on the lam," Doc said, sounding very Cagney.

An unintended smile brushed her lips. Doc returned it.

"Does anyone know you're here?" Father Jake asked.

"No. I didn't tell anyone where I was going. Arnie's panicking, and my friend Ashleigh is worried that I can't handle America. Other than that, I doubt anyone even cares I'm gone. Except maybe creepy Burt, hypothetically."

"Then you should be safe, at least for now. Let me see what I can do. I can talk to someone for you. If your stepfather assaulted you, he should answer for it."

"He did, and he won't. He *never* has. You don't know Burt. He doesn't know the word quit. He won't stop with police. It's personal for him. An insult to his maleness. But thanks for trying, Father Jake the Priest. I feel better talking to you. You're very good at this."

"It must be hard," Doc said, "being alone in a strange place."

"Yes. Harder than I thought it would be."

"So, what part are you up for?"

"Scarlett in the new *Gone with the Wind.*"

"No kidding? That's huge."

Paradise shook her head. "My agent says it's in the bag, but he says that about everything from big parts to toothpaste commercials. It's a one-in-a-million long shot. Although the toothpaste commercial came through, come to think of it."

"I think you'd be a perfect Scarlett."

"You don't even know me."

"I know enough. So, Paradise Jones. Paradise, Arizona. Coincidence?"

"My father was an actor," she said. "He grew up here. He named me after this town. So I came because I wanted to see it."

"Wait," Doc said. "Your dad was Gregory Jones?"

"Yes."

The men looked at each other.

"Why?" she asked.

"This may sound like a strange question," Father Jake said, "and I hope you don't find it insensitive, but your father, did he ever mention a coin? An old one? Gold?"

"You mean the Dos Escudos?" Paradise said.

Father Jake's mouth opened.

"That's right," Doc said. "The Dos Escudos. You know it? Your father told you about it?"

"He never told me about it, but he left it to me. To tell you the truth, that's another reason I came. A man at a coin shop told me there was another one like mine. Here, in a museum. And they went together somehow."

Doc tipped his coffee cup toward Father Jake. "You mean *his* museum. You're counseling with the head honcho museum man, although the other coin's usually *behind* the museum. In my trailer."

"Your trailer? Why do you have it?"

"Because I found it. And now you found me. Like in a movie. It was meant to be."

"Like I said before, you need to learn to focus."

Father Jake touched her arm. "Listen, this could be very important. Where is your coin now? Do you have it with you?"

"Because of the treasure, you mean?"

Father Jake's eyebrows arched. "You know about that too? How?"

"The man at the coin shop told me—a strange little man. And I looked it up on the Internet at the library in Phoenix. There are lots of articles about it. Do you think the treasure is real?"

"No one knows. Probably not, but even if it isn't, the coins are a substantial historical find. I'd love to see them in the same room."

"I don't have it here. I left it at my room. I'm staying at the Venus Motel."

"No one's seen these coins together in nearly three hundred years. This is a small miracle. Tomorrow, then. Could you bring the coin to the mission tomorrow?" Father Jake said.

Doc reached into his pocket. Gold glinted in the air as he flipped a coin and popped it on the table with a sharp smack. Just like hers. She picked it up.

"My good luck charm," Doc said. "Nice night for a drive. What do you think?"

"C'mon, little brother, don't push it. It can wait till morning. Heaven knows it's waited this long. And you don't invite yourself to a lady's room," Father Jake said.

Paradise turned the coin in her fingers. For the first time in days, Burt faded to the back of her mind. His creepy, tanned face crowded out by newfound curiosity. She liked these two brothers, and the thought of her dark motel room depressed her. "I'm game, fellas. Let's do it. It's not like I have a busy nightlife. I'm on the lam, remember?"

Chapter Thirteen

The Beginning of the World

Doc followed Paradise's taillights as they headed out of town down First Avenue. Out past the commercial district and a tract of new homes, the landscape gave way to scrub oak and sage. First Avenue turned into Juniper Road and wound down the mountain. She drove fast, and Doc had to push his truck to keep up. At Highway 30, the taillights turned left—no blinker—and the moonlit desert stretched out to the west like an infinite sea floor. The moon shone full, lighting the wispy clouds stretching horizon to horizon. So bright that Doc could just make out the shadows of the San Angelo mountain range miles away to the south.

Jake spent the drive talking about the coins and sounding almost excited—at least as excited as Jake ever got. Doc tried to track, but his mind took a hard right down another road and it had nothing to do with Spanish coins.

Paradise Jones changed everything.

As of tonight, the world was bigger and spun faster. More solid and tenuous at the same time. It had become, in a single moment, a world where a girl like Paradise Jones could walk through the door of Shorty's Café and Restaurant. He went over the details again. Her fingers, long and perfect, nervous as they toyed with the spoon in her coffee cup. The little hollow at the base of her throat that flexed when she spoke. The way she talked and how her mind flitted through sentences like a butterfly trying to find a place to land. Even how she dismissed him so handily. He laughed aloud in the dark cab.

"What?" Jake said.

Doc glanced at him. His brother's face shone dull green in the dashboard glow.

"What, what?" Doc replied.

"What do you think? What if?"

"What if *what?*"

Jake shook his head and eyed Doc from beneath his hat brim. "You haven't been listening to a word I've said."

"Of course, I'm listening. What if *what*?"

"What if it's real? The story? What if it leads to something? It's a possibility."

"Oh, that. Yeah. What if?"

Doc's attention focused on the taillights now a quarter mile ahead, but he felt Jake's stare. No, scratch that. *Father* Jake's stare.

"Don't do that," Doc said.

"Do what?"

"Look at me like that."

"Like what?"

"You know like what. Like a priest."

"I am a priest."

"You know what I mean."

"Be careful, Doc, that's all. You just met the girl. Don't get ahead of yourself."

"Weren't you the one who wouldn't stop telling me I should go talk to her? That I needed a distraction? What happened to that?"

"I just want you to be careful. She's in trouble. Maybe a lot of trouble. *Law* trouble. Don't get in over your head."

Doc let a half mile or so slip beneath the truck's wheels before he answered. "Yeah. She's in trouble. But you heard her story. She's alone. And it wasn't her fault."

"We don't know her, Doc. Maybe it's not the whole story. I'm just saying, go slow, that's all. You're not in control. It's not baseball. This is not Fenway, and she's not the Green Monster."

"That's what Mickey told me the other day just before I hit that bomb."

"I'm serious, Doc."

"I know you are."

"The Green Monster," Doc said, half to himself.

"What?"

Doc clapped Jake on the shoulder. "I said I'll be careful, Father Jake the Priest. Don't you worry about a thing."

The Venus Motel had been a Paradise landmark since the early '40s. The motel's sign, a two-story, flashing neon Venus, stood guard over Highway 30 and beckoned travelers for a mile in either direction. Once rundown and half forgotten, a couple from Tucson recently purchased the property and gave it a much needed facelift. The motel lounge and retro piano and music bar filled to capacity most nights with locals and weary pilgrims alike. Tonight, a biker club joined the fray, parking their Harley Davidsons tight in among the pickups, BMWs, and Toyota Priuses. Doc followed Paradise as she rolled past them to the end of the motel and parked in front of room thirty-one. He threw the truck into park, opened the door, and slid out.

In the pool across the parking lot, a young mom and dad laughed and splashed with their daughter, all three glowing blue-green in the shimmering light. The sight brought a pang of the old familiar restlessness. Paradise Jones standing next to her Olds Eighty-Eight drove it away like Jesus with his scourge.

"Home sweet home," she said.

Doc's world fell around him when heard the sad edge in her voice. Then she smiled and built it again.

"Isn't she beautiful?" Paradise's face turned to the glow of the smiling Venus, neon light playing across her features.

"I guess I never thought about it," Jake said. "How did you find this place?"

"Where else? It's perfect," she said simply.

Jake nodded as if this made perfect sense. "How long have you been here?"

"A few days. Not long. I love it."

"And you haven't come to the museum?"

She crossed her arms, leaned back against the Olds and lifted her shoulders. "One day I just sat by the pool. Then another I drove out into the desert. It's so quiet out there, isn't it? Like the beginning of the world. Like there's nothing else. Only possibility."

"I see," Jake said, though Doc knew he didn't.

"I started to go to the museum today, but by the time I got to town it was getting late. I walked around the park for a while. Under that big tree."

"The oak," Jake said.

"I suppose it was. Then I got hungry and went to the diner, but I saw you and got nervous and wasn't hungry anymore. It's a good thing, don't you think? That I went in?"

"Absolutely," Doc said.

Paradise glanced at him, then back to Jake.

"Why didn't you bring the coin with you if you were going to visit the museum?" Jake said.

"I don't know. I don't think I was going to tell anybody I even had it. I wanted to see the other one first. But then you were so nice, so I told you."

Spanish guitar from the lounge floated across the balmy evening. The Venus hummed and flickered beneath the glowing desert sky. A beautiful night made even more so with Paradise Jones standing squarely in the middle of the universe.

"Get it together, man," Doc mumbled.

"What's that, Doc?" Jake said.

"I said, how about we see the coins," Doc said.

Paradise moved to the door of room thirty-one, then fished through her purse and came out with a key. "I love that they have real keys here. Not those card things. And real Cokes in the machine."

She moved to insert it into the doorknob, but the door swung open at her touch, creaking slightly on its hinges. She took a startled step back. "That's funny. I know I locked it."

Doc moved forward and placed a hand on her shoulder. She didn't move away, but he felt her tense.

"Let me take a look," he said.

She nodded and moved another three steps away from the door.

Doc felt around until he found the light switch. It took a few seconds. Lower than it should have been. A table lamp next to the bed flicked on. The bed had been stripped, blankets, sheets and pillow scattered. A large, red suitcase lay open and upside down on the floor. Clothes sprawled over the otherwise bare mattress. The nightstand drawer hung open, and a Gideon Bible rested among some of its own torn-out pages.

"Oh, no." Paradise said.

Jake stepped in behind her. "What in the world?"

"It's Burt. I know it's him. He found me." Paradise wrapped her arms around herself as if trying to make her body as small as possible.

"It could have been random," Doc said. It sounded hollow, even to him.

"We need to call the police," Jake said.

Paradise touched his arm. "No. Please. It's okay. I just need to go. I'll find somewhere else to go. The police will take me back to LA. To Burt. I can't go back. Not until it's all sorted out, and I know he won't hurt me."

"It's all right. No one's taking you anywhere," Doc said.

Behind Paradise, Jake's brow furrowed, and he shook his head at Doc.

Paradise moved into the bathroom and Doc followed. A flower-patterned makeup case lay on its side next to the sink, its contents scattered across the Formica counter. Paradise shuffled through them frantically.

"It's gone," she said finally. "It's not here."

"What's gone?" Jake said, standing in the bathroom doorway.

"My dad's coin. It's gone. He got it—Burt. How could he know? Why would he even care?"

"You're sure it's gone?" Doc said, studying her profile.

She didn't turn but continued to stare straight ahead. Doc followed her gaze. A tube of lipstick, the same shade Paradise wore, lay uncapped by the faucet. Above it, again the same shade, the mirror had a smeared kiss mark and next to it a pink, scrawled message.

C + H.

CHAPTER FOURTEEN

We'll Leave the Light on For Ya

Hollister scratched his arms while he counted to one hundred in his head. The arm-scratching, he knew, was psychosomatic, left over from a run-in with bedbugs ten years ago at a Motel 6 in Montana. The counting, however, constituted a regular blocking-out-Crystal's-voice exercise and wasn't psychosomatic at all. In fact, it very well may have saved her life on more than one occasion.

"I hate Motel 6," he said when he could force a word edgewise into her current diatribe—something about interval training. He'd gotten to seventy-three in his head so far and had no clue what she was talking about.

Crystal flopped her body onto the polyester bedspread, picked at a thread, and showed her shark-teeth. "It's not a Motel 6. It's a Motel 5."

"I never heard of a Five. I heard of a Six. And a Super 8, but not a five anything."

"Yeah, well, this is a Motel 5. Get over it."

Hollister scratched harder. "That's one worse than a Six." He started counting again, picturing the numbers floating up into a cloudless sky as big balloons.

His cell rang. Old-fashioned ring-tone, the loudest one. Lately he couldn't hear the others.

"Yeah?" he said.

"Where are you?" Dr. Simmons' voice rankled.

Hollister started his count over at one and released a balloon. "Arizona."

"Where in Arizona?"

Two . . .

"Who is it?" Crystal mouthed, elbow on the bed and head propped on her hand.

Hollister shook his head and held up a finger. Crystal hopped to her knees and mimicked him, holding up her own finger. *A forty-year-old kindergartener.*

Hollister turned his back on her. "Paradise. No, let me rephrase that. Middle-of-nowhere-godforsaken-you-can-see-hell-just-down-the-road-from-here Paradise, Arizona. In a Motel 5—no joke. A *five*, not a six."

Crystal disco-danced around in front of him and air-punched twice, coming within half an inch of his nose. "Who is it?" she mouthed again.

"You've got to be kidding," Simmons said. "She's in Paradise? That's where she went? So you've got her then?"

"Not exactly, but it's just a matter of time. She's here. We found her motel, but we missed her."

"What do you mean, missed her?"

"You're the one with the doctor in front of your name. I have to explain *missed her*?"

"Do-o-o-o-o-ctor Simmons … " Crystal sang the name to the tune of "Play That Funky Music White Boy."

"Is that Crystal?" Simmons said.

"Nice chat. Gotta go," Hollister said.

"You know, Hollister, I paid you forty thousand dollars. That means you work for me. You can show a little respect."

"You want the money back?"

"I want the girl. That's what I want."

Hollister shrugged, though he knew Simmons couldn't see him. "I am who I am. You get what you get. I told you I'd get the girl, and I'll get the girl. You want to give me grief, and I'll hand you your money back and walk."

"Big—tough—Hollister," Crystal sang, still in her groove. She caught her reflection in the mirror, stopped dancing and started a series of flexes.

Hollister turned his back to her again.

"When will you have her? How long?" Simmons said.

"Soon. We're leaving again now."

"Just get her. Let me talk to Crystal."

Hollister turned around. Crystal grunted, in the middle of a set of push-ups. "She's busy."

At this, Crystal hopped up and reached for the phone. Hollister dodged her.

"Busy doing what?" Simmons said.

"Putting on makeup."

An iron forearm snaked around his neck, and Crystal tried to pry the phone from his hand.

"Just get the girl, you hear me, Hollister?" Simmons said. "And tell Crystal to make it painful."

"Yeah, adios. I'll let you know." Hollister jerked his phone hand out of Crystal's claw and hung it up. "What's the matter with you?"

"Why didn't you let me talk to him?"

"Just let me handle the deals, cool? Which, by the way, isn't easy with you dancing around like Michael Jackson on a sugar high."

Crystal air-punched at him again, and he flinched. She laughed. "You're a moron."

Hollister released a balloon.

Crystal flopped onto the bed again. When she rolled over to face him, she had the gold coin wedged into her eye socket like a monocle. She saluted and shouted "Hogan!" in a thick German accent. "Who am I?" she said.

"Knock it off."

"Colonel Klink from *Hogan's Heroes*. Remember that? Or was it the other guy? The fat one?"

"Shultz," Hollister said.

"What?"

"Shultz, the fat one. No, it was Klink. He was the one with the monocle."

"What's a monocle?" Crystal said.

"An eyeglass."

"Who cares?"

"What do you mean, who cares? *You* asked *me*."

"Moron," Crystal muttered. "Old man." Crystal loved the word *moron*.

"Let me see the coin." Hollister reached for it, but Crystal leaned back.

"Let's go find the girl," Hollister said.

"Nope, the Little Princess can wait. She'll get hers. I can't wait to get a fist on that chick. But we got other business first." Crystal stood and headed for the door.

"I told you before. Not a mark on her or we don't get the rest of the money. And what other business are you talking about? Let's get the girl and be done with it. Get back to LA. All this open space gives me the willies."

Crystal held up the coin. "What's this?"

"What do you mean? It's the coin."

"Yeah, moron. *The* coin. *One* coin. Not *two* coins. What did the guy at the shop say? You gotta have two if you're gonna find the Mexican's gold."

"Spanish gold. And he don't even know if it's gold. Or if it's real. Let's just get the girl and go."

"Shut up, sweetie. We're going to the museum. We're gonna get the other coin, and we're gonna be rich. Easy peasy, nice and cheesy."

"You think this is some dumb movie? What that guy at the shop told us is just a story. Besides, the museum's probably closed."

"Of course, it's closed. That's the point. You want people watching while we steal the other coin? What happens in that rock of a head of yours? Anything?"

"I do a lot of counting."

"What?"

"Nothing."

Crystal opened the door and Hollister followed the *Game Over* tattoo out onto the sidewalk.

"We'll get the coin, and then we can slap—arou—ound—Pri—in—cess— Pink." Now Crystal sang to the tune of "Jive Talkin'" with a John Travolta disco side-shuffle.

"No marks," Hollister replied.

"Yeah." Crystal pounded her fist into her palm. "No marks."

CHAPTER FIFTEEN

Someone to Watch Over Me

Jardin de Dios Mission. Arizona. United States. Planet Earth. Universe.

Paradise liked Paco the moment she saw him. She liked his office, too, filled with the comfortable smell of old books and pipe smoke. Like Spencer Tracy would have smelled in *Boy's Town*. But Paco was more intense than Spencer. Living color, not black and white at all. Alive, but *more* than alive. His was a beautiful calm. Here, in this office, she felt safe for the first time since she'd launched Burt's car. The break-in at the motel room shook her emotions more than she wanted to admit, and she hadn't argued when Doc and Father Jake packed her things and brought her to the mission. They'd mentioned her staying here, and though she had no idea what that might look like, she instinctively trusted the brothers.

Doc stretched his body across a leather couch while Paradise opted for an armchair, hugging her knees to her chest. She'd changed clothes before leaving the Venus, first picking out a black dress and pearls—Eva Marie Saint in *North by Northwest*, excellent hideout look—but switched at the last minute to Marilyn in *The Seven Year Itch*, capris and matching cotton sateen blouse.

Paco listened to her story with the same patience that Father Jake had shown back at the diner, nodding but making few comments. Now, silence hugged the room save for the muted puffing sound from Paco's pipe as he reclined behind his desk.

At length, he blew a smoke ring, watched it climb and dissipate, then leaned forward and placed his forearms on the oak desk. "I knew him, you know—your dad. He was a good boy. He had it rough. I never blamed him for getting out of town. I'm very sorry you lost him. And even sorrier you didn't get to know him." He paused and puffed again. "Now, let me say this—Paradise, Arizona isn't Los Angeles ... or Beverly Hills ... or Malibu. We'll take care of you. You're safe here at the mission. At least for now."

Paradise blinked back unwanted tears. "Thank you."

Father Jake leaned against a bookshelf with his arms crossed. "One thing I don't understand is who got into your motel room? It wasn't the police. And why the coin? Why not anything else? Who else knows about it?"

"I'm sorry. I should have kept it in my purse. I didn't think," Paradise said.

"What do you think's going on, Doc?" Father Jake said.

Paradise sniffled and raised an eyebrow at Doc. "He's asking you? I thought you played baseball."

"It's like chess on grass and dirt," Jake and Doc said in unison.

Doc shrugged. "You're right, the police didn't break into the room. That probably means Paradise's stepdad put someone on her trail. Luckily she wasn't there. But, yeah, why the coin? How did they know? It seems like they were looking for something specific, the way they trashed the room. Jake has a good question. Who else knew about it?"

Paradise toyed with the strap of her white patent sandal as she thought. "My friend Ash was there when I found it, but she wouldn't say anything to anyone. Eve—my mom—she knew about it. She was surprised he'd kept it all those years. She pretended like she didn't care, but she's good at that. I don't know if she would have told Burt about it. I doubt it. There was the man at the coin shop …"

"The coin shop guy, what did he say about the coin when you took it in?" Doc asked.

"He recognized it. And he told me the story about the treasure. And about your coin, too. He wanted to buy mine, but I said no because it was my father's. He even gave me an estimate."

"And he didn't say anything else?"

"Um … Go Dodgers, I think."

Doc tossed a baseball in the air and caught it. "Was it a written estimate?"

"Yes. On a piece of yellow paper. He had very neat handwriting."

"Okay. What did you do with it?"

"I don't remember. I think I left it on my kitchen counter. Or in a drawer. Why?"

Another ball toss. "If Burt hired someone to go after you, the first place they would have gone was your apartment. If your room at the Venus was an example of their work, they would have turned over everything, looking for anything they could. An estimate for a coin, especially a valuable one, and recent, would have been a good lead."

"You think they went to the coin shop?" Father Jake said.

"I would have." Doc glanced at Paradise. The corner of his mouth lifted. "And I'm just a ballplayer. If Burt *did* hire these guys, we can assume they're pros. If they found the estimate, then they knew Paradise either had the coin or the cash from selling it. They'd figure there was a chance she might have mentioned where she was heading to the guy at the coin place. Anyway, it'd be worth checking. If the coin guy told them the same story he told Paradise, it would've been a fairly good bet she'd come here. Not many motels in town, so it wouldn't be hard to track her down. The only thing we know for sure is that one way or the other somebody found her room and stole the coin."

Paradise rolled her head back and groaned. "I registered under my real name. I was Veronica Lake until then."

"Who?" Father Jake asked.

"An actress. Big in the '40s. But when I got here, I just wanted to be me. Just for a few days. I don't know why. I'm so stupid," Paradise said.

"No," Paco said. "You want to belong somewhere. We all do. It's how we're made. Don't feel bad for wanting what you were created to have."

"If we could bring the police in …" Father Jake said.

"That's not a good idea. At least not yet," Paco said.

"I know, but if they could catch the guys … They've got the other coin."

"Not guys. It's a man and a woman," Doc said, still tossing the ball.

"How do you know that?" Father Jake said.

"C+H. The lipstick kiss on the mirror. Some kind of bounty hunter lovebirds."

"A couple? You think so?" Father Jake said.

Doc tossed the ball again. Paradise sucked in a breath as he caught it a fraction of an inch from his nose. "Seems like it. The question is, where are they now? Did they leave? What's their next move?" He sat up. "Paradise, you thought the other coin was in the museum, remember? You said you read it on the Internet?"

"Uh huh. I saw it on a coin collector's page. A whole article. The story of the Spanish brothers' treasure and about the museum."

Doc turned to Paco. "They didn't hesitate to break into the Venus, right? They might go after the museum—try for the other coin. They could find it on the web as easy as anyone else."

"That's true. And if they're still in town …" Jake said. "I think I'll go check downstairs. Make sure everything's locked up tight." He stood and headed for the office door and the stairs.

Paradise rested her chin on her knees. "I've brought you trouble, and you've been so nice to me."

"If there's trouble, it isn't your fault," Doc said.

"He's right. And we're happy to help," Paco said.

"Doc! Paco! Come down here!" Father Jake's voice echoed up the adobe walls.

Paco hit the doorway in four steps. Doc followed with Paradise close behind. Paradise's heart sank as she rounded the corner at the bottom of the stairs. Across the vestibule the museum door stood open, the knob hanging at an unnatural angle.

"I'm in here," Father Jake called from the museum's interior.

"Doc, wait with Paradise till we know for sure they're gone," Paco said as he headed through the broken door.

"You sure nobody's here? You didn't see anyone?" Paco's muffled voice found its way across the vestibule.

"They wrecked the place," Father Jake said. "It'll take me a week to put this all back together."

"These walls are thick. No way we could have heard anything from my office. Only bright spot is they wouldn't have heard us, either. They wouldn't know Paradise is here," Paco said.

The men came back into the vestibule, and Doc flipped his coin up into the air. Light glinted off it as it fell back to his hand. "They didn't get what they were looking for." His eyes found Paradise. "Not the coin and not the fugitive."

Father Jake turned toward the thick front doors. "What was that? Did you just hear something?"

"Yeah ... Someone singing the Bee Gees," Paco said.

Outside a car door slammed, an engine revved, and a car sped into the night.

Chapter Sixteen

The Second Most Beautiful Thing

There are a lot of sunsets. In fact, if you think about it, there's one happening every second of every day somewhere in the world. The old man eases his body down on jungles, plains, and mountains. He sinks, hissing into rivers, and casts his fading gold over the summer children who laugh and splash in the shallows. He bounces off sheets of ice and sets oceans on fire. The sun dies a hundred, a thousand, a million deaths a day—yet remains a grand and eternally optimistic Romeo, offering his dying breath to lovers and poets around the globe.

When Doc closed his eyes, he felt his heart beat, and for the first time in years, it beat with purpose. When he opened them, he looked out on the second most beautiful thing in the world, a red sun setting behind a sandlot baseball field.

The first most beautiful thing, Paradise Jones, sat on a lawn chair four feet away from him in front of his old Airstream trailer.

"They don't act it, do they?" Paradise said.

"Who doesn't act like what?"

"Father Jake and Paco. They don't act like priests."

"Paco isn't a priest; he's a pastor. Did you know you have a habit of picking up a conversation in the middle of one that never existed before except in your head?"

She shielded her eyes from the last rays of the falling sun and turned to him.

He felt his heart thumping hard in his chest, though this time his eyes weren't closed.

"I do?" she said. "Is that bad? I wish they'd caught them."

"Caught Jake and Paco?"

"Whoever broke into the museum ..."

Doc nodded. "It might have made things easier."

"They'll find me, won't they?"

Doc considered. "No, they won't. What are priests and pastors supposed to act like?"

"I don't know. Calm. Holy. Godlike, I suppose."

"You think God's calm? Tame?" Doc pointed toward the western sky, a riot of yellows and oranges fading to deep purple far above. "I wouldn't call a God that does that, calm and tame."

"God does that?"

"I think so, don't you?"

"Paco ran out into the night like he wanted to tackle somebody."

"He probably would have. I wouldn't get on his bad side."

"You believe in him then?"

"Paco?"

She rolled her eyes. "God."

Doc watched a bird flit overhead. "Yeah. I believe in him."

Two perfect, small lines formed between Paradise's brows. "How? How could you? I mean, if he's real he took your parents. Then baseball. And you love it so much. How can you believe in a God like that?"

"Maybe when he takes things from us, he brings along something better."

"Like what? What could possibly make up for what you've lost?"

Doc looked at her but didn't answer. If she understood his intent, she gave no indication.

"I don't think I could ever believe in him," she said.

Doc shrugged. "If he's out there, and he is who he says he is, then he believes in you."

"How can you be sure? That he's out there?"

"When we were kids, Paco used to take me and Jake fishing. He was Police Chief Hollis then. Now that he's a full-time pastor, everyone just calls him Paco because he says he's not comfortable with titles. He told us stories out there. Miraculous ones. Things that happened right here in Paradise a long time ago. A lot of people around here still talk about it. I think I've always believed on some level, but listening to Paco made it real. He never talked about God like some idea. Some theory out of a book, you know? He talked like he knew him, like a friend. About conversations they'd had and things they'd done together."

Silence passed. The purple above the orange grew and deepened.

"Do you always talk to people like this?" Paradise asked.

"Never. Except maybe Jake."

"Really? I'm not sure what to think about that."

Doc shrugged. "Do you? Talk to people like this?"

"No. Well, maybe Ash." Paradise pointed to the ball field. "You were good out there today."

Doc glanced down at his sweat-stained T-shirt and sweats. "You watched? I didn't think you liked baseball."

"It's like chess on grass and dirt. You played hard."

"Yeah, well, go big or go home, you know?"

Paradise smiled. "I like that," she said. "Go big or go home."

"Yeah? That's how I see things. I mean, if you're gonna do something, give it everything you got." He looked out over the ball field again. "So you were watching, huh?"

Paradise looked at him and nodded. "What else was I supposed to do? You guys have me locked away in a trailer like the man in the iron mask."

"*Man in the Iron Mask*, 1939. Louis Hayward and Joan Bennett. How do you know I was good?"

"You hit the ball when the guy threw it at you. That's good, right?"

Doc laughed. "I guess that's the idea."

"Do you miss it? Playing professionally?" she said.

"Every day, all day. It's the greatest game in the world. I fit there. It was home."

"A home where people throw things at you?"

He laughed again. "What about you? Is it hard to be away from Los Angeles?"

"If I get the part, it'll be everything I've ever worked for. I'll be a star. I've dreamed of it my whole life."

Apprehension stirred. "I'm sure you'll be a star whether you get the part or not."

"It's different, though, isn't it? You love baseball for baseball. For what it is."

"You don't love acting for acting?"

Paradise crossed her legs and looked out at the sky. "I don't know. It's just different. It's the whole thing. The life, the clothes, the happiness—everyone knowing you and loving you. It's not just the acting."

"I play ball out here on a dirt lot. No crowds, no money, no fame. Just baseball because I love it. But I won't lie. I miss the Majors."

"It would be wonderful to have something like that. I *want* to love acting like that. I think I did before—maybe. Everything is so strange since my father died.

Like it's all a dream. And here I am, camping in the middle of Arizona, talking to you. Burt's car, someone chasing me, it's hard to know how to feel."

Doc leaned back and put his hands behind his head. "It's not actually camping. I live here, you know."

"As close as I've ever come. And now I've kicked you out."

"I don't mind. I've bunked with Jake before. And I like having you here. Can I ask you something?"

"I suppose, since I'm camping in your camper."

"Trailer. What do you want?"

She turned sharp eyes on him. "Why do you ask that?"

"I don't know. I'm curious. Are you happy?"

"I'll be happy someday. Soon, if I get the part. Right now, I don't have time."

"I know what that's like. I felt it all the time working my way up to the Majors. But I'm happy right now. Right here, watching this sunset. Maybe you could be, too."

Paradise turned to the desert and the lights of the homes in the valley. "I feel bad for Father Jake. It meant a lot to him, didn't it? Solving the puzzle? The coins?"

"Sure, but he'll live."

She turned back. Her lips parted, and she started to speak but stopped.

"What?" Doc said.

"Nothing."

It's enough. Just this. Sitting with this girl out here in the night.

The sky was more purple than orange now. Stars began to poke through the darkest parts.

Paradise sighed and looked up at them. "If he *had* the coins, what then? If there *was* a treasure, what would he do with it?"

"I don't know. It depends on what it was, I guess. Why?"

"I wish there was a way to get the coin back."

"It's not that big of a deal. And it's not your fault."

A single tear slipped down her cheek, and Doc died a little. "Hey, really, it's not your fault."

"It was all I had left of my father. All I had left of anybody. Did you know he had an article about me hanging on his wall? I don't know why that makes me so mad. Sometimes I want to hit him. And sometimes I wish I could hug him. It's all so confusing."

"I'm sorry I said that … about it not being a big deal. I didn't realize. I didn't think."

Paradise didn't answer. "Why are you helping me?" she said at last.

What could he say? That two days ago she'd walked into Shorty's and the world stopped? That in the hours that followed he'd found a purpose to get up in the morning and breathe in and out?

"Because you need it." *Lame.* "And you're worth it." *Better, but still lame.*

"How do you know? You don't even know me."

"You asked for help. That's enough."

"Are you sure it's not because you're in love with Lana Turner?"

Blood crept up his neck, and Doc silently thanked God for the gathering darkness. "You're you. That's enough."

"You never answered my question."

"Which one? It's hard to keep track."

"Why do they call you Doc? After a baseball player?"

"It's not anything that cool. Doc's my real name."

She laughed. A welcome relief from the tension. "You mean like on-your-birth-certificate real name?"

"Yup."

"But why?"

"My mom was only in labor for thirteen minutes. It happened so fast, and she was so happy about it, she named me after the guy who delivered me, Doc Longston, right there on the spot."

"So she named you after the doctor? What if he'd been Horace? Or Percival?"

"Doc wasn't a doctor. He was the mailman. I was born on a bench in the post office about half a mile from here. But *he* was nicknamed after Doc Crandall, a guy who pitched for the Giants. So it kind of works out for me in the end."

Paradise crossed her arms and bit her lower lip as if trying to decide whether to believe him.

"Scout's honor," he said.

"People who tell the truth never say 'scout's honor.'"

"Okay, that's true, but I wouldn't kid you."

"You were a Boy Scout?"

"Nope. Were you?"

"What would *you* do if you had the answer? To the treasure puzzle? Would you try to find it?"

Doc scratched the back of his head and thought. "I guess if we found the other coin then yes, I'd be curious to see if it led to anything. Doesn't matter now. It's gone. I doubt whatever bounty hunters are after you are gonna give it up anytime soon. Right now, the important thing is keeping you out of sight. You're more important than some coin."

Paradise scanned the empty horizon. "Not much chance they'd be looking in a dilapidated camper on the edge of nowhere."

"Trailer. Airstream. It's restored, well, kind of restored. Not dilapidated. And home is where the heart is. With a great collection of classic movies included at no extra charge."

"Still, I feel bad chasing you out of your tin can."

"The bunks at the mission aren't bad. Like I said, I'm happy to have you here."

Her face softened. She sat up and unbuttoned the top two buttons of her blouse, and Doc's heart went to his throat.

"Relax, Junior. It's not what you think," she said.

Turning on her chair, she dropped the fabric of her blouse a few inches revealing the back of a very beautiful shoulder. "Take a look."

Two dark circles. He moved closer for a better look, and she leaned into the light that spilled through the trailer window. There—side-by-side—two circles, both a little bigger than silver dollars. The detailed front and back of a *Dos Escudo* coin tattooed onto smooth skin.

CHAPTER SEVENTEEN

God and Old Men

Paradise used the phone in Doc's trailer to call Ash. A rotary. She loved it.
Ash's Boston-ese cracked across the line, sounding like home. "Where are you?"

"I'm on the lam, doll." Paradise offered the Cagney.

A sigh came through the phone. "*When* are you?"

Paradise gave herself a once-over in the full-length mirror mounted on the closet door. "Rita Hayworth, *Affair in Trinidad,* 1952."

"You're killing me."

"You'll survive. I've made some friends."

"Friends? What kind of friends?"

"A preacher, a cowboy priest, and a broken baseball player. Nice friends."

"Are we talking about a movie again?"

"Nope. They're real flesh-and-blood friends. I think the baseball player's a little in love with me."

"Listen, Eve called me."

"Eve? Why?"

"She's worried about you, for one. We all are. She told me Burt sent a couple of real pieces of work after you. Some sort of P.I. bounty hunter and his lunatic wife. She used to be a cage fighter, if you can believe it. You need to be careful, Paradise. Eve wants you to call her."

Paradise paused, surprised to find that the thought of calling Eve appealed to a part of her. For a fleeting instant, she became five years old again. "She'll spill anything I tell her to Burt. I can't talk to her."

"What if they find you? I'm really worried. I'm afraid you'll get hurt. The police are still looking, too. Eve said they think you might go to the house in Cabo. They're watching the border and everything. Are you going to Mexico?"

"Can't say, doll, but they'll never take me alive, see."

"Be serious."

"Don't worry. I'm hiding someplace no one can find me."

"Wait … Back up. Did you say the ballplayer's in love with you?"

"Like a lovesick puppy. It's kind of sad."

"What's he look like? Handsome? Do you like him?"

"I did mention he's a washed-up baseball player, right? From the middle of nowhere? Who lives in a camper? I mean, trailer?"

"Handsome?"

"I suppose. In a washed-up ballplayer sort of way. Horrible timing. Not interested."

"You're lying. You like him. I know you. I can tell."

"I have a career to think of. And who knows? I might get that part. I don't have time for that sort of thing, and if I did it wouldn't be here and it wouldn't be with him. I just want to get back to LA. Back to normal."

"Don't have time for what sort of thing?"

"The romance sort of thing."

"Uh huh. There's always time for love, chickie. I'm just saying keep your options open. And LA isn't one of them at the moment, by the way. Why wouldn't it be him? You too good for us little people now that you're on the cusp of stardom? Baseball players are cute. Have you seen them in those uniforms?"

"I didn't mean it like that. To be honest, he's probably too good for *me*. And even so, running around after an aspiring actress isn't fair to anybody. Trust me, he's not the LA type."

"You've decided all this for him or does he get any say in the matter?"

"I'm not interested. Can we please drop it? Okay?"

"Okay. Just *don't* tell me he played for Boston."

"No, the Red Sox."

"I may have to kill you. You understand that, don't you?"

A sharp knock sounded on the trailer door.

The bounty hunters? Her heart skipped until she saw Doc's head through the window.

"I have to go, Ash. The baseball player's at the door."

"He played for the Red Sox. Marry him right now, do you hear me?"

"No marriage. Just a hot date with two three-hundred-year-old brothers."

"You're really weird, you know that?"

"Bye, doll. Call you soon." Paradise hung up and swung the trailer door open.

Doc gave a low whistle.

"Rita Hayworth," she said.

"Nope. Paradise Jones."

Her effort to ignore the compliment crumbled beneath the weight of her smile. "At ease, soldier. What's the word from project headquarters?"

"Getting close. C'mon, you don't want to miss history, do you?"

She didn't take the hand he offered but followed a step behind.

"Can I ask you a question?" Doc said as they walked.

"Curiosity killed the cat."

"When did you get the tattoo?"

"You'd make a lousy cat."

"More of a dog guy, anyway."

"Yes, you would be. Back in Los Angeles. It made me feel closer to my dad, I think. It was a strange time for me."

Doc glanced back over his shoulder. "I get that. It's hard to lose someone, especially parents."

"And you lost both of yours."

"I had Jake. That helped."

"But no tattoos for you." A statement rather than a question.

Doc paused a beat. "Not all tattoos are on the outside."

He led her through the back door of the mission, up another staircase and down a hallway to a large, bright room. Paco and Father Jake hovered over a massive wood table that dominated the space. Papers, both whole and crumpled, covered with notes and equations littered its surface and spilled onto the floor. An old-fashioned blackboard mounted on wheels stood next to the table, the words *Gato Negro* chalked on its center in clean, block letters. White lines radiated from the cipher-key in all directions, terminating at various letters and words, all of them either punctuated with question marks or crossed out with hard scribbles.

"Look at those two," Doc said. "They're having the time of their lives."

"C'mon, Doc. Give us a hand here." Father Jake crumpled another sheet of paper and tossed it toward a corner trash can, missing by a full foot.

"And ruin it for you? Nah," Doc said.

"Forget it, Jake. We're close. Let him miss the fun. He can cry about it later," Paco said.

"Yeah," Doc said. "I'll cry later."

Father Jake's eyes narrowed. "There something you want to tell us, Doc?"

"Not that I can think of at the moment." Doc dropped onto a couch against the wall and stretched out with both hands behind his head. "But I think you should give Paradise a huge thanks for her permanent preservation effort."

"The only tattoo I've ever been happy to see," Paco said.

"I'll second that. Paradise, you're the woman of the hour," Father Jake added.

"Wait, Jake, look at this!" Paco sucked in a breath and began writing something. Father Jake pressed close to see over his shoulder.

Sweat beaded on Paco's forehead. "Here! What if this was a zero? Not an O?"

Father Jake nodded. "How could we have missed that? You could be right." He picked up a pen and added to Paco's page. "That would make this a ... wait ... no ... here." More writing.

At length, he finished, and both men stepped back, staring at the page.

"What?" Paradise asked. "Did you find an answer?"

"That has to be it," Paco said.

Jake put a long arm around the older man's shoulder. "No doubt. I can't believe it. After almost three hundred years. The brothers really did it."

"What does it say?" Paradise strained to see across the wide table.

Paco turned the paper toward her. "*Mission Del Dia Perdido*. It must be a church."

To Paradise, this elicited more questions than answers. "But why? What's there? Where is it?"

Father Jake reached across the table, pulled an open laptop in front of him and began typing. "Wait, here—"

"Dia Perdido," Doc said. "It's a town in Mexico. The Yucatan—jungle. And, yes, the church is still there. Only now it's a children's home run by a mission group out of Seattle."

Paco looked confused. "How did you ..."

"I knew it." Father Jake smacked a hard palm on the table. "That smug look of yours. Why didn't you tell us you already figured it out?" His voice was hard, though he didn't look altogether displeased. Maybe even a little proud.

Doc sat up, dropping his feet to the floor. "You were having too much fun. Am I wrong, Paradise?"

"You *did* look like you were enjoying yourself," Paradise said.

Doc's teeth shone white against his tan. His eyes, almost black, crinkled at the edges. "Just breathe in that sense of accomplishment! How could I rob you of that?"

"Shut up," Father Jake said.

Paco laughed. "Doc's right. I enjoyed figuring the thing out. So did you, Jake. But now that we have an answer, what do we do with it?"

"We could publish it. It's just the name of a church, but even that's a historical find," Father Jake said.

"Look," said Doc. "What we need to do is obvious. There's a chance whatever they were trying to hide might still be there. Or found a long time ago. But I'm thinking those brothers were smart and didn't put all their eggs in one basket. The cipher wasn't hard to figure, and it might only be the first step. Whether there's something hidden or another piece of the puzzle, I say we go look."

"Go look?" Paradise said. "To Mexico?"

"Why not? We've gotten this far with it. I want to see the end of the story. These guys went to a lot of trouble to hide *something*."

Paco dropped into a chair and scratched his chin. "Of course, Jake and I couldn't go, we're needed here. But you, Doc ..." He leaned back and studied the ceiling, then eyed Doc. "You could go. Your story, remember? Maybe God's handing you a pen." His gaze found Paradise from beneath his dark brows. "And you, young lady. You're going, too."

Did he just say that?

"Me? No, I have to get back to Los Angeles. I have things to do there. I have my life waiting for me," Paradise said.

Paco nodded. "And yet here you are, hiding out in a camper in Arizona. Seems to me that Los Angeles isn't exactly waiting with open arms."

"It's a trailer. And Ash says the same thing about LA."

"So what do *you* say?" The excitement of the chase glinted in Paco's eyes.

Paradise tried hard to ignore the curiosity flooding her from head to toe. Could her father's coin really mean something? *I can't go, can I?* But it *would* be nice to see where the coins led. After all, he'd kept it all that time. Maybe this was something she could do for him. Kind of a goodbye tribute. And she already felt a connection with these men. Maybe Gregory Jones unwittingly left her more than a gold coin the day his soul fled the planet.

Her brain and heart played tug of war. On one hand Los Angeles, *Gone with the Wind*, and all her dreams. On the other, Ash and Paco had a point. Los Angeles meant creepy Burt and the police.

"The police are looking for me," she said. "And Ash says they're even watching the border. I wouldn't get very far if I tried to get into Mexico."

Even as she spoke, disappointment crept in. Could it be she really wanted to do this?

But Paco smiled at her. "Tell you what. You leave that part to me. Loosely quoted, with God and old men, all things are possible."

Chapter Eighteen

A Shift in the Stars

The crisp pre-dawn air made Doc's muscles twitch in anticipation of an early morning run, a habit since high school.

No run today.

Stars danced in the clear mountain air, having lost none of their intensity though nearing the end of a long work night. The eastern sky streaked gray as the sun grumbled, still a good half hour from breaking the horizon.

Should the light find them there next to the old Airstream, they'd make an odd pair. Paradise resplendent in a World War II era swing outfit—skirt, blouse, short jacket, and shoes to match. Doc's old jeans and T-shirt made him feel like a poor country relative.

Headlights cut the darkness, and Paradise's Olds Eighty-Eight crawled to a stop in front of them, Jake behind the wheel. He killed the motor.

"You guys about ready?" Jake said through the open driver's-side window.

Doc glanced down at Paradise's huge red suitcase and his old duffle bag, a holdover from his American Legion Baseball years. "Yeah. Traveling light. Ready to hit the road."

Doc popped the trunk and loaded the bags.

Jake climbed out of the car and met him in the back. "You know where you're going?" Concern colored the edges of the question.

Doc hugged his brother and grinned. "Hey, we've got a member of the clergy praying for us. What could go wrong? And I don't think we'll get lost between here and Brownsville. GPS all the way."

"Be careful, Doc. These people that are after her don't mess around. They've shown that in spades. Keep your head down and drive."

Doc pointed to the front of the Olds where Paradise had already slid behind the wheel. "Too late. I think I'm riding shotgun."

"It is her car."

"She let you drive it, didn't she?"

"Uh huh, fifty yards. All the way from the shed."

"Yeah." Doc stalled as unexpected sadness crept through him.

"You're gonna be okay, little brother. And I'm always here."

Jake always could read him like a book. This time, Doc had to force the grin. Jake was family. All he had.

"Yeah, I know. Write the story, right? The one off the diamond."

"You bet."

Jake patted Doc's shoulder, then pulled him into another hug. Paradise turned the engine, and the Olds roared to life. At the thought of her, Doc's sadness ebbed a good bit.

Paco appeared through the door in the mission wall. He shook Doc's hand and then waved at Paradise. Her return smile carried with it a bag full of nerves.

"You two be careful," Paco said. "Stop as little as possible. Just get yourselves to Brownsville. You'll be fine once you get there. Call when you're close, and I'll give you instructions on what to do."

Doc had a hard time letting go of the old man's hand. "Thanks, Paco, for everything. We'll call you. But what about you guys? What if they come after the coin again? They have one. They're gonna want the other."

Paco shrugged. "Maybe, but we'll keep a sharp eye out. Jake's gonna replace the museum lock system with something more substantial—about time if you ask me. The coin will be behind glass. And the police say they'll swing by at regular intervals."

Jake put his hand on Doc's shoulder again. "Listen, you need to focus on protecting Paradise, little brother, not the coin. And if it's here, it'll be one less thing for you to worry about. Besides, the word's out. I've got a couple of professors from U of A coming up to see it tomorrow. Even got a call from the Smithsonian. It needs to be in the museum. It's the right thing. History should belong to the public."

"Don't worry about us, Doc," Paco said. "You just go solve it. You're the perfect man for the job."

"Solve which? The brothers' mysterious stash or are you talking about my life?"

"Both. Trust God. He won't leave you hanging."

"You've been telling us that since we were kids."

"A smart old man used to say it to me. And he was right. Now I'm the smart old man."

Doc opened the car door and slid in.

Jake shut the door and leaned forward, hands on the doorframe. "It's good that you're on the road before the sun. I'm betting they're keeping an eye on things."

"I'll call you."

"Any time. Love you, Doc."

"Love you too, Jake."

The dirt back road behind the mission curved around the ball field and a row of single-level ranches. Doc directed Paradise down the mountain until the car bounced onto pavement as it hit Apache Road. In the passenger rearview mirror, streetlights lit the huge oak tree dominating the town square. As it grew smaller with the distance, Doc wondered whether he'd ever see the town of his youth again. *Where did that come from?* Of course, he would. They weren't driving off the edge of the world. Still, the sense of something huge, a shift in the stars, pressed hard on him.

"What are you thinking about?" Paradise asked.

The question surprised him. "The Green Monster."

She arched an eyebrow without taking her eyes off the road. "What's the Green Monster?"

"It's the left-field wall at Fenway Park. It's what makes up dreams. Everything possible and impossible rolled into one."

"Is it in Boston?"

"Yup. Boston Red Sox. Why?"

"Just something Ash said. She asked if you played for Boston. She's from there. It makes sense now. So then, you're a baseball poet. Why are you thinking about the Green Monster?"

"Because I have a feeling we're driving right toward it."

She sighed. "On the lam, kid."

"Yeah. On the lam."

"Have you ever been to Texas?" A slight tremor in her voice.

"Sure. Lots of times. I played ball all over Texas. Before that, I traveled with Jake while he rodeoed. Texas, New Mexico, California, Nevada. The Midwest too. Couple of times to the deep south."

"You and Jake were in California?"

"That surprises you?"

"I guess I just can't picture it. Where did you go?"

"All over. Even LA. Once we stopped right in the middle of Hollywood. Had the trailer behind Jake's truck. Parked right down there on Sunset Boulevard. Ate at a Denny's."

She stared at him so long he thought she might run off the road. "You went to Denny's on Sunset? You and Jake?"

"Sure. We wanted to check it out. See some movie stars and all that."

"Did you? See any stars?"

"The guy that waited on us said he'd been in a commercial. He was a dancing tooth or something."

"That doesn't count."

"No, I guess it doesn't. You're right. Not many movie stars at Denny's."

Paradise shrugged. "You might be surprised. I saw Dustin Hoffman there once."

"You're kidding. Really?"

"Uh huh. He had a grand slam breakfast."

They hit Highway 30 and turned south. A route that would take them past the Venus Motel and eventually drop them to Highway 70 and then Interstate 10 in New Mexico. Neither spoke for a mile or two.

"What's it like?" Paradise broke the silence.

Doc did a mental rewind through the previous conversation, although he was getting used to her *Breakfast at Tiffany's* verbal shifts. "Denny's? Better than the Waffle House, I guess. Why? Good enough for Dustin, apparently."

Doc might have been speaking Swahili by her expression.

"No, not Denny's."

He loved the raspy edge in her voice.

"The Green Monster?" he said.

She offered the exasperated sigh of an adult dealing with a two-year-old. "You and Jake. To tell someone you love them? To have them tell you?"

Doc searched for a reply. Slim pickings. "No one's ever told you they love you before?"

Paradise studied the road. "My friend Ash, I guess. But that's not the same as you and Father Jake. Not like real family."

"Your mom?"

"Eve? Hardly."

"Jake and me. We're all we have. Each other, you know? He's always had my back, and I'll always have his."

"I guess that's what love is, isn't it? An *I'll have your back* sort of thing?"

"Sure, that's part of it."

"Ash has my back. At least, I think. Still, it's not like you two."

"I'm sorry."

"So am I when I think about it."

"Is that why you do it? The '40s movie star thing?"

She didn't answer right away. Had he gone too far?

They passed the Venus Motel and its unlit sign. To the east, the sun made a brilliant debut as it peeked over the mountains.

"I like the '50s too. What time do you think?"

"Time?"

The exasperated look again. "The time when we'll get there? To Texas?"

"Oh. Texas today, but Brownsville late tomorrow night. At least, I hope."

She gave a satisfied nod. Not, Doc suspected, so much at his answer as at a successful change of subject. She ranked expert on that score.

She turned on the car stereo and swept across the dial. Rap in Spanish—a couple of words there that Doc knew, but wouldn't repeat. A preacher shouting and Taylor Swift pouting. Paradise settled on Johnny Cash's comfortable baritone letting everybody know he still missed someone. On the dash, catching the first bold rays of morning sunlight, a bobble-headed Jesus smiled and gave Doc a cheerful thumbs-up.

"Where'd this little guy come from?" Doc gave the Savior's head an extra wobble.

"The Virgin Mary. Conceived by the Holy Spirit. Your brother's a priest; you should know all that."

"I stand without excuse."

"I picked him up awhile back near some dinosaurs. I thought I could use a friend, and he looked friendly. He's been keeping me company," Paradise said.

"I'm not even going to start with the symbolism in that."

"Do you think they're following us?"

"Dinosaurs?"

"Dinosaurs are made out of cement. Everybody knows that. I mean the bounty hunters."

"Who knows? I don't see how they could be. We'll make good time and hope for the best. Paco says we'll be okay once we get to Brownsville. Some friend of his will help us out there."

"How?"

"I have no idea, but Paco's always on top of things. If he's holding his cards close, he has a reason, so I didn't really ask."

I-10 cut the deep emptiness of the desert, skirting the northern border of Mexico. The vintage Olds purred along without a hiccup.

"Are you sorry to be here?" Doc said.

"It's strange, all this empty space. I don't know. I get nervous thinking about the movie. It's hard not to be in Los Angeles right now. I think it's because I don't know what's happening there."

"We'll figure it out."

"It's not your problem. Besides, we're just following the coins. That's why you're here." She moved the sun visor to the side to shade her eyes.

"Jake says I'm a sucker for movie stars. I'm not here because of the coins."

She glanced at him out of the corner of her eye. "You're out of line, soldier."

Eventually, Las Cruces loomed up brown and windswept, and Paradise pulled the big car into a gas station on the outskirts of town. Doc filled the tank and watched a plastic bag bounce across the highway, jerked along by the wind, while Paradise disappeared into the market looking for a restroom. She emerged a few seconds later holding a key attached to a green, plastic flying saucer large enough for Doc to read the words *Welcome to Roswell* on it from across the parking lot. She jiggled the key in a door on the side of the building. When it finally opened, she went in and closed it behind her.

A dirt-crusted pickup pulled up to the pump opposite the Olds, and an old man climbed out, long silver braids framing a lined face that spoke age and stories, though his body had the lean and muscular look of a younger man. He tossed a wave at Doc and pulled the handle from the pump. Behind him, another car pulled in. This one a late-model silver Crown Victoria—the kind the police used to use. The man at the wheel didn't look Doc's direction, but the woman in the passenger seat gave him the once-over. The two exited the Crown Vic and stretched. They were both large. Not fat but muscular. The desert sun glinted off the man's bald, tattooed head. The woman's Elvis-black hair was shaved close on the sides and pushed up into a spiky Mohawk. She wore Spandex workout shorts and a sweat-stained, tie-dye tank top. Uneasiness touched Doc as the couple headed for the gas station store. He twisted the cap onto the Olds' gas tank and returned the gas nozzle to the pump, then took a closer look at the Crown Vic.

Cold fingers touched him.

California plates.

CHAPTER NINETEEN

Welcome to Roswell

Hollister made a quick sweep of the gas station store, not that there was much to look at. The place consisted of a counter manned by a skinny, pimple-faced teenager staring at his cell phone, a glass case holding a few exhausted hot dogs and a piece of pepperoni pizza with a bite out of it, and five aisles offering everything from candy bars to motor oil to feminine hygiene products. A large framed poster above the soda and beer cooler sported a jackalope with a cartoon bubble above his long ears that read, *Welcome to Las Cruces, why don't you stay a while?*

"No thanks," Hollister mumbled.

His rubbed his neck with his right hand and his lower back with the other. *Just focus, man—eighty thousand dollars.* Maybe he'd demand the second half in cash just to get under Simmons' skin. That would be a sight—forty grand in pretty stacks of twenties.

As long as they'd been together, Hollister couldn't remember the last time he and Crystal had been alone twenty-four-seven for days on end. How much more of it could he take? He watched her reflection in the round, fish-eye mirror above the door. She flexed her shoulder muscles right-left-right while scrutinizing the ingredients listed on a can of peaches. She shuddered, put the can back on the shelf, then reached over and smashed a bag of chips with a single, quick squeeze. The crunch was loud, but the kid behind the counter only scratched absently at his acne-covered face, eyes never leaving his phone.

"Hey, old man, you want an apple?" Crystal said.

"Nah. Grab me a Snickers bar and some chips. And not the bag you smashed."

Crystal came around the corner with four apples. "She must be in the bathroom."

"You got a mind like a steel trap. Can't slip nothin' past you, can they?"

"Don't be cranky, moron. What'd you do? Forget to take your Geritol?"

Hollister walked around the corner and picked up a bag of Doritos and four Snickers bars. Crystal rolled her eyes.

She shoved the apples into his arms. "You pay, and I'll go round up the princess."

"No need to round anybody up. Just hang loose a minute."

"What do you mean?"

Hollister jerked his chin toward a sign above the counter. "Says to ask for the key. She'll be back. She has to return it."

"Huh," Crystal said. She pulled the food from his hands. "Give me some money."

He tossed her his billfold and walked to the front window. The pane was coated with a thick layer of dust behind neon beer signs. A small army of dead flies populated the sill. He rubbed at the window and tried to see the Oldsmobile, but a big, redneck pickup truck blocked his view. He rubbed the back of his neck again and rolled his head back and forth. In LA, he had a La-Z-Boy recliner and a flat screen. He could be there right now, maybe watching a rerun of *Magnum P.I.* or *Miami Vice*. The thought of the long, empty miles between Las Cruces, New Mexico and Los Angeles, California depressed him even further. He missed the smell of the ocean. Missed the traffic. Missed the smog. Missed Tommy's Burgers chili. Missed everything.

Las Cruces, New Mexico. Oh, man. It might as well be the moon.

Crystal appeared at his side and tossed him an apple.

"Where's the other stuff?" he said.

"Can't let my sweetie go putting that junk in his body, can I?"

Hollister gave her a long look. "What color is the sky in your world? Am I sweetie or moron?"

Crystal put up a fist and air-punched at him. "Pow! Wham! Hey, remember the old Batman show? Where the bubbles came on when they punched somebody?"

Hollister shook his head in wonder and took a bite out of the apple. Crystal set a few more apples down next to a cardboard rack of green suckers with scorpions in the middle, dropped to the ground and did a few push-ups.

"Would you get up? The floor's filthy," Hollister said.

Crystal showed her wifely obedience by putting an arm behind her back and knocking out five one-handed reps, then five with the other. She climbed to her feet and said, "I hate to admit it, but it was a good idea to put the tracker on her car. But how did you know it'd be at the church?"

"She had the coin when she got to Paradise, didn't she? She'd have to make contact with the museum guys at some point. I figured one of those priests or preachers or whatever they are might have decided to help her out. Especially if she told them a sob story about Simmons. She knows someone's after her, especially after you trashed her motel room. I just poked around and found her Olds in that shed. Got lucky."

"We should'a just grabbed her at the church. Who's gonna say anything?"

"Yeah, but we don't have the other coin. And I doubt the Arizona cops would look kindly on us smacking around a couple of preacher guys to get it. It wasn't in the museum, so they must have it hid someplace. You keep talking about that treasure, and I'll admit it's got me curious. Those preachers, I bet they figured the whole thing out already. And the girl and this guy are headed someplace. What do you wanna bet they know where it is?"

"Or maybe she's just running after we trashed her motel. She's got to be freaking out."

"But she didn't take off right away. They had her hidden someplace. Probably in the mission. Why not just stay there? Nah, they figured something out. They know. They're going after whatever the Spanish guys hid."

"My sweetie's so smart for an old man." Crystal talked around a mouth full of apple. Juice dripped off her chin. She made no effort to wipe it.

"Give me a break."

"So now we grab her, beat the secret out of her, and drop her off at dear old dad's. We get the rest of our eighty grand *and* the gold."

"First of all, we don't hurt her. Second, the guy at the coin shop didn't know if there even *was* any gold. Nobody does. It might be nothing. But if she knows anything about it, she'll tell us. She'll be too scared not to."

"What do'ya think's taking her so long, anyway? Did she drown?"

Hollister shrugged. "I can't see anything with this stupid truck in the way."

"Well, I'm sick'a waiting. I'm gonna go see."

Crystal shoved her remaining two apples in the waistband of her workout pants. Hollister sighed, made a mental note not to take one of them if she offered, and followed her out. Once through the door and past the big pickup, he saw what he'd started to half expect.

The Olds was gone.

"Hey, old man!" Crystal called.

Hollister moved around the building as fast as the pain in his leg would let him.

Crystal stood by the open door to the women's restroom holding a green, plastic flying saucer. She tossed it to him. "Welcome to Roswell, moron."

CHAPTER TWENTY

Have a Willie Nice Day

Paradise leaned her head back against the seat and closed her eyes—a weak attempt at calm. Shadow and light played through her lids as telephone poles cut the rays of the sun in regular, perfect intervals. She cracked an eye and glanced at the speedometer. The needle pushed a hundred as the Olds hurtled down a desert back road, Doc's knuckles white on the wheel.

"You're sure it was them?" Paradise said over the whine of the tires.

"I have a feeling. Anyway, I'm not taking any chances."

"I almost jumped out of my skin when you pounded on the door of that restroom."

"Sorry."

"I don't understand. How could they find us? I didn't see anyone follow us when we left Paradise. I looked for headlights behind us. The road was empty."

"I don't know. But, however they did it, they might do it again. We'll stay on back roads as much as we can. It'll take longer, but I think it's worth it."

Paradise looked behind them. "You can probably slow down now, Mario Andretti. There's no one back there."

Doc's foot eased off the gas pedal, and the speedometer dropped to a reasonable seventy-five. The desert spread out in every direction, blanketed by a deep, ocean blue. Doc pushed on for several miles. Eventually the asphalt turned to gravel, and he slowed to fifty. The GPS showed nothing. It didn't even show a road, just brown space. Paradise pulled the Rand McNally from the glove compartment. No highway, byway, trail or footpath seemed to match their location, no matter how hard she scrutinized or which direction she turned the page.

"You have any idea where we are?" she said finally.

"Southern New Mexico?"

"Is that a question?"

"The way I figure it, we just keep moving east. Eventually, we'll have to hit a road that'll drop into Texas."

"How do you know which way is east?"

Doc pointed to the sun.

"You're kidding," Paradise said.

"It's been working for thousands of years."

Paradise leaned her head back again. *Paradise Jones. Guided by the sun. Gravel road. New Mexico—probably. Southwest United States. Planet Earth. Universe ...*

On the dash, Truck Stop Jesus smiled. *"What do you want, Paradise?"*

Good question.

What was she doing here? Everything she'd ever dreamed of waited in Los Angeles. She was on the way to becoming a star. Yet here she was, bouncing along a dirt road in the middle of who-knows-where with a broken ballplayer.

The unbroken rumble of gravel beneath the tires made her eyes grow heavy. Would she take it back if she could? Dumping Burt's Porsche? Maybe. This had seemed an adventure at first, but on further inspection, adventures might be better enjoyed in a dark movie theater with popcorn and Milk Duds than having to actually live them out in real time.

She squinted an eye at Jesus. "Why do you ask what I want? You're supposed to be the one with all the answers."

Jesus jerked a thumb at Doc. *"Okay, how about him?"*

"What do you mean?"

"He's good for you."

"He's sweet. So? You know what's waiting for me in LA. I just need to get back and get my name cleared. Doc's not the tag-along-on-the-red-carpet type."

"You're here, aren't you? You decided to come with him."

"How about you? Are you happy? To be out of the truck stop?"

"No, Paradise, you can't change the subject."

"What was the question again?"

Jesus laughed. *"I said, you're here, aren't you? You decided to come with him."*

"That's not really a question."

"Okay, let me rephrase it. Paradise, didn't you decide to come?"

"Nope. Not by choice. Unless it was Burt's."

"Mm-hmm. We'll see. You're curious, and you know it."

"What's *we'll see* supposed to mean?"

"What if Doc loves you? What then?"

"Loves me? He's known me five minutes. He might have a schoolboy crush, but he doesn't love me. I'm Lana Turner to him. Or Audrey. You heard him. Real love has your back. And why do you have to ask all these questions?"

"He's driving you through the desert just to keep you out of Burt's paws. That seems like having your back to me."

"You know what? I'm having a conversation with a piece of plastic. What's wrong with me? Besides, Doc's after the answer to the coins, whatever that is. That's why he's here. Not for me."

"You know better than that."

"Speaking of treasure, Mr. All Knowing, is there one?"

"Of course! There's always a treasure. But it might not be the one you think."

"You know what? I don't care about it anyway. I *know* what I want. Like I told you, to get the part, to be famous. Can you help with that?"

"Be famous to me. Be famous to him."

The Olds came to a stop, and she opened eyes heavy from sleep. They were at an intersection, a four-way stop. The western sky burned, blazing yellows and reds brighter than she'd ever seen. Just outside the passenger window, a whitewashed, adobe shrine to some saint glowed in the sideways sunlight, casting an endless shadow behind it. A bent Mexican woman sat on a bench in front of it, clutching a rosary and mumbling prayers.

"Where are we?" Paradise asked.

"Smack dab in the middle of where we are. You really slept. At least, we hit pavement a while back. That's a good sign." Doc pointed across the road. Kitty-corner to the shrine stood a long, low building. The sign above it read *Manhattan Bar.* "I say we grab a bite to eat. What do you think?"

"There? At a bar?"

"Take a look around. Not exactly a lot of options. This is the first sign of life I've seen in two hundred miles."

"You think they have food?"

Doc swung the Olds into the dirt parking lot in front of the place. "Only one way to find out. People have to eat, even in the desert."

"What if that couple shows up? The bounty hunters."

"No one followed us. I made sure of it. They're probably still looking for us in Las Cruces. Let's grab a bite, get some gas, then head for Texas. We can find a motel across the border and make a long push for Brownsville tomorrow." Doc gave Truck Stop Jesus a wobble. "What do you think, amigo?"

Thumbs up.

"So now you don't have anything to say?" Paradise said.

"What?" Doc said.

"Nothing. I was talking to Jesus."

"Really? Huh."

"Long story, sailor. Let's find some food."

Three other vehicles sat in the dirt lot in front of the Manhattan Bar. A newish Dodge pickup with a lumber rack on top, a school-bus yellow El Camino, and a low-slung Harley Davidson motorcycle. The whine of country pedal steel spilled loneliness through the building's open front door. Long plastic strips hung in the opening, most likely an effort to repel insects. Coolness laced the evening air. A rust-pocked van crunched to a dusty stop next to them, and a heavy, bearded man climbed out, pulling a guitar case across from the passenger seat after him. His black leather vest, covered with biker club patches, hung loose over a dirty T-shirt.

Paradise eyed the man. "Do you think this is safe?"

"I thought you were from the big, tough city." Doc smiled. "It's fine. I grew up in places like this. C'mon."

At the door, Doc pulled the plastic strips aside and Paradise stepped through the entrance. She paused to let her eyes adjust to the dim light. The building's interior presented much larger than it appeared from the parking lot. A long bar stretched the entire length of the back of the room. Neon beer signs and glassy-eyed deer heads peppered the wall above it. One enterprising taxidermist had gone so far as to stuff the back half of one of the animals and mount a sign underneath—*The Other Side of the Wall.* To the left, a stage stood sentinel over a well-used wooden dance floor. The biker from the van stood talking to another man who tinkered with a drum kit. The bass drum proclaimed *The Rio Kings* in large, hand-painted block.

Doc took Paradise's arm and guided her to a table. His hand lingered a little longer than necessary, and she leaned away. *No use giving the poor guy the wrong idea.*

"I need to use the restroom," Paradise said.

Doc nodded.

The washroom was small but clean, and she found herself staying longer than she needed. It wasn't like there was a line waiting to get in, and she wanted a few minutes to herself. She fixed her hair twice and reapplied her makeup. Her stomach made a noise. *Hiding from Burt, the ultimate weight loss program.* She should write a book—go on Oprah.

Doc stood up from the table as she returned. "No waitress around. I'll go see if there's someone here to take our order. Be right back."

"You better hurry, sailor, before I eat your arm."

He disappeared around the bar and through a pair of bat-wing doors that presumably led to a kitchen.

The man at the drum set began to tap the snare and tune it with a silver key while the bearded biker eyed Paradise, looking her up and down. She averted her eyes, then realized she still wore her swing ensemble. She must look a sight in a place like this. Heavy footsteps approached, and the biker cleared his throat. Paradise looked up, clenching her fists in her lap and feeling blood pound in her temples. The man towered over her, his gray beard streaked reddish brown. He smiled, and Paradise was surprised to see he had straight, white teeth.

He indicated her outfit with a purple-nailed forefinger. "You like swing music?"

The last thing she expected to hear.

Air eased back into her lungs. "It's Paulette Goddard. *Second Chorus.* 1940. Did you smash your finger?"

"Yeah. Wrench slipped, and I hit it good. My name's Hap. I'm part of *The Rio Kings*, the band playing tonight."

"Hap as in short for Happy?"

Hap shrugged. "If you want. Anyway, we'll try to get a couple swing numbers in. Just for you, Paulette Goddard 1940. What do you say?"

Before she could answer, he turned and sauntered back toward the stage. Paradise thought about calling after him to say she wouldn't be there long enough to hear the band but was interrupted by Doc's return. A woman followed him with a couple of menus, her face hard and brown as the New Mexico desert beneath a short shock of snow-white hair. She wore Levis and a T-shirt with a caricature of Willie Nelson on the front, and the slogan *Have a Willie Nice Day.*

"Sorry, hon. I should've been out here." The woman pointed a finger in the direction she and Doc had come. "Leaky sink. Your boyfriend had to track me down. Afraid all he found was my legs. The rest of me was shoved under the cabinet. I'm all present and accounted for now, though."

Paradise raised an eyebrow. "Where are you from?"

The woman's leathery skin crinkled with a million lines. "Yeah, everybody asks. Big Apple—Upper West Side. I never shook the accent. Welcome to the Manhattan. I'm Doris."

"I'm Paradise. And he's not my boyfriend. We're just traveling together."

Doris' smile didn't dim. "Okay. Whatever you kids call it these days. Look over the menus and order anything you want as long as it's chili, 'cause that's all I got right now. You want anything to drink?"

Paradise ordered a Coke. Doc asked for ice water.

"And a couple bowls of chili," Doc added.

"Excellent choice, travelers." With a spin, Doris headed for the kitchen.

"You don't drink?" Doc said.

"All the time, when I'm thirsty."

"Alcohol, I mean."

"Take a joke, Doc." Paradise thought of Burt and Eve and shook her head. "No, I don't. How about you?"

"Nah. I was always too focused on being an athlete."

"My mom, Eve, and Burt, they drink … a lot. Burt was drinking that night he came after me. He reeked of it. If I close my eyes, I can still smell him, and it makes me feel sick. When I left there, Eve was passed out on the couch. Good old Eve. My friends used to call her the martini mom."

"I'm sorry. At least your stepdad can't hurt you here."

"So that's why I don't drink." Paradise pointed toward the stage. "That biker over there? His name's Hap. He plays swing music. Can you imagine?"

"Paradise. Listen to me. I mean it—I won't let anything happen to you."

"See? That's just it. That's the problem."

"What's just what?"

"You—how you do that. Say those things."

"What things?"

"You're not, you know."

"Will you take a breath, please? I'm not what?"

"My boyfriend. You're not my boyfriend. I'm going back to LA as soon as I can. By myself—no ballplayers allowed. I have a life there. You understand that, right?"

Doris appeared with the Coke and ice water. "Be right back with the chili. Hope you like it hot. This is pepper central."

When she was gone, Doc shrugged and said, "Saved by the chili. I'm not going to pretend this is all nothing, if *that's* what you want. Or that I don't feel something."

"It's not me you like, Doc. It's the *idea* of me. I'm an act. A costume. Come to think of it, *I* don't even know what I am."

"Wrong. It's you. I see the girl behind the curtain. I'm not a kid."

"You can't know. Not this fast."

"Why not? What's wrong with fast? Who makes the rules about how fast or slow a person should feel something?"

"I don't know. But somebody should."

"You feel it too."

"I feel hungry, that's what *I* feel."

"You feel it."

"You're an impossible person to talk to, do you know that?"

"Nah, I just know what I want."

"I'm not some challenge, buddy. I'm not a baseball game. I'm not a Green Monster."

"You're Paradise Jones."

Doris returned and slid two huge bowls of chili onto the table, along with a plate of bread and a couple of salads. "Okay, I lied. We have salad, too. Hope you like Italian dressing. If you don't, we also have Italian. Eat your vegetables. Enjoy. If you need anything, yell or yank one of my legs. I'll be in back under the sink."

"Thanks, Doris," Doc said.

"You bet," Doris said over her shoulder as she trotted away, boot heels clopping on the floor.

Doc sipped his water. "Back to the subject at hand. Why can't I know how I feel this fast?"

"Do you *like* swing music?"

"Why can't I know?"

"Ugh ... I don't want to talk about this anymore."

"About swing music?"

"Doc ..."

Doc picked up his spoon with a half-smile.

Why couldn't the guy be pimple-faced and fat? It was exasperating.

"Okay, let's not talk about it," he said.

Paradise's stomach growled as the rich smell of chili wafted up. She blew on a spoonful to cool it.

"But I knew the second you walked into Shorty's," Doc said.

"We're not talking about it, remember?"

"Yeah. But I knew."

She smiled. "Shut up, Doc."

CHAPTER TWENTY-ONE

The Rio Kings

Wide open country, particularly the independent American Southwest, plays its cards close to the vest. It can, and often does, hold a deceptively large amount of people scattered across its plains and tucked into its crevasses and canyons without advertising the fact. By the time Paradise finished her salad, the Manhattan Bar had filled to about half capacity. By the time she sopped up the last bit of chili in her bowl with a piece of soft sourdough and leaned back with a contented sigh, the place was as full as her stomach felt.

The Rio Kings tuned up on stage. They were a mixed lot. Hap stood talking with a drummer in a white tank top and cowboy hat. Several Mexican men with nylon-stringed guitars of every conceivable size stood on one side of the stage. On the other, an elderly African-American gentleman in a pin-striped suit and dirty tennis shoes slouched over an upright piano, poking one key repeatedly. Next to him stood a full horn section made up of more Mexican men and one blonde woman—the blonde woman squeezed like soft cheese into a floral-print evening dress that threatened to rip a seam.

"What kind of music do these guys play?" Paradise asked as Doris cleared the dishes from the table.

"The Rio Kings?" Doris watched them for a beat or two. "Yeah, hard to tell by the look of 'em, isn't it? I'm not sure how to answer that. A mariachi-country-rockish sort of thing, I guess. Anyway, everyone likes it. They pack the place, and they play for beer and tips. Price is right, and they make me money. Works for everyone. "

The band kicked off. A sombrero-wearing horn player set his trumpet on the piano and took the vocal mic. As he rolled into a ramped up version of Garth Brooks' "Friends in Low Places," bar patrons headed for the dance floor. Garth was followed by Bonnie Raitt's "Let's Give Them Something to Talk About," lead vocals ala soft cheese floral-print. Bonnie passed the baton to a mariachi version of U2's "Lemon."

"Want to dance?" Doc shouted over the blare of horns.

"We should really get going."

Doc nodded, but neither of them stood to leave. Doris brought another Coke for Paradise and coffee for Doc. Paradise watched the band, but could feel Doc's eyes on her.

"Stop it, Doc."

"Stop what?"

"Stop looking at me like that."

His eyes glinted, black in the dim light of the bar and contrasting his blond hair. Handsome. Handsomeness paired with annoying persistence. *Which is exactly the problem with broken ballplayers.*

The music dropped in intensity. Biker Hap stepped up to the vocal mic as he strummed the first few riffs of the Rolling Stones' "Wild Horses."

"I like this song. C'mon, let's dance," Doc said.

"No, thank you."

"It's just a dance. One."

"No, thank you."

"What if I promise to keep daylight between us? Like in junior high?"

"No, thank you."

"Look, I snuck you out of town in the middle of the night, rescued you from bounty hunters, and found the best chili you've ever tasted. The least you could do is dance with me."

Paradise sighed. "All right. But if I look like I'm enjoying myself, I'm not. I'm an actress. I know how to fake it."

"Got it."

Doc led her to the packed dance floor. His arm, hard and muscular, slipped around her waist. His big right hand took her small left. Butterflies danced inside her, and she forced herself to focus. *Think about something else. Anything but how good his arm feels.* She looked at the stage. The big biker sang with his eyes shut.

"What do you want, Paradise?" he sang.

The words hit her. Pure Mick Jagger-esque.

She pressed her face against Doc's chest and whispered. "Here we go again ... To be loved, that's all. That's all I've *ever* wanted. How many ways do I have to say it?"

"What?" Doc said.

"Nothing."

"You sure?" Doc said.

"Shut up, Doc." She felt his heart beat against her cheek.

"To be loved? You're sure? Because you look pretty loved to me ..." Mick faded back, and Truck Stop Jesus' voice replaced him.

"I'm going to make a movie. I'm going to be a movie star. Everyone will know me. Everyone will love me," Paradise mouthed, taking care not to let Doc hear.

"Wild, wild horses, could not drag me away ... Whatever you say, Paradise, but I love you already ... So does he ... Wild, wild horses, we'll ride them someday..."

She looked up into Doc's face.

"You look peaceful," he said. "That's new."

"Acting," she said. "Remember?"

"Yeah. I remember."

The Stones ended, but Hap kept the mic. "This one goes out to Paulette Goddard, *Second Chorus,* 1940."

The mariachi horn section leaped into a very passable version of "Don't Be That Way" by the Benny Goodman Orchestra, and Paradise felt an actual, genuine laugh break her lips. When was the last time that had happened?

"I guess we're dancing again," she said.

Momentary concern touched Doc's face. "What if I don't know how to dance to this?"

"It's easy. I'll show you. You've seen the movies. Think Hal Takier in *Twice Blessed.*"

By the end of the song, Doc had actually started to get the hang of a few basic moves.

"What do you think?" he asked.

"I think Gene Kelly would smack you. Quit stepping on my feet."

The Rio Kings seamlessly transitioned into Glenn Miller's "In the Mood" and then, "Straighten Up and Fly Right."

"They know a lot of swing," Paradise said. "I'm getting tired."

"Could've fooled me."

"And you're getting worse. Pay attention."

"Give me a break. You're the one who wanted to do this, so stop whining."

"Whining? I'm going to have to ice my toes."

The song ended, and Paradise started for the table. Doc caught her hand. "You giving up?"

She smiled at him. "I think you've had all the swing lessons you can handle for one night, sailor. Too much to retain all at once. I don't want to hurt your brain any more than I already have. Or my feet, come to think of it."

"One more dance. C'mon, I promise I'll do better."

The band kicked in again with a ripping version of "Stompin' at the Savoy."

"All right. One more. But that's it. My toes can't take it."

"One. And I promise to be careful."

Doc grabbed her hand and swung her out onto the floor. A move that surprised her.

And he didn't stop there. For the next five minutes, he tossed her around the worn wooden boards with some of the best swing moves she'd ever seen. When the song ended, they stood facing each other, both breathless.

"What was that, sailor? You *are* Gene Kelly," she said.

"I wanted to surprise you. Maybe you're not the only actor around."

"The way my toes are aching from before, you should win an Academy Award. Where did a broken ballplayer learn to dance like that?"

Smile lines creased the corners of Doc's eyes. "Aunt Katie. She used to torture me with it. Jake too. We still take her dancing once in a while. At least, as much as my knee lets me."

"Aunt Katie's some teacher. I'm stunned."

"It's getting late. We really should get on the road."

"I suppose so."

Hap ambled up and flashed his even, white teeth. "How'd we do, Doc? That was a heck of a show, brother."

"Perfect, Hap. Thanks, man."

The big man laughed and patted Doc on the back, then headed toward the bar.

"How do you know Hap?" Paradise said, arching an eyebrow.

"Talked to him while you were in the bathroom. We hit it off."

"When I was in the bathroom? You asked him to play swing?"

"I wanted to dance with you. Surprise you, you know?"

Onstage, floral print dress sang the first few lines of "Angel of Montgomery." Doc made a move to leave, but Paradise caught his hand.

"Hey, sailor. How about one more?"

He studied her. "You sure? It's a slow one."

"You better start dancing before I change my mind."

Doc put his arm around her, and she pushed Los Angeles and Burt and movies out of her head. *One dance. What can it hurt?*

Okay, two dances.

Maybe three ...

By the time the last Rio King packed away his guitar, Paradise's face was sore from smiling, and her legs were tired. She couldn't remember having had so much fun in her life. She and Doc hadn't left the dance floor nor had they switched partners. Doc's arm was still around her as they moved toward the door. She moved away.

C'mon, Paradise. What had she been thinking? Simple—she hadn't.

"You okay?" he said.

She hesitated. "Look, Doc. I had fun, okay? But so you know, nothing's changed. I *still* don't want you to get the wrong idea about anything. If there were a way for me to go back to Los Angeles right this second, I'd do it. We're on the lam, right? It was a moment, that's all. Do you understand?"

"Hey, I didn't propose marriage. We danced. Relax."

Doris called to them from the bar. "Hey! You two. It's late, and there's nowhere for you to land for a few hundred miles. Why don't you stay here tonight? I have rooms in the back. We proudly offer full-service accommodations for the weary traveler."

"That actually sounds good to me," Doc said to Paradise. "I'm exhausted. What do you say we stay here and hit it early tomorrow? You can stick a chair under the door to keep me out."

Weariness pressed, and Paradise nodded. "Don't think I won't, sailor. All right, let's stay. I'm tired, too."

Doris hadn't lied. The rooms were clean and perfectly done up. Paradise chose the one without deer antlers mounted on the paneled wall.

"Shampoo, soap and clean towels in the bathroom," Doris said. "I'm just down at the end in the last room if you need anything."

"Thanks, Doris," Paradise said.

"You're welcome, sweetheart." The leathery woman exited. Through the open door, Paradise heard her say, "Go Yankees." Out in the night, Doc laughed. Paradise stepped out onto the cracked sidewalk that fronted the rooms. Doc sat on a plastic lawn chair next to his own door, gazing out toward the ink black of the desert.

"Hey, Doc. I had fun tonight. Really. Thank you."

"On the lam, doll," Doc said. "Makes for exciting times."

"Yeah. On the lam. How do they do it, do you think?"

Doc leaned his head back against the brick. His eyes smiled. "Okay, I'll bite. How does *who* do *what*?"

"Them." Paradise pointed toward the Manhattan. "All of them. How do they live out here? What do they do? There's nothing here."

"There's everything here. And you just said it. They *live*. That's what people do. Not everybody lives in the tomorrow. Not everybody is waiting for their dreams to come true to be happy. These people—what you saw tonight—they just *are*. They find joy in the here and now. You could do that too if you wanted. You were happy tonight. I bet happier than you've been in a long time."

"Why do you talk like that? Do you just automatically say everything that goes through your brain? Put everything out there?"

"Not how they do it in LA?"

"I don't think that's how anybody does it anywhere."

"You and I ... what's happening. It's too important to do any other way."

Paradise tried to read his face, but the darkness prevented it. "But Doris. She's from *New York*! Have you ever been there? Look at the darkness out there. The quiet. How does she stand it after Times Square?"

"I guess she's writing her story. Just like me. Just like you. Right here, right now. In the moment." Doc stood. "Good night, Paradise Jones. I enjoyed our dance. And not only the one on the dance floor."

"Okay, sailor. See you tomorrow."

Doc looked at her for a long moment. Then he turned to his room and closed the door softly behind him.

Paradise sighed. "Yeah, good night, Doc Morales. Thanks for the dance."

Long after the lights were off and the deep desert night offered nothing but silence and ghosts, Doc's words played through her mind. Was she writing her story? Or waiting ... always waiting for the day when she would finally feel whole? Finally feel loved? As her eyes got heavy, she imagined she could feel Doc's heart beat through the motel wall like it beat against her cheek as they danced to the rhythm of The Rio Kings.

The desert spoke to her through the open window. *What do you want, Paradise?*

"I want to dance."

So dance ...

"I'm going to be famous."

Be famous to me. Be famous to him ... Dance.

Hours later, a short while before dawn, gravel crunched beneath tires in the lot outside, although no headlights touched the window. Something pulled the edge of her sleepy awareness. Some thought in a passing dream that she should be frightened.

But then she dreamed of The Rio Kings.

Doc's strong arm circled her waist, and she danced.

Chapter Twenty-Two

Indians in the Hills

Doc opened his eyes with the daylight. How long since he had slept that hard? His mind went immediately to the night before.

He loved her. No question. And she felt something for him as well. He'd seen it in her eyes. Her face. Felt it in her body. He'd never stop her from chasing her dreams, and maybe, just maybe, that meant at some point he'd have to let her go. But the fact remained, he loved Paradise Jones with everything in him.

She'd said it was the clothes he saw, the movie star thing. But it wasn't. It was her smile. The laugh that never quite covered the sadness in her eyes. It was the way she jumped subjects every five seconds. It was the way she walked, the way she blew the stray hair out of her face as she danced. It was how she looked at the desert night, or the sign from the Venus Motel even though there was nothing there to see. It was simply Paradise Jones. She had been made for him, and him for her. Something had happened between them, and she had to see it, to recognize it for the gift that it was. He had to make her see.

Doc showered and brushed his teeth. He could hear no movement through the wall. He'd probably have to wake her. They'd need an early start, though even so, he doubted they'd make Brownsville before sometime tomorrow.

Lan, Paco had said. They were supposed to meet someone named Lan, who apparently had a way of getting them across the Mexican border without Paradise getting picked up by the authorities. None of it sounded promising—or legal for that matter—but Doc trusted Paco and he'd go anywhere if it meant five more minutes with Paradise. Mexican prison? Why not?

The smell of frying bacon drifted through the window. Doris must start things early at the Manhattan. Like many rural watering holes, along with being a bar, the Manhattan probably served as breakfast-and-lunch joint, post office, church, and general clearing house for local gossip. Some of that talk was probably about Paradise and him this morning. Fresh coffee added its aroma to the frying meat.

Doc's stomach growled. He knocked lightly on the wall and called to Paradise but received no response.

Deep sleeper.

He finished cleaning up and re-packed his few belongings. Carrying his duffle out to the Olds, he popped the trunk and tossed it inside.

No red suitcase. No surprise.

He knocked on Paradise's door, but again received no response. He waited twenty seconds or so, then tried again. Nothing.

Worry began to rise. He tried the door and found it unlocked. It swung open under his touch. She wasn't in the room. Her suitcase stood at the foot of the unmade bed, but no Paradise.

Doc exited the room and headed for the back door of the Manhattan, his pace quick.

She must be in the Manhattan.

Doris stood in front of a large commercial stove covered with about every breakfast food imaginable. She sported an apron that said *Kiss the Cook*.

"Morning, sunshine. You ready for some coffee?" she said, Brooklyn thick in her voice.

"You're speaking my language. Is Paradise in the bar?"

Concern creased Doris' brow. "Haven't seen her. She's not in her room?"

"No. Just her suitcase. Where could she have gone?"

"The car's here? There isn't anywhere *to* go. At least not on foot."

A jolt of fear punched Doc, and a cold sweat broke. "I think something's wrong. I have to find her."

Doris set her spatula down. "Are you two in some sort of trouble? You need to tell me what's going on, kid."

"It's a long story. But yeah, there are some people after Paradise. They're not good people."

"And you think these people took her?"

"Maybe. I have a feeling, yeah. It's the only explanation."

"Who are they?"

Doc clenched his fists, mind racing. His words of explanation tumbled out in a rush. About Burt's come-on, the Porsche, and the twisted accusations. He finished with the bounty hunters.

"They must've taken her. Where else could she have gone? The thing is, I can't figure out how they found us."

"C'mon," Doris said when he'd finished.

She led the way into the bar, which this morning looked more the country café than nightlife hot spot. Hap sat at a table with a few other bikers, as well as about half the mariachi horn section of The Rio Kings. This included the floral-printed female trombonist who, this morning, was more suitably attired to the area in Wrangler jeans and a faded, pearl-buttoned plaid blouse.

"The girl's missing, Hap," Doris said. "Doc thinks it might have been bounty hunters from LA."

Hap raised a bushy eyebrow. "Paulette Goddard 1940?"

"Yeah," Doc said, sharper than he'd intended. "Paradise." He wanted to run, to chase after her, but had no idea where to start. Panic choked him.

"And these guys are bounty hunters?"

Doc nodded. "Kind of. A couple. A man and a woman. Paradise's stepdad hired them to track her down. I'm pretty sure we saw them in Las Cruces. That's why we came this way."

Doris jumped in and quickly recounted Doc's story.

Hap didn't waste time. He turned to one of the bikers. "Jack, check that Olds Eighty-Eight. Find the tracker and bring it here. Doc, what were the hunters driving? Did you see?"

Tracker? "A Crown Victoria. Silver. California plates."

"All right. Reverb, get on the phone and round up the guys. Tell them to saddle up and find that Crown Vic. If they took her sometime in the night, they're probably still in New Mexico." Hap kicked out a chair for Doc. "Now Doc, you sit down and have some breakfast. This is liable to be a long day."

Doc's hands shook. "I don't have time, Hap. You don't understand. I have to find her."

"Kid, you ain't gonna help her by having a stroke. We'll get her back. Just relax."

Doris brought coffee and a plate of food. Doc looked at it, but didn't at all feel like eating. "What did you mean by tracker?"

Hap smiled. "This ain't our first rodeo, Morales. Big, bad bounty hunters from LA? They just met some bigger, badder ones. Right now, I got guys headed out in every direction. We cast a wide net. Indians in the hills, you might say. They see all. We'll find Miss Paulette. The electronic tracker's an old trick. I'm betting they put one on your car. They can follow you with a simple cell phone app. They know where you are all the time. Easy stuff."

The biker called Jack came back in and tossed what looked like a large black button on the table. "Stuck to the frame."

Hap picked it up and turned it over in his hand. "Good job. 'Preciate it."

"Uh huh," Jack said.

"So that's it? That's how they followed us?" Doc said.

"Yup. I would've done the same if I found your car somewhere," Hap said.

"Wait a minute. You called me Morales. How did you know my last name?"

Hap grinned and unbuttoned his leather vest revealing a blue T-shirt with a faded pair of red socks screened on the front. "You kidding? We had season tickets when I was a kid. Right behind the first base line. Ate, slept and breathed the Sox. Still do. Go out for spring training every year. Saw you play out there a time or two. We had high hopes for you, man. I knew you as soon as you walked in yesterday. Even have your rookie card someplace. By the way, how's the knee?"

"Sore."

"Well, suck it up. We got us a movie star to find."

CHAPTER TWENTY-THREE

Desert, Dust, and Disco

"I have to go to the bathroom," Paradise said from the back seat of the Crown Victoria.

Hollister and Crystal—those were their names. Although Crystal seemed to prefer calling Hollister 'moron' and Hollister didn't call Crystal much of anything.

"Oh, c'mon, old man. Let me slap Barbie around," Crystal said for what must have been the hundredth time in the last twenty minutes.

"I told you, no," he replied.

"Please, can we stop someplace? I really need to go," Paradise said.

"Listen, Miss Jones, one more time—the coins. What did the puzzle say? Where were you going?" Hollister said.

Paradise leaned forward. "Do you even know what happened? Did you know Burt tried to molest me? That's why I hit him with the lamp. And crashed the Porsche. Can't you understand that?"

Hollister's eyes shifted to the rearview mirror, then back to the road. "He didn't say nothin' about any lamp."

"Couldn't you just let me go? He'll put me in jail. Or worse. Please?"

"I feel for you, kid. I really do. And Lord knows I'm no fan of the good doctor, but the money he's paying for you is just too good. You're a big fish, you understand? It's not personal. Now tell me about the treasure."

"I already told you. You stole my coin before I could take it to the museum. I don't know what else I can tell you. Please, can we stop? I really have to go."

"What coin did we steal, Princess?" Crystal said, rolling the Dos Escudos across her knuckles. Paradise reached over the seat for it, but the coin disappeared as fast as it had come.

"Ooh! Magic!" Crystal said.

Hollister sighed and pulled off the road onto a rough dirt track. He stopped the Crown Victoria in a cloud of dust, threw the stick into park, and rubbed his temples. Opening the glove compartment, he pulled out half a roll of toilet paper and tossed it back to Paradise. "Fine, find a bush if there is one in this godforsaken moonscape. That's the best you're gonna get." He leaned back against the seat with a groan.

"Thank you," Paradise said.

"And you go with her," he said to Crystal.

Crystal hopped out of the car, gave the desert air a roundhouse kick, and sang, "And slap the princess around if she tries anything funny," to the tune of "Jive Talkin'."

Paradise found a scraggly bush and was relieved to see that Hollister turned his back. She managed to accomplish the task successfully even with Crystal watching. Hollister's phone rang as the women walked back to the car.

"Yeah?" he said. "Yeah. We have her. Like I told you earlier."

Paradise could hear Burt's unmistakable baritone on the other end of the line, but couldn't make out what he said. Cold touched her insides.

"The coin? Yeah. But how ..." Hollister turned to Crystal with a glare.

Crystal shrugged her shoulders, lifted her hands, and mouthed, "What?"

Hollister shook his head. "Look, I know as much as you do about the coins. Which is pretty much *nada*. There's some story about a treasure, but this ain't the movies, you know? It's probably bogus. We just want our eighty-thou and we're done, *bueno*?"

Crystal danced up to Hollister. "Do-o-ctor Simmons ... what is he saying?" Still to the tune of the Bee Gees. This woman definitely had issues.

"Why?" Hollister said into the phone, sticking a finger into the opposite ear in an effort to block out Crystal's disco. "Look, I understand, all right? Just lay off. We got her, and we'll deliver her as agreed upon. Just have the other forty grand ready ... Yeah, yeah, okay. Whatever." He pocketed the phone and pulled out a bottle of pills. He shook a couple out and swallowed them without water.

"What did the dear doc have to say?" Crystal said.

Hollister's face burned red. His voice, though not quite a shout, sounded loud in the still air. "You told him about the coins?"

"I answered the phone when he called. You were in the john. Who cares? Don't get your boxers in a knot."

"Don't you get it? Now he wants to know about the treasure. He says anything that the girl has is his."

"Well, she don't have no treasure. So it don't make any difference, moron. And don't yell at me or I'll cave your ribs in."

Hollister's eyes rolled. "Let me talk slow so you understand. If ... he ... knows ... about ... the ... coins ... he'll ... want ... the ... treasure! That means competition! C'mon, Crystal, use your stinking head."

"Know what? You're cute when you get mad, sweetie cheeks."

"Sweetie cheeks? Seriously? I thought you were gonna cave my ribs in."

"Hollister and Crystal sitting in a tree ... " Crystal did a passable moonwalk that kicked up dust from the dry ground.

"What is it with you and 'Jive Talkin' today, anyway?" Hollister said.

Crystal gave a one, two, three punch so close to Paradise's face, she could feel the wind.

"Shut up, moron," Crystal said. Whether directed at Paradise or Hollister, Paradise had no idea.

"He wants a picture," Hollister said.

"Huh?" Crystal replied.

"Simmons. He wants a picture of the girl. I don't know why. Maybe just 'cause he's a perv."

"What do you think, sunshine? Why does the good doctor want a picture of you?" Crystal said.

"Because he's a fan of wide-leg trousers and monochrome flats?" Paradise said.

"Maybe he's a fan of me throwing you into the middle of next week and stepping on your head," Crystal sang, punctuating the melody with another air punch.

"Knock it off," Hollister said. "Just hold her still. Make yourself useful for a change."

Crystal did as she was told, grabbing a fistful of Paradise's white, cotton collar, although Paradise had no thought of trying to escape. Hollister snapped a couple pictures with his phone.

"Wait a minute," Crystal said, yanking Paradise's blouse. "Little Miss Perfect has a tattoo. What d'ya think about that?"

Paradise felt the back of her blouse rip, baring her shoulder.

"Hey, moron, look at this. She's got the coin tattooed right on her. Right here! She had a picture of it the whole time, the little liar."

Hollister studied Paradise. Then walked behind her. She heard the click of his cell phone camera.

He came back around and met her gaze, his eyes hard. "You know where the treasure is, don't you? Do you realize how much Crystal would like to beat that little tidbit of info out of you?"

"Yes, but you won't let her."

His eyebrows rose half an inch. "And why do you say that?"

"Because I've been listening to both of you. I don't think you're a bad person. Not like that, anyway. You don't want to hurt me."

Hollister looked out over the desert. "I'm not as nice as you think."

"Yes, you are, sweetie pie. You're a softie old man these days," Crystal said. "But I'm not. And I'm telling you now, Miss Thing. If you don't spill, I'll take you apart a little at a time until you do."

"Nobody knows if there even is a treasure. It's most likely nothing," Paradise said.

Crystal grabbed a handful of Paradise's hair. "You know where the gold is, and I'm gonna pound you till you beg me to let you tell."

The unmistakable sound of tires on dirt caused all three of them to turn. Crystal let go of Paradise's hair. The Olds rolled to a stop not ten feet from them. Doc drove, and Doris sat in the passenger seat.

Doc opened the door and swung out of the car. "Let go of her. C'mon, Paradise. Time to go."

Crystal laughed. "You've got to be kidding. Ken's here to collect Barbie."

"C'mon, Paradise," Doc repeated.

"Look, man," Hollister said, "we got a legal right here. She's a fugitive, and we're taking her back to LA. I've been very patient with all this and so far it hasn't gotten violent. Let's not let that happen. You just drive on down the road, and neither you nor the girl will get hurt. All I want to do is return her to her father. Hopefully in one piece, but that's up to you."

Doc made no move to go. "You're not taking her anywhere."

"Why're you even talking to this guy, moron? I'm finished with this." Crystal walked to the Crown Vic and reached through the open window. She pulled out a short baseball bat and headed for Doc.

Doc gave no ground. Not an inch. Paradise held her breath.

The sound of engines filled the afternoon, and Crystal stopped short. A group of twenty or so rough-looking men on Harleys rumbled in and formed a loose circle around both cars.

Hap swung a leg over his bike and approached. He grinned. "Paulette Goddard 1940. Where you been? Why don't you go get in the car?" His tone offered no room for argument.

Paradise quickly crossed to the Olds and got in. The convertible top was down, and she sat on the top of the back seat for a better view. Doris reached back and squeezed her hand.

Hollister eyed Hap. "Who are you?" He didn't look scared, but he made no sudden moves either.

The biker grinned. "I'm Hap, and you have a busted taillight. That's illegal."

"What are you talking about?" Hollister said.

Hap grabbed the bat out of Crystal's hand before she could protest, and walked to the back of the Crown Vic.

Hollister put up a hand. "Okay, okay. I get it. The girl goes with you. Crystal, get in the car. Let's go."

Crystal didn't move. "And let eighty grand drive away with Ken and a bunch of wannabe Hell's Angels? I don't think so."

"Just do what I tell you for once in your life!" Hollister said.

Crystal shrugged. "Why start now?"

Paradise was surprised when Doris exited the Olds and walked toward Hollister.

"You're bounty hunters?" Doris said.

"I'm a cop," Crystal said.

Hollister shook his head. "Don't listen to her, she's not a cop. The girl's father hired us to bring her back. I'm a P.I."

"Licensed in the State of New Mexico?"

Hollister's face reddened, and he rubbed his temples again. "No. California."

"Can I see your license?"

"Who are you exactly?" Hollister said.

Doris pulled out a wallet and showed a badge. "Doris Demarco. Chief of Police."

"You gotta be kidding me," Hollister said. "This just gets better and better."

"Actually, she's the *only* police," Hap said. "And the judge."

"Perfect. Of course, she is," Hollister said.

"She's also the minister," another biker added.

Doris smiled. "And I sell Mary Kay."

"God help me, I'm stuck in a twisted episode of *Dukes of Hazzard*." Hollister reached into his wallet and pulled out a card. He handed it to Doris.

"This is expired," Doris said. "Not to mention, it looks kinda fake." She held the card up to the sun. "Either way, this whole deal feels like kidnapping to me."

"Kidnapping?" Crystal said. "What are you talking about?"

"You know you don't smell good?" Doris said, then turned to Paradise. "Hon, did you leave with these two willingly?"

"No, ma'am," Paradise said.

Doris shrugged. "See? Kidnapping. The judge'll have to sort it out."

"I thought you *were* the judge," Hollister said.

"Not at the moment. Right now, I'm the police. It's complicated."

"Yeah, I'll bet it is," Hollister said.

"Why don't you two come with us? Tell you what, you can even drive your own car. Whoever said New Mexico wasn't a friendly place?"

"That's not gonna happen," Crystal said.

Hap still held the bat. "Oh, it'll happen. In fact, you're getting an officially deputized police escort."

"And where're we going?" Hollister asked.

"Jail. You'll love it. Doris makes great biscuits and gravy," Hap said.

Hollister grunted. "Lovely. How long?"

Doris shrugged. "Day? Couple of days? Could take a while. We'll see what we can do."

"This ain't over, you know," Crystal said.

"Oh, I'm sure of that," Hap said. "But by the time you two see daylight again, Miss Paulette Goddard 1940 and the Swing King will be long down the road." He tossed Crystal the bat. "You can even keep this."

Crystal started to say something, but Hollister grabbed her arm and pushed her into the Crown Vic. The bikers fired up and formed a tight circle around it.

Hap walked up to the Olds. "Hey, Paulette 1940, you ever rode on the back of a Harley?"

"Nope," Paradise said.

Hap shrugged out of his leather vest and draped it around Paradise's torn blouse. "Well, now's your chance."

Chapter Twenty-four

Pink Cadillacs and Whitewashed Prayers

Doc started the Olds and followed the unlikely entourage onto the pavement and back toward the Manhattan Bar. In front of him, Paradise's hair lifted in the wind as Hap hit the throttle.

"You're a minister?" Doc said.

"I wear a lot of hats. Need any Mary Kay?" Doris replied.

"Not that I can think of at the moment."

"Too bad. I dream about that pink Caddy."

Doc pointed to Paradise. "Thanks, Doris. For everything."

"You're welcome, Doc. I hate bullies. Tell you the truth, that's the reason I came out here in the first place all those years ago. One particular bully. Story for another time. But now I got Hap. How about you? You ever going to play ball again?"

Doc shook his head. "Even if I was a hundred percent, I don't think so. My priorities seem to have shifted."

"They tend to do that. Looks to me like your priority is about a hundred feet in front of us on the back of a Harley Davidson Panhead."

"I won't argue. But she's damaged, you know? I'm not sure I can give her what she needs."

"Nah. She may be chipped—a couple of dents, but nothing that can't be fixed. And something tells me you can give her *exactly* what she needs. She'll be good as new."

"I hope you're right."

"I am. Trust me."

"And I hope I have the time. She's dying to get back to Los Angeles."

"*Amigo*, we're all dying for something. Sometimes for the right thing, sometimes the wrong. I've seen her story before. I've *been* her. She doesn't know *what* she's dying for. You be you. She'll come around."

The jail, a tiny block-shaped adobe, stood only a few hundred yards from the Manhattan Bar. Doc watched as the tough-looking Los Angeles couple was ushered inside by a handful of Hap's crew. What would have happened if Hap and his guys hadn't found Paradise? Doc considered this. Easy, he would have followed her back to Los Angeles. Man, he was in deep. Paco told him to write his story, but the story was writing him. He'd known this girl only a short time, and already he couldn't imagine his world without her. He knew she didn't feel the same, but she felt something; he could see it in her eyes. But then again, she'd told him straight out she wasn't interested. And why should she be? Who was he, anyway? She was primed to be a star. Destined for fame and fortune. He'd had one at bat in The Show. So what? Thirty seconds in the batter's box at Fenway constituted the pinnacle of his life. How could he blame her?

Lunch was served in the bar, and Paradise took a chair next to Doc.

"How was the ride?" Doc said.

"A little scary. But I figured if Barbara Stanwyck and Elvis could pull it off, so could I."

"*Roustabout*," Doc said.

"You've seen it?"

"You remember who you're talking to?"

Doris exited the kitchen, a bottle in hand, and parked herself across from them. Her white hair stuck straight up. "Look what I found. Coke in a bottle for Paulette Goddard."

"Barbara Stanwyck," Paradise said.

Doris chuckled. "Okay. Babs Stanwyck—whatever. Listen, I figure since we went out and saved your skin, you two are regulars now. You want anything, help yourself, got it? I got things to do. Kitchen's yours."

"Got it, thanks," said Doc.

"So where're you headed next?" Doris said.

"Brownsville, Texas. Supposed to meet a guy there," Doc said.

"What kind of guy?"

"Wish I knew."

"You in a hurry?"

Doc nodded. "Yeah. But maybe not as much of one now that those two aren't breathing down our necks."

"Real couple of lovebirds. Hollister and Crystal Finch. I can hold 'em in the nest for a few days, but that's about it. Anyway, long enough for you to get to

Brownsville. Why don't you stay till tomorrow? The Rio Kings are playing again tonight."

Doc tried to get a read on Paradise. "What do you think?" he said. "You up for another night on the town? Except there's not really a town …"

She smiled. "I could be talked into it, if you try hard."

"Okay then. We'll leave first thing in the morning," Doc said.

Doris moved on to talk with Hap a few tables away.

"What would you have done?" Paradise said.

"You mean tonight? Stayed here or waited till morning? I don't need an excuse to dance with you," Doc said.

"No, if she would have come after you. Crystal—with the bat."

"I'm not sure. Gotten nailed with a bat, I guess."

"You weren't scared?"

"I wasn't *not* scared. But you needed help. Like you did back in Paradise. Doesn't matter whether I was scared or not."

"You mean you had my back."

"Yeah. I did."

"Sailor, I think you hit one over the Green Monster."

"Four-fifty if it was a foot."

Paradise sipped her Coke. "Because we're on the lam."

"Yup."

She finished the Coke and stood. "I'm going to rest awhile. I have to make sure I can keep up with the Swing King." Her eyes met his. "Thank you, Doc. I can't go back to Burt."

"You're welcome. And you won't."

Doc watched her go, then turned at the sound of a chair scooting out. Hap stood over him.

The big biker spun the chair around backwards and straddled it. "Made a couple of calls to some friends in Cali. Your buddies over in the jail are the real deal. Bad news—especially the woman. She has a rep for hurting people, man. The police are looking hard for Paradise, too. You're okay out here in the boonies for a day or two, but once you get on into Texas, you really have to keep it low."

"We'll be careful. We just need to get to Brownsville. I'm gonna try to make it there by tomorrow night. Then on into Mexico."

"Doris says you have someone getting you across the border?"

"Yeah. A guy named Lan. Friend of a friend."

"Can you trust him?"

"I trust the friend. Trust him completely. That's good enough."

"Look, there's something else. Her stepdad, this Dr. Simmons guy, has offered a big chunk of a reward for her return. Fifty grand. That's a lot of cash, man. The kind that makes even friends think twice, you know? I'd be careful, amigo. Don't trust nobody."

"What about you? You're not tempted by that much money?"

"Me? I got everything I want right here. What would I do with fifty grand? Besides, I like a good love story."

"Thanks, Hap."

Hap leaned over and slapped Doc on the shoulder. "You got it, Red Sox."

Later, Doc met Paradise at the door of her room. She wore a black, off-the-shoulder dress. How in the world did she fit all those clothes in that one suitcase?

Doc gave a low whistle.

"Lauren Bacall," she said.

"Paradise Jones," he answered.

"Shut up, Doc."

He offered his arm. She took it.

The Rio Kings thumped, and the Manhattan filled with people of every age, shape and size. Once in a while, Hap left the stage to the other musicians and danced with either Paradise or Doris. Doc's heart thrilled at the sound of Paradise's laugh. On one particularly slow song, she hugged Doc so tight her strength surprised him.

"Thank you, Doc," she said.

Whether for the rescue or the dance, he wasn't sure. He answered by holding her a little tighter.

They danced till midnight, then retired to their rooms. Doc lay awake for a long time, hands behind his head, thinking of her just a few feet away. He imagined he could hear her breathing through the wall.

Rain came just before he slept.

The early desert sun followed the rain with an act of its own, drawing the pungent odor of sage and earth out of the brown hills and into the fresh-scrubbed morning air. Doc knocked on Paradise's door, and she answered, suitcase in hand. Across the road, the bent Mexican woman once again sat on her bench and prayed toward the whitewashed shrine. Doc noticed Paradise watching her as he loaded the bags into the trunk of the Olds.

"What do you think she prays about?" Paradise said.

"I don't know."

"Do you pray? Talk to God?"

"Sometimes. You could too, you know."

Her eyes shifted to the dash of the Olds where Truck Stop Jesus smiled in the morning sunlight. "I'm not sure ... Maybe I already do. Sometimes."

Hap and Doris came out of the Manhattan to see them off.

Doris tossed Doc a couple of black T-shirts. "A parting gift from Manhattan, New Mexico."

Doc shook one open. It said *I Spent a Year at the Manhattan Bar One Weekend.*

Hap removed his leather vest and dropped it around Paradise's shoulders. "This one's yours to keep, kid. You earned it yesterday."

Paradise put her arms around the big biker and hugged him tightly. She pulled off the vest and traced *The Rio Kings* patch with a red nail. "Are you a band or a motorcycle club?"

Hap laughed. "Lines tend to get a little blurred out here." He put a thick arm around Doris' shoulders. "Does this lady enforce the law, marry people, or sell makeup? It's fuzzy." He turned to Doc and handed him a cell phone. "Only one app loaded on this, Doc. There's a tracker on the Crown Vic hidden a heck of a lot better than the one they put on the Olds. If they follow you, you'll know it. I doubt they will, though. A trucker buddy of mine is giving *their* tracker a lift to North Carolina."

Paradise hugged Hap again. "Thank you. And thanks for helping me. I'm not sure what to say. Thank you isn't enough."

Hap shrugged. "You just said it. Now get down the road. And when you get back this way, we'll have a few more swing songs in the repertoire."

"It's a date," Paradise said.

Doris handed Doc a lined piece of paper. "Directions to get you to Texas. Back roads. Be careful, huh, Red Sox?"

"We will. And you're sure you can hold our California shadows long enough for us to get to Brownsville?"

"No problem. Court can't even hear their case for a few days. I have to run up to Truth or Consequences to see a lady about a makeup order."

"We owe you one, Doris. A few, actually."

"Go Yankees."

Doc laughed. "Yeah, go Yankees."

The Olds' engine rumbled as they left the Manhattan. A four-way intersection—four possible directions. But the right road stretched before them, both literally and figuratively. Somewhere up ahead, a guy named Lan waited for them. And in the rearview mirror, the Mexican woman still prayed in front of the gleaming shrine.

Maybe she'd toss one up for him and Paradise.

CHAPTER TWENTY-FIVE

Kermit, Texas

The Texas border town of Kermit welcomed Doc and Paradise with a water tower painted green and adorned with massive, one-dimensional ping-pong ball eyes. A fitting tribute to the amphibious star that shared the town's name. Billowy white clouds rolled across the sky. Doc pulled into a Dairy Queen to stretch his legs and find something cold to drink. Paradise borrowed his cell and dialed Ash's number. Her friend answered on the fourth ring.

"It's me," Paradise said.

"You know I've been worried sick. Where are you?"

"Traveling. Hollister and Crystal are in jail. At least for now."

"Burt's psycho trackers? How did that happen?"

"It's a long story."

"You with the ballplayer?"

"How did you know?"

"I think it's romantic. Are you okay?"

"Yes. And it's not romantic. Except maybe the dancing. That's kind of romantic."

"What dancing? Spill, sister."

"Nothing to spill."

"C'mon. It's me."

"It's not like that. He's helping me, that's all."

Was it? Was that all? There'd been a couple of times on the dance floor last night ...

"Yeah, okay. I get it, no details," Ash said. "Listen, Eve calls me every thirty seconds, asking if I've heard from you. She's actually worried sick. Why don't you call her?"

"Maybe I will. I don't know."

"Just do."

"I said maybe."

"Uh huh. So what's it like out there in the big bad world, just you and the ballplayer who's only helping you and you don't have feelings for him so help you God on a stack of Bibles?"

Paradise squinted her eyes against the sun and looked up at the giant Kermit water tower. "I could really use a turkey on rye from Cantor's. You know there's only a few months before they're supposed to start shooting *Gone with the Wind*?"

"Tell me about it. Arnie's going berserk, calls a gazillion times a day. If you don't get back soon, I swear he's gonna lose his mind."

"Have they announced who got the part yet?"

"Not that I've heard, but Arnie's been talking to them. He still thinks you'll get it—so do I. And what if you do? What about Burt? Will you come back?"

"I can't think about it. Besides, if I really got it, I would have heard by now."

"Maybe, maybe not. So who are you wearing today?"

Paradise caught her own reflection in the Dairy Queen window. "I don't know, that green dress. You know the one."

"The Elizabeth Taylor? Are you sure you're okay? You don't sound good. You love that dress."

Paradise focused past her reflection and watched Doc as he placed his order. He laughed at something the girl behind the register said.

"Maybe once in a while, I'll just be me. Or maybe half Elizabeth and half me."

A long pause on Ash's end. "I don't think that's a bad idea, but ... what's going on? You don't sound very ... I don't know ... you."

"I just need to get home. Back to LA. I'll be fine. Everything feels so strange right now."

"Paradise, it's okay. Relax a little. LA's not going anywhere."

"Even if they *were* going to give me the part, I'm sure this thing with Burt has messed it all up. What does Arnie say about that? And don't forget, *you* were the one who told me not to leave LA in the first place."

"You know Arnie. Always a spin. He's been selling the studio on the publicity angle. Kind of a *Free Paradise Jones* sort of thing. And I told you not to leave LA because I was worried. But now it seems like things are changing. I don't think they're bad changes either."

"Why do you say that?" Paradise said.

Doc backed through the Dairy Queen door with a bag and a couple of Styrofoam cups in his hands and headed for the Olds.

"Because you're only half Elizabeth Taylor."

"That doesn't even make sense."

"It makes perfect sense."

"Ash, I have to go. We need to get on the road."

"'Kay. Say hi to Red Sox for me."

"Bye, Ash." Paradise hit the end button and handed the phone to Doc.

"Everything okay?" he said.

"Everything and nothing. It seems impossible, doesn't it?"

Doc's eyes searched her, a line deepening slightly at the edge of his mouth. "What does? Escaping from crazy bounty hunters? Finding the answer to a three-hundred-year-old puzzle? Or an almost-movie star driving through Texas with a nobody like me?"

Paradise turned her gaze up and shielded her eyes with her hand. "The sky. That it could be so blue. Deep, dark blue, like water. I don't think I've ever seen anything like it."

"Yeah. The sky. That was my next guess." He held one of the cups out to her. "I got you a malt. Strawberry. Did I guess right?"

"Close enough, but I'm a chocolate person."

"In that case," he held up the other cup, "I got you a malt. Chocolate. Did I guess right?"

Paradise took it. "Nail on the head, sailor."

In the car, Doc sipped his malt and made a face.

Paradise squeezed ketchup on an onion ring. "You don't like strawberry?"

"Of course, I do. Who doesn't? Strawberry malts are the reason I get up every morning."

She handed him the onion ring. "Two chocolate fugitives on the lam. Here, onion rings make everything better."

"You bet. Breakfast of champions."

"Except it's afternoon."

"Never argue with Paradise Jones. So listen, I figure if we take back roads, we have between ten and thirteen hours or so to get to Brownsville. That's if we push straight through and don't stop except for gas. I think we should just go for it tonight."

Paradise handed him another onion ring. "Okay. You're not, you know."

"I'm not what?"

"A nobody."

Lines deepened on both sides of Doc's mouth. "Know what I think? You like me."

"Don't get ahead of yourself. It's just the chocolate malt talking."

Doc guided the Olds south out of town, and the country spread out before them, brown and hard. Occasional pump jacks dotted the landscape, bobbing their big, dinosaur heads up and down with dogged persistence as they sucked oil from the West Texas depths.

"Jim Sharp is from Kermit," Doc said. "One of the greatest bull riders of all time. Jake and I saw him ride once."

"Why in the world would anyone ever do that?"

"Ride a bull?"

"Name a town after a Muppet."

"Pretty sure the town came first."

"Well, why would they, then? Ride a bull?"

"Why would someone want to be an actress? Or hit a baseball?"

"The Green Monster, right?"

Doc nodded. "Mostly. We've all got one."

Paradise leaned her head back. Truck Stop Jesus smiled at her.

"What?" Paradise said.

"Nothing," Jesus answered.

"You want to know what I want, right?"

"I already know what you want. I'm just waiting for you to figure it out."

"What's that supposed to mean? We've already talked about this. Anyway, stop being a dead horse."

"You mean *beating* a dead horse."

Paradise shrugged. "Either way, lousy news for the horse."

"Okay. I'm patient."

"Oh, brother. You're as impossible as he is, do you know that?"

"All things are possible."

"That's exactly what I mean ..."

Doc's cell rang. He picked it up off the dash and looked at the incoming number. "Los Angeles, I think." He handed it to Paradise. "Is it your friend?"

Paradise looked. "No. It's Arnie, my agent. Ash must have given him this number."

The ringing stopped. Ten seconds later it started again.

"Maybe you should talk to him," Doc said.

"Maybe ..." Paradise contemplated for a few seconds, then answered. "Hi Arnie, what's up?"

Arnie's affected Brooklyn accent slammed off the satellite. "Don't you dare play cute. Do I even want to ask where you are?"

"You could, but I won't tell you. And I wish you wouldn't."

"Do you realize what's at stake here? The studio's asking questions. I can't keep holding them off, Paradise."

"I can't come back right now. You know that."

"Look, here's the straight dope. I just got word that Scarlett is down to three girls. And I think the producers are leaning toward you. They like you for this, you understand? But your being MIA isn't helping. It's like I'm juggling cats here!"

"Do you think I want to be out here? I don't have a choice, Arnie. I don't want to go to jail. What's hard to understand about that?"

"Yeah, okay. Listen, I talked to Burt. He's agreed to drop the charges if you come back. He'll take payments for the car over time. Heck, you'll be able to write him a check for two cars when you get the part. All he wants is for you to come back and stay in the pool house where you can all be a family again. Does that sound so bad? Free rent in Malibu?"

"No, Arnie. He started it. He came on to me ... don't you understand? That's why he wants me back there."

"Look, kid, it's all a little blurry, you know? He'd been drinking ... You were tired ... Call it a misunderstanding. I promise it'll be okay. Burt promises, too. Just come back and let's seal this movie deal, okay?"

"It'll be okay? What's the matter with you? Are you deaf? The man tried to molest me! It will never be *okay*, Arnie."

"Paradise, quit being dramatic. We *all* have a lot riding on this deal."

"All? Is that why you want me back? Just so you can get your commission if I get the part? I thought you were my friend."

"I am your friend, Paradise. But I'm also your manager. It's my job to take care of you. To help you know what's best for you which, frankly, you almost never do."

Paradise glanced at Doc. "I'm being taken care of at the moment."

"Look, let's back up. Take a rewind, okay? So don't live with Burt. Maybe I can talk him out of that. Just come back. I'm telling you, we'll work something out. Just get back here."

Paradise looked at Doc and sighed. "I need time, Arnie. A few days, maybe a week."

"For what? If Burt will back down, then why …"

"I have to go, Arnie."

"Paradise, I …"

Paradise hung up.

"A few days?" Doc said.

"I don't know what to do."

Doc shrugged. "We'll work it out."

"We?"

"Yeah, we. Let's find this Lan guy. If he can get us across the border, it shouldn't take long to get to Dia Perdido. We'll find the answer to the puzzle and then see how LA's looking. If things have blown over, we can go back."

"Why do you keep saying *we?*"

"You think I'm gonna let you tackle Burt by yourself?"

"Why are you doing this, Doc? It isn't your concern."

"I told you, I have your back, that's all."

Paradise sighed.

Pump jacks bobbed, silhouetted against the evening sky.

Jesus smiled.

"Don't say a word," Paradise said.

Jesus gave her a thumbs-up.

The hours rolled on as the Olds reeled in mile after mile of Texas highway. Evening caved in to a night filled with stars. Paradise slept, then woke again to a preacher on the radio. The man pontificated with a slow, southern drawl, sounding bored with his own voice.

"What time is it?" Paradise said.

"Around two."

"How much longer? Do you want me to drive?"

"I'm hanging in there. You just go back to slee—"

Doc's foot hit hard on the brake, sending Paradise's body forward and her heart to her throat as the Olds, tires screeching, went into a slide.

Chapter Twenty-six

Hallelujah, Jesus Saves

Doc woke to a faint knock on the car window, and squinted against the early morning light. Two bloodshot, hound dog eyes peered through the glass at him from beneath the wide brim of a cowboy hat.

Doc cleared his throat. "Paradise, wake up. Somebody's here."

Paradise stirred as Doc rolled down the window.

The eyes were set in a deeply lined face of a man about sixty. He removed the cowboy hat, revealing thin, sweat-dampened gray hair, and wiped his brow with a faded, red bandanna. Tiny purple veins laced his faded roadmap of a face. He replaced the hat, spit a stream of tobacco at the ground, and spoke with a slow, Texas drawl. "You two all right? Looks like you had yourself a long night."

"Only a few hours," Doc said. "A truck crossed the line into our lane last night, and we slid off the road to miss it. He just kept going. We weren't hurt, but it trashed one of our wheels. Car won't budge. We decided to sleep for a while till somebody came along. Pretty empty out here."

"Uh huh. It's them trucks comin' up from Mexico. I seen 'em bump a car from behind and push 'em right through an intersection to hurry things along. Ain't no manners anymore. So you sure you ain't hurt? Both in one piece?"

"Yeah, we're fine."

The man straightened, removed the hat again, and scratched his head. His eyes traveled the length of the car and back. "Don't reckon you're wrong about your car. From the angle of that tire, I'm guessing you got yourself a busted axle. Lucky I was out this way. You could'a sat here a while."

"Axle? That doesn't sound good," Paradise said.

The man's words rolled out slow, laced with gravel and sun. "It ain't, 'less you're in the mechanic game. Then I guess it might be a mortgage payment." He spat again. "Maybe two, dependin' on the house. Three, if it's a dirt-lot trailer." He held out a gnarled left hand to Doc. "Name's Cal Sloan. Why don't you two hop on in the truck, and we'll run ourselves up to town. We'll get ol' Elwood down to the Texaco to come pull you outa the ditch. He's just the man to patch her up, if we can drag him away from his biscuits."

"Sounds good. I'm Doc Morales, this is—"

"Elizabeth," Paradise interrupted.

"How long do you think it'll take? To fix the car?" Doc asked.

Cal squinted out toward the horizon line. "No telling. You're on South Texas time down here. But let's go rustle up Elwood. He'll give you an idea."

Doc climbed out of the car and stretched his stiff muscles. "Thanks, we appreciate the help."

"Hey, you bet."

The mild, rolling hills of South Texas spread around them, dotted with brush and low trees. Power lines paralleled the two-lane road, fading into distance in both directions.

"Cal, you have a ranch around here?" Doc asked.

"Used to, long time ago. Was my old pop's, and his afore him. His pop's afore that, too. Family fought off banditos, red Indians, grasshoppers, and dust storms just to keep it. Had a bad spell a while back. So dry the Baptists were sprinkling, the Methodists were spitting, and the Catholics were giving rain checks. Couldn't make the taxes no more. Developers—worse than any bandito, let me tell you— they dropped out of the sky like a flock of vultures. I'd have shot 'em if I could. We live in town these days. Me and Mary Martha—that's my wife. Hate everything about it, too."

Cal moved with the comfortable rolling limp of a man long acquainted with injury. He opened the passenger door of his rusty Ford pickup for Paradise. "In you go, girl." He used only his left hand and arm. His right hung at his side like a dead weight.

Doc set his duffle and Paradise's suitcase in the bed of the truck and climbed into the cab next to Paradise.

Cal walked to the driver's side door and hoisted himself in, tossing a half-empty tequila bottle onto the floor as he did so. "You know what they say, breakfast is the most important meal of the day."

"You want an honest reply to that?" Doc asked.

Cal shrugged. "That old bottle's been drinking out of me a long time now. I'm an old dog, amigo. Not much for new tricks."

Doc gazed out at the country. "Been through this way a couple of times back when my brother was rodeoing."

Cal started the truck. "Your brother rodeoed? What's his name? I remember most of 'em. 'Specially if it was around here."

"Jake Morales, out of Arizona."

"Ah, that Morales kid. Saddle bronc rider. Good cowboy, really something. I thought he had a future in it. He ain't ridin' no more?"

"He retired. Became a priest."

"No kidding, a priest? Huh. Well, we all got to skin our own buffaloes. I'd say you got the better time of it, driving Texas with the prettiest girl I seen around here in a year's worth of Sundays … If you don't mind my saying, miss."

Paradise smiled. "I don't mind at all. Thank you, Mr. Sloan."

"Call me Cal. Everybody does. That way, I'll know who you're talking to. And don't you tell my wife about that little compliment either. I won't get dinner for a month."

"My lips are sealed."

"Atta girl."

"Can I ask what happened to your arm?" Paradise said.

Cal grinned. "Ain't pretty, is it? Used to rodeo myself 'bout a lifetime and a half ago. Bull rider. Made of rubber and leather and pure bulletproof, ain't no lie. Got so hung up on my last ride, I thought I never would get free. Old arm's just hung there ever since like a dead piece of meat. Nothing the docs could do."

"Hung up?" Paradise said.

"Yup. Bull rope. That's what you hold onto for dear life, trying not to die when that old rascal comes out of the chute like a ton of dynamite. Took a third wrap around my hand that day. Suicide wrap, they call it. Wanted an extra edge, and I was feelin' lucky. But feeling ain't being. Bull threw me, and I couldn't get my hand loose. Banged me around like a rag doll till I was out cold. Tell you the truth, I don't remember much of it. Wish I could take it back, but there ain't no rewind button on life, know what I mean?"

"I'm sorry," Paradise said.

Cal smiled. "Thank you for that. My day just got brighter. So, you two picked a danged empty part of the world to be driving through so late at night. Where y'all headed?"

"On our way to Brownsville," Doc said.

"Ain't many people on their way to Brownsville come this a'way. Interstate's a whole lot faster. You get lost?"

"Let's just say we were taking the scenic route," Doc said.

Cal eyed him. "All right, son, let's just say that, then. I ain't one to hang my wash on another man's line. Can't say the same about everyone in Agua Loco, though. People down here grow some real long noses when strangers show up. 'Specially when they look like the young miss here."

"Agua Loco?" Paradise said. "Is that where you live?"

"Home sweet home. It's Mex for *crazy water*. Used to be a bad spring around here. Cow drank from it, she'd lose her mind. Run till she dropped and died. No good for people neither. Dry now, though, thank the good Lord."

The road ran straight for several miles, then twisted and turned through a series of sandy washes. They passed a sand-blasted double-wide trailer sitting lower on one side than the other. A couple of kids, one still in diapers, kicked up dust as they chased each other around a car mounted on blocks. A little farther on, a tract of single-level, stucco ranch homes huddled together, their generic facades the same brown as the dirt lots they sat on. On the horizon, a water tower took root and sprouted, growing taller with each mile. Eventually, a town appeared beneath it, the buildings the same dull brown as the tract homes.

Doc had seen a hundred main streets of a similar bent. Dirty and windswept, waking up to a sun-drenched day. The place appeared deserted, except for a man sleeping on the sidewalk beneath a barroom window. On the building next door, an unlit neon sign proclaimed *Hallelujah Jesus Saves*. A rancher and a Mexican man with a truck full of irrigation pipe chatted over the gas pumps at a corner Circle K—the only other sign of life.

It didn't take a genius to see that Agua Loco was no tourist mecca.

Cal drove through the small downtown, then turned right. A quarter mile later, he swung into the gravel parking lot of the Busy Bee Diner. "Elwood'll be here at the Bee sure as shootin'. I imagine you two could use a bite to eat as well."

"Sounds good to me. I'm starving," Doc said.

Paradise smiled and took Cal's hand as he helped her down from the cab.

Doc pointed at the dozen or so cars that filled the small lot. "Looks like the whole town is here."

"Most, usually. Least this time of day," Cal said.

The Busy Bee lived up to its name. Of the ten booths laid out in an "L" shape along the walls in front of the plate glass windows, nine were full. Several patrons sat on stools in front of a counter as well.

"Elwood. Got a couple of customers for you," Cal called.

A fat man with a Caterpillar cap pushed back on his head swiveled his stool with effort, then grunted as he stood, cup of coffee in hand. His gut spilled over the front of his belt-line between a pair of thick suspenders struggling to hold up his jeans. "Hey'a, Cal. Shop's closed till I finish my coffee."

"You bet. But when you're done, these two have a car stuck in a ditch with a busted axle 'bout twenty miles or so out on Meyer Road. Doc and Elizabeth, meet Elwood. Only grease monkey in town, so he's what you get. Good news is, he ain't half bad at it."

"You have time to go out and get the car?" Doc asked. "We'd appreciate it."

Elwood finished his coffee with a long swallow. "I'll head out. Coffee's cold anyway. What kind of car?"

"It's a 1949 Olds Eighty-Eight," Paradise said.

Elwood narrowed an eye and nodded. "No kidding, 'forty-nine? Ain't fresh off the showroom floor, is she? Busted axle might take some time. I'll have to order parts from San Antonio. Maybe even Houston."

"How long do you think?" Paradise asked.

"No telling. If I had to guess, a day or two to get the parts, maybe more. Then another couple to get her back on the road. Let me go get the old girl, and we'll see where we stand."

"Fair enough," Doc said.

"Well then, let me ride." Elwood waved as he waddled out of the diner. Doc watched through the plate glass as the fat man hefted himself up behind the wheel of a tow truck, started it, and rumbled out of the parking lot onto the road.

The food was the kind of good that can only be found in small-town diners. Doc offered to buy Cal breakfast, but the rancher said he'd eaten and accepted a cup of coffee instead. Once it arrived, he stirred in a package of Sweet'N Low, then spent the next hour entertaining them with good-old-days stories of ranch life, rodeos, and mean bulls. When they finished, Doc paid the bill, and the trio headed back toward Cal's truck.

"Reckon you two can camp out at our place till we get word on your car. Mary Martha would be glad for the company," the old rancher said.

"We'd appreciate it, thanks," Doc replied. "But we wouldn't want you to go to any more trouble. We can find a motel."

Cal fished his keys from his pocket. "Uh huh. You sure can. Be lookin' for a good spell, though. Only motel around here closed about ten years back."

"Your place it is, then. Thanks again," Doc said.

The parking lot had emptied substantially. The day offered deep-Texas quiet, and the sun warmed Doc's shoulders. Since they had time, maybe he'd go for a run. The sound of tires on gravel and loud country music pushed into his thoughts as a lifted, late-model Chevy pickup dusted by him and skidded to a stop in front of the diner. The music stopped with the truck's engine, and the air went quiet again as three laughing young men climbed out.

The driver ogled Paradise and whistled. "Hey, Cal, who's your friend?" He was tall, with wide shoulders and an arrogance that usually comes with too much alcohol. The other two laughed.

"You Callaghan boys have beer for breakfast, or ain't you been to bed yet?" Cal said.

"You're one to talk, Cal. Let's just say we had us a good night in Old Mexico," the driver said.

"C'mon, King Jr. Let's go in, man."

The driver threw a mock punch, and the boy ducked, laughing.

"Knock it off," Cal said. "King or no King, you ought to be getting to work. Your old man'd have your skin if he saw you here in town,"

King Jr. grinned. "King's at a stock show in Dallas. What he don't know won't hurt him. So you gonna introduce me to the lady or what?"

Cal pointed a finger at them. "You can call me Mr. Sloan. And you boys has been spoiled since you stepped out of the womb." Cal addressed the driver. "*King Jr.*, my sweet hind end. You ain't no King Jr. You don't hold a candle to your old man. This lady's out of your league. Go on home and get you some sleep. Sweat Old Mexico out of your bloodstream."

King Jr. grinned. "You sure talk big for a little old man livin' in a townie trailer."

One of the others, tall and freckled, slapped King Jr. on the shoulder. "C'mon, King Jr. Leave the old boy alone. Let's get us something to eat. I'm hungry."

Irritation flashed across King Jr.'s face. "Go on ahead, then. I'll catch up."

Freckles kicked at the dust with his boot but didn't leave.

Doc gauged King Jr. carefully. Well over six feet. Wide shoulders. Used to getting his own way. Cock of the walk.

Well, it's a small walk.

"Doc, why don't you two hop in the truck?" Cal said.

King Jr. moved to his right, blocking the way. "Nice dress, girl. Looks just right on you, too. You want to take a ride with me? See some real Texas cowboys?"

He reached for Paradise's arm, and Cal slapped his hand down. Surprise registered in the young man's eyes. He shoved the rancher and laughed as Cal stumbled back, then reached again for Paradise.

Doc took King Jr. in the gut with his shoulder, and they both went down hard onto the gravel lot. Doc scrambled up first and watched the dazed King start to his feet.

King Jr. spat and looked at Doc as if he were a cockroach. "You're a dead man. You think you can—"

Doc punched him in the mouth, and King Jr. doubled over, hand to his face. Blood streamed through his fingers and dripped into the dust.

When King Jr. didn't straighten, Doc turned quickly to check on Paradise.

Her eyes widened. "Look out, Doc!"

Lights flashed behind his eyes, and the Texas morning went black.

Chapter Twenty-seven

All Hat and No Cattle

Doc struggled to put his thoughts together. Sunrise? Where was he? Light seeped through his eyelids in increments. It started out dull purple, then orange, then yellow, then crashed with the full weight of the sun.

He cracked a lid.

Not the sun. A bare light bulb surrounded by a metal cage glared down at him, giving a boost to the pain throbbing through his brain. With effort, he lifted his head and felt the back of his skull with careful fingers. He winced, finding a knot the size of an egg.

"You awake there, Mike Tyson?" Cal's drawl reached him through the haze of pain.

Doc turned his head. The rancher sat on a bunk across from Doc. The room was small and colorless. A wall made up of thick metal bars separated him from an office furnished with a few industrial looking, gray metal desks. Sunlight filtered through dirty windows.

A sheriff's office—and a jail cell.

Through another wall of bars to his right, a second cell sat unoccupied.

"Where are we? What happened?" Doc said.

"In the hoosegow, amigo. We been picked up on a dual charge of disturbing the peace and generally irritating a Callaghan—King Jr. being one of 'em. Irritating Callaghans is pretty much a capital offense around here."

"Are you kidding? That guy assaulted *you*. What are you doing in here?"

"Like ol' King Jr. said, I'm a trailer park townie. Not to mention, I got me a reputation for dancing with the bottle. He's the son of the biggest rancher in South Texas. Clear-cut case of wrong place, wrong time. Plain truth of it is, what Jr. wants, Jr. gets, and what he wants right now is for me and you to have us a luxury vacation here at Hotel Graybar. You embarrassed him."

"Where's Paradise?"

"You mean Elizabeth? Had me a feelin' that wasn't her real name. Guess now that we're cellmates, we got no more secrets, huh? Young miss is over with Mary Martha." The old man's craggy face clouded slightly.

"What is it, Cal? Is she safe?"

"Aw, it ain't nothin'. I could just use a drink, is all. Dry as a powder house."

"Listen to me, she's in trouble. She didn't do anything wrong, but it doesn't matter. People are looking for her. We need to get to Brownsville as soon as possible. How can I get out of here?"

"Don't reckon either of us is going nowhere for now. I'm afraid your travel plans been shut down for the immediate future."

"What happened to my head?"

"Chevy Callaghan—ol' King Jr.'s brother—happened to it. Caught you with a rock when you was turned around. Sheriff showed up right after, brought us here. Had the boys toss you in the patrol car for him."

"Why me? Didn't you tell him what happened?"

"This is Agua Loco, kid. We try never to confuse the story with facts. Good news is, once King Sr. gets back from that Houston stock show, I imagine he'll straighten things out. Till then, we just got to make ourselves comfortable."

The station's front door opened, and a tall, thick man in a sheriff's uniform ambled in. "Well then, Sleeping Beauty's back from the dead." He tossed Doc a bag of frozen corn through the bars. "Picked it up at the market. For the knot on your *cabeza*."

Doc touched the bag gingerly to the back of his head. "You know the other guy started it, right?"

"Don't matter who started it. Matters who made the complaint. In this case, it was King Jr. That means game over for you, amigo. You lose. You threw a punch at the wrong *hombre*. Not that I doubt he deserved it. Elwood has your car over at the garage, by the way. Gonna be a few days, he says."

"And I get to spend them with you?"

The sheriff shrugged. "Cheaper than a motel, not that there is one. King Sr.'ll be back by then and Jr.'ll back off. You'll be better off here. For your own protection and all."

"You're that afraid of the Callaghan family? You do whatever they say?"

"Listen, kid. You're not from here, so I'm gonna give you the benefit of the doubt. Chalk it up to regional ignorance. What the Callaghans say, goes. Period.

Mark it down in ink. It's natural selection. Kind of a survival-of-the-fittest sort of deal. I'm Sheriff Rome, by the way."

"Doc Morales."

"Doc's brother used to saddle bronc," Cal said.

"You don't say? He any good?" the sheriff said.

"He was. Now he's a priest," Doc replied.

"No joke? Caught religion, huh? Let me ask you, Doc," Rome said, "where are you and … what was the young lady's name again?"

Doc glanced at Cal. "Elizabeth."

"Yeah, that was it. Where are you headed, anyway? How'd you wind up in Agua Loco?"

"Hey, Sheriff," Cal interrupted before Doc could answer, "why don't you round up the young miss and bring her here, too? You got an empty cell. Let these two lovebirds sing."

"She ain't in trouble. Got no cause to bring her in."

"Be a decent thing, though. To let 'em be together. Protect her from King Jr."

"King Jr. ain't gonna bother her. Ain't she with Mary Martha?"

"Uh huh."

Rome blew off Cal with a wave and turned his eyes on Doc. "Anyway, like I was saying, where are you and the miss headed? You're out here where the buses don't run. You get lost or what?"

"Does that have anything to do with my charges?" Doc asked.

"Nope. Just curious."

Doc closed his eyes. "In that case, my head hurts. Can we talk about this later?"

"Ain't no law says you have to answer. I'll be back in a little while to check on things. Y'all just stay where you are, all right?" Rome laughed at his own joke as he left, letting the station door swing shut behind him.

"Who's after you? The law?" Cal asked once the sheriff was gone.

"Her stepdad tried to molest her. She hit him with a lamp, wrecked his car—a Porsche—and ran. He's a big shot in LA, and he lied to the police about what happened. I don't know where it stands legally at this point. Worst part is, he hired some bounty hunters to find her and bring her back. They're not nice people."

"You listen to me. You keep all that stuff under your hat, you hear? Rome, he comes across like a nice enough fella, but he's crooked as a dog's hind leg. Man's well acquainted with the bottom of a deck, and if he thinks he can squeeze a nickel out of turnin' you over, he'll toss you to the sharks without thinkin' twice."

"Okay, I hear you. I just want to get out of here and down the road."

"I'll do what I can to help, but I think you already seen I don't draw much water."

"Thanks, Cal," Doc said, then groaned as a fresh wave of pain swept through his head. "What'd the kid throw, a boulder?"

"Ah, just a little rock. Come to think of it, though, Chevy Callaghan does throw a ninety-mile-an-hour fastball. Kid's got a wing."

"Feels like every bit of ninety. Do you think King Jr. will try to bother Paradise?"

"I don't think so. Jr.'s mostly talk. All hat and no cattle, if you get my drift."

"Why did you want the sheriff to bring Paradise here? You think they'll harass your wife?"

Again a shadow brushed the old man's eyes, and he hesitated a beat. "Naw, she's fine. Lucifer himself wouldn't cross Mary Martha."

Doc closed his eyes again and dozed. He dreamed of Fenway Park—the Green Monster taunting him from left field. A giant pitcher hurled a rock at him the size of a grapefruit and Doc jerked back, dropping into the dirt in a desperate move of self-preservation. The crowd roared, and the pitcher laughed. Standing, Doc searched the stadium seats for Paradise, but she was nowhere to be found.

Chapter Twenty-eight

Mary and Martha's Barc-O-Lounger

Cal and Mary Martha's trailer gave Paradise the impression it had been transported through time from 1971, complete with worn, avocado-green shag carpet, orange Formica countertops, and dark wood wall paneling. A velvet portrait of John Wayne hung above the couch where Paradise sat. A wooden bowl filled with potpourri sat on the coffee table.

Paradise realized she'd never been in a mobile home before.

In the movies, trailers were, for the most part, trashy places. If that was true in the real world, this one defied stereotype. Old, but neat as a pin. A place for everything and everything in its place.

Paradise glanced down at her green Elizabeth Taylor dress, creased and wrinkled from the night spent in the Olds. She didn't even want to imagine the damage to her hair and makeup. How strange to feel underdressed in a mobile home.

She took a sip from the teacup warming her hand. *Delicious.* "This tea is wonderful. What kind is it?"

"Old family recipe—little of this and a little of that. Glad you like it. It'll calm your nerves. You just relax now."

The woman was right. As Paradise sipped, calm slowly but steadily began to talk her anxious heart off the ledge.

"Thank you for bringing me here. I don't know what I would have done," Paradise said.

"Nonsense. You would have done what women always do when our men are in trouble—figured it out. But I won't lie, I'm happy for the company."

Mary Martha spoke from behind the counter that separated the kitchen area from the living room. At least, Paradise supposed it *usually* functioned as a kitchen. At the moment, an incredible variety of herbs lined every inch of counter space. Bushels of drying plants hung from the ceiling and cabinets. The collection filled the trailer with a wild, earthy smell. Mary Martha moved through this natural abundance with purpose. Stripping stalks, crushing flowers between her fingers, and dropping the remnants into small plastic baggies.

At length, she removed her gingham apron and hung it on a hook. She poured a cup of tea of her own, then exited the kitchen. Mary Martha Sloan wasn't a big woman or remarkable in appearance. Average, really. Her mouse-gray hair was tucked back into a bun. She wore a long cotton skirt and a denim blouse open at the collar, revealing a silver chain looped through a turquoise stone. Average, yet something about her spoke confidence. Complete control. She smiled, but her black eyes were sharp, missing nothing.

Paradise scooted back on the couch the tiniest bit. *I think I'm in the presence of Mother Nature.*

Mary Martha took a seat on a wooden rocker opposite. "Sorry. Not trying to ignore you. I have a show up in San Antonio next week. Behind on my bagging."

"A show?"

"Yup. Trade show. Herbs are all the rage these days in the city. Most likely sell everything out on day one. Months of picking and drying and it goes just like that." She snapped her fingers.

"How did you learn to do that? Collect herbs? What to pick?"

Mary Martha sipped her tea. "My grandma on my papa's side was Coahuiltecan Indian. She showed me all kinds of things. Comes in handy now. Seems like a long time ago. Another lifetime."

"I never met my grandmother."

"Wouldn't lose any sleep over it. Could've been good or bad, depending on the situation. I had one on my mama's side I *wish* I never met, and that's no joke."

"I suppose that's a good way to look at it."

"One way, for sure. So, hon', what's your real name?"

The question came out of nowhere, and it caught Paradise off guard. It hadn't felt right, lying to this woman. Still, what choice did she have? "But ... I thought I told you."

"You said your name was Elizabeth, yes. And mine's Lady Bird Johnson. Don't hold out on me, now. I ain't a'gonna tell nobody. I'd just like to know who you are, that's all. No agenda here. I ain't gonna eat you."

"Paradise Jones." Relief flooded as soon as she said it. "I'm sorry I lied. It wasn't right of me. You've been so nice."

Mary Martha dismissed this with a wave. "We've all been known to bend the truth once in a while, Lord knows. Long as it's just bendin' and not breakin', ain't no harm. And you were scared, what with King Jr. drunker'n who-shot-John. I ain't holding nothing against you."

"Why do you have two first names?"

Mary Martha sipped her tea and gazed at Paradise with dark eyes. "You're good at slipping in the subject change, ain't you? No matter. You ever read the Good Book? You know, the Bible?"

"No. I don't think so. I've seen movies about it. *The Ten Commandments*. And *King of Kings* by Cecil B. DeMille."

"Uh huh. Ol' Cecil did a bang-up job for a silent picture. Anyway, there's a story 'bout a family in the Bible. Not sure Cecil touched on 'em in his telling of it. Two sisters and a brother. Lazarus, that was the brother's name. He had him a story all his own as well, but that's another deal. See, he up and died one day and the Holy Savior Jesus had to come and raise him up again. Pretty slick."

"From the dead? And you believe in that?"

The old woman shrugged. "I don't know, but shoot, girl, I've seen stranger things than that right here in South Texas. Ain't no stretch. Now the sisters—they were named Mary and Martha. Sound familiar?"

"Not other than the fact that those are your names."

"Trust me, it's in there. Story goes, one day Jesus comes to visit. Don't know if this was before or after Lazarus' dance with the reaper, but that ain't here nor there. Jesus drops in on a social call, and Martha gets impressed that the God of the universe is sitting on her Barc-O-Lounger, so she runs around busier than a funeral home fan in July making sure everything's just so. But Mary, she just sits there at Jesus' feet, listening to all the wise things he's saying, which I imagine were quite a few. Now that upsets Martha to no end, so she asks Jesus, shouldn't Mary get on the stick since Martha's doing all the work? But Jesus says no, Mary's fine where she is. Fact is—according to him—Mary's doing just the right thing."

"So your parents named you Mary because she did the right thing?"

"Nope, that was obligatory. Family name on my mother's side. All the way back to Ireland. Can't break tradition; you know how it is. But my papa, he was a preacher, poor sap, and he always felt bad for old Martha. Figured she was doing her best with what information she had to go on. He also figured Mary might have been a bit spoiled as a child, but he never mentioned it from the pulpit, so far as I can remember."

"So he named you Martha because he was sympathetic?"

"Yup. He held to the old adage that idle hands was the devil's playground; so here I am, Mary Martha."

"Do you believe all that? The Bible stories?"

Mary Martha's face was bland. "I believe and don't believe in lots of things."

"Does he talk to you? Jesus, I mean. Not your father."

The black eyes narrowed slightly. "Why? Does he talk to you?"

"I didn't lie about my name because I was scared of the man Doc punched."

"Okay …"

"People are looking for me. People who aren't nice."

Mary Martha arched an eyebrow and sipped her tea as if considering. She set the cup down and studied Paradise with a shrewd gaze. "You in trouble with the law?"

Unease flitted, light as a bird. Had she said too much?

"I suppose. I'm not good at keeping secrets. Doc says we're on the lam."

Mary Martha leaned forward and patted Paradise's leg with a boney hand. "Don't you worry none. I'm a good judge of people. Always have been. My grandmother said it was a gift, but I think people are mostly obvious about things. When I look at you, I don't see a troublemaker. I think you're confused, don't know what you want, but not a troublemaker."

"Why do you think I'm confused? I'm not. I *do* know what I want, and there's a good chance of it happening soon."

Mary Martha's dark eyes bored into her. "I asked you a question, and you changed the subject. Does God talk to you?"

Paradise stared into her teacup and became small. *Paradise Jones. Crazy Water. Texas. America. Earth. Universe …*

"So he does?" Mary Martha pressed.

"I think I'm losing my mind. He just asks questions. Or someone does. Or it's all in my head. And when I give him an answer, it's never good enough."

"Like I said. You don't know what you want."

"But I do! I have a life. A career. This trip is just a detour. A short one, hopefully."

Mary Martha laughed. "Some detour! This place is about as desolate as hell with everybody gone to lunch. Let me give you a little advice, darlin'. That voice you hear? You're not crazy, just under stress. Ignore it. It'll pass. God don't usually come right out and talk to people."

"But I thought you said you believed in him?"

"Did I say that? You finish that tea. I'm just gonna duck in the back and use the little girl's room. Can I get you anything else? You comfortable?"

"I'm fine, thank you."

Mary Martha gave Paradise's leg another pat, then rose and disappeared into the recesses of the trailer. Silence hung heavy in the place, save for the dull hum of a swamp cooler fan on the other side of the exterior wall. Exhaustion crept through Paradise's body, and her eyes drooped. She set her teacup on the coffee table next to the potpourri, laid her head back against the couch cushions, and allowed her eyes to close. Was Doc okay? Mary Martha had assured her that he and Cal were fine. Could she trust the old woman? It wasn't like she had a choice. *Helpless* was the word that came to mind. From the back of the mobile home, she thought she heard a muffled voice, but couldn't be sure. Mary Martha talking to herself? Someone outside?

Or stress.

No matter. Sleep settled around her like a warm blanket.

Chapter Twenty-nine

Maybe Just a Salad

Dulled by the thick layer of smog that hovered over the Los Angeles basin, lazy sunlight filtered through the plate-glass windows that made up the front wall of Auggie's Gym.

"Uh huh," Hollister said into his cell. In the mirror, he watched Crystal pump out arm curls with sixty-pound dumbbells. "Yeah, yeah. I got it. We'll be there. No, just email the tickets, and I'll print them off before we head for the airport. Yeah, goodbye." He hit the end-call button with a beefy thumb, then rubbed his temples.

Crystal stopped pumping and dropped the dumbbells onto the rubber mat covering the gym floor. The sound rumbled through the building.

Auggie, the gym owner, yelled at her from across the room. "Hey! Crystal! I've told you a hundred times not to drop the weights! C'mon!"

Crystal threw a rated-R-for-language hand gesture in Auggie's general direction, then looked at Hollister. "Who was on the phone, sweetie?"

Hollister squinted at her. She smelled like sweat and old socks. He considered lying, then caved to the inevitable. "Simmons."

Crystal's Mohawk lay sweat-plastered to her head. Today she'd skipped the obligatory tank top and wore loose basketball shorts and a black sports bra. Her skin shone with perspiration, and thick rivulets of it ran down her sides. Veins stood out on her pumped-up biceps. She eyed herself in the mirror and flexed. "What did he want?"

"Some old lady down in Texas called. Got his number from that missing-person website Simmons set up. Says they have his daughter down there and wants the reward money. Simmons wants us to fly down there and collect the girl. Tonight. Already bought tickets."

A devilish light touched Crystal's eyes. "The princess? And we get the rest of the eighty grand?"

"Yeah, we get the money."

"Hey, Texas! Let's get cowboy hats, want to? We can lasso the brat and brand her like on *Bonanza*."

Hollister rolled his eyes and sat down. He laid back and pushed out ten reps on the bench press. It was his fifth set, or fourth … or sixth. Simmons' call had interrupted him, and he'd lost count. He dropped the bar back onto the steel arms that held it and sighed. Sure, the second half of eighty grand sounded good, but somewhere in his heart of hearts, he'd been rooting for the kid. Hoping for a happy ending for her, if things like that still existed.

"Let's go pack," Crystal said. "And get a smoothie or something. I'm starving."

"Maybe a burrito. I'm not drinking any of that slime."

Crystal pinched his cheek. "That's 'cause you're a moron."

"Whatever."

"And you're getting fat."

Hollister glanced at the mirror. Okay, maybe he had put on a pound or two—or twenty—but hey, stress would do that to a guy. "Yeah, okay, maybe a smoothie. Or a taco salad."

Half an hour later, the two of them sat under a thatched umbrella in a roped-off section of a strip mall a block from their Northridge apartment. Crystal sipped a thirty-two-ounce blended concoction of what looked like grass and mud while Hollister took his third bite of a *carne asada burrito*.

Crystal sucked her straw and peered at him over the rims of a pair of dime-store reading glasses. "Your life insurance all caught up?"

"Why? You making plans to do something criminal?"

"Uh huh, always. But those burritos will kill you before I do. And you'll be so fat, we'll have to bury you in a piano crate."

Hollister grunted and poured salsa on his prize from a small plastic cup.

"Anyway, it dawns on me that you may be worth more dead than alive," Crystal said.

"I'll make sure to list Auggie as the beneficiary. Help him pay for a new floor after all the weights you dropped. Where'd you get those stupid glasses?"

"Walmart. They make me look smart."

Hollister started to reply, then swallowed it. Why bother? Instead, he dipped his burrito toward Crystal's smoothie. "What's in that thing, pond scum? It smells awful."

"Ancient Chinese secret, sweetie. Plus four scoops of protein powder so I can help push your eight-hundred-pound carcass up the stairs in your old age. Or trade you in on a younger model. Either way, I have to keep up my strength."

"The glasses look ridiculous."

"Between you and me, I'm leaning toward the younger model."

"Ain't no younger model. When God made me, he broke the mold."

Crystal poked his burrito with a dirty nail. "Don't matter. You wouldn't fit in it now anyway."

An hour later, a cab dropped them at the departure curb of the Burbank Airport with another hour to spare before the flight to Texas. Other than a handful of sunburned tourists dragging huge, rolling suitcases through the double glass doors, the place was deserted. Hollister appreciated the fact Simmons had booked out of Burbank rather than Los Angeles International. LAX was always a zoo, and Hollister hated crowds.

Once through security, the two of them sat facing each other on the black, vinyl airport seats—the kind manufactured by malicious TSA workers to torture Hollister's bad back.

Crystal still wore the reading glasses balanced on the end of her nose. In addition, she'd rounded out the look with a black cowboy hat. She studied Hollister from beneath the brim. "Penny for your thoughts, moron."

"I'm just wondering if there's some extra from a Roy Rogers movie bleeding in an alley after you mugged him to get that hat."

"Don't be jealous. It's Marco's. He let me borrow it."

Marco was their actor neighbor, although most of his acting gigs were for a singing telegram service and kids' birthday parties.

"Marco. Figures. Listen, here's how this is gonna go. We fly into San Antonio, pick up a rental car, buzz down to some town called Agua Loco—wherever that is—pick up Miss Thing and come home. No messing around. Do not pass *Go*. Do not collect two hundred dollars. I just want to get there, get back, and be done with it, *comprendes?*"

"And slap her around."

"We've been over all that. No damage to the girl. Just get her, get our money and be done."

"We'll see," Crystal said as she began to whistle the theme from *The Big Valley*.

CHAPTER THIRTY

The Legality of Lone Stars

"What's the matter with you, Mary Martha?" Cal said.

Doc looked the old woman over through the bars, then glanced at Paradise who sat on a mattress-less, metal cot in the cell next to his. She still wore the green Elizabeth Taylor dress. It hung rumpled and torn at the shoulder. Her hair was a mess and tears had streaked makeup down her cheeks. She returned Doc's gaze with large, frightened eyes.

A mess—and her beauty stole Doc's breath for the thousandth time.

"I'll tell you what's the matter with me," Mary Martha said. "Fifty thousand dollars is what's the matter with me, you fool old drunk. You know how many baggies of leaves and roots I'd have to sell to make fifty thousand dollars? And if you quit yammering, maybe I'll buy you a couple bottles of tequila. The good stuff, too. Not that poison you get down on the border."

"It's just *wrong*, that's what it is. These are nice people. It's just plain *wrong*. And I'm quittin' the bottle. Keep your money *and* your hooch."

"Quittin', my eye. You'll be tighter'n bark on a log an hour after Rome lets you out. Fifty thousand! I can't believe it."

Sheriff Rome interrupted from behind one of the gray metal desks. "Twenty-five thousand. You're splittin' that reward with me."

"What are you talkin' about? I found her," Mary Martha said.

"And I apprehended and detained," Rome countered.

"Only 'cause I called you, you greedy slug. You didn't even think to check if these two might be on the run."

"And how was I supposed to do that?"

Mary Martha barked a laugh. "Oh, I don't know, run their license plate? Ask a question or two? Like maybe her real name? Look on the Internet? They have that now, you know. It's in these magic boxes called computers. You should get yourself one."

"You can cackle all you want, you ol' witch, but this is my jurisdiction, and I'm the one collecting. I'm willing to split it, and you're lucky to get that."

"I'm sorry, Doc," Paradise said. "I thought I could trust her."

"You've got nothing to be sorry about." Doc wanted to pull the bars apart and hold her.

"Nothin' personal, girl," Mary Martha said. "Anyway, they ain't gonna do nothin' to a pretty young thing like you. You'll be fine. You got to understand, we're talking about a lot of money here."

Paradise offered the old woman a defiant stare. "You tricked me."

Mary Martha's eyes were flat and indifferent. She might as well have been looking at an insect. "I did no such thing. But you're gonna have to learn to keep your secrets better. You're young yet. You'll figure it out."

"What now, Sheriff?" Doc said.

Rome turned and shrugged. "They're sendin' a couple private investigators from Los Angeles to pick her up. Should be here tomorrow sometime. That's all I know. That and the fact I'm about to be twenty-five thousand bucks richer. That's a lot of *frijoles,* amigo." He shifted toward Mary Martha. "C'mon, Double M. I'll buy you a cold one over at the Cantina. Celebrate our newfound wealth."

"I'll pass," Mary Martha said. "What about Cal? How long you keepin' him?"

"Don't know. Still have King Jr. to worry about. Probably a day or two."

Mary Martha didn't even look in Cal's direction. "Suit yourself, but I'll be waitin' on the money." She walked out the door without a backward glance.

"Well, guess I'll have one for both of us, then. Adios, jailbirds." Rome chuckled as he followed Mary Martha's exit.

Doc stood and gripped the bars of the cell, looking down at Paradise. "Are you all right?"

She nodded. "Other than feeling stupid."

"It's not your fault, girl," Cal said. "It's mine. I never should'a let you go there. Should'a knowed better. That tequila breakfast had me thinkin' a little crooked. Still, ain't no excuse."

"You were trying to be kind," Paradise said.

"I meant what I said to the old witch. I ain't touchin' a drop after this. I said it before, but this time it's gonna stick."

"The question is, what now?" Doc said.

"Ain't much choice, is there? Can't walk through walls. And even if we could, that Olds of yours ain't goin' nowhere for a few days, at least."

"I'm not letting Paradise go back to Los Angeles."

"Don't see that it's your call. You got a plan?"

"Yeah. Play chess."

"Just because a chicken has wings don't mean it can fly, boy. Hard to play chess from a jail cell."

"It's okay, Doc," Paradise said. "Arnie says Burt will drop the charges if I come back and live in his pool house. I'll just make it work."

Doc noticed his white knuckles. He hadn't realized he gripped the bars so tight. "Drop the charges? He's the one that should be *facing* charges."

"Arnie told me on the phone yesterday. I should have told you."

Doc shook his head. "What difference does it make if he drops the charges? He tried to molest you. Rape you! You can't go back there. Why would you?"

"Like Cal said, I don't have a choice."

"I won't let you."

Paradise traced a seam on the Elizabeth Taylor dress with a pink nail. "I *did* enjoy it, Doc. Dancing with you."

"Don't change the subject, not this time."

Her eyes met his. "I'm not changing the subject. I'm trying to tell you. Burt will let it go ... I'll get the part of a lifetime ... and I'll find a way to fend him off. If it's meant to be, it's meant to be. But I want you to know that the time I've spent with you meant something to me. Something very special."

"No," Doc said.

"No?"

"No. Not like this. If you want to go back of your own choice, and there's no danger to you, I won't argue. But I won't let you give up." Doc turned to Cal. "And you! Why didn't you tell me about your wife? I *knew* something was bothering you."

"Sorry, boy. Didn't see any point in it. I figured Mary Martha might see somethin' weren't right. That woman can practically see through walls. Guess I hoped it wouldn't come to this."

Doc sat back on the cot. He put his face in his hands and closed his eyes. The back of his head pounded like it might blow off. "I need to think."

The idea of Paradise going back to her stepfather caused his insides to twist. But was that it? Or was it the idea of Paradise going anywhere, period? At least without him? Probably both. He loved her, utterly and hopelessly. And she had the world waiting for her. A bad joke, that's what it was. A useless baseball player dreaming a dream that could never come true. The Green Monster in full force.

Doc's thoughts went on like this for a long while. Circling, jumbling, then splitting again. Never organizing into a rational line. He would've traded his right arm for an aspirin—or five. Cal whistled away the monotony, and the sound reverberated through Doc's skull like a buzz saw.

At length, the station door banged open and Rome returned carrying a couple of Lone Star beers, wet with condensation. Cal eyed them dully.

The sheriff rested an ample hip on one of the desks, popped the cap off one of the beers and tipped the bottle in toward the cell. "Sorry, Cal, no alcohol for prisoners. Federal law. At least, I imagine it is."

"Ain't no law about a sheriff tippin' a Lone Star in the station?" Cal asked.

"None I ever heard."

"Don't believe you was listenin' all too careful in sheriff school, then."

"You got a point. Don't reckon I was," Rome said, taking a long pull.

The front door squeaked on its hinges again, and Rome stood, slapping the bottle down so fast Doc was surprised the thing didn't shatter. A man filled the doorway, blocking the light. After a moment, he entered the room. He didn't quite have to duck under the frame, but by Doc's estimation the guy stood at least 6'5" or 6'6", and there wasn't much room to spare. His face belied his age— not a young man—at least seventy, maybe older, but he exuded strength. He wore camouflage-patterned cargo pants and military style boots. A T-shirt, once probably black but now a faded gray, stretched tight over shoulders heavy with muscle. His sun-bleached blond hair was streaked with gray and pulled back into a loose ponytail. A hawk beak of a nose and a thick white-gray beard accentuated the deeply lined face of someone long acquainted with the sun.

The man took in the room with a glance, pale eyes landing on Doc, then Paradise.

"Howdy. Can I help you with somethin'?" Rome asked.

Gray eyes shifted to the sheriff. "You in charge?"

"You bet."

"Doc Morales and Paradise Jones. These your prisoners?"

"They are."

The man pulled a folded envelope from his back pocket and tossed it on the desk next to Rome. "Not anymore."

"What's that supposed to mean?"

"Paperwork's all there. I'm taking 'em into my custody."

Rome's eyes narrowed. He ignored the envelope. "You the PI? I thought there was supposed to be two of you. Where's your partner? The woman?"

"Flight got hung up in LA." He pointed a huge finger at Paradise. "The authorities and the girl's stepfather want to move this along. They hired me locally. Out of San Antonio."

"And you are?" Rome stood, apparently feeling his oats.

The pale eyes tightened, and the man took a step toward Rome. The sheriff sat back down on the desk as quickly as he'd stood.

"It's all in the paperwork," the man repeated. "Now, I'd like to get on the road. I got a long drive."

Rome's fingers trembled the slightest bit as he opened the unsealed envelope and pulled out an official looking document. "Wha ... what about the money? The reward?"

The man picked up the Lone Star bottle and dropped it into a metal trash can with a loud thump. Rome jumped. Drops of the liquid splashed across the sheriff's pants.

"Isn't the satisfaction of bringing a dangerous fugitive to justice enough for you, Sheriff?" the man said.

Mental scrambling played out across Rome's face. "Well, sure ... sure it is. It's just that a local citizen, Mary Martha Sloan, is responsible for the recovery. Fair's fair, ain't it?"

The man reached into the side pocket of his cargo pants with a sigh and retrieved another envelope. "Hmm. That might be a problem. See, this cashier's check is made out to a Thomas Rome. No Mary Martha Sloan mentioned. Fifty thousand dollars. Don't want to make a mistake, do we? I'd better make a call."

"No, no, that's right. I'm Sheriff Rome. The check *should* be made to me. All legal and proper channels. That's important. Keep it neat. I'll pass on the funds to Mary Martha."

The man shook his head but handed Rome the check. Rome studied it for a long minute then stuffed it into his shirt pocket and began fumbling with a ring of keys attached to his belt.

He walked to Paradise's cell. "One Paradise Jones, fugitive, coming right up."

"I said both of them. Jones and Morales," the man said.

Rome looked confused. "Morales is in here on local charges. Nobody said nothin' about him."

"Look at the paperwork. The police want him, too. I'm taking them both."

Now Rome's confused expression turned to doubt. "Look, mister, there are pending charges to be dealt with here. I can't just let a prisoner go on your word."

The big man shrugged. "There's a fifty thousand dollar check in your pocket that says you can. And like I said, it's all in the paperwork. Morales has aided and abetted a fugitive. He's coming back to Los Angeles. The authorities want him."

"You got any I.D. other than that paperwork? You never even gave me your name."

The man pulled out a billfold and opened it, revealing some sort of official identification card, then closed it again and dropped it back into his pocket. He leaned over to Rome's desk and picked up the original paperwork he'd produced. As if putting on a mask, his demeanor gentled. "You know, Sheriff. You're right. You're just doing your job. Due diligence, I get it. Tell you what, give me back that cashier's check, and you can keep both of them. You work it out with Los Angeles. I think they're getting tired of the whole thing anyway. Between you and me, the officer I talked to sounded like he'd rather just forget the whole deal. They might even drop the charges there. Either way, that fifty thousand doesn't mean anything to me. I'm getting a lousy day rate for this. Not even expenses on top. I drove all the way down here from San Antonio for what's probably gonna be a break-even. Give me back the check, I'll tear it up, then they're your problem. You can negotiate, and if the girl's father still feels she's worth the reward, good for you. If not, just let Jones go and do whatever you want with Morales. That way you're covered here. Cool?"

The man held out a large hand. Rome didn't take it but put his own hand over the check in his pocket. The panic in his eyes almost made Doc smile.

"*If* they still offer the reward? No, listen, you go ahead and take them. Charges against Morales are weak anyway, and it's the taxpayer's dime he's living on here. I need to think about what's best for the county. Fiscal responsibility and all. Yeah, you take 'em both. I don't want to cause any trouble for you, and I'll make sure Mary Martha gets this reward money. Gonna change her life, that's sure."

The big man shrugged. "Have it your way, then. Like I said, don't matter to me either way."

Rome hastily opened the cell doors, and Doc and Paradise stepped out. The hard eyes in the bounty hunter's bearded face showed nothing. From a pocket, the man produced a pair of handcuffs and tossed them to Doc. "One for you and one for Miss Jones. I'm not as young as I used to be, but let me tell you, if you run, and I catch you—which I will—you'll be praying to your Maker you hadn't, understand?"

Paradise nodded, wide-eyed. Doc said nothing, but attached the cuffs to both their wrists.

The man walked to the door and held it open. "Remember what I said."

Doc turned to Cal, still in the cell. He couldn't help feeling sorry for the old man. "See you, Cal."

Calvin raised his good arm. "Adios, Doc. Sorry 'bout it all."

"Stay off the bottle, huh?"

Cal sighed and nodded. "Sober as a judge. Bank on it."

Doc offered a smile. "Even if she buys you the good stuff with all that reward money?"

"Even if, boy. Even if."

Outside, the big man ushered Doc and Paradise into the back seat of a Lincoln that had seen better days. Faded brown paint oxidized by the sun peeled off the hood and roof.

The man eased into the driver's seat, started the car, and electronically rolled down all four windows. "Sorry, no AC. Lucky the windows still work on this piece of junk. It's a loaner."

The Lincoln whipped onto the street and within minutes, the tiny town of Agua Loco became a memory.

Paradise leaned forward. She spoke loudly, fighting the noise of the open windows. "Please. At least hear my story before you send us back."

Doc put a hand on her leg. "I don't think we're going back. None of that made sense back there. Something's up." To the big man, he said, "Who are you?"

The man laid a muscular right arm across the top of the front seat and turned, left hand still on the steering wheel. Smile lines crinkled around his eyes. "Name's Lan," he said. "Oh, and Paco says hello."

CHAPTER THIRTY-ONE

Satellites and Home-Made Tortillas

Hollister gazed through the café window at Agua Loco. Main Street consisted of an ancient adobe courthouse, a bar, a Circle K, the sheriff's office, and several boarded up businesses. There were also no less than three Mexican restaurants, and the one he and Crystal sat in at the moment had a reputation for excellent *carne asada* tacos. They made their own thick, corn tortillas—just the kind Hollister liked—and marinated the meat in citrus juice, garlic, and peppers. A symphony of flavor—complete joy. All in all, the town wasn't a bad place.

At least, it wasn't until his cell vibrated on the table next to his beer, and Simmons' face registered on the screen.

"Hello?"

"What happened?" Simmons' voice echoed slightly as it bounced off satellites and South Texas cell towers.

Hollister purposely took a bite and chewed in Simmons' ear, letting his words slide around tortilla, cheese, and grilled beef. "Don't know. Some guy showed up with fairly official-looking papers and a reward check. I looked 'em over. Both bogus. He conned Barney Fife down here into handing over your daughter and the guy who's helping her."

Simmons' shouting distorted the earpiece. "How! How could this be happening? Can it really be that hard to track down my half-brain freak of a stepdaughter? It's not like she's firing on all eight cylinders here! She thinks it's the 1940s, for God's sake! What am I paying you for?"

Hollister set his phone down and let Simmons rant. Truth be told, he was glad the girl skipped. Across from him, Crystal tapped her dirty fingers on the worn Formica table. She crunched a salsa-dunked chip, swallowed and grinned her crazy grin, one tooth covered with something green. "Let me talk to him," she mouthed.

Hollister shook his head at her and followed his taco with a long cold swig of Tecate beer. He picked the phone back up to make sure Simmons heard the swallow. "Look, Dr. Simmons, I don't know what to tell you. We flew in. We picked up the car. We drove to Who-knows-where-or-why-it-even-exists, Texas, and went to the sheriff station. All exactly like you asked, right? And we find the local-yokel sheriff and some beat-up old cowboy sitting in an open jail cell surrounded by empty beer bottles and singing about the lone prairie. It's like a spaghetti western down here. What do you want me to tell you?"

"So now what? She couldn't have gone far! Who picked her up? That's what I don't understand. Give me answers."

"Some guy. Big. Old. Long hair and a beard. Tough looking, they said. He about made the sheriff wet his Wranglers. Tell you what, though," Hollister realized he felt good—headache free for the first time in weeks, "I'm glad you sent us down here. I'm telling you, best tacos I ever had."

"The problem," Simmons went on, "is that you're not taking this seriously. I paid you a lot of money to bring my daughter back to me. You called yourself a finder. Now I expect you to *find-her*!"

Hollister took another bite. "Relax. We found out from the sheriff who the guy helping her is. Kid named Morales. I got connections. We're tracking his phone right now. Soon as he makes a call, we'll know exactly where they are. We'll get them. Give us a day or two. Just keep our other forty grand handy."

"After all your screw-ups, I should just keep it."

"Don't even joke."

"I'd better see some results, Hollister, I'm telling you. This is getting very old. And when you find my brat, make sure Crystal uses her for a punching bag. I've had it! I want her black and blue and dragged back here in a sack."

"Uh huh. Call you soon." Hollister hung up.

Crystal didn't comment. Whoever said there was no such thing as miracles?

"Where do you think they were headed?" Hollister thought out loud, directing his question at no one in particular.

"Pretty out of the way down here. Maybe they thought they could hide till things cooled off," Crystal said.

Hollister took another drink of his beer.

"Or they're headed for Mexico," Crystal said.

How could he have been so stupid? "Wait, yeah … Mexico. That's got to be it. The coins. The puzzle. Must have something to do with Mexico. Why else come this way? Drive all the way down here? If it were farther, they'd probably try to figure out some way to fly."

Crystal crunched another chip. "Got your passport, moron?"

Hollister waged inner war. On the one hand, he couldn't stand the condescending Dr. Simmons. Besides, he was sure the man was a perverted womanizer. But on the other hand, a payday of eighty thousand dollars total couldn't be argued with. Add to that the possibility of an actual treasure—which looked more and more likely with every ice-cold *cerveza*—and no real choice remained to be made.

Another buzz from his phone interrupted his reverie. He picked up—his call tracker back in Los Angeles.

"You got something?" Hollister had never been much for small talk. "Uh huh. Yeah, got it. Keep me up to speed."

"What?" Crystal asked.

Hollister pointed to her plate of rice and beans. "Shovel it down, bruiser. They're headed for the border."

Chapter Thirty-two

Fast Lincolns and Personal Saviors

A pothole roused Paradise from deep sleep. She rubbed bleary eyes and tried to get her bearings. Humid air blasted through the open windows of the Lincoln. She leaned forward, bracing herself higher by planting a hand on the seat, and attempted to catch her reflection in the rearview mirror. Hair flew in her face, and she dropped back on to the seat and raised the white flag. What was the point?

"You look beautiful," Doc said.

"And you're a liar."

"Nope. No glamour, no movie star, just Paradise. I like you that way."

The car careened around a corner, and both of them grabbed for an armrest.

"Isn't he driving a little fast?" Paradise said.

"You slept through the best parts," Doc said. "I accepted Jesus as my personal savior at least five times so far just to be sure I'm covered. I'm thinking our new buddy must have raced stock cars in a past life."

"No point in wasting time," Lan said from the driver's seat.

"Nobody'll ever accuse you of that," Doc replied.

Lan laughed.

Doc reached over and brushed a strand of hair from Paradise's face. "I talked to Jake while you were asleep. He told me you called him right after Rome took us in. That was good thinking. Paco called Lan. That's how he found us."

"I'm just glad I called. I didn't know what else to do. I'm sorry. I should have seen something was wrong with Mary Martha."

"Don't be sorry. People can surprise you, especially if money's involved."

"I'll bet Jake was glad."

"About Mary Martha?"

"That Lan found us."

"Yeah. And also that we left the other coin back at the mission. The thing would have wound up in Sheriff Rome's pocket for sure. It's better off in the museum."

Doc's earnest face moved sadness in Paradise. They'd part ways soon; no other outcome made sense. Still, she couldn't forget the feeling of his strong arms around her as they'd danced at the Manhattan. Over the past days, she'd maintained distance although, she admitted to herself, there were moments it hadn't been easy. The reality of someone caring—really caring—touched her in places she hadn't known existed.

"*Well?*"

The voice came from nowhere and everywhere at once. Paradise looked around. Truck Stop Jesus grinned at her from the dashboard of the Lincoln.

"Lan, where did you get that Jesus?" she said.

"Paco told me about your Olds breaking down. I stopped at the garage. Only one in town—wasn't hard to find. I grabbed your bags. They're in the trunk. Grabbed this little guy too. Figured he'd seen some miles with you, maybe he'd like to see a few more."

"Our intrepid mascot," Doc said.

The right side of the Lincoln edged another bump in the road, and Jesus' head wobbled.

"*Well?*" the voice pressed.

"I'm tired," Paradise said.

"*No, you're not.*"

"What do you want?"

"*Funny, I was about to ask you the same thing.*"

"You really need to get some new material." Paradise focused her attention on the scenery. As they drove, buildings rose out of the Texas landscape with greater and greater frequency beneath a wide blanket of deep blue.

"So, Lan, is the plan to get us across the border at Matamoros?" Doc said. "Head south?"

Lan glanced up at the mirror. "That what Paco told you? That I was gonna smuggle you across the border?"

"I guess ... Pretty much. At least, I assumed. The authorities are watching for Paradise. Paco said you could help."

"Huh. Well, I'll get you to Mexico, but it might not be what you're expecting."

Doc's cell phone rang, and he glanced at the screen, then handed it to Paradise. "I think it's your guy in LA. Same number as before."

Paradise took the phone. "Hello?"

"Where are you?"

"Fine, thanks, Arnie. How are you?"

"Knock it off, Paradise. This is important. Where are you? How fast can you get back?"

Paradise closed her eyes and leaned her head back. "I'm not living with Burt, Arnie. Please stop. I told you I needed some time."

A long pause on the other end. "You got it, Paradise. They want you for the part. I have a contract sitting in front of me *right now*. You're the next Scarlett O'Hara. This is it. I'm telling you, everything you've dreamed of is happening, starting now. I need you back in Los Angeles. Like yesterday."

Blood roared in her ears. Had she heard right? "Are you serious, Arnie? This isn't some card trick to get me back to LA?"

Doc glanced at her with concern.

"No way. I wouldn't jerk your chain about this, kid. This isn't *might*. You *have* the part. You have a read-through in two weeks. Then costume fitting and you start filming. This is happening, Paradise. Get back here; we have a lot to do. The press is already pounding my door down. You're front page! No lie, I mean it!"

"Two weeks? What about Burt? What about the police?"

"You're a star now. *What* Burt? What can Burt do to you? The studio will make him back off. They'll buy him if they have to. He's crying big crocodile tears in your dust. A non-issue. Just get back here."

Doc's dark eyes asked questions.

"Paradise? You there?" Arnie said.

Why on earth was she conflicted? She fought the feeling by flooding her mind with images of cameras flashing and designer dresses. Press conferences and premier nights.

Stupid Doc and that Manhattan Bar. Get out of my brain!

How could dim lights reflected off a worn-out dance floor possibly compete with the flashbulbs of Oscar's red carpet?

Are you kidding me? This is it. Get back to LA.

"All right, Arnie. I just need to—"

A loud crash from the back of the Lincoln cut Paradise short. The Lincoln swerved and started to slide, but Lan corrected and the big car straightened.

"What the ..." Lan said.

Doc turned to the back window. "It's them. The two that grabbed Paradise in New Mexico."

Another crash, but, this time, Lan was ready and the Lincoln stayed on track.

Paradise turned. The chrome grill of a Hummer closed in fast. "Arnie, I'll call you back," Paradise yelled before hitting the End Call button.

"You two hang on back there." Lan hit the throttle, and the Lincoln surged forward, the Hummer close on its tail. Lan swung the wheel hard, and the car skidded to the right, charging down a street between lines of industrial buildings.

Another hard right threw Paradise against Doc. His arm went around her like an extra seatbelt. Fear coursed through her, drowning out everything else.

"Are they still back there?" Doc shouted.

Tires screeching behind them answered Doc's question.

"Hold on tight. I'll lose 'em!" Lan swung a hard left. Still, the Hummer howled the chase.

A large trash truck loomed to the left and Lan swerved wide to miss it. Braking tires sounded behind them, then a loud crash. Lan hung a right into a parking lot, then a left into an alley. The Lincoln broke onto a main street with the Hummer nowhere to be seen. Doc still held Paradise tight as Lan floored the car through several more turns before entering a four-lane highway.

"Those guys are crazy," Lan said.

Doc surveyed the road behind. "At least we lost them for now."

As they sped along, urban gave way to wetlands, then low-lying dunes peppered with brush. Eventually, more town loomed ahead.

"Brownsville?" Doc asked.

"Nope. Port Isabel," Lan said.

In town, the four-lane divided, separated by a wide swath of grass and palm trees, then came back together as the Lincoln climbed onto a long bridge. To Doc's Arizona-bred eyes, it looked like it headed straight out to open ocean.

"Queen Isabella Causeway," Lan said. "South Padre Island coming up. End of the road."

Two miles later—still on the bridge and over water—Lan grabbed a cell and thumb dialed. "Easy, listen up! Fire her up, drop the lines, and stand by. We're coming hard and fast." He hung up, apparently satisfied with the reply.

"Who's Easy? What's going on, Lan? Where the heck are we?" Doc asked.

The causeway dropped again to solid land of sand and brush. Lan veered right, then another right into a gravel parking lot and stopped hard in front of a low concrete wall. A scattering of masts and fishing boat towers stood out against the blue sky.

Lan plucked Truck Stop Jesus from the dashboard as he swung open his door. "Great day for a sail, boys and girls."

CHAPTER THIRTY-THREE

Fair Winds

Doc grabbed the bags and followed Lan, checking to be sure Paradise was behind him. They passed through a metal gate and ran down a long dock, collecting some strange looks from boat occupants and sightseers along the way. The dock ended at an end-slip where a long sailboat—ninety feet at least—rocked gently in the water. The craft spoke of age, but not in a run-down way, and though Doc knew next to nothing about boats, he immediately appreciated the graceful lines of this one. It looked out of place among the dozens of modern, fiberglass vessels bobbing on the liquid parking lot. The sailboat's hull shone white, contrasting the varnished teak deck. Brass and stainless steel glinted in the bright Gulf sun. Two thick, wooden masts touched the sky, high above it all.

"Cast off, Easy. Time to get wet." Lan pushed the words out between heavy breaths.

A small, dark man, barefoot in loose, khaki shorts and a faded *Cancun Spring Break '96* tank top, stood holding a bowline. "Yes sir, boss. Fair winds today, I tink."

His accent rolled thick, and Doc couldn't quite place it. Maybe Caribbean, but something else in the mix as well.

The smell of diesel tinged the air, and from deep in the sailboat an engine chugged. Lan climbed on board and put a thick hand back for Doc and Paradise.

Paradise grabbed Doc's arm from behind, and he turned to her. Uncertainty and worry creased her pretty face.

"Doc, I can't go."

"What do you mean, you can't? We have to go. You saw those guys."

"No. The part. In *Gone with the Wind*. That's why Arnie called. I got it, Doc. It's a sure thing. I have to go back."

"You can't, Paradise. What about your stepdad?"

Paradise bit her lip. "I'll be okay. It's too big for him. The studio will protect me. They'll get the police to listen. Arnie's sure of it. You see what I mean? I *have* to go."

"What about the coins?" Doc's words hung like weak wisps of smoke in the sea air. Who cared about the coins? This was it. He'd lose her now. He'd been a fool to imagine the lure of a mystery—or a baseball burnout—would be enough to interest a girl like her.

Her words confirmed his fears. "You go, Doc. Figure it out. Then call me and tell me what happens. Visit me in LA sometime. I want to hear all of it. And thank you for everything. Really, I mean that."

Doc reached deep for words, but they slipped through his fingers like water. His lungs emptied, the reason clear—Paradise Jones gave him breath. Before she walked into Shorty's, life had been nothing but hazy black and white. Like some dark Raymond Chandler film noir. But she was 1939 *The Wizard of Oz*—bursting forth in blazing Technicolor. Stars had shifted. The world had changed. *He'd* changed. And this woman was responsible for all of it.

Lan spoke from the deck. "Guys, I hate to break up a good thing, but your buddies are back. Picked us up somehow. Persistent sons-a-guns, I'll give them that. Paradise, maybe you need to go back to La La Land, but not with those two Neanderthals. Get on the boat."

Sure enough, the Hummer, right fender caved in, sped across the gravel lot and jolted to a stop behind the Lincoln. Hollister and Crystal hopped out and headed in the direction of the docks. A shout of recognition rang out, and the two broke into a run, Crystal leading the way.

"Get on ... now!" Lan said.

Doc threw the bags onto the deck. "Paradise, they'll hurt you. Let's get out of here and talk this through later when you're safe."

Paradise hesitated, lips tightening, but she reached for Lan's hand. Doc helped from behind and jumped on after her. Lan hurried to the wheel and gunned the throttle as the man he called Easy let loose the bowline and swung himself aboard with an athletic leap. The boat shuddered slightly, then started forward in slow motion. The couple from the Hummer still ran, only fifty feet or so separating them from the end of the dock.

"You got any more juice in this thing, Lan?" Doc said, his throat tightening.

"Relax, junior. Ol' *Lazarus* won't let us down. Been in tighter spots than this, believe me."

Short seconds later Crystal, with Hollister just behind, stopped at the dock's edge, breathing hard. Only six feet or so separated them from the rail of the boat. For a second, face-to-face with the woman's wide-eyed, crazy grin, Doc thought she'd jump, but Hollister grabbed a fist full of her shirt and pulled her from the edge.

"Don't you want to play, princess?" Crystal called.

"Shut up, Crystal," Hollister said, his face unreadable. His eyes met Doc's. Was there a touch of empathy in the man's expression?

Crystal shot an elbow back, catching Hollister squarely in the ribs. "Old man moron."

The man replied, but several yards now separated the boat from the couple, and Doc could no longer make out the words over the chug of the diesel. The couple turned and headed back up the dock at a fast trot, the man pulling a phone from his pocket and stabbing in a number.

Paradise took a seat on a bench against the rail behind Lan. Doc crossed the deck and sat across from her. Forward, near the bow, the man called Easy moved with the quick, practiced grace of a seasoned deckhand, stowing loose items and coiling line.

Doc studied Paradise "You okay?"

Tears touched her eyes. "I don't know anymore. It's all upside down. Like a dream but not a dream at the same time. Where are we going?"

Doc reached for her hand, but she pulled it back.

The harbor mouth lay straight ahead, and Lan stood relaxed at the wheel. Once through the opening, he brought the craft left and throttled back slightly. "Might as well get ready to hoist sail, Easy."

"Yes, boss." The small deckhand moved nimbly, removing canvas sail covers with quick hands.

A short time later, Lan brought the craft left again and entered a wide channel. The boat began to rock slowly back and forth.

Lan turned toward Doc and Paradise. The wind tugged the big man's beard and hair, giving him a wild look, like some time-traveling Viking. He moved his index finger in a wide circle above his head. "This is the Brazos Santiago Pass we're motoring through. That's the Gulf of Mexico dead ahead." Deep lines creased the corners of his eyes—a man in his element. "Welcome aboard the *Lazarus*, amigos."

CHAPTER THIRTY-FOUR

Pirates and Idiots

Burt Simmons stared through his plate glass office window above Beverly Hills. The day spread before him clear as a bell, unusual for smoggy Los Angeles.

Clear day ... offshore winds ... blah, blah, blah ... who cared? The problem with dealing with idiots—and most people invariably turned out to be idiots—was that you received idiotic results. Forty thousand dollars? What a waste.

Oh well.

Burt leaned back against the cool leather of his oversized office chair and allowed his eyes to close. Exhaustion blanketed him from head to toe. He hadn't slept well in days. Not since the night in the pool house when the trampy brat hit him with the lamp. Who did she think she was? He'd practically spoon-fed the girl.

Business suffered as well. He'd begun to cancel appointments and spend long hours staring at the LA skyline through the office window.

Staring, but never seeing.

Her face—that's what he saw. Couldn't get it out of his head. What a laugh. The shrink needs a shrink. Among his colleagues, he'd become a joke. Burt never heard them, but he knew they talked about it. And they probably got a good laugh gossiping about his Panamera sailing over the cliff.

Well, they were idiots, too.

Who cared about them? And who cared about the car? Insurance had already replaced it with a newer model anyway. No. It was her stupid, beautiful face—the tramp-brat. That's the thing that wouldn't leave him alone—the thing that brought torment. He had everything he wanted ... except for her.

And she was *the* thing. When had it started? Not at first, certainly. The girl was just an awkward kid when he'd married Eve. Nothing much to look at. And he wasn't a pervert, right? He couldn't pinpoint exactly when, but sometime in her teens—the budding beauty, the aloof work of art. The dresses, the swimsuits

217

... Paradise Jones. Right under his roof and a million miles away. Sure, maybe there were times his hugs had lasted a little too long, or his pats and brushes had "accidentally" strayed a little, but he'd never crossed the line ... At least not one *he* was drawing. But things were different now. She was an adult. They were *both* adults. What was wrong with her?

And why *her*? Why was it her face that tortured him? It wasn't for lack of available women. Even young ones. He could have women any time he wanted. *Had* had them, in fact. Nah, in the end, it came down to one sad, simple truth. He ached for what he'd never possessed.

Story of his life.

True, he couldn't care less about the car, but speaking of newer models ... Eve came to mind. Talk about needing a trade-in. The woman hovered around the house like a wraith, reeking of booze, expensive perfume, and depression. Almost as if she blamed him for her daughter's exit. Talk about nuts. Well, all good things must come to an end, including Eve. The divorce papers were already in the works. Hey, maybe he'd even marry Paradise?

Burt pressed his hands together to stop them from shaking.

Yes, lack of sleep. That's what it was. That's what caused his thoughts to ricochet around his brainpan like bullets in a cave. The Spanish coins dropped in and did their own brain dance. What about them? An afternoon of web searches had educated him quite well on the subject of the legendary treasure story. He could practically write a thesis. Hey, who knew? Maybe—just maybe—a stash of Spanish gold would be the pot at the end of the proverbial rainbow.

Get the gold and the girl. Every pirate's dream.

It was like playing with children. Burt knew people that knew people; that was the thing. He was a *doer*. Even his *people* knew people that knew people. He'd had one of them contact the priest at the museum in Arizona—another idiot, by the way. It had been almost too easy. A phone call to hire a couple of actors—have them pose as college professors from the U of A—arrange a visit to see the coin— one distracts the priest while the other snaps a few pics with his iPhone... and presto. Burt opened his top desk drawer and pulled out two glossy, color photos of the second coin. One front shot and one back.

People that knew people ... Also not hard to hire the best of the best to compare cipher and key and crack a three-hundred-year-old Spanish code.

The beauty of being Dr. Burt Simmons—a few calls and you're two moves ahead in the game. Easy. Especially when you played with idiots.

He picked up his phone and scrolled his contacts. Hollister's gravel voice answered on the second ring. "Yeah?"

"So I've been thinking."

"Good for you. Give the man a prize."

"Where are you now?"

"Sittin' in the sun, cracking crab legs at a joint called Dirty Al's. Where are you?"

"Shut up. You have your passports with you?"

"Always. Why?"

"Because—the tramp and her entourage—they're headed for Mexico. That's why they got on the boat."

"Yeah, I thought Mexico at first. But shoot, it's a boat, man. Why not somewhere else in Texas? Or Florida? Or the Carib? They could go to Antarctica if they want."

In the background, Crystal said something about a moron.

Burt dropped the photo back into his drawer. "Because I *know*. It's Mexico. And now *you* know. And that's *all* you need to know till I tell you more. Now shut up, get in your car, and drive south. To the Yucatan. Town called La Dia Perdido. Check into a hotel if they have one and call me when you get there."

"All right, whatever. Mind telling me why?"

"Just do what I tell you. I'll meet you there."

"Wait, you're coming?"

"See? There's that brilliant deduction skill. I knew you still had it. Listen, Hollister, I might need your muscle, and Crystal's particular brand of crazy, but now you're going to have an actual brain with you. It'll be a new sensation. Now get down there."

"You've got a lousy bedside manner for a doctor. Anybody ever tell you that?"

"Just do what I tell you. You want the rest of the money or not?"

"Yeah, okay. Whatever. See ya there."

"La Dia Perdido. You better write it down."

The line went dead.

Burt pulled another picture from the desk drawer. This one of Paradise. It had been taken at a dance of some sort, maybe her prom. No date stood next to her. It was a cameo, snapped as she laughed at something off camera. So beautiful she tied his insides into square knots. He thought of her out on that boat with that man—Morales—and the picture shook in his hand. He rubbed the spot on the back of his head where the lamp had connected. It throbbed the same rhythm as the blood pounding in his temples. He glanced again at the picture but saw a crumpled wad of paper. When had he done that? He threw it at the Los Angeles skyline, but it bounced off the plate glass and rolled back between his feet.

You think you can run, Paradise? Enjoy it while you can. Because I'm coming.

Chapter Thirty-five

Lost Tacos

Paradise felt alive. Really alive. And not because of Arnie's big news, she realized with no little surprise. The sun and ocean and the rolling boat—a completely new experience—sent a thrill through her body. How strange that she'd grown up next to the ocean but had never sailed. Not that this could officially be called sailing, she supposed. Just motoring, really. But she could love this.

Not that she could say the same for Doc. The poor guy lay against the rear rail of the boat, his face a pale green color.

Truck Stop Jesus remained above it all, securely fastened with industrial-strength Velcro above the narrow doorway that led to the cabin. He dripped with salt spray and gave his cheerful thumbs-up to the distant horizon, head moving and jiggling with the slap of the waves and the roll of the deck.

"Why do you call your boat *Lazarus*?" Paradise asked.

Lan, hands firm on the boat's wheel, threw her a glance and raised a bushy eyebrow. He waved at Easy. "Easy, come take the wheel, would ya?"

Easy stopped turning a crank long enough to look up and reply. He sported a wide grin, one that never seemed to leave his face. "Yah, boss. You want to hoist the main?"

"Not now. We'll just motor a while. I think the wind'll die before long."

Easy nodded, then coiled a loose line.

"Where did you meet him?" Paradise said.

"You're a curious cat, aren't you?"

"I'm just interested."

Lan adjusted the wheel slightly to the right. "Little reprobate tracked me down in a bar in Costa Rica back in '81. I needed a deckhand, and he was in bad need of a job. He challenged me to a game of checkers, bought me a Red Stripe or two, and by the time the sun came up, we'd shaken hands and come to a temporary agreement. He's been with me ever since."

"That doesn't seem very temporary. You seem more like friends than employer and employee."

"Maybe. The pirate still beats me at checkers. I keep him around hoping for a little payback.

"Why do you call him Easy? It's a strange name."

"Given name's Eztli—a Mayan word—hard to pronounce for us Americans. I started out calling him *EZ*. Then Easy, and it stuck. He likes it, and don't let him tell you different."

Easy finished with the line and jogged back to the cockpit, nimble as a mountain goat. He slid behind the wheel as Lan stepped back.

"All right, just hold her on course."

"You got it, boss," the little man said.

Lan motioned Paradise to follow. "Let me show you something below." He led her through the cabin doorway and down some wooden steps into a wide, well-appointed salon.

Paradise's feet stopped of their own volition, and she gazed in wide-eyed wonder. Polished brass shone. Wood, thick with layers of varnish, surrounded her. Plush couches lined the walls. Forward, a galley stood ready for service, complete with a dining table that could have accommodated a small army—or large crew.

Lan put his hand on her shoulder and gave it a squeeze. "You like my little hideout?"

"It's the most beautiful thing I've ever seen. It really is!"

"I never get tired of this boat. She's been a faithful friend for a long, long while."

"She? Then why *Lazarus*? It's a man's name."

Lan waved a dismissive hand. "Not much for semantics. More about the meaning. Come over here." He led her forward to where a mast came through the ceiling and down into the floor. "Look at this."

A brass plaque adorned the thick beam. In engraved script it read, "*The Banana Coast, Paramount Pictures, 1934.*"

"*The Banana Coast*? Paramount? As in the movie?" Paradise said.

"You know it?"

"Of course, I know it! Who doesn't? Clive Granger and Madaline Lemieux. They were the biggest stars in the world. The rumor was that they fell in love making that movie."

"Yeah, good-hearted but degenerate rum runner sees the error of his ways, thanks to the influence of the Mosquito Coast missionary lady. Classic shmaltz. And it wasn't a rumor. They fell in love right here. Filming on this boat. She was the *Gladys Myrtle* then. Can you believe that? Who'd name a boat the *Gladys Myrtle*? The captain married them right where we're standing. Just a few close friends and crew, all sworn to secrecy. Clive bought her the next day—the boat, not Madaline Lemieux. Let me show you something else."

Lan led Paradise back down a hallway past a couple of closed doors to what must have been staterooms. The short passage ended at a master suite built into the rear of the boat. Built-in drawers and closets lined the walls. A writing desk faced one of several oversized portholes with views of the sea. A large bed stood as the centerpiece to the room.

Lan pointed to a beam above the bed. "Look there."

Another plate of brass and more graceful engraving.

Clive + Madaline
Our Love is a Shoreless Sea

Paradise's breath caught in her throat. "You're kidding me."

"Ain't no joke, kid. That's the real deal. Been there for eighty years."

"So this is actually *the* boat from *Banana Coast*?"

"Yup. A more faithful old girl you'd be hard pressed to find. Keel laid in nineteen-oh-three. Launched in oh-five. Ninety-five feet stem to stern. Gentleman's yacht—cruised the Keys and Bahamas mostly till the studio needed a boat and bought it. Clive and Madaline honeymooned on her before they took off back to Beverly Hills. I think they flew down to the Carib and visited her once or twice after, but that's about it. Busy life, I suppose—stardom and all. Not much time for the simple things. The things that matter."

Paradise searched his face for motivation behind the statement—nothing showing.

"What did Paco tell you about me?" she said.

Lan laughed. "Not much. I think he's got a little crush. Very protective."

"That's not an answer."

"He told me he wants you to be safe."

"Still not an answer. How did you get it?"

"Get what, a crush? Sorry girl, I'm out of your league."

Paradise smiled, liking the man. "No, the boat."

A glint came to his eyes. His boat was clearly something he enjoyed talking about. "Ah, that. Found her dry-docked at an end-of-the-road Puerto Rican boatyard about a million years ago. All blocked up and falling to pieces. Nobody'd touched her in years. Clive was long dead, and as far as I know, Madaline was holed up somewhere in Vegas doing the Howard Hughes and vodka thing. The boat had been through a few different owners, but the last one died, and I guess he didn't have any relative ambitious enough to come all the way down to claim a crumbling relic. The yard had a lien on her, but three cases of Bacardi rum delivered to the yard manager made it disappear. The rest is history."

Paradise ran her hand over the smooth wood. "I can't imagine her ever being run down."

"Ha! Trust me, sister, she'd been rode hard and put away wet. And after that, she'd sat baking in the sun for who knows how long. I spent three years of my life right there in that boatyard before I even got her in the water again. Did it right, though. And I've kept her up. She's old, but state of the art. I even rigged her so she can be handled by just a couple of seasoned sailors."

"When was that? When did you get her?"

"Nineteen seventy-three. Vietnam was over, and the US was trying to pick up the pieces. Heck, the whole world was picking up pieces. Chaos everywhere, you know? I'd been knocking around for a few years down there in the islands and figured, why go back? Why not just lay low, drink rum, play cards and mess around on an old boat? So I did. Let the planet solve its own problems without old Lan. Nobody missed me, and I've been sailing ever since. Me and *Lazarus* have seen this globe many times over."

"And Easy."

"Yup. Easy, too. Along with extra crew we pick up once in a while for longer crossings."

"That's why you named her *Lazarus*. Because you raised her from the dead?"

"You know the story?"

"Only as of recently."

"Yup, thus the name. I think it fits."

"Me too. Thank you."

"For what?"

"Rescuing us back in Agua Loco. You raised *us* up, too. They would have taken me. The woman—Crystal—I think she'd like to hurt me."

"You're welcome. But don't worry, you'll earn your passage. Easy and me, we can sail this girl just the two of us, but an extra hand or two makes it easier. And more fun, frankly."

"I don't know anything about sailing. I've never been on a boat before now."

Lan headed out of the stateroom toward the salon. "You're on one now and no place to go. You'll learn fast enough. You're already doing better than your sick buddy up there."

"I hope he's okay."

Lan chuckled, the sound coming from deep in his chest. "He'll live. Not the first *hombre* to lose his tacos over that rail."

"He's so nice. I feel sorry for him."

"Let me ask you—I couldn't help but hear your conversation back in the harbor—you're going back to LA? For a part in a movie?"

"That was my agent that called just before Hollister rammed us. I got a part, a *huge* part. They want me back there right away. I have to start in two weeks. A read through. Do you know what that is?"

"Heard of it once or twice, yeah."

"So I need to get back. Can we? Go back right now?"

"We can do anything you like, darlin'. This isn't a kidnapping. But you say two weeks. That gives you a little time. Why not let the dust settle?"

"Well, that's true ... technically, I suppose. But I have to go sometime, and my agent is about to have a stroke. Why prolong it?"

"Look, kid. I might be an old reprobate pirate, but I'm not blind. I don't even have an eye-patch. Seems to me the answer to that question is up on the deck, tossing his cookies into the drink."

"What did you do? Before you found the *Lazarus*, I mean? Why were you in Puerto Rico?"

Lan squinted an eye at her. "So you don't want to talk about Doc—I get it. But I'll tell you what, you've got two weeks; give me a day or two at sea before I take you back. Watch a sunset. Sleep with the sound of whales swimming beneath your pillow. All that Moby Dick stuff. Easy's got a nice grouper on ice. He'll grill it up, and you'll think you've died and gone to heaven. I'll even give you the Lan's-sordid-life highlight reel. I got a sea story or two up my sleeve. What do you say?"

Paradise again felt the roll of the sea beneath her. A gust of salt air breathed through the open door of the salon and brushed her face. "*What do you want, Paradise?*" it whispered.

She smiled. "Just a day or two? You promise?"

"Cross my heart," Lan said.

"And then we go back to shore?"

"Yup."

"Then I say you've got a date for the sunset, Captain Ahab."

CHAPTER THIRTY-SIX

Dancing With the Princess of Luxembourg

The breeze eased as the sun inched down toward the warm water of the Gulf of Mexico. Texas—or Mexico, maybe, Doc couldn't be sure—lay in that direction, but the *Lazarus* had traveled far enough so that the sea now spread out on all sides with no sight of land or boat.

As the waves died with the wind, Doc came to the happy realization that he might survive seasickness, after all, a sentiment that would never have crossed his nausea-addled mind half an hour earlier.

Hallelujah, brothers and sisters. A miracle on the high seas.

Doc hoisted himself to a sitting position on the bench where he'd been lying and leaned back against the rail.

Oh, the rail … his nearest and best friend for the last half day.

Finding his head and stomach fairly steady upon sitting, he threw caution to the wind and stood.

The smell of grilling fish, onion, and pineapple reached him, and his stomach growled.

"Hey there, Rip Van Winkle." Paradise emerged from the doorway leading below deck. "Lan said the sleep would help. Did it?"

"I think I might live to see tomorrow. That's a new development within the last few minutes. And something smells good."

"You've got to be hungry. There's certainly no food left inside you."

Doc cringed. "Not my finest hour."

Paradise pointed toward the bow of the boat where Easy manned a barbecue. "Easy's barbecuing. I've been helping Lan in the galley. That's a kitchen on a boat for you landlubbers."

"I know what a galley is."

"Don't pout. It's a nice evening, and we thought we'd eat out on the deck. Are you up for it?"

"With fear and trepidation, but I'm in. Aren't you queasy at all? Even being down below?"

"Lan says I'm a born sailor."

"Huh. I guess I'm a born landlubber."

"You feel better now, though. You'll be okay. Lan says you just need to find your sea legs."

"I'll keep my eyes open. Let me know if you run across them, too."

"Aye, aye. Listen, you've got to hear the story of this boat. It's really amazing. Remember *Banana Coast* with Clive Granger and Madaline Lemieux? This is the boat!"

A smile came unbidden to Doc's face at the excitement in her voice, then he sobered. "Look, Paradise, I understand that you need to go back to Los Angeles, I really do. Believe me, I know what it's like to have a dream. And I'm the last guy to stand in your way. I just want you to be safe, that's all."

"I will be. Arnie says the studio will take care of everything. Even Burt can't compete with them."

"Then it's settled. We're going to LA. Who knows? Maybe I'll be an extra in your movie. I bet I could pull off a Confederate uniform."

"No, Doc. *I'm* going to Los Angeles. Not we."

"Hey, it's still a free country, right? And LA's part of it, last time I checked a map."

"Yes, it's free. LA's being part of it is debatable. But I can't see you being there."

"Maybe it's time for a change."

Lan emerged from below. "Back with the living, huh, Doc? Good to see your bow for a change. Lord knows we were getting tired of your transom."

"Transom's the back of a boat," Paradise said.

"So I gathered," Doc replied. "What'd you do, take a crash course?"

"You up for some food?" Lan asked.

Doc nodded. "I'm up for giving it a try. We'll see how it goes."

"That's the spirit. I talked Miss Scarlett here into staying afloat for a day or two. Wasn't easy, either. Had to appeal to her romantic side. You know how these artistic types are."

"So I'm finding out," Doc said.

Paradise squeezed Doc's heart with a smile as she turned to Lan. "And you have vast experience with people of the arts playing hermit on your floating hideout for the last fifty years?"

"Oh, you'd be surprised, girly. Everyone from paupers to princes have graced the deck of old *Lazarus*." Lan pointed a thick finger forward. "I once danced with the Princess of Luxembourg right there next to that mast. What a night! Full moon over the Aegean Sea. She had my heart, that one. I still look for her face in a crowd. I've ferried poets and missionaries, aid workers and rock stars. Keith Richards fell asleep one time up on the bow. Wrapped himself up in a jib cover and bam, out like a light. Some marina in the Bahamas, I think that was. He stayed with me over a week."

"You've got to be kidding," Doc said.

Lan's hair and beard glowed in the setting sun. "And now? Paradise Jones. Or should I say, Miss Scarlett O'Hara? As I live and breathe. Prettier than Vivien ever could have dreamed."

Paradise plopped onto a bench and tucked her legs under her. Doc couldn't remember her looking so relaxed.

"You talk like you knew Vivien Leigh. Was she one of your imaginary guests too?" Paradise said.

"Vivien passed in '67. Me and *Lazarus* hadn't met yet. But you never know, girly, you never know. There are plenty of ghosts hovering around the edges. Now if you two will excuse me, I'm going to go play house with Easy and set a table on the foredeck. Doc, there's a spare cabin for you right through the salon, then the first door on the left. You can clean up if you'd like. I threw your bag in there on the bunk. We'll eat in fifteen minutes or so. Sound good?"

Doc and Paradise both answered in the affirmative, and Lan moved off along the deck to where Easy was arranging a white cloth over a long table.

Gulls screeched and circled overhead. The boat lay still on the water. No sail aloft. No engine running. Lights strung along the rigging bathed the scene in a soft glow.

"You look happy," Doc said.

Paradise looked at him for a long moment before answering. "I don't want to think tonight, okay, Doc? My brain is tired. My heart's tired, too. But I guess so. In this moment, I *am* happy. No Burt. No Hollister and Crystal. Just the boat and the sky."

Breeze touched her hair. She must have showered and changed her clothes while Doc slept. Shorts and a loose blouse, both white. Her feet were bare—*very* un-Paradise Jones.

"You're beautiful," Doc said.

"You really need to stop saying that."

"You don't like it? I say what I feel."

"Have you ever been on a boat before? Out at sea like this?"

"I said, I say what I feel. You're beautiful."

She surprised him by reaching for his hand. "Doc, you're special. You really are. And you mean something to me. A lot. I have feelings for you, but not how you'd like me to. Please, I appreciate your help. Everything you've done. But I haven't led you on. You know who I am. You know what I have to do. And it's not a life for two. At least not now."

"That's just it. I *do* know who you are. Maybe better than you do."

"Everything I've dreamed of, Doc. Everything I've wanted since I was a little girl. That's what's waiting for me in Los Angeles. Don't you see? I'll *matter*. I'll *mean* something. I won't be just an atom floating. I won't be lost anymore. I'll be *somebody*."

Defeat pressed and Doc stood. "I think I'll take Lan's advice and clean up. I could use it." At the door leading down to the salon, he paused and turned. "You already are somebody, whether you know it or not. And to me you don't just mean *something*—you mean everything."

Chapter Thirty-seven

The Life and Times of Landon Prescott

Paradise stared at the opening where Doc's broad shoulders had been moments before.

Don't think. Don't feel. Not tonight.

Truck Stop Jesus reflected the fading rays of the sunset off his plastic frame. *"Really?"*

"Really what? Wait … no … I don't want to hear it."

"What do you want, Paradise?"

"For you to quit asking me stupid questions. I don't want *anyone* to ask me questions tonight."

"What do you want, Paradise?"

"I've never been on a boat before. I'm glad this is my first one. It has to be the most beautiful boat in the world."

"Don't dodge the question."

"Well, I love it."

"I was on a boat, you know."

"When? An Olds Eighty-Eight doesn't count."

"There was a storm. I spoke to it, and it calmed. You've heard the story?"

"That was the *real* Jesus. Not a plastic one. Are you the real Jesus?"

"Are you the real Paradise?"

"Yes."

"No, you're not. But she's close. Just like me. I'm close. I'm always close."

Opposite the last vestige of the dying sun, a thin edge of the moon broke the watery horizon, sending a silvery trail toward the *Lazarus*.

"I don't want to feel tonight."

"Too bad. We always feel."

"Even you, my little plastic buddy?"

"Especially me."

"I suppose that must be true when I think about it. At least, the *real* Jesus must feel—if he exists."

"*What do you want, Paradise?*"

"I want to be famous. I want to matter."

"*You matter to me. More than the stars. More than whole worlds you've never seen or even dreamed of. I love you. Be famous to me. Be famous to him.*"

Hope surged, then faded just as fast. "But you're just in my head. Aren't you? Just in my head?"

"*Of course, I'm in your head. Now open your heart.*"

"This is crazy. I bought you at a truck stop. You cost $5.99. On sale, too. I'm losing my mind, that's what's happening. Ash always said I would, and now I am. I've gone over the edge just like Burt's car."

Paradise stood and stretched. The water lay like glass against the hull of the boat. Air warm on her skin. She closed her eyes and let her mind drift.

Paradise Jones. A boat called Lazarus. Gulf of Mexico. Planet Earth. Universe ...

"*No, Paradise,*" Truck Stop Jesus said.

"No? What do you mean, *no?*"

"*You're wrong. Very wrong. You didn't buy me ... I bought you ...*"

"Paradise!" Lan's voice rang loudly in the still evening. "Rustle up Doc. Time to eat."

Saved by the bell. Relief and disappointment thumb-wrestled. "Okay. Coming."

Doc emerged through the doorway. "I heard him."

Doc's hair was wet and combed back from his face. His brown eyes caught the light. He really *was* handsome.

Stop it ... Don't think. Don't feel ...

He put his arm out toward Paradise. "Shall we?"

"Do I have a choice?"

"Not tonight," Doc said.

Lan and Easy had pulled out all the stops. The table presented as beautiful as any posh LA restaurant. White tablecloth. Silver. Real crystal.

"Wow! Do you always do this?" Paradise asked.

"It's not every day we have a famous movie star onboard, right, Easy?" Lan said.

Easy's face blended into the dark, but his eyes and white teeth shone. "That's true, boss. Sort of. Only the best tonight, huh?"

"What do you mean by *sort of*?" Paradise said.

"These place settings have been part of this old girl since they splashed her in oh-five. We only bring them out on special occasions," Lan said.

Centerpiece on the table, a platter of grilled grouper gave off a wonderful aroma. Brown rice, grilled onions, pineapple, and a spinach-tomato salad rounded out the meal. Lan insisted on serving everyone. When all had a full plate before them, Lan held out his large hands. "As is tradition, let's thank the good Lord for his provision."

"Tradition?" Paradise said.

Lan laughed. "Even Keith Richards bowed his head on the *Lazarus*, sweetheart. No exceptions."

Prayers complete, light from the boat danced on the water. A very slight breeze gently rustled the tablecloth. Paradise took the night deep into her lungs. From below deck, Spanish guitar drifted up through open hatches and into the air. Stars, brightly visible even through the hanging lights strung through the rigging, spread themselves to all points of the compass.

"I've never seen stars like that," Paradise said. "The sky at night in Los Angeles glows. Brown and orange. You don't see stars very often."

"A whole other world out here," Lan said. "Nothing like open water. Especially when it's calm like this."

"It's like a lake," Doc said.

Lan poured cold water from a pitcher into his glass. "Uh huh, at the moment. But don't let it fool ya. The ocean can change on a dime. She's a fickle lady."

Evening moved on. The big grouper whittled down to bones. Music and laughter lingered and blessed.

"Lan," Paradise folded her napkin and laid it across her empty plate. "You were going to tell me your story tonight, remember?"

Reflected light danced in the old man's eyes. "I knew Vivien well, you know. I read something later about her being bipolar, but I never saw that side of her. I found her to be a gracious woman."

"Vivien?" Doc said.

"Sure, Vivien Leigh. Scarlett *numero uno*," Lan said.

"How did you know her?" Paradise said.

Lan pulled a pipe and package of tobacco from his pocket. He filled, tamped, and lit it with a silver lighter. He set the lighter on the table. It had an oblong, polished piece of turquoise ornately embedded in the side. He blew smoke into the night, and the sweet smell of vanilla and figs mingled with sea air.

"Hey'a, boss?" Easy said.

"Right, forgot. Used yours last time, didn't we?" Lan tossed the tobacco package to Easy, who produced a short, stubby pipe of his own.

Lan puffed again. His voice rolled deep and rich. "All right then, my story for what it's worth. Let's see, to start with, I was thrown into this world in nineteen hundred and thirty-five—sinner head to toe. To save you from hurting your brains with math, that makes me a ripe old eighty years young. Grew up around Austin. My given name was Clarence Gene Hardy. Strange, I haven't thought about that name in a long, long time."

"You don't look eighty," Paradise said.

Lan winked and puffed again. "I love you very much. My mother was a dust-bowl-days farm wife. I never knew my dad. Mom's story was he got himself killed in a farm accident when I was a baby. I later came to find out he'd lit out for California before I was even born. Killed in a knife fight over a poker game in Salinas. By a woman, no less. My mom, she married again. The way I see it now, with a few miles behind me, she plain old made bad choices as far as men were concerned. My stepdad, he was a real piece of work. He could knock you in the head from the next room. I worked every summer. Saved my dimes and nickels, and when I turned fifteen, I bought myself a pile-of-rust Indian motorcycle. Took a month to get the thing running, but once it did, I headed west and never looked back. Wound up in Los Angeles in '52. Washed dishes, waited tables. Worked the docks down in Long Beach for a while and from there I wound up getting a job on a tramp steamer making runs to the South Pacific. That's where I learned to love the sea."

"Nineteen fifties in Los Angeles. That must have been quite a time," Doc said.

"Oh, it was. Good time to be young and alive. One day, I bumped into an ex-shipmate of mine in a bar in Torrance. He'd gotten a job on a movie set as an extra. In a western—those were the thing at that time. Asked if I was looking for work. I wasn't particularly. In fact, I was planning on shipping out again in a few days, but the thing sounded interesting. I thought I might meet John Wayne or Gary Cooper, maybe. So I tagged along with my buddy, and before I know it, I'm dressed like a cowboy and standing in a fake saloon on the Warner Brothers lot."

Doc leaned forward, elbows on the table. "Really? What movie was that?"

"*Dead Man's Bluff.* Never made it to the screen. But they did ask me to come back again. The next day that shipmate and I got into a bit of a scuffle over one of the saloon girls. Not on camera, mind you. I laid him out flat. Dropped him like a dead fish. Felt bad about it. Funny thing is, he wound up marrying that dame and the way she turned out, I figure I dodged a bullet. They didn't invite me to the wedding—imagine that."

"Did the studio fire you, then?" Paradise asked.

Lan took another puff. "Nope. In fact, the director wound up giving me a line. I was big and tough looking. Definitely not shy. The whole thing came pretty natural. That one line led to another and then a small part in a picture. That's when a studio producer asked me if I'd be averse to changing my name. He said Clarence Hardy was a lousy cowboy name. I said sure, why not? I'd never really liked Clarence anyway. He said since the movie we were on was set in Arizona, what would I think about Prescott for a last name? Sounded good to me, so there it was."

Some hint of recognition tugged at Paradise. "Wait ... Prescott? Lan? Were you ... are you ... are you saying you're Landon Prescott?"

Another puff from the pipe. "Ding, ding. Lady wins a prize."

Paradise looked at Doc, who seemed to be having a hard time picking his jaw up off the table.

"You're actually saying you're *the* Landon Prescott?" Doc said.

"The one and only, as far as I know."

Paradise studied the craggy face carefully. "Yes. I see it now! Landon Prescott! Lan, you were the biggest movie star on the planet! You were everywhere! A-list of A-lists!"

Doc picked up, sounding just as excited. "Then you disappeared into thin air. When was it? Nineteen seventy? 'Seventy-one?"

"March, 1971. Remember it like yesterday. I'd just wrapped *The Longest Night* in Rome with Lana Lee as my leading lady."

"But why would you leave? I mean, you're Landon Prescott! You had everything anyone ever dreams of!" Paradise said.

"Not everything, girl. And not everyone dreams the same. I had more money than I could spend in two lifetimes. I had fame. Everybody knew my name, or, at least, my film name."

Paradise struggled to understand. "But what, then? What didn't you have? Why run from all that?"

"I didn't have the quiet of a South Pacific island beach. I didn't have the thrill of a squall line on the horizon and a sail full of wind left over from a spun-out Atlantic hurricane. Or the satisfaction of tired muscles after a hard day's work. By then, I'd spent so much time acting out life I'd forgotten what it felt like to live it for myself. To be a man. I didn't have love. Or family. Lana Lee was America's sweetheart and my love interest for three consecutive films, but off camera, she was a real piece of work. More interested in chasing rock stars and dropping acid than anything else. It was all fake, you know?"

Doc sipped from his water glass. "But how? You just disappeared and never surfaced. I've watched TV specials, read articles—everyone thought you were dead. Maybe even murdered."

"My favorite was abducted by aliens," Lan said.

"For a while, you were supposed to have holed up in a hotel like Howard Hughes," Paradise said.

Lan shook his head. "The answer is D—none of the above. It wasn't that dramatic. I laid low in Italy for a while. Grew a beard. Romanced a local girl till her father gave me a swift kick out the door. Then one day I went to sea. Just another lowly deckhand—no offense, Easy."

Easy puffed his pipe and showed his white teeth. "None taken, boss."

"I bummed around on this ship and that—worked a schooner off the African coast for a while. Old school, that one. Practically pirate stuff. Hiked around in Central America. Then somehow I found myself in Puerto Rico. That's where I found the *Lazarus*. Although, like I told you, she was the *Gladys Myrtle* then. Cruel, cruel name."

Doc leaned back in his chair. "*Landon Prescott*. I just can't believe it. How did you meet Paco?"

"Ah! That's a story for another dinner. Suffice it to say, New Orleans, some crates of medicine. A bottle of rum—that one was my fault. Oh, and a British missionary lady with a very persuasive way about her and a need to get to Honduras under the radar. Paco and I had some long talks on that sail. And what he said made sense. We've kept in touch ever since. He talked about you a lot, Doc. In fact, I saw you get that hit with the Red Sox. Watched it on a TV with an antennae made out of a clothes hanger. Glorious black and white on a guy's back porch in Havana."

"You knew Doc played baseball?" Paradise said.

"If you knew Paco, you heard every detail about Doc and Jake. But even without Paco's press, Doc here was the next big thing. Golden boy of the sports world. Red Sox said you'd take them to another World Series."

Paradise raised an eyebrow at Doc. "You were that good?"

"Better than good," Lan said. "Great. Doc was the talk of the MLB for a while there."

A sense of loss stirred deep within Paradise. An odd feeling because it wasn't for herself this time, but for another lost dream. "I'm sorry, Doc. How can you bear it? It was everything to you."

His eyes met hers. "Not anymore."

Easy dropped down through one of the hatches, and the stereo grew louder. Flamenco guitar accompanied by heartfelt raspy Spanish.

Lan stood. "Ah, the Gypsy Kings. Let's dance, Miss Scarlett."

Before she could respond, Paradise found herself swept off her chair and into the big man's arms.

"You can cut in later, Doc. But let me take her around the mast a couple of times."

Paradise couldn't swallow her laugh. "Do I get a say in this at all?"

"You're my date for the sunset, right? Argue, and you walk the plank. You know what? You're a pretty good dancer ... You ever been to Luxembourg?"

Chapter Thirty-eight

Good Day for a Sail

Paradise usually took sleeping in to the level of an art form, but dawn stars still dotted the cabin's portholes when her eyes opened to her first morning at sea.

Roll over and go back to sleep? Would have worked normally, but the Sandman dodged and skirted, taunting from the edge of the abyss.

Her feet found the smooth, wooden floor. There were a couple of built-in drawers under the bunk, and she opened them out of curiosity. One held a few worn pairs of men's swim trunks, a pair of size thirteen flip-flops, and a puka shell necklace—the other, only a double extra-large white men's dress shirt. Opening her big, red suitcase, she dug out one of her Esther-Dash-Williams-Dot-Com swimsuits and slipped it on. She used the dress-shirt for a cover-up and put the puka shells around her neck for good measure.

Very *Starlet goes Caribbean.* She was sailing, right? What did Doc say? Go big or go home …

The delicious smell of fresh coffee drew her to the salon. The galley was empty, but a percolator bubbled on the gimbaled stove. She found a mug in the cupboard and some coconut flavored creamer in the refrigerator, poured, then made her way to the salon door, trying hard not to spill against the rocking of the boat. Sea air whipped her curls into her face as she stepped out onto the deck. She pushed them away with her free hand, still balancing the coffee mug in the other.

"Miss Jones … Fresh wind today, huh?" Easy manned the big wheel. His smooth brown face crinkled in the growing light. "You like da' coffee?"

"It's wonderful."

"Honduran. We get it from a friend in San Pedro Sula. Best in the Carib. Why you up so early, anyway?"

"I don't know. I'm not usually. I couldn't sleep."

"Ah, dat's cause you a saila'. Born to it. I seen right away. You feel fresh wind in your bones dis morning. Me too."

Paradise loved the lilt of his voice. "The wind *has* come up, hasn't it?"

"Oh, yes, ma'am. Look up!" Easy stuck a boney finger forward.

Paradise turned. She'd seen movies, television, but nothing had prepared her for the sight that rose into the heavens above her. What seemed to be a square mile of sail stretched up along the towering wooden mast against the graying sky. Two more sails caught the wind forward. Words caught in her throat.

"It's beautiful, yes, Miss Jones?" Easy said.

"More than beautiful! And please, call me Paradise."

"Ah. Yes, Paradise, ma'am. I call you dat. Look now, dat big sail on the tallest mast? Dat's the main sail. This smaller one, it's da' mizzen."

"What about the ones on the front?"

"Ain't no front on a boat, Miss. Fore and aft. But dem two sails are jibs. Carry a lot of wind, ol' *Lazarus* does."

"It's beautiful," Paradise said again.

"C'mere, now. You steer dis lady. Let you feel what it's like to hang between wind and sea, heaven and earth, huh?"

"Really? I can steer?"

"You bet! I'll stand right behind to help. Don't worry, now!"

Easy took her mug, and she moved behind the wheel. It tugged slightly in her hands and shuddered just a little. She looked up at the sails again. "Am I really driving?"

"No, miss. You're *steering*. You're *sailing*! Men been doing the same for t'ousands of years, you know?"

"Where are we going?" Paradise asked.

"We going west. See dat compass dere? Away from da sun comin' up. Land out over dat way somewhere. We hit it sooner or later. Got to get you off here, Lan says. Send you on to da movies. Me? I'll keep sailin'. Nothin' on land hold any interest for ol' Easy no more."

The wind picked up and blew spray in her eyes. She wiped it with a quick hand. "Don't you have a family, Easy?"

"Used to. Before AIDS came. Disease everywhere, dough. So many people! My wife and son, they up and died. I wished I had AIDS back den, too. Wanted to die with dem. But Jesus, he decide who come and go. He say, not yet! So I got drunk instead. For years I got drunk. Den I found da boss, and he brought me on board here. We went sailing. Da boss is my family now. One day I'll see my wife and son again up in Heaven. Till then, I'll go sailing. Help Lan with what he needs. I love him. He's a good man."

"He seems wonderful. I'm sorry about your wife and son, Easy."

"Me too. But I'll see again. Dey in the arms of Jesus."

Truck Stop Jesus drew Paradise's attention. Water dripped from his plastic beard. He smiled.

"Easy, do you believe in Jesus?" she asked.

"Oh sure. My wife? She always talked about him. I laughed at her. Told her Jesus was a story for children and white people. I asked her, where was Jesus when she was sleeping around with all da sailors? Back in da old days? But she don't listen. She just prayed. She just smiled and prayed. Prayed for me, prayed for my son, prayed for everyone. I knew she was different from da old days. I knew she changed when she met Jesus, but I didn't want to admit. I was afraid he'd take my rum, ya know? When da sickness took her, I was so mad. Den my son, too. I wanted to die. I asked Jesus—why? Why dem? My son was just a little ting! No bigger than a mango! And my wife was kind … I got a bottle and went to da cane fields." Easy reached out and corrected Paradise's steering slightly to the left. "Watch dat compass now. Western heading."

The *Lazarus* leapt into a wave and crashed down the backside.

"She's picking up. Good sailing today!" Easy said. He handed Paradise her coffee, miraculously all still in the cup, and took back control of the wheel.

Lan appeared in the doorway, hair wild in the wind. "Good morning, Miss Scarlett! How did you sleep?"

"Wonderfully. Really, wonderfully. This is a different ocean from the one last night, isn't it?"

"I told you she's a fickle lady," Lan said. "Fair winds today, though. Good for sailing. This old girl loves a good wind. Thanks, Easy. I got her now."

"Yes, boss. My eyes is heavy. Quick nap, eh?"

Easy waved at Paradise and headed below deck.

"He's got a room down there no bigger than a closet," Lan said. "I told him years ago to take any cabin he wanted, but he loves his little spot next to the engine room. He's a good man, that Easy."

"He says you rescued him."

Lan glanced at her, then up toward the sails. "See that handle there to your left? Crank it clockwise a couple turns. We'll trim her up a bit."

Paradise did as she was told.

"That's good," Lan said.

"What did I do?"

241

"You trimmed the main. That means you pulled it in a little tighter. More power from the wind."

Paradise sat and leaned back, letting her hair fall loose in the wind over the rail behind her. "I love this, Lan."

"I can tell."

"Why?"

"Why do you love sailing?"

"No, why did you leave? The films? You had it all. I still can't understand it. Was this it? Is this enough?"

Lan's weathered face focused on the horizon. The sun crept out of the sea behind him, backlighting his blowing hair.

"It's a wide world, girl. A never-ending horizon. Yeah, for a year or two there, I thought I was happy. I thought, like you say, I had it all. Money, women, attention. Things I couldn't have imagined back on the farm. But then I got this feeling. Crept up gradually, I guess. Like I was wading around in the shallow end of the pool. Getting my knees wet, but I couldn't find the deep end. You know, the place where real life happens. Like I was hungry, but couldn't get enough to eat. The parties, the awards, the movies—they became two-dimensional."

"So you left. Just like that."

"Always been my modus operandi. If you decide to do something, do it. You find something that makes you happy, grab on and don't let go."

"Like the girl? In Italy? Did she make you happy?"

Lan's smile lines deepened. "Oh, for a minute or two. I was on the run, though. Didn't know it, but I was. I needed the sea. Her father did me a favor, really."

A hard gust of wind pushed the huge sails, and the ketch leaned hard to the right.

Tiny fingers tickled Paradise's insides. "You're sure it's safe? Leaning like this?"

"On a boat, we don't lean. We *list*. And yes, it's safe. This is a good day for a sail, girl."

"But we're headed back to shore? To Texas?"

"Should be able to see it pretty soon. Gotta get you back to La La Land, right? Although I do hate to waste a day like this puttering through that oily harbor drink and all those plastic party boats around Corpus Christi."

The *Lazarus* crested a swell and salt water blew high into the air, splashing onto the teak decks before running off in sheets.

"Well, you said a couple days ... I have two weeks, right? At least, sort of. Arnie's going to lose his mind. Let's sail today ... spend one more night, maybe. But only if I can steer again."

"Ha! That's my girl! Here, take her. Hold this course. I'm gonna go grab a cup of joe. Be right back."

The wheel felt good in her hands. It filled Paradise with a sense of control. The boat crested another rolling swell, and an unintentional gasp broke her lips.

Jesus grinned.

"What now?" Paradise said.

"*You. You can't stop smiling.*"

"So?"

"*So I'm glad ...*"

Chapter Thirty-nine

The Queen of the High Seas

Paradise didn't leave the *Lazarus* cockpit all day. Lan stood with her, pointing out parts of the boat and giving her instruction. She learned that left was port and right starboard. She learned that rope was only rope until it found its way onto a boat, then it was *line*. Lan told her the lines that adjusted the sails were called sheets and showed her what winches controlled the main, mizzen, and two jib sails, and how some of the winches had been converted from manual to electric to make the boat easier for a small crew to handle.

A fascinating new world. Like stepping back in time. Even Burt, pounding on the walls of her subconscious, couldn't dampen the enthusiasm and joy flying freely on the Gulf winds.

"Prepare to jibe!" Paradise shouted.

Easy and Doc scrambled to the lines and sheets.

"Jibe ho!" she said.

She swung the wheel, and the men ducked as the big booms hesitated, then pulled to the opposite side of the boat as the sails reversed in the wind. Easy, Doc and Lan cranked to trim, and the *Lazarus* leaned hard to starboard.

"You're becoming a regular old salt, Miss Scarlett," Lan said, laughing. "So is your boy up there. Told you he'd find his sea legs."

Paradise glanced at Doc. He'd found a pair of deck shoes somewhere that fit. His cargo shorts were soaked, and water ran down his shirtless torso. He stood out on the bowsprit, one hand on the forestay and back to the forward horizon. He laughed at something Easy said.

"I have to admit, he looks better than yesterday," she said.

"No doubt about that. A *whole* lot better. Not green. The fish are disappointed he's not feeding them, though."

Turning the boat while sailing upwind, Paradise learned, was *tacking*. When away from the wind, *jibing*. At the moment, the *Lazarus* dug into the swells on a *broad reach*, with the wind off the port rail and a little behind them.

"I think I'm beginning to understand a little," Paradise said.

Lan reached around her and made a slight direction adjustment to the wheel. "And what's that, darlin'?"

"The attraction. Of being out here. The sun and wind. The horizon … It makes me want to see what's on the other side of it."

"Ah, now *that's* the stuff that dreams are made of, isn't it? Same feeling that pushed the Vikings across the Atlantic. Columbus to the Americas. Lewis and Clark across a continent. That horizon is an elusive mistress, let me tell you."

Doc made his way aft and dropped into the cockpit. "I could get used to this."

"You look like you're having a good time up there," Lan said.

"This is great, Lan. And how's our girl doing? She yells like she's the queen of the high seas."

"Like a fish to water," Lan said.

Doc lay across a bench and propped himself up on an elbow.

Paradise looked down at him. "What are you grinning about?"

"Are you glad that you decided to stay out here today?"

"Prepare to Jibe! Jibe ho!" Paradise shouted.

Easy and Lan grabbed sheets and trimmed as Paradise turned the wheel and the huge wooden booms swung hard across the deck.

"Okay, I admit it. I'm having fun," she said.

Doc dropped to his back and put his hands behind his head, looking up at her.

"Stop that," she said.

"Stop what?"

"You know what."

As the western sun wandered away from the Gulf in search of the Pacific, the wind began to die again, though big swells still rolled under the *Lazarus*. Very unlike last night's glass. Paradise, finally willing to leave the cockpit, helped Easy in the galley. Nothing fancy tonight—sandwiches, chips, salad and a pot of fresh coffee.

Lan and Doc dropped down the steps into the salon, and Doc headed off to find some dry clothes.

Lan poured himself a cup and took a seat at the table. "Dropped everything but the main and lashed the wheel. Old girl's on her own for a bit. I'm starving, kids. Good day, yes?"

"Aye, good day, boss," Easy said.

"*Great* day," Paradise said. "So, Lan, after all that sailing, where are we now? I still can't see land."

"Funny thing about the ocean, isn't it? I figure we made about a hundred and twenty-five miles today. But—and here's the good news for you, Miss Scarlett— we're right about the same place we started. We can get some sleep and then tool over toward Corpus in the morning."

Doc came back in. Barefoot in a T-shirt and dry shorts.

Lan reached from his chair, poured from the pot and slid Doc a cup of coffee. "How about you, Doc? We still headed for the Yucatan? You, me and Easy? Find all that gold and the meaning of life?"

Doc sipped the coffee. "The coins indicated a place called Dia Perdido—the mission there."

"I know Dia Perdido well," Lan said. "Close to the coast but tucked back in the jungle and forgotten, really. Tourist business missed it somehow. The locals like it that way. Been a while, but the folks at the mission are friends of mine. It'll be good to see them again. So that's a yes? We sail to Mexico?"

Doc's eyes searched Paradise's. She focused on cutting a tuna sandwich. "Of course, he's going." She didn't look up. "It's important, Doc. You have to."

"And you? You're really going back? You can't give it a few more days?"

"There's no point. If the studio can protect me like Arnie says, then there's no reason for me to be here."

His sadness was palpable.

"Doc, I didn't mean it that way. You know I didn't."

"*What do you want, Paradise?*"

She thought the question came from Lan. The knife dropped from her hand to the counter, causing her to jump.

"What, Lan?" she said.

Lan sipped his coffee. "Did I say something?"

"Didn't you just ask me what I wanted?"

Lan eyed her with curiosity. "Nope."

Later, food gone and dishes done, Lan opened a cabinet and turned on the stereo while Easy made his way topside to check on things. Nat King Cole reported that it was only a paper moon. Easy dropped back in and pulled a deck of cards from a drawer. The four of them played rummy for the next couple hours, Easy winning almost every hand. No one seemed anxious to turn in. At last, Easy put the cards away and headed back up topside to take first watch. Lan stood, stretched, said his own goodnights, and ambled toward the aft cabin.

"So. Tomorrow, then," Doc said. "You're really going?"

"Yes, tomorrow … Will you come visit, Doc? I'll miss you, you know. I really will."

"I'll come *with* you if you want. All you have to do is ask."

"I'll be okay. Burt won't bother me."

"Burt has nothing to do with it."

His face—so earnest in the dim light of the salon.

She bit her lip. "We'd better get some sleep."

Doc sighed. "Yeah. But I'll always tell you how I feel. I don't care if you're the biggest movie star in the world or living out of your Olds. I won't hide my feelings or lie to you."

"I know. I'm sorry."

She managed to force emotion down but later, alone in her bunk, listening to the water rush by just inches away, a tear slipped down her cheek. She wiped it with a hard hand. What was going on? The situation had gotten out of control. For years, she'd dreamed and worked, hoping against hope that this day would come. Now here it was, and all she could think about was the way a baseball player had danced with her in a bar.

Ridiculous. *Pull yourself together!*

"What do I want?" she whispered to the darkness.

No one answered.

"So now you're quiet? Too busy, suddenly? Out saving the world or something?"

She rolled over and stared through the porthole. Spray blew up, glowing green with luminescence.

"Shouldn't I go? It's so hard. What about Arnie? What about Ash? No, I have to go. I'll be happy … finally."

Her muscles ached from the long day. Fatigue cracked the door, and sleep crept in on quiet feet.

"*Be famous to me, Paradise,*" the water whispered as it met hundred-year-old wood.

Then she dreamed of the ship's wheel and the sails and water dancing in the sun high over the bow.

Chapter Forty

Whales

A loud knock jolted Paradise upright. Then Lan's voice. "Paradise, you there? Wake up. Need everyone on deck."

Paradise hung her legs over the edge of the bunk and started to stand. Something boomed against the hull and the *Lazarus* listed to a crazy angle. She tumbled onto the hard floor.

Lan knocked again. "Paradise! You coming?"

"Yes!" She struggled into her clothes. "What's going on?"

No answer. He must have headed up. Paradise followed, reeling down the hall and through the salon. The view through the cockpit door seemed something right out of a Landon Prescott movie. The big man gripped the wheel like some insane pirate king. Rain and seawater streamed off his hair and beard. As Paradise climbed through the door, the force of the wind struck—a giant fist. Lan grabbed her and pulled her to him, strapping her into a harness and placing her body between his and the wheel.

He shouted into her ear, the wind yanking his words into the wild night. "You hold tight here! Hold this course, you hear me? Watch the bow and don't wander if you can help it! We want to quarter the waves. See what I mean? At about a forty-five degree angle."

She nodded. *Please let this be a dream!*

Lan shouted again. "We're in it now, girl! This is a real blow. Came out of nowhere! Nothin' on the satellite. Gonna take all of us on deck for a while! I need to help the boys reef the sails. Set her up for the storm before it shreds the canvass. You just do as I tell you and hold her here!"

Again she nodded. "I'm scared, Lan!"

"Ha! You should be, girl! This is the ocean! This is God in his glory! You're scared, but you're alive! Really alive!" He turned his face to the sky and gave a great rebel yell.

Lightning turned the night to instant daylight, followed by the deafening roar of thunder.

Lan moved to the front of the wheel, and his eyes met Paradise's. Even through her terror, his smile was contagious.

"Be alive, girl. Be alive!" Over his shoulder a massive mountain of water rose, dwarfing the *Lazarus*. Paradise's heart leaped to her throat.

"Lan!" she screamed.

Turning, he grabbed the wheel again. "Hold on, girl! She'll ride it out!"

Lazarus rose, climbing up the face of the monster wave. The boat crested, then raced down the other side, a ninety-foot child's toboggan on a watery slope.

Lan gave another yell. This time Paradise followed suit.

"You got her?" Lan shouted.

"I got her!"

Lan patted her shoulder, then half ran, half crawled over the bucking deck to where Doc and Easy were scrambling to secure the sails and lash things down, the three of them wearing harnesses of their own.

Lightning crashed again. Truck Stop Jesus grinned from the bulkhead.

"You don't look worried!" Paradise shouted.

Thumbs-up.

The storm raged on, and the *Lazarus* crested mountain after mountain of raging water. Eventually, the three men made their way back to the cockpit.

"It don't look like it's letting up, boss!" Easy said.

"Nope, it's a wild one, sure enough. Well, boys and girls, you said you wanted to go sailing! We're sailing now!"

Lan took the wheel again, and Paradise collapsed to the cockpit bench next to Doc. He put his arm around her, and she didn't pull away.

"You did great up there, Doc!" Lan said. "Glad you were here!"

"What now?" Doc shouted.

"Now we hold on and wait! There's no off switch for a storm! You might try to get some sleep if you can. Me and Easy will get her hove to and keep the mast-side up."

Paradise gratefully tumbled into her bunk. Though she'd manned the helm but a short time, her body felt as if she'd run a marathon. The *Lazarus* yawed and heaved, creaking against the elements. She listened for a voice in the rushing sea and wind but heard none.

"You picked a heck of a time to check out of the conversation," she mumbled.

"*I didn't know we were having one. I do most of the talking.*"

"Where have you been?"

"*Everywhere. You need to go with Doc to Mexico.*"

"What? Are you *telling* now? No more asking?"

"*It's just my opinion. Not that any others matter.*"

"What if I don't?"

"*You ever heard of Jonah?*"

"You're kidding, right?"

The storm raged, unabated and unconcerned by any conversation going on in Paradise's fatigued brain. The sky lightened only a fraction, with the coming dawn bringing a pale, green light to the porthole by the bunk.

Sleep came.

And Paradise dreamed of whales.

CHAPTER FORTY-ONE

The Lost Day

Hollister stared out at the soggy day. "I hate rain."

Crystal counted out sit-ups on the tile floor. "Ninety-nine ... a hundred." She stood and flopped onto the bed.

Not even out of breath. The woman was a machine.

"Enjoy, moron. Don't be a whiner. Look how pretty the jungle is," she said.

"I hate the jungle."

"Think of it as a second honeymoon. Free trip to Mexico."

"I hate Mexico. And what do you mean second? When was the first?" Hollister said.

"The first was Catalina Island."

"Catalina? You got drunk and almost killed that bouncer, remember? I spent three days sitting around waiting for them to let you out of jail."

"That's what made it so sweet, moron. You waited."

While everyone on the planet had heard of Cancun, no one north of the border ever heard of Dia Perdido, or "Lost Day" in English, according to the tourist maps. At least not outside of a few rum-soaked ex-pats and surfers who somehow found their way down here. A thirty-mile, rut-riddled road wound through dense jungle, providing the only way into the place. The road turned to potholed asphalt and stone on one edge of town, then back to dirt again at the other where a sign made from a broken surfboard said "Beach-3K."

Who knew how the ancient buildings edging what passed for Main Street withstood the insane heat and humidity of the Yucatan Peninsula? Let alone how any human being survived? These were mysteries above Hollister's pay grade. And somehow—he especially couldn't wrap his brain around this one—the drenching rain brought no relief from the heat.

Ain't life grand ... What is it they say? This ain't hell but you can sure see it from here ...

Lost day? More like a lost *world*.

Casa Vieja Cabra. The name rolled off the tongue like it should be a five-star hotel. The desk clerk informed Hollister it meant the Old Goat, then eyed him like he'd be a good fit for a mascot. Whatever—the place offered the only reasonable option for accommodations, and after a bone-jarring, two-day road trip through the cheerful opulence of the Third World, Hollister accepted the place, if not with gratitude, then at least with resignation.

And then it had started raining.

And raining ...

And raining ...

Hollister groaned. "What is it, like a hundred and eighty degrees? How do people live in this? I feel like I should swim instead of walk."

Crystal ignored him.

Sweat streamed off every exposed part of her body in rivulets, soaking her spandex workout clothes. Her Mohawk lay sideways—tired and limp.

"What happened to Simmons, anyway?" Hollister said.

"He'll be here. Quit whining."

"I still can't believe you told him about the coins. You know the greedy idiot is gonna try to take anything we find at that church. Assuming there's anything *to* find."

Crystal took a long swig of some concoction she'd managed to wrangle the poor woman who worked in the kitchen to blend for her. She proceeded to burp the alphabet, only making it to G. "What's your problem? We get the princess. Get the forty large. Find the gold with Simmons' clues—which we wouldn't have had, if I hadn't told him, by the way—beat the snot out of him and his daughter. Dump 'em in a ditch and live happily ever after. Why do you always have to make everything so complicated?"

"This is Mexico, Crystal! You ever been in a Mexican prison? It's not a day spa."

"Who said anything about prison, moron? Anyway, Simmons already said I could pound Little Miss Muffet—which you lied about—so that's not even a crime. And who's he gonna tell? Since he's the one telling us to beat her up?"

Hollister rubbed his temples. "As usual, none of what you just said makes any sense. I don't know what you're talking about half the time anymore."

"'Cause you're a fat-old-man-soft-lazy-moron. I'm gonna take a shower." Crystal dropped for thirty more push-ups, hopped up, shadowboxed the mirror, then headed for the bathroom, stripping off her sweat-soaked clothes and humming the theme to *Footloose*.

Hollister went back to staring out the window. "What's the point of anyone showering in this dump? You're always wet anyway." Not that he'd complain about Crystal cleaning up a little.

What had happened? Where had life gone? There'd been a time—a hundred years ago—when he and Crystal were happy. *Was that possible?* Or as happy as a stuntman and a cage fighter could be. Which, come to think of it, was pretty happy. He'd even liked her stupid humming back then.

At what point in a relationship does cute become crazy? Well, they'd passed it, brother.

A knock on the hotel room door jerked him to the present. Must be Simmons.

It wasn't.

"Hola, señor."

"Who are you?" Hollister said.

A tall, thin man stood on the veranda. He wore loose-fitting, black cotton slacks and a white guayabera shirt. Rain and sweat rendered the guayabera semi-transparent, showing a dirty undershirt beneath. A gold crucifix hung around the man's neck, and a nasty scar split his thin mustache.

The man removed an American ball cap from his head and shook the rain off it. "Señor Simmons, he sent me."

Hollister ran his eyes over the man again. "Man, what did Simmons do, look in the local yellow pages under B-grade Mexican thug?"

The man gave a slow blink. "You don't have to be rude, señor."

"Excuse me?"

"Maybe you hurt people's feelings sometimes, talking like that."

"You carrying a purse?" Hollister said, nodding at a canvas bag looped over the Mexican's shoulder.

"No, it's a carry-all."

"Huh, same difference if you ask me."

The man's droopy eyes watered. Tears, or remnants of last night's tequila binge?

"What's the matter with you?"

"It only seems to me you could be kinder to others, señor."

"Are you kidding me? Who are you, Barney?"

"Who is Barney?"

"A big purple ... Ah, never mind." Not worth the effort.

The shower stopped.

"Who you talking to, moron?" Crystal called.

The Mexican's eyes shifted toward the bathroom door.

"Hey, Jack. No free show today, comprende?" Hollister said.

"I wouldn't tread on a lady's honor," the thin man replied.

"Trust me, brother, she ain't no lady, but the rule still stands."

"Moron! I said, who is it?" Crystal shouted again.

"I don't know! Some Mexican daisy Simmons sent."

"What does he want?"

Hollister turned toward the bathroom door. "I don't know!" Then turned back. "What do you want?"

"First of all, my name is Sammy, not Jack. Dr. Simmons hired me to be your guide."

"Guide? Guide to where?" Hollister said.

"And to bring you this." Sammy pulled the bag off his shoulder, reached inside, and pulled out a pistol roughly the size of a refrigerator.

Hollister took a step back. "What the ... ! What does that thing shoot, mortar rounds?"

"It was my great grandfather's—from the revolution. Dr. Simmons said you have need of a *pistola*, so I loan it to you. You're welcome. Now, be polite and say thank you."

Hollister eyed the gun but didn't take it. "Why does Simmons think I need a pistola?"

Crystal emerged from the bathroom, a towel wrapped around her body.

Sammy bowed at the waist—very old school. "Hola, señora."

Crystal raised a tattooed brow. "You're right. It *is* a Mexican daisy. What's with the grenade launcher?"

"Simmons thinks we need it. No idea why."

Crystal reached for the gun. "Cool. I like it. Let's go shoot something. Maybe the daisy?"

Hollister held it away from her. "Newsflash, Annie Oakley, here's one thing that *ain't* happening—you getting your mitts on this cannon. Might as well drop a nuke on the whole Yucatan Peninsula."

Hollister shot an eye back to the Mexican. "Where's Simmons, anyway?"

"He says we meet him at breakfast. He is waiting in the café."

Crystal moon-walked to the bathroom and emerged ten seconds later in the same tie dye tank and spandex workout shorts she'd worn before her shower.

"Seriously?" Hollister said. "You're not gonna change your clothes?"

"If I want your opinion, moron, I'll give it to you."

Apparently rain in the Yucatan stopped as quickly as it started. The world steamed in the fresh sun as Sammy led the way across a cracked concrete sidewalk that cut through a courtyard filled with bushes and low, hardy looking grass.

"Holy! What the … ?" Hollister took a panicked leap backward, grabbing for the pistol he'd shoved down the waistband of his pants. A three-foot lizard ignored him from its perch on a small boulder. "Is that an alligator?"

Sammy blinked his big, watery eyes. "Put the pistola away, señor. It's just an iguana. A baby one, at that."

Hollister edged around the beast, keeping a wary eye. "You're telling me they get bigger than that?"

"Of course. Much bigger. Don't worry, the snakes keep the population down."

"Snakes and alligators. I'm in hell," Hollister mumbled.

Sammy continued down the sidewalk without a backward glance.

"What kind of Mexican name is Sammy, anyway?" Hollister said to the man's back.

Sammy didn't turn. "What kind of gringo name is Hollister?"

Crystal gave an appreciative grunt.

"You got something to say, Crystal?" Hollister said.

"The daisy's got a point. Hollister *is* a stupid name."

Casa Vieja Cabra's lobby, a separate structure from the rest of the hotel, sprawled with haphazard abandon in several directions. The café and bar sat open to the air, sending the aroma of coffee and bacon wafting from beneath a free-standing roof of posts, beams, and palm fronds.

Burt Simmons, looking fresh in a cream-colored linen suit, Panama hat and glossy Italian loafers, reclined at one of the tables reading a newspaper. He folded it as the group approached and set it down next to a coffee mug. Sunglasses covered his eyes, hiding his expression. "You're late. Sit down."

Crystal pulled out a chair to Burt's left and Sammy to his right, leaving Hollister directly across from Simmons. His own dual reflection stared back at him from the doctor's mirrored shades.

"I see you've met Sammy," Simmons said.

"I find Mr. Finch very rude," Sammy said.

"You and the rest of the free world," Burt said. "Forget it. You brought the gun?"

"Sí, señor. He has it in his pants."

"Bueno," Burt said, letting the word roll out slowly.

Getting right into the spirit of things, Mexico style.

Hollister pulled out the hog-leg and dropped it on the table with a loud thud, barrel pointing at Simmons. "What do we need this thing for? I don't do guns."

Simmons scooted out of the line of fire. "Put that thing away, you idiot! Is it loaded?"

"Sí, señor," Sammy said. "It has been loaded since 1921."

"Nineteen twenty-one? You mean this gun hasn't been fired in almost a hundred years?"

The Mexican shrugged. "You wanted a pistola? This is the only pistola in Dia Perdido."

Simmons turned to Hollister, then Crystal with a can-you-believe-this-guy look—an actor in a made-for-television courtroom drama. "Isn't this Mexico? Haven't you heard of the Cartel? Whoever heard of a gun shortage south of the border?"

Sammy offered Burt the watery-eyed stare and spoke with slow deliberation. "Sí, this is Mexico. Sí, this is Dia Perdido ... And that is a pistola, yes? What more can I tell you?"

Simmons threw up his hands. His eyes rolled skyward. "Lord, help me."

A waitress appeared with a large tray loaded with plates of eggs, bacon, beans and sliced papaya. She served them, dropped a basket of corn tortillas onto the middle of the table, then poured coffee all around.

"Are these beans low-fat?" Crystal said.

The woman gave Crystal a why-don't-you-drop-dead glare, then arched an irritated eyebrow at Sammy, who shrugged.

Simmons put a hand on the woman's arm and offered a cap-toothed, Don Juan smile. "Hey, beautiful, I'm looking for someone to show me around town. You available?"

Another arched brow. "Sorry, I don't speak English," the waitress said in un-accented English, then sauntered away, all hips and attitude. Simmons sipped his coffee and watched her go till she exited the patio café through a door to the main building. He gave a low whistle.

"Talkative gal, ain't she?" Hollister said.

"She is my cousin," Sammy said as if this constituted an explanation.

Hollister's stomach growled. He scooped a huge bite of beans and bacon into his mouth, chewed, swallowed, then pointed his fork at Simmons. "You never said what the gun was for."

Simmons dropped his shades to the end of his nose with a manicured index finger and drilled Hollister from over the rims. "My daughter won't be alone, and I'm sick of all this messing around. So, simply put, the pistol is to shoot the guy—or guys—that are with her. Dead men don't make trouble. No fuss, no muss."

Hollister shook his head. "What do you think this is, some whacked-out *48 Hours* mystery? Are you off your nut? We ain't shooting nobody."

"I'm your therapist, Hollister. You've told me things. I know you haven't been a choirboy. What's the problem?"

"Yeah, well, I've never been locked away in a Mexican prison either. And besides, that stuff was a long time ago in a galaxy far, far away. You ever heard of doctor-patient confidentiality?"

"Kill the kid that's putting his filthy hands on what's mine. He's got it coming. Maybe I'll even up your payday. We clear?" Simmons said.

Hollister shook his head. "No deal."

Crystal slurped a bite of fruit from her plate, burped the word *papaya*, then picked at a dirty fingernail. "Don't listen to the old man, doc … I'll shoot 'em."

Simmons grinned. "Atta girl."

Chapter Forty-two

The Problem with Walking on Water

The thing about movies, as realistic as they could be in the modern days of computer-generated imagery and multi-million-dollar budgets—they were powerless to capture the true experience. Sitting in a comfortable theater, sure, you might see and hear an actor clinging to the wheel while the ocean raged—but what about the smell? What about the bucking deck beneath your feet? The salt water, wild on the wind, stinging your skin?

Will it ever stop?

Two full days now and not a break in the storm. Wet hair whipped Paradise's face. She'd stared at the rolling horizon so long her eyes threatened to cross. The bright side? She'd learned to sip coffee from a to-go mug on the slamming deck of a ninety-foot ketch.

Doc poked his head out of the salon door and shouted over the wind. "You ready to come in?"

"Third time you've asked in the last ten minutes!"

"I'm worried about you."

"I'm harnessed in! As long as the boat keeps floating, I'm fine."

"Then how about some company?"

"Go to sleep, Doc! You have another hour before it's your watch. My turn!"

Doc gave a reluctant nod and dropped back down.

Ten minutes later, he popped up again. "I'm taking over. Don't argue. I know you're tired."

She wanted to argue, but he was right; her muscles, rubbery with exhaustion, confirmed the fact. With reluctance, she shuffled over and let him take the helm. "Thanks."

He smiled. "Just get some rest."

Paradise climbed down the steps to the salon on wooden legs and collapsed onto a couch.

Lan sat sipping coffee and fiddling with the knobs on the ship's radar at the navigation station. "Great day for a sail, eh?"

Paradise pushed hair from her face. "So you keep saying."

"You're not letting a little weather dampen your enthusiasm for yachting, are you?"

The *Lazarus* crested a wave and took a stomach-churning drop.

"Is that what this is?"

"It's life, Miss Scarlett. You take the bad with the good."

"Don't remind me about the movie. Arnie's practically sitting in the corner sucking his thumb, he's so worked up. So much for getting back to Texas."

"You were able to reach him? On the satellite phone?"

"Yes. Everything's still on schedule, providing I can get home."

"Well, girl, home is a funny word. Maybe somebody's trying to tell you something."

Paradise pointed at the life vest stretched tight around Lan's big frame to the point of exploding. "Don't they make those in extra large?"

"This is a double XL. Struck a nerve, did I? About somebody trying to tell you something?"

Paradise rolled her eyes. "That's the problem. *Everybody's* trying to tell me something. Nobody ever *stops* telling me things. Are you joining the chorus?"

"Want to know the real reason I left the business?"

"I'm not sure I want to hear it anymore."

"Bottom line—I was lonely. Surrounded by a constant barrage of friends, agents, press, you name it. But lonely, nonetheless."

"Sometimes I feel tiny. Like a single atom lost in the universe. At least, that's how I picture it."

"Yes, sort of. The thing is, my loneliness was not for people. It was for someone or something I'd never even met. Didn't even know existed."

"And you found that something? That someone? Out here on the sea?"

"I did. Thanks to our friend, Paco. See, I'd never really thought about God. And Jesus was just the joker on the cross the Catholics lost sleep over. None of that was for me. Then Paco hitched that ride out of New Orleans, and everything changed."

Paradise studied Lan's craggy face. "What changed? Did he talk to you? Jesus?"

"Tell you the truth, I think he'd been talking for a long time. I'd just gotten good at ignoring it."

"Then you really heard him?"

"I did, in a way. And guess what? I wasn't lonely anymore."

"What if he wants me to do something I don't want to do?"

"Are you sure you don't want to do it?"

Paradise leaned her head back and closed her eyes. "I know I want to act, to be a star. And here it is right in front of me. I can't ignore that."

"Why do you have to? Look, if you're hearing the voice of the Creator of the Universe, he's not telling you not to be you. He's just saying, *Come home, your Father misses you.*"

"I've never known a father like that."

"That's the thing. He knows *you*."

"What about Doc?"

Lan sipped his coffee and shrugged. "Doc's no accident. But that's your call. The man's head over heels for you, obviously."

"Funny. I never think of Doc as a man."

Lightning crashed—a thousand flashbulbs outside the portholes.

"I think you do. And I think that's part of your little conundrum."

"How long will it last?"

"Your feelings for Doc?"

"No, the storm. It's been two days, hasn't it? It feels like a year."

Lan shoved the cup back into the holder. "I'm not sure. Easy figures the weather radar's down. Storm doesn't even show up. I'm messing with it now. See if I can't figure it out. Might have been the lightning or something. Why don't you go get some sleep? You look exhausted."

"I'm fine. But I *could* use the rest."

"All right. I'll rouse you when it's time again."

In her small cabin, she stripped out of her wet clothes and slid beneath the blankets. Had she ever been this tired? On the dresser, securely fastened with his Velcro strips, Truck Stop Jesus' head bobbed like a bull rider on a rodeo bull.

Inches away, the fury of the wind and waves buffeted the bulkhead of the ketch.

Paradise cracked an eye and glanced at Jesus. "You're still smiling."

"*Why not? You brought me down here where it's warm and dry. I think you're starting to like me.*"

"I just didn't want you to blow away and waste my five dollars and ninety-nine cents."

"You'd miss me."

"You heard, I suppose, what Lan said in there?"

Truck Stop Jesus bobbled. *"I did."*

"Will I be small forever?"

"Not if I can help it. Will you go to Mexico?"

"I don't know what to do. I can't lose the movie."

"I didn't ask you to. I asked you to go to Mexico. Don't get off the subject. You don't want to go to Mexico because you love Doc, and every minute you stay with him you come closer and closer to admitting it. You're stubborn."

"How can you say I'm stubborn? I thought you were supposed to be kind ... loving and all that."

"Love tells the truth. I knew another stubborn person once. I came to him—in a storm a lot like this."

"I saw the movie. Walking on the water, right? It always bothered me that your robe must have gotten wet."

"Not the most comfortable thing, I'll admit. That Peter, he was stubborn like you. But he was good like you, too. I told him to get out of the boat, remember?"

"Yes. And he did," Paradise said.

"He walked on the water for a while. Then he stumbled."

"And you caught him."

Jesus bobbled. *"I did."*

"You want me to get out of the boat, don't you?"

"I do. In Mexico."

"I can't even *get* to Mexico. All I can do is wait for the storm to stop. That and try to keep my eyes open when Lan says it's my watch."

Jesus' permanent grin widened. *"I'm the Calmer of the Storm, remember? And do you really think a breath of wind on a speck of a planet hanging in space is an issue for me? I imagine galaxies into existence just for the joy of it. Why don't you come home, Paradise? I miss you."*

Something broken and long forgotten stirred deep. A tiny vestige of belonging. *Something to steal dreams. Something to be fought off. But ...*

"What if I agree to go to Mexico? Just for a day or two?"

"Are you saying you will?"

"I don't ... Oh, all right. I'm saying I will."

Something changed she couldn't immediately place. Then ... yes. The sound. That was it. The shrill whistle of the wind through the rigging above, a constant aural companion for over forty-eight hours—so long that her ears had become numb to it—was gone.

Silence deafened.

"What happened?"

Jesus shrugged his plastic shoulders. "*Why don't you go up and take a look?*"

Paradise dropped from the bunk, threw on dry clothes and scrambled to the *Lazarus'* cockpit where Doc and Lan already stood.

Only a happy tropical breeze touched the sails above. Long gentle rollers stretched out on the open ocean.

The sun smiled. A gull offered a celebratory cry.

Easy's head popped up through a hatch, his eyes wide.

Lan did a slow turn. "What happened? What in the world is going on?"

Paradise dropped to a bench. "I told him I'd go."

"What? Told who?" Lan said.

Paradise watched Doc for a long few seconds. His rain-soaked hair dripped and his body steamed in the sun. He had a five-day beard and a coffee stain running down the front of his T-shirt. So handsome he made her heart hurt.

"Let's go to Mexico, Doc," she said.

His smile lines went deep. "All right, beautiful. Let's go to Mexico."

Chapter Forty-three

Drawing Moustaches on the Saints

Sammy seemed infinitely proud of his ancient diesel Toyota Land Cruiser. Hollister thought the back seat could have used a little more leg room.

Plus the stinking back window wouldn't roll down, and Crystal was beyond ripe.

Simmons rode shotgun up front, listening to Sammy's non-stop informal tour.

Yeah, of Dante's nine levels of hell. Ugh, Mexico. What Hollister wouldn't give for an In-N-Out burger right about now.

"So, Sammy," Simmons said. "What would a guy have to do to get a little time with your cousin?"

Sammy didn't turn. "What cousin?"

"I thought the waitress at the café was your cousin?"

"I have many cousins, señor."

"Yeah, but what would I have to do to get some time?"

"That one? You'd have to crawl back in your mother's womb and come back out Mexican. She doesn't like gringos. Even rich ones."

"Now who's rude?" Hollister muttered.

"You ask, señor. I tell you the truth. It is what it is."

Sammy steered, bounced, and verbally tortured them through a never-ending maze of adobe, metal, and even cardboard shacks. Hollister grudgingly admitted to himself the Mexican's usefulness. They'd never have navigated this place on their own, and the GPS in the Hummer had handed in its resignation a day and a half ago, suggesting with irritation that they make a U-turn in two-hundred-thirty-seven miles.

Simmons wiped his brow with a silk handkerchief. "What a dump. Sammy, please tell me you don't live in one of these shacks."

A boy, snot running down his face, ran into the narrow dirt street chasing a soccer ball, and Sammy slowed. The boy smiled and waved, and Sammy gave a couple toots on the horn.

Simmons reached over and added his own long blast. "Get out of the way, you little brat! C'mon, Sammy, move. Let's get there, already! I'm roasting in here."

Hollister pressed down the strong urge to break the good doctor's arm.

The boy joined a small army of others like him on a large patch of dirt that served as a field. Jungle pressed in around.

"How much farther?" Crystal asked.

"Just ahead," Sammy said.

The barrio gave way to bigger, very old buildings.

"This part of Dia Perdido has been here for four hundred and fifty years. Before the United States of America was even a gleam in George Washington's wooden eye," Sammy said.

"Teeth," Simmons replied.

"*Qué?*" Sammy said. "What?"

"*Teeth*. He had wooden *teeth*. How could he see if he had wooden eyes?"

Sammy shrugged. "That's *your* problem. That over there?" He pointed toward a graceful, two-story adobe building. "That is the Mission Del Dia Perdido."

A high arch topped the mission, holding a large bell, green with patina.

Sammy parked the Land Cruiser on the street. The engine clacked and sputtered for a full ten seconds after he switched off the ignition.

Hollister swung the door open and breathed in deeply, trying to purge Crystal from his nostrils. Out of nowhere, a small army of children engulfed his legs. Sammy shouted at the hoard in Spanish, and they began to disperse, though with obvious reluctance.

"Aggressive little ankle biters, ain't they?" Hollister said.

"They're excited. It's not often visitors come to the home," Sammy said.

"Yeah, Simmons said something about that. It's a home for children, right?"

"Sí. Some orphans live here, and some come from the barrio to have a meal and to play. The staff is very good to them. I hope you will not give them trouble."

"What a daisy," Crystal said.

Hollister shot her a warning glance. "No trouble. We just want to look around."

"We're very interested in the history," Simmons added.

"Please don't insult me, señor. I'm not a fool. You paid me well to guide you and provide with the pistola. I do these things. I ask no questions. I tell no one. All I ask is that you make no trouble for the staff and the children here."

"Or?" Crystal said.

Sammy waved an arm back toward the barrio. "Or my cousins will be very upset. And like I said before, I have many cousins."

"We just want to look around. That's it, okay?" Hollister said. "No trouble. Like the doctor says—consider us just a few curious gringos."

"Sí. Okay. I'll wait with the car. I've seen the church."

A white woman emerged from the mission. Young. Pretty in an I-live-in-Mexico-and-couldn't-care-less-about-makeup sort of way. Thin blonde hair pulled back into a severe ponytail. "Welcome. Sammy told me you'd be coming. I'm Leena Rogers, the orphanage director. Can I show you around?"

Simmons stepped forward, making introductions all around. His hand lingered too long on the girl's, and Hollister's skin crawled.

The thick, adobe walls kept the sanctuary surprisingly cool. Pews filled much of the available space. Thick columns rose floor to towering ceiling, on either side of the center aisle. Two confessionals beckoned and threatened from one wall, and a stage, altar, and pulpits fronted the airy space. Niches stuffed with statues of saints filled the high wall behind. Frescos covered other walls. "This is the main chapel, of course," Leena said. "Built by Spanish missionaries around 1560."

"And it's still a Catholic church? I thought it was a children's home. Run by Protestants or Baptists or something," Hollister said.

Leena squinted up at him. "Baptists *are* Protestants."

"Oh, okay. Sorry."

She laughed. "Don't be. Just think of most of the Christian faith outside of Catholicism as Protestant. It's not important. But yes, the home is run by a non-denominational church based out of Seattle. That's where I'm from. I oversee things, but teams from various churches come down from the States about every other month to fill out the staffing. Some people come more often or even spend the whole winter down here. They do Vacation Bible School, puppet shows—all kinds of things. It's no end of work. We also have a few locals on the full-time payroll as well. We've built dorms, a kitchen, common rooms, a playground—all kinds of things—out on the back of the property. That's where the kids and staff live. Do you want to come see? The children love visitors."

"Not particularly. What's upstairs?" Simmons said.

"I do," Crystal said. "Let's go see the kids."

Hollister raised an eyebrow. "What are you talking about?"

She flashed her shark teeth. "I want to see the kids, sweetie dear."

Leena's eyes flicked between the two. "Um ... upstairs ... some offices nobody uses, another small chapel, and the stairway up to the bell tower."

Simmons fanned himself with the Panama. "Fascinating. No need to trouble you. Do you mind if we look around on our own? Do some exploring?"

Leena reached up and tightened her ponytail. A nervous habit, maybe. "But I thought you were here to take a look at the ministry."

Simmons made his way to a wall and studied the fresco. "Yeah ... well ... you thought wrong. We just want to see the church."

"I'll see 'em," Crystal repeated. "I'll see the kids."

Visible alarm bells registered in Leena's eyes. "Yeah. Okay. The church is public and never locked, so you're free to look around and take as long as you like. I'll be getting back to the kids then, if you don't mind. Nice to meet you." She glanced at Crystal. "You sure you want to meet them?"

"Love 'em. Love the kids." Crystal rolled her head back and her neck cracked. "Let's see 'em."

Simmons turned to Hollister once the ladies had exited. "What was that about? Since when does Crystal like kids? Or *anybody*, for that matter?"

"I have no idea," Hollister said. "She's an interesting bunch of women. That head of hers is a strange and scary place."

"Is she safe with them? The kids? Out there?"

"Absolutely not."

"Oh, well. Leave it alone. Let's look for the gold. Where do we start?"

Hollister shrugged. "You're the doctor. You tell me."

"It's been, what, three hundred years since those brothers had the coins? I bet this place looked pretty much the same back then. Lucky for us, they built separately out back for the little riffraff. If they had torn into this place to remodel or something, they might have found it already."

"You know, nobody ever said whatever those guys hid even *was* gold. It might have been worthless. Or a map to some stupid myth like the Fountain of Youth. I read it online. Those Spaniards ran all over the place looking for junk like that."

"Nah, it's gold. Has to be. Otherwise, why go to all the trouble?" Simmons took a slow three-hundred-sixty-degree survey of the room. "Our advantage is that the locals never knew anything was ever hidden here, so they wouldn't have thought to look. *And* we got here first. Before my tramp daughter and her friends."

If there *was* gold, there had to be a way of cutting Simmons out. Maybe Crystal was right about pounding the guy and leaving him in a ditch. It certainly would be an enjoyable workout.

"Yeah. I guess."

"Let's start upstairs and work our way down."

"You're the boss, boss."

The bell tower proved to be solid adobe and offered nothing but a crystalline view of the Caribbean where a large island rose up on the horizon. From the tourist map back in the hotel room, Hollister marked it as Cozumel. Closer in to shore, a double-masted sailboat approached the mainland, sails white against the sea and sky.

What would that be like? To sail off without a thought?

The search through the upper rooms continued to disappointment. Solid bare walls of thick, mud brick offered no opportunity for a hiding place.

Nothing, nothing, and more nothing.

That left the sanctuary ...

Once back downstairs, Hollister moved to the center of the space, trying to put himself in the brothers' shoes.

Where?

"Don't just stand there like an idiot. Start looking. You know, false walls, loose bricks—you've seen the movies." Simmons began moving along the edges of the room, tapping as he went.

Hollister ignored him. The brothers had been both careful and smart, secreting the location of whatever-it-was on two separate coins. Clue and cipher—both useless without the other. This was too easy. Besides, why hide something of value in such a public venue? Even if you were planning on returning for it soon, as the brothers must have been, why risk such a public place where the chances of someone stumbling on it would be high?

Simmons moved to the platform, tapping, and stomping.

Good, knock yourself out.

The wall-to-wall frescos pulled Hollister's eyes upward. Even the ceiling. Blue sky filled with angels soared high above the tile floor.

No. Hollister wouldn't have hidden treasure here ... But maybe another clue? Yeah, definitely another clue. One that could be in the frescos. He moved his eyes along the closest wall with forced deliberation, and he began to take the scenes apart in his mind inch-by-inch, stroke-by-stroke. Some of the scenes he recognized from stories he'd heard or read. Peter denying Christ in the courtyard. Judas and his thirty pieces of silver. Along the wall, scene after scene, story after visual story, he went.

Nothing.

The fresco on the high wall behind the pulpit made little sense. Some biblical epic he apparently wasn't familiar with. A muscled, bearded man in the midst of a nasty battle held a sword above his head. The weapon dripped with enemy blood, and the slain lay around him in piles of limbs and other body parts. High above, both a sun and moon hung over the gruesome scene.

More like a late night horror flick than Sunday morning material. Real *Elvira* stuff. Hollister studied the depiction for long minutes, but nothing jumped out. Nothing, nothing, and more nothing.

It had to be there somewhere.

Simmons grunted from the stage as he threw his weight against the massive altar. "Hollister, when do you think was the last time anyone moved this thing?"

"Probably never. Must weigh at least a ton."

"C'mon, get your head in the game. You have to think like the brothers. If you wanted to hide something in here, where would you do it? I'd say behind something like this. Give me a hand."

Hollister sighed but threw his considerable weight into moving the piece away from the wall.

Maybe a ton wasn't an exaggeration.

The altar creaked and budged a fraction of an inch. Hollister moved his hands, searching for better purchase, found it, then heaved again. The wood groaned as it slid, but once inertia kicked in, the thing kept sliding.

Burt knelt down, examining the wall and floor. "There's a good chance nobody's seen this wall in hundreds of years."

Hollister still studied the fresco above. "Yeah. I've got chills."

Dull thumps from Burt ... "Wait. Did you hear that?"

Another thump. This one hollow sounding.

"There's a hollow place back here." Burt reached up and grabbed a silver candelabra from the altar and started beating at the adobe wall. So much for respecting sacred places. The guy never ceased to amaze. What was next, mustaches on the saints? Still, Hollister couldn't help crouching for a better look. Maybe Simmons was onto something. Hey, even a broken clock is right twice a day.

"I'm through!" Dust rose as Simmons yanked dirt and chunks of adobe brick from a hole about a foot high and two wide. "Definitely something in here. This has to be it!"

Hollister rocked back and forth, trying to see around Simmons. "What is it?"

"A box. Yeah, it's a wooden box. Heavy. Old, too. But it's locked." Simmons pulled the object from the hole, and it dropped to the floor with a heavy thud— and the unmistakable jangle of coins.

Lots of coins.

Chapter Forty-four

Dominoes and Tequila

Doc stood on the bow holding a line, ready to make landing. Lan guided the *Lazarus* around a rough, limestone breakwater and motored into a small harbor nestled against the jungles of the Yucatan Peninsula.

Doc stole a glance at Paradise, who watched the shore from the rail, shading her eyes with a hand.

Scarf and cat-eye sunglasses—Audrey today.

Birds screeched in the dense forest, and the air hung heavy and hot as if shaking off the natural law of gas form and opting for solid instead. A narrow beach stretched out on either side of the breakwater, dotted with a few shacks and a thatch-roofed cantina. Five rust-streaked fishing boats and an oxidized, fiberglass sloop—waterline heavy with hanging marine growth—populated the crooked, sun-baked docks.

"Hey! Chuey!" Lan called from his perch behind the wheel.

A tin-roofed, stained stucco building sulked in the heat at the edge of a sand and crushed shell parking lot. A man stepped out of it into the bright day. He blocked the sun from his eyes with his hand. "Ah! Señor Lan! *Bienvenida!* Welcome, my friend! Welcome!" He scurried toward them at a fast trot, pumping short, bowed legs.

"Dat's Chuey, the harbor master." Easy stood at Doc's elbow, ready to climb down and catch the line on Lan's order.

"Isn't he hot?" Doc said, taking in the man's grease-stained jeans and long-sleeved shirt.

"No. He was born here. Right on dis beach. Dis ain't nothin' to him."

The man arrived at a patched and splintered dock at the same time Lan dropped the *Lazarus* into reverse and edged up. The boat inched slowly to the side and gently touched the berth.

"Look at that," Lan said. "Wouldn't have cracked an egg."

Easy tossed a line to Chuey, who caught it and wrapped it around a cleat. Several days' worth of gray beard covered the man's face. A ragged captain's cap that had the word *Harbormaster* handwritten on it in English with a black permanent marker was cocked down over one eye. An old Pepsi bottle with a cork stuck in the top hung around his neck, fastened with a piece of twine.

"What's in the bottle?" Doc said, his voice low enough that only Easy could hear.

"Don't know, mon. But if he offers you some, don't take it. Trust me, I spent a bad, bad night on dis beach one time cause of dat nasty, little bottle."

Chuey spoke passable English, though with a heavy accent. "Señor Lan. It's been too long, amigo. I begin to wonder did you drown or something?"

Lan's reply had the easy familiarity born of long friendship. "No dice, Chuey. Davy Jones hasn't got me yet. Listen, my passengers want to go to Dia Perdido. Does your car still run?"

"Does it run? Does the sun still come up? Does my wife hide my tequila every Friday? Of course, it runs! And I still owe you one, eh? From last time? But you have to give me a ride to my sister's casa first. Feeling too old to walk today—most days, I think. And my sister, she likes to play dominoes."

Lan hopped to the dock with the agility of a much younger man and dropped a big arm around Chuey's shoulders. "No problem. And you owe me more than one, amigo. I took quite a chance for you. The Cartel is probably still ticked off about that whole deal."

Chuey laughed and waved a dismissive hand. "Those guys are always ticked off. But sí, I owe you lots. Ha! You're not bad for an old gringo hippie, eh?"

Easy jumped down and tied off the line Doc tossed him, then three more. With the *Lazarus* secured at five separate points, he gave a satisfied nod, then unfastened and lowered the wooden steps from the boat to the dock.

"Easy, take Chuey to his sister's and bring the car back, will you?" Lan said.

"Yes sir, boss," Easy replied. With Chuey leading the way, the men headed toward the parking lot, talking and laughing as they went.

Lan boarded again, and Doc and Paradise began helping him secure the sail covers.

"What did you do to make them mad, Lan? What did you call them, the Cartel? How did you help that man?" Paradise said.

"I've known Chuey for years. I like this place. There's a big, modern marina ten miles down the coast, but this one's more my style, me and Easy and the

Lazarus. The Cartel—they're bad news. Don't bother people out here in the sticks too much, but somehow Gomez—that's Chuey's nephew—got on their bad side. Something about a dice game and somebody's sister. Never quite got the details sorted out. Anyway, Gomez—he comes tearing down here one day in an old Plymouth and runs out of road in the marina lot. They'd broken his arm before he got away from them, and the guy was really hurting. He was yelling for Chuey, but Chuey'd gone into Dia Perdido to buy a present for his granddaughter's *Quinceañera*—that's a party they have when a girl turns fifteen. Gomez wasn't what you'd call smart, but not a bad guy. I got him on board, but those Cartel guys came screaming down in a big, black SUV a minute later and started yelling and waving guns. I told 'em I'd seen a guy run into the jungle, but they insisted on taking the *Lazarus* apart looking for him. Eventually, they settled down, and I guess decided not to shoot me, which was a bonus. Still don't think they ever believed me."

"I don't get it," Doc said. "If they took the *Lazarus* apart, why didn't they find Gomez?"

"Ah. The million-dollar question! This old girl has a few tricks up her sleeve. Come on down below, let me show you something."

Doc and Paradise followed Lan through the salon and down the hall to the aft cabin.

At the head of the four-poster bed, he laid his palm against part of the paneled wall. "Acts as a lever. Found it by accident one day."

A dull click sounded, and a section of the floor at the foot of the bed rose an inch. At Lan's tug, the section opened on hidden hinges, revealing a long, deep cavity.

Doc crouched at the edge, peering in. "Amazing. You'd never know this was here in a million years."

"The design's clever," Lan agreed.

"The *Lazarus* was used for smuggling?" Paradise asked.

Lan dropped the door, pushed the floor down again, and the hole disappeared without a trace. "Sure she was. Ran booze during Prohibition from Canada all the way down to the Keys. Cuba, Bahamas—it's a boat, man. The world is your backyard. Heard rumors about opiates in the South China Sea. This girl's been around a long time. When something's available in one place and discouraged in another, there'll always be someone around willing and able to capitalize on it."

"What about you? Have you been willing and able?" Paradise said.

"Let's just say I've made a wake in some gray areas, but only for worthy causes. I don't need money, and I've seen the damage people can do to one another in the name of profit. Drugs? Weapons? No thanks. But ... medicine, books, Bibles a couple times, a wandering soul here and there—we've reunited a few families. I figure I'm on this planet to help, not hurt. And now here I am playing a supporting role in *The Continuing Adventures of Doc Morales and Paradise Jones.* Might win another Oscar for this one."

"Yeah, there is that. And it's appreciated," Doc said.

A car horn blared from the direction of the marina parking lot.

"Sounds like Easy's back with the car." Lan threw Paradise a wink. "C'mon. You're gonna love this."

Back on the deck, Doc couldn't help but laugh. "You're kidding? An Olds Eighty-Eight?"

Paradise's eyes shone. "Lan, I may be in love with you."

"Well, you know, I'm lovable. Now, the Mission Del Dia Perdido is only a few miles from here. I know it well. What d'ya say we go wrangle you kids some answers?"

Chapter Forty-five

What Happens in Mexico Stays in Mexico

"Shoot him!" Crystal mouthed for the hundredth time since they'd gotten back in Sammy's Land Cruiser.

Thankfully, Hollister had managed to get the windows down, and the wind and barrio noise drowned out any communication going on in the back seat, whispered or otherwise. He eyed the back of Simmons' head and the perfect haircut. *Probably cost five hundred bucks.* He also noticed the doctor kept a tight grip on the wooden box on his lap.

"Shut up!" Hollister hissed, exaggerating the words with his mouth so Crystal would get the picture.

Crystal showed her shark-toothed grin, eyes wide. "Shoooooot hiiiiiim!"

"Shuuuuut uuuuuup!"

Not that the idea didn't appeal on some level. Just the sight of the back of the guy's head almost sent Hollister over the edge.

Burt turned in his seat. His eyes narrowed at the expression on Hollister's face. "What?"

Hollister conjured blandness. "What, what?"

"I was going to suggest we open my box over a nice bottle of merlot. Although I suppose you'd probably prefer a beer."

"What do you mean, *your* box? And why would I prefer a beer?"

Simmons shrugged. "There are wine people, then there are *good* wine people, and then there are beer people. No offense."

"And never the twain shall meet," Hollister said.

"Sweetie doesn't drink anyway," Crystal said.

"What?" *Since when?*

Simmons' eyes tracked a group of white-bloused, plaid-skirted schoolgirls crossing the rutted road. "Did you just call him *sweetie*? Very nice, Crystal. Looks like our counseling time paid off, yes?"

Crystal put her hand on Hollister's arm. "We think we'd like to continue our sessions. Could we meet later today?"

Hollister shook his head and let it fall back to the headrest. The woman was one hundred percent certifiable.

Simmons wiped the back of his neck with a handkerchief. "I'll be happy to continue our time when we're back in LA. Maybe we can work a fee schedule out of the remaining forty thousand. That is, if you do indeed contribute something to finding the little tramp, which I'm beginning to doubt."

Hollister stared at Crystal. *Counseling?*

Crystal did a car-seat dance move—churn the butter—and mouthed, "Shooooot hiiiiiim!"

Hollister rubbed his temples. "You know, Doctor, the girl may not even show up here. Why do you care, anyway? We found the gold. Why not just leave well enough alone? Let her go live her life. Why do you need her?"

"Need her? Interesting choice of words. Psychologically speaking, that's fairly accurate. I *need* her. Bravo, beer man. Let's just say the little tease has been begging for my affection since she was twelve. Prancing around in those movie costumes of hers. Showing off by the pool. She's not going to walk away from me and get away with it."

Forty grand, forty schmand. How fast could I get an arm around the guy's throat? "She walked away? I thought you were the one who turned *her* down? You got a thing for young girls, Burt?"

Simmons turned, eyes widening a fraction. "Burt? It's *Dr. Simmons* to you. And it's not my fault. From a medical perspective, I mean. Young girls, women ... it's a condition. I'm a victim."

"And that *condition* makes you get handsy with your daughter?" *This guy makes me wanna puke.*

Crystal tried to pull the gun from Hollister's waist, but he pushed her hand back.

Simmons' face flushed. "You know what, Hollister? I'm getting sick of your stupid comments. Handsy? First of all, she's my *stepdaughter*, not daughter—so get your mind out of the gutter. Good schools, clothes, vacations—I *own* her. Get it? Besides, she practically begged for it that night. My wife was stone-cold passed out on the couch as usual. I'd had a few greyhounds myself. Just enough to get myself feeling loose and good. So I went into the pool house and—good timing—she was changing. Sending all the signals with her body but pretending that insipid innocence of hers, just like when she was a kid. So I told her what time it was. She could finally pony up, or I'd cut her off. Her choice. Then she had the gall to hit me with a lamp as if we weren't two consenting human beings. If she says I forced myself on her, so what? My property, my money, my way. Besides, she's nuts. And it's her word against the most respected psychiatrist in LA."

"So you admit you assaulted her."

"Oh, brother. Call it what you want. She's a woman. I'm a man. I have urges."

"Yeah, well, leave us out of it."

Simmons' eyes rolled. "I'll talk slow so you can understand. I hired you, and you do what I say. Simple. If I want a cup of coffee, you'll bring it. If I want you to do jumping jacks, you'll do them. If I want you to bring my tramp of a stepdaughter home so I can take her over my knee and spank her, then you'll do *that*. What I do with her is none of your concern. And *whatever* it is, she deserves it. She probably even *wants* it. This is exactly what I mean by *beer* people. You always insist on overlooking the obvious." Something on the street caught his gaze, and his head swiveled left. "Hey, Sammy. Wasn't that your cousin? The hot tamale from the café?"

"Why?"

"She's walking with a white man. With his arm around her."

"Yes, so? That's her husband. He's from Michigan, I think. She married him last year."

Simmons turned, drawing his brows together. "Husband? I thought she hated gringos?"

Sammy raised a shoulder. "She does. She hates *him*, too. Women, you know? Who can figure them?"

Simmons craned his neck through the open window. "Tell you what, Sammy. You bring that chile pepper to my room later, and I'll see if I can't cool her off."

Sammy's knuckles turned white on the steering wheel.

"Take it easy, Simmons. You're talking about the guy's family," Hollister said.

Simmons shrugged. "You know the old saying. What happens in Mexico *stays* in Mexico, right?"

"That's Vegas," Crystal said. "And it doesn't work. Trust me, I tried it."

Simmons turned in his seat. "Hey, Crystal, I've got to ask. What's with the orphans? Since when do you like kids? You know, I mean other than for snacks. Why'd you want to go see the brat factory back there?"

Crystal bolted forward, but Hollister caught her with his thick forearm.

Simmons lifted his hands in mock surrender, grinning. "Down, girl! Good thing your owner's got your leash! Geez, I'm just kidding. Relax."

Hollister pushed Crystal back, eyes drilling Simmons. "I ought to let her bite your head off and spit it down your neck. She grew up in an orphanage. Keep your mouth shut."

"Or what, beer man?"

"Or I'll knock your teeth out of the back of your skull."

"Ha! I love you guys. You're non-stop entertainment." Simmons turned away and started to whistle *La Cucaracha* through his teeth.

The drop of sweat dripping from the five-hundred-dollar haircut, the insults, the perverted disrespect ...

Hollister's fingers brushed the big pistol shoved in his waistband. "Hey, Sammy. Pull off onto that road up there. Find us a place back in the woods. I saw a toolbox in the back. Let's crack this box open and see what we have. I'm sick of waiting."

Simmons's eyes rolled. "See? Beer people. No patience. No sense of the dramatic. All about the instant gratification. Okay, children, since we can't wait, we'll do it your way. And I'll tell you what. I'm feeling generous. If it's a lot of money, I may even give you some kind of finder's fee. Not that you actually *found* anything."

"What do you mean, finder's fee? Whatever's in that box is ours," Hollister said.

Simmons ignored him. "Up there, Sammy. Pull off right there."

Sammy cranked the wheel, and the Land Cruiser came to a stop in a small clearing pressed in on three sides by dense brush and jungle.

The four exited the car, and Simmons placed the box on the hood while Hollister fetched the toolbox. No hammer, but the socket set contained a large ratchet that seemed heavy enough. That and a screwdriver should do the trick.

Simmons grabbed the tools out of Hollister's hands. "I'll do the honors. Sammy, hold it steady." He placed the screwdriver against the lock and gave it a smack with the ratchet. The sound rang loud in the still afternoon, and a flock of birds lifted from a tree, wings beating.

"Piece of junk didn't budge," Simmons said.

Crystal crowded close. "Hit it again."

The next swing of the ratchet brought a cracking sound.

"Ha! Side of the lid broke in. Must have been rotten. Moment of truth …" Simmons put his hand on the lid, preparing to open. "Drum roll, please …"

Everything's a production with this guy. Hollister gripped the butt of the pistol. If the box turned out to be a fluke of some sort, he'd keep the doctor around to assure they'd get the second half of the eighty-thou. But one glint of gold and Simmons was on his way to shake hands with the devil. With the whole world revolving around him, the good doctor would never see it coming. The forty grand they already had and a box of gold? Hollister could live with that. And Simmons said it himself—what happens in Mexico *stays* in Mexico. *One less pervert loose on the street.*

"What's this?" Simmons said, staring into the box.

Crystal pulled the box to her. "Don't look like gold. Coins, though."

Hollister relaxed his grip on the pistol, but only slightly.

Sammy reached in and pulled out a coin. "Congratulations, Señor Simmons. You've found yourself a box full of pesos. Must be two thousand. Maybe three. That would be close to two hundred dollars US."

Simmons' ears reddened. "Pesos? Just pesos? But they're at least old, right? They must be valuable?"

Sammy held the coin up to the light, squinted and chuckled. "Oh, sí! Pretty old! This one says 1983."

Chapter Forty-six

Falling Through the Cracks

No nieces or nephews. Kid-less single friends. The fast paced, audition-filled life of an aspiring Hollywood actress—Paradise could probably count the hours she'd spent around children on one hand. But the cacophony of noise and tiny bodies that engulfed her in front of the Mission Del Dia Perdido made up for a lifetime of juvenile deprivation in five seconds. She tried her best to focus on one child at a time, but the situation overwhelmed her. She found a small brown hand in each of hers. Girls no taller than her waist, big brown eyes staring up at her.

Doc, Lan, and Easy received no lighter sentences. Doc—on his knees in earnest conversation; Lan—a little girl in each arm and a boy seated like a king on his shoulders. Easy trotted up the street with a group of boys, working a soccer ball between his feet like Beckham.

The pint-size army crowded and shrieked, laughed and tugged all the way to the front door of the mission where a young, ponytailed blonde woman waited, smiling. She shooed the children away in machine-gun Spanish.

"I heard the noise! Welcome to Mission Del Dia Perdido. Lan! It's good to see you again. It's been way too long," the young woman said—English this time.

"You, too, Leena. Brought you some visitors." Lan made introductions all around.

"Lan, do you know everyone in the Caribbean?" Doc said.

"I get around, kid. I've dropped off a few necessities here at the mission a time or two. Last time it was a few cases of antibiotics, if I remember right. Picked 'em up in the Keys."

"And much needed, along with all the toys he's not mentioning," Leena said. "Lan's a long-time friend and, honestly, a hero here. Our southern Santa Claus. He's even taken some of the children sailing. Where's Easy, by the way?"

"Headed up the street with a soccer ball and a million kids, last I saw. He'll be back when he wears 'em out," Lan said.

"They're a non-stop adventure, no doubt about it." Leena turned to Doc. "Are you here to see the facility?"

"Kind of. We'd like to look around the mission, if you don't mind," Doc said.

Leena's expression narrowed. "Seems like a popular thing to do today."

Doc paused a beat. "Someone else was here?"

"Can I ask why you want to see the mission?" Leena said.

Doc glanced up and down the street. "It's kind of a long story. Can we talk about it inside?"

Leena raised a questioning eyebrow but nodded and led the way inside.

The cool interior of the adobe building belied the Yucatan heat, caressing Paradise's skin. Something warm moved against her hand, and she looked down, realizing with a start that one of the little girls had failed to flee with the rest of the retreat and had slipped a tiny hand in hers. Wide, pool-of-chocolate eyes stared up, unblinking.

"Hello! Where did you come from?" Paradise said.

"That's Sofia," Leena said. "She's just come to us in the last couple weeks. Her mother hopped a bus for Mexico City and didn't look back. Only seventeen, if you can believe it. No one knows what happened to the father or even who he was. Common story around here, I'm afraid. This is the first time Sofia's made any connection with anyone here. That's a big first step! But is she bothering you? *Ven aqui,* Sofia! Leave the nice lady alone!"

The tiny hand squeezed tighter.

"No, no! That's okay! I don't mind at all," Paradise said.

"You're sure?"

"Oh yes. She's adorable."

Leena turned to Doc. "Like I said, we had some others come today. Quite a popular spot for the middle of the Yucatan jungle. I left them alone, and they vandalized the place. Who would do that? To a church?"

"Vandalized?" Doc said.

"Yes! They moved the altar and caved in the wall with a candlestick. Can you imagine? I called the priest, and he's beside himself. He's a nice man, but I'd be very careful about your intentions here."

"Can we see where they did the damage?" Doc asked.

"Sure." She led the way.

On the platform, Doc knelt and examined the hole. He looked up at Lan and Paradise. "A false wall. There was something here for sure. You can see marks in the dust where they dragged it out."

"Something hidden?" Leena asked. "You know, I had a feeling about them from the start. And then they were so rude!"

"A couple, by any chance? Big guy? Bald? And a lady that looks like she spends all her time lifting weights and torturing babies?"

"Oh, yeah, that's them. Absolutely. Hollister and Crystal were their names. But it was the other guy—Burt, I think—that was so rude."

A chill danced up Paradise's spine. "Burt?"

"Uh huh. The three of them in here, plus Sammy, who was driving. He waited in the car," Leena said.

"Burt Simmons?" Paradise said.

"He didn't mention a last name. Older, tan, good looking. Wealthy, I think. Fancy shoes and a linen suit. Who wears a suit in Dia Perdido?"

Strength fled Paradise's legs, and the room closed in. All the brave talk about going back to Los Angeles flew out the window with the realization ... *Burt is here? So close?* "Doc, we have to go! Get back to the boat. Go somewhere. Please, anywhere!"

Doc put his arms around her and pulled her to him. She didn't resist.

"Nobody's gonna hurt you, okay? I promise," Doc said.

The sanctuary door opened, and Easy stepped in, shirt soaked with sweat.

"Easy, watch the front, would you?" Doc called. "We may have company close by, and we need some time to look around. They're Americans. Two of them are the ones that chased us in Texas. May be three of them now. Yell if you see anybody coming."

"You got it, Doc. I sound de alarm, don't worry." Easy ducked back out the door.

"I don't know, Doc," Lan said. "Looks like they found what they were looking for. They're long gone now. I'm thinking we're a day late and a dollar short."

"I don't think so. Look at the fresco behind the altar—where the hole is. The paint around the edge, it's brighter—newer. Doesn't look original. If somebody hid something there, it was recent. Or at least, more recent than our Spanish brothers. I'll bet it had nothing to do with them."

"Brothers? What brothers? What in the world's going on?" asked Leena.

"Tell you what, Doc," Lan said. "I'm pretty sure I've got all the pertinent details down. Why don't you and Paradise take a look around, and I'll fill Leena in on the where, who, and why."

Doc nodded. He turned to Leena. "You're sure it's okay if we look around?"

"Of course. Now you've got me curious," Leena said.

"Thanks," Doc said as he headed toward the back of the sanctuary.

Paradise followed. "What are we looking for exactly?"

"I'm not sure. But I know this—I would never have hidden something I really didn't want to be found here in the building. It wouldn't make sense. Too many people in and out. Too much chance of someone stumbling on the hiding place."

"But they must have thought they'd come back for it. And that whatever it was wouldn't be hidden for too long."

"Even so. It wasn't like they traveled in planes back then. They'd be away for months. Maybe years. They couldn't know how long."

Doc stepped back and studied the floor-to-ceiling mural before them. The first of several giant depictions of Bible stories covering every wall.

"The biblical account of creation. In layers representing the seven days, from bottom to top, see?" He moved down the wall to a depiction of a ship surrounded by perishing humanity begging for rescue. "Here's the flood. And this next must be Christ in the Garden of Gethsemane. No particular order, New or Old Testament, I guess."

"You know these stories that well?" Paradise said.

"Sure. I've heard them all my life."

Paradise followed as Doc moved around the room, narrating as he went. The artist had spared no detail in his visual storytelling. Sofia tugged and held up her arms—universal kid sign for *pick me up*. Paradise leaned down and scooped the little girl into her arms. Light as a feather.

Leena and Lan joined them as Doc scrutinized a giant Judas throwing coins to the floor in front of a group of stern looking men.

"Imagine. Jesus betrayed for thirty pieces of silver," Leena said.

"Hard to fathom. God in flesh," Lan added.

Doc reached out and touched the painting lightly with his fingertips. "Not silver, though. These coins look like gold."

"It's a trick of the light," Leena said. "It filters in at different angles as the sun moves, and the color of the coins changes through the day. It's one of the things we show to tourists and pilgrims. In the early days of the mission, people thought it was a miracle. Now we know the artist used several different composites of metal flake in the paint to catch the light. Very clever."

Doc studied the wall intently.

"What is it, Doc?" Paradise said.

"Twenty-eight," Doc replied. "There are only twenty-eight coins. Not thirty."

"That's right, good eye," Leena said. "One of the painter's little curiosities—the missing coins. There've been lots of theories over the years. My personal opinion is that he was going for realism and figured at least two out of thirty would bounce away or fall in a crack between the stones."

"Two coins. Gold. That might not be a coincidence." Doc started down the wall, scrutinizing one scene after another.

On the platform, he paused before the massive mural of Joshua's lost day.

A thump sounded from beneath the front pew, accompanied by a child's laugh. Sofia swiveled in Paradise's arms and giggled.

"I think we're being spied on," Leena said, then pointed to the wall. "*Dia Perdido*—The Lost Day. When the sun stood still. In the Book of Joshua."

Behind them, another bump and another giggle. Above, Joshua—sword dripping blood, the slain army at his feet.

Doc scanned the fresco back and forth for a full minute, then stopped and took five steps forward, leaning to examine something he'd seen.

"What is it, Doc?" Lan said. "Coins?"

"No. But this dead soldier, look what he's holding."

The man in the painting lay sprawled and bloody, blank stare cast skyward. Falling from his outstretched, lifeless hand was what appeared to be a small sack.

"The bag?" Paradise said.

"Yeah, exactly. That looks identical to the leather sack we first found the coin in."

"So?" Lan said. "It's a sack. No coins or anything. What could it mean?"

"It's open. And angled downward. Look at the crack in the rock below it. As if any contents might have fallen out and through the crack ..."

"So whatever we're looking for might be hidden in the crack of a rock somewhere?" Lan said.

The thump and laugh came again, and Doc turned back, scanning the floor. "Leena, where are our spies hiding?"

The floor gapped slightly under the front pew, revealing the tops of two heads and four bright, brown eyes. Another giggle, and the trap door fell shut.

"There's your answer. Basement. These little guys have this place wired. A regular miniature Mexican CIA."

Doc looked at the open sack on the wall again, then back at the trap door. "There's a basement?"

Leena nodded. "Yes. It's not open to the public anymore. In fact, it's been sealed off for more than two hundred years. It's kind of morbid actually. But the kids slip in and out through a crack in a boarded window. Usually on a dare. Or to spy, obviously. It's harmless."

"The sack is open right above the crack in the rock. Like whatever was in it slipped down below. Can we see the basement?"

"I suppose so. But the only way in big enough for an adult is through the trap door. We'll have to move the pew. I've only been down there once, years ago, when they moved the pews for some renovation."

Doc waved. "C'mon, Lan. Help me move this thing."

In the end, it took all four of them to move the heavy wooden bench.

Leena pulled the trap up. "There's a ladder. C'mon down." She started her descent.

Two boys stuck their heads through a side door of the sanctuary and laughed, then ducked back out, letting the door shut behind them. The same lurkers from the basement, no doubt, publicizing their escape. Sofia giggled and chased after them with a squeal that echoed in the big room.

Paradise watched her leave, then followed Doc and Lan down the ladder.

True to the rest of the ancient church, the basement offered floor-to-ceiling murals. These, however, spoke no comfort to the observer. A chill washed over Paradise as she turned in a slow circle.

"See what I mean by morbid?" Leena said.

"Are these things in the Bible?" Paradise's voice sounded forced, even to her own ears.

"Uh huh. That's Stephen being stoned—Apostle Paul is standing by with the coats in his arms. He was *Saul* then, though. There's the ground opening and swallowing disobedient Israelites. Remember that? And this one's pretty gross, Jezebel being eaten by dogs after she fell off the wall. Good old King James, warning—adult content. No one ever said the Bible was rated G. You can see why the kids dare each other to come down here."

Doc moved to the wall that would have been directly beneath the sanctuary platform and the Lost Day mural. "And this one?" he asked.

"Ezekiel's bone yard. The Valley of Dry Bones. That's Ezekiel with the beard. The angelic looking figure behind him is God, both giving and explaining the prophecy."

"And over here, these are bones rising up and coming to life?"

"That's the idea. But this one's another mystery. The guy in the back that doesn't match, see him? The priest? He's rumored to be Father Salazar, the Jesuit, who first came here to build Mission Del Dia Perdido. If you look close, you'll see he's handing gifts to children. He was known for his kindness and loving demeanor. Of course, the artist had to go and paint the children half skeletal, which is spooky."

Sparse light from cracks in the boarded windows made the painting difficult to see. Doc leaned down for a closer look.

"What happened to Father Salazar?" he said.

"Oh, Father Salazar's a big deal! He became a local legend. Still is. A saint in the minds of the people. The story goes that he never really died, but God took him up in a ball of flame. Kind of like an Enoch thing. They call him *El Fantasma* around here—the ghost. Supposedly, he leaves gifts—candy, coins, little toys— for good children while they sleep. Kind of a Yucatan Tooth Fairy. They have a parade every year in his memory."

"So he disappeared?" Lan said.

"The truth isn't so exciting. He's buried out in the old cemetery. It's back in the jungle a few hundred yards down a dirt track. Nobody goes there anymore. Doc, why do you ask about him?"

Doc straightened and turned. "Because the gift he's handing that little guy there? Two gold coins. And we're right below the empty leather sack. I bet Salazar's the key. He has to be. And he's standing in the middle of a biblical graveyard. Leena, you say nobody goes to the old graveyard?"

"Not that I've ever heard. There's a new one now. In town. Although even that's a hundred years old. It's much closer."

"So Salazar's grave is completely isolated unless you go looking for it?"

"Uh huh. Which nobody does."

Doc smiled. "This may be a long shot but, Lan, you and Easy feel like helping me dig up a Spanish priest?"

Lan grinned back. "I'd be lying if I said I haven't done stranger things."

CHAPTER FORTY-SEVEN

Dancing in an Alternate Universe

Hollister sipped his *Negra Modelo* and considered his wife over a shadowed corner table at the open-air Vieja Cabra café.

Clean clothes tonight? Sure, they were still workout clothes, but clean nonetheless.

Quiet, too. No burping or humming disco tonight. No *moron* or *old man*.

All very un-Crystal. It rattled his nerves.

The temperature was almost bearable. Not cool but close. They'd arrived with the sunset, and now the place had completed its metamorphosis from restaurant to full-blown bar. A sombrero-topped man about five years older than the nation of Mexico sat on a stool in the corner, singing and playing guitar along with an electronic drum machine.

"Is that guy singing 'Material Girl?'" Hollister said.

Crystal stared absently out toward the night. "Yeah … Madonna."

Weird how tropical moonlight could make out-of-tune, broken English somehow sound good. A few tourists and ex-pats shuffled to the rum-soaked rhythm on the tiny dance floor.

Crystal's detachment unnerved him.

"What's eating you?" Hollister said.

"Nothing."

"You're not hungry? You haven't eaten all day."

She pushed a plate of tamales toward Hollister. "You eat 'em. I don't want the MSG."

"What MSG? This is the middle of the jungle. They never even heard of MSG here."

"Not organic. High in fat. Gross. Smelly. Looks like a dead fish. Fill in the blank. Who cares, anyway?" She rubbed her eye with the hard heel of her hand.

"Are you crying?" *Yeah, very un-Crystal.* "What's with you, man? What's going on? You're starting to freak me out."

A big tear rolled freely, and she didn't try to hide it this time. She faced him. "Why didn't we ever have kids?"

Now, this WAS *The Twilight Zone*. Hollister glanced around for the hidden cameras.

Sombrero Methuselah finished with Madonna and began a fresh round of musical abuse—"Living on a Prayer" by Bon Jovi.

"Are you serious? You and me? What are you talking about? We're the last people who should have kids."

"Why? You don't think I'd be a good mom?"

If ever there was a loaded question …

"Are you saying you'd *want* to? Wait a minute … Is this a serious conversation? Knock it off. We can barely stand each other."

"Those kids at the orphanage. I picked 'em up and everything. I shoulda broke that stupid Simmons' neck for calling them snacks. They're so cute and happy! And that lady, Leena? She wasn't bad. Something about her reminded me of Sister Jan from the orphanage. I don't know; maybe there's more important things than the cage. Anyway, don't be a moron, moron."

"More important things than two people trying to murder each other in the name of entertainment? That's something I never thought I'd hear come out of your mouth. This is absolutely insane. Listen to yourself. Who are you tonight?"

"Shut up, Hollister. Don't act like you don't remember the way it used to be. You know who I am. It's just been a long time. Besides, you'd be a good dad, even if you *are* older than dirt."

How long since she'd used his name? It sounded strange.

"Me?" An exasperated sigh escaped him. "Crystal, what are you talking about? What is this?"

"Here's what I'm talking about, moron; let's have a baby."

She might as well have punched him in the face. Or hit him with a bat. Or kicked him in the crotch. In fact, all of them at once would've at least been more Crystal-like—instead of a let's-have-a-baby nuclear bomb exploding in his face. This conversation was already weird, but the word "baby" shoved it out of the spaceship and into plain old alternate universe territory.

"Wha … What about *old man? Moron? Soft? Stupid?* And worse! What about all that? Now suddenly you want to have a baby? Out of thin air? You're yanking my chain."

Crystal shrugged a shoulder. "It's not out of thin air. It's the kids. Listen for once and get over yourself. I don't mean those things I call you. Well, maybe I mean them a little, but mostly I just like to watch the back of your neck turn red. It's cute." She absently scratched an armpit. "C'mon. Have a baby with me."

The look in her eyes ... Something he hadn't seen in years.

Or maybe hadn't wanted to see.

Or maybe *had* wanted to see ...

It all scared him way more than normal Crystal crazy.

Something inside shifted and softened a fraction. "Crystal, look. A baby's serious business, you know? It ain't something you take lightly. It ain't a toy. Or a dog. It needs a mom and dad to actually take care of it. Ones that love each other! You of all people should understand that. Think back when *you* were a kid. Look at us! It takes time to make a decision like that."

"*You* look at us. You don't think we love each other? Why do you think I stuck around all these years? And I *have* taken time. Ever since this afternoon."

Hollister leaned forward. *I gotta get a hold of this.* "Let me spell it out for you, okay? A—You're crazy. B—You dance around and sing all the time, and not in a normal way, in a weird way. C—You burp half the things you say. D—You like to hit things. E—You're crazy. F—You're nuts ... What else? I could go to Z and start backward again. It's not a short list! You think I love that? You get more whacked by the minute."

Crystal leaned forward and squinted.

Is she deaf?

"That's crap, moron. All that stuff is exactly *why* you love me. C'mon, let's have a baby."

Hollister reflexively put his fingers to his temples and started to rub, but stopped short.

The headache was gone.

"Wait, did you just say you loved me?"

Crystal dug in her ear with her ring finger and made a show of watching the dancers. "Actually, I didn't come right out and *say* it."

"But you do. You're telling me you love me now. *You.* Crazy Crystal."

Crystal's eyes rolled. "What are you talking about? Why are you making a big deal out of it? I tell you all the time."

"No, you don't."

"In my own way ..."

"Your own way—like a right hook? Or a body shot?"

"Yeah. Love taps. But only you, you know. Never a kid. 'Cause that's not what moms do."

"Is this why you got dressed up tonight?"

"What an old man. You want me to say it? Fine. 'Cause I love you. And I loved the way you told Simmons off. Even the way you kept me from killing him. And then how you didn't kill him either 'cause the gold wasn't in there, and you still want the other forty grand. See? I love everything about you. Including your dumb, red neck."

Hollister stared. Blood throbbed in his temples. Crystal reached over the table, put her hand on his, and grinned her pointy-toothed shark grin.

Years with this woman but the thought came, a tidal wave over long-frozen ground. Blame it on the Yucatan night, or the bad music that sounded good, but yeah, he remembered … she was beautiful.

"This is crazy," he said.

"Shut up, moron."

For once in his life, he did.

Crystal gulped and swallowed air. "Let's have a baby," she burped.

A dam broke in Hollister. *The Twilight Zone?* Yeah, but who cared? He remembered love. "Yeah. Okay, why not? Let's have a baby."

Sombrero Guy switched the drum machine rhythm and started a chipper, mariachi rendition of "Stayin' Alive." Crystal's eyes lit.

Hollister shook his head. "The answer's no, so don't even start. This guy's killing me. Did you tell him to play that? Do I look like John Travolta?"

"Ask me."

"Ain't gonna happen."

"Ask me."

"What did I just say?"

"Ask me."

"Geez … Geez, all right! You wanna dance? Like all the other stupid tourists? You happy now?"

Crystal reached over and grabbed a tamale. She stripped its husk, ate half of it in one bite, and washed it down with a gulp of Hollister's Modelo beer. "Yeah, baby. I'm happy. Let's boogie."

Chapter Forty-eight

Riding Stars

A couple of dogs on the beach barked and yipped, and that started the jungle howling. The sound sent a tingle of fear through Paradise's legs.

"Howler monkeys," Lan explained. "They sound scarier than they are. Actually cute little guys."

Howling monkeys, birds screeching and singing, the constant, never-ending whine of locusts—the jungle rang with life though the sun had long since retreated.

Fifty yards from shore and safe on the Lazarus. Thank you!

"*You're welcome,*" Jesus called from the cockpit.

Paradise rolled her eyes.

Lan had invited Leena for dinner, but she'd needed to stay with the children at the mission and politely declined. Sofia, however, occupied a chair padded with a stack of sailing magazines, a Chapman Piloting manual, and a 1994 Key West phone book for added height. She occupied the head of the table with queenly command. Her dark, serious eyes reflected the deck lights above as she surveyed her subjects with graceful benevolence.

Easy had whipped up a simple meal on the grill. Chicken and fresh vegetables provided by Chuey's sister.

"So how long do we wait?" Lan said. "Curiosity's killing me. Do you really think something is in that grave?"

"I wish I knew," said Doc. "But two coins missing from the Judas mural, the same leather sack pointing down, Father Salazar in the fresco below in a graveyard with the two escudos coins. May be wishful thinking, but I think it adds up. Salazar would have been long dead when the brothers arrived. The grave would've been accessible."

"Or, like the locals say, he's still alive. Sneaking around the village leaving treats for kids," Lan said.

"Don' talk like dat, boss," Easy said.

"Relax, amigo. I won't let the boogie man get you."

"That's another thing that got me thinking," Doc said. "Most legend is born in some fact, or perceived fact, right? For some reason, a story formed around here over the years that Father Salazar isn't really down there, or at least not all the time. Either way, it's worth a look. Leena suggested midnight at the earliest. Shouldn't be any prying eyes around then. We definitely don't want to rock any boats. The locals won't take kindly to somebody digging up the bones of *El Fantasma*."

Easy put a hand to his forehead. "Midnight! You just asking for trouble, mon. Hey, Easy, dey say. Why we don' go dig up a dead mon's bones at midnight? Be fun, don' you tink?"

Lan laughed. "We'll put 'em back! You remember Aruba, don't you?"

Easy groaned, stood, and began collecting empty plates and glasses. "You all a bunch of crazy white people." He headed for the door and dropped down into the cabin with his load.

"He's superstitious, but don't let him kid you. He wouldn't miss it. Why don't you two entertain future Miss Universe here while I go help with the dishes?"

"Thank you, Lan," Paradise said. "Everything was wonderful."

Lan patted her shoulder. "Everything usually is, sweetheart. Don't you forget that." He scooped up an armful of dishes and headed for the galley whistling.

Paradise leaned back and took in the blanket of stars. "He's right, you know."

"Everything's usually wonderful?" Doc said.

"No. Sofia. She's beautiful."

"Yeah. She is. And so are you."

Paradise looked at him. "Stop, Doc."

"And everything *is* wonderful," Doc said.

"Burt's out there somewhere. He's close. I can *feel* him."

"He's not gonna hurt you."

"Maybe he'll get eaten by howler monkeys."

Doc laughed. She realized she liked the sound of it. When had that happened?

"Keep your fingers crossed," he said.

Doc reached for her hand. So strange the way their hands looked, flesh intertwined. Hers delicate—nails painted pink. Pale skin stark against his, so brown and strong.

She traced a fine white scar running down his index finger. She would miss this man.

He *was* that—a man.

"You could, you know. Tonight. With the smell of the jungle. And the lights. With all these stars—you could," she said.

"I could what?"

"Talk me out of it. The movie. Los Angeles. Everything. But only now. Only here. Right now, you could talk me into anything."

His expression hardly changed, but his shoulders dropped a fraction, and his gaze went to the sea. "No, I couldn't."

"Why do you say that?"

"Maybe I could, but I wouldn't. When you walked into Shorty's that night, life changed for me. I won't hide it—*haven't* hidden it. It was like someone had hit the pause button on my life when I blew my knee out. Then you started it again—pushed play. It was life but *more*. Louder. More colorful. More *alive*. I'm not here to solve some puzzle. I don't care about a treasure. I've already found it. I'm just trying to protect it."

Paradise pressed into her chair. Everything spun. Too much. Too close. Why couldn't she keep her mouth shut?

Paradise Jones, Lazarus, Yucatan Peninsula, Mexico, Earth, Universe.

"*What do you want, Paradise? Think now,*" Jesus called from the cockpit.

"Don't interrupt. It's too confusing!" she snapped back silently.

"You're you," Doc said. "Dreams, clothes, the way you see things, your way of jumping subjects that makes me crazy—all of it. You're you, and your dreams are part of it. To try and change it wouldn't be love, and that's the thing—I love you. So no, I wouldn't talk you out of anything. You go be who you are, and I'll love you because that's who I am."

"You know all the wrong things to say, you know that?"

"Jake always tells me the same thing."

"You'd hate it. Los Angeles, I mean."

"Probably."

"You don't care?"

"Not even a little."

"Still ... Oh, stop it, Doc. What are we talking about?"

What was she thinking? *None of this is real! You're drunk on starlight and ocean. His laugh. The way he smells. Get yourself together! It'll all be over tomorrow.*

"*Will it?*" Jesus called.

"I just can't think," Paradise said.

"I don't want to upset you. That's the last thing … " Doc stood and picked up Sofia. "I'm gonna give this girl a tour. Sí, señorita?"

Sofia giggled.

Alone on the deck, Paradise made her way to the cockpit and leaned against the ship's wheel.

Truck Stop Jesus smiled.

"Oh, what now?" Paradise said.

"*We have to stop meeting like this.*"

"Amen to that, brother."

"*Ha! I get it—amen … So, do I have to ask?*"

"No. You know what I want. But he'd be miserable, wouldn't he? Doc? In Los Angeles?"

"*No. He'd be with you. He'd be with me.*"

"You? You're in my head," Paradise said.

"*At the moment. But I see your heart. It's softening.*"

"I'd never see him, anyway. I'll be working night and day."

"*That's true.*"

"You're not going to try to talk me out of it? You're Jesus, right? Why don't you just snap your little plastic fingers and change my mind?"

"*Would you want me to?*"

Paradise surveyed her hands on the wheel. Delicate, pale pink nails … All the parts yet incomplete somehow. Doc's hand missing … "Maybe …"

"*Love, unless it's freely given, is no love at all. Look up. Look at those stars. Wild and free like me! Unbound and unchained. Sure, I could snap my fingers. I could speak a word and shift time and space. I paint sunrises with my fingertips. I ride stars through the sky. But I want your love, daughter. I want it freely given and joyfully received. I'm waiting for you to come home.*"

"Daughter?"

"*Yes.*"

Lan's head appeared in the salon doorway. "It's time, girl. You ready to crash a bone yard?"

It took a second for Paradise to pull herself from her heart to the present.

"Am I interrupting something?" Lan said.

"Oh, no. Just daydreaming."

"Good. Time to ride."

His enthusiasm was contagious, and a thrill touched her. "Ready when you are, skipper."

CHAPTER FORTY-NINE

Play That Funky Music White Boy

Hollister's head spun. For not being John Travolta, he'd done a passable job. Better than passable. Play that funky music white boy ...

If I don't say so myself ...

They'd danced to the magical sounds of Sombrero Man till Hollister's legs began to turn to rubber, at which point Crystal had suggested they return to the room and begin the baby-making process posthaste, if not sooner.

Closing the bungalow door behind them, he'd told her she was beautiful. She'd shark-tooth grinned and sucker-punched him in the gut. *Ah, true love ...*

Now his wife lay next to him in a tangle of sweaty sheets and post baby-making bliss.

And Hollister was in love again.

He stood and walked to the window, looking out at the dark jungle. What a trip, man. He whisper-sang his best Louie Armstrong. *What a wonderful world ...* Yeah, a wonderful, cool, trippy, headache-free world. Amen and pass the biscuits, what could he say?

How could this have happened? Who cares? Don't ask.

Crystal gave a loud snore.

So she was nuts. So what? *He* was nuts. The whole world was nuts. Maybe between them, they'd have a halfway normal kid. Anyway, somewhere between the dance floor and the lumpy bungalow bed, he'd made a decision. He'd be a great dad or die trying. Shoot, make it two kids. Five. Ten! Bring 'em on.

His cell phone buzzed, and Crystal stirred.

He grabbed it. Simmons ...

"Yeah?" Hollister said.

"You sleeping?"

"What d'ya want? Take us out on the town with all your new pesos?"

"They're here. And they're on the move."

"Who, the girl?"

"Of course, the girl, you idiot. One of Sammy's cousins called when they went to the church today. I've had someone watching them ever since. They were in there forever, then they came out and walked around an old cemetery."

"And you think they figured it out? The treasure? You think it's in the cemetery?"

"I have no idea. If I did, you think I'd be talking to you now? But I had them followed. They're staying on a boat at some dumpy marina. But right now, they're on the move again. This time of night they must be going after the gold. It's the only thing that makes sense. Meet us out front of the hotel. And bring the gun."

"I gave it back to Sammy."

There was a muffled conversation on the other end of the line.

"Okay. Sammy still has it in his truck. Just c'mon."

Hollister considered blowing the good doctor off and suggesting what he could do with the gun, but curiosity reared its head. What if there really was gold? Even a little? After all, he was going to be a dad. The responsible thing to do would be to explore the option. Raising a family could be expensive. At least, that's what he'd heard.

"I ain't shooting nobody. Let's get that straight," he said.

"Okay, whatever. Just get a move on."

"Neither is Crystal."

"Look. Just get your butts out here. Forget the gun. I'll use it myself if I have to."

"One more thing. I'll help you look for the gold, but I'm done with the girl. You're on your own on that one."

A pause. "Then I want my money back."

"How about if I break your legs instead?"

"For crying out loud, Hollister! Whatever! Keep the money, just get out here! I need a show of force."

"Yeah. Cool. See you in three minutes." Hollister thumbed off.

Crystal sat up, burped, and rubbed her eyes. "Who was that?"

"Simmons. The girl's here. They're going for the gold—right now."

"Well, they say private schools are expensive."

"They do. But only the best for our little ankle biters, right?"

"More than one?"

"Why not?"

Crystal stood and pulled her workout clothes on.

"You're beautiful," Hollister said.

"Shut up, moron." She laughed and swung for his ribs, but he blocked the shot with a quick elbow.

"Let's go get rich," Hollister said.

"Rich, rich, leave Simmons in a ditch."

Chapter Fifty

Go Big or Go Home

Doc maneuvered the car by the light of one dim headlight and a full Caribbean moon. Chuey's battered Olds needed shocks, and the back roads of the Yucatan jungle reinforced that fact. In the rearview mirror, Lan and Easy came a foot off the seat as the car nailed yet another pothole.

"Sorry," Doc said for the hundredth time in the last three miles.

Lan rubbed his head. "Let the lady drive, would you? You drive like you played ball, all or nothing."

"Go big or go home," Doc said.

"You're gonna have to skip the graveyard and take us straight to the hospital," Lan said.

"Don' tink so, boss. We be dead by da time we get dere," Easy said. "Jus' dig a hole and bury our poor broken bones."

"Paradise can't drive anyway. She's carrying precious cargo." Doc glanced down at Sofia, sound asleep in Paradise's lap.

"How anyone could sleep through this is beyond me. I feel like I'm in a B-52 dodging enemy fire," Lan said.

Doc looked up at the mirror again. "Listen, ladies. Quit whining, or I'll hit the next one on purpose."

Doc parked next to the prefabricated dorms that backed the mission property. He exited the car and walked to the passenger door, lifting Sofia gently when Paradise handed her to him. The little girl didn't stir.

"Out like a light," Doc said.

"It's been quite a night for her. I doubt she's ever done anything like this before. I'm glad Leena let her come," Paradise said.

Leena met them at the door. She reached for Sofia, but Paradise asked if she and Doc could put her to bed.

Leena led them to a room full of bunks and sleeping children and a handful of volunteer staff.

Doc stared. "How many do you have here?"

"Just over a hundred," Leena said. "These are the younger girls. You know the crazy thing? I love every one of them."

"It would be hard not to. I'm sad just bringing Sofia back. I miss her already," Paradise said.

"Visit any time! They'd love it. Especially Sofia."

Doc laid the tiny girl carefully in her bunk. She stirred slightly and reached for a stuffed lion, pulling it close.

Paradise opened her mouth as if about to speak, then shut it again.

"Hey, they have airplanes, you know. Especially for movie stars," Doc said.

"I suppose ... She's just so precious. They all are. I wish there were something I could do for them."

"They do have a way of changing a person's perspective," Doc said.

Paradise arranged the blanket around Sofia one last time and kissed the little girl on the forehead. At the door, she thanked and hugged Leena.

"You're welcome," Leena said. "Like I said, the cemetery's isolated. No one will bother you out there. Just let me know what you find. The curiosity's killing me! And make sure you leave everything the way you found it. Oh, and if you get caught, I'll deny ever knowing you."

Doc laughed. "Point taken. Don't worry."

Back in the Olds, Doc maneuvered the car down an overgrown path into the jungle behind the mission. After a half-mile or so a limestone wall rose up in front of them. Night noises pressed in as he killed the engine.

"Three hundred years, give or take, since the brothers were here. If they even *were* here. This is wild," Doc said.

The four of them climbed out of the car.

"It's quiet, mon," Easy muttered. "Just jungle noise. We all alone out here. It ain't good."

"We need to be," Doc said. "I don't imagine the locals would look kindly on us tampering with their tooth fairy."

Lan opened the trunk and handed out shovels and crowbars, as well as a flashlight for Doc and a lantern for himself. "Let's get to it," Lan replied. "And we'll put it all back just like it was when we're done. No harm, no foul. Lead the way, Doc. See if you can find the grave."

An opening that might once have held an iron gate led to a worn, gravel path winding through a tight maze of low, mounded graves and above-ground mausoleums, eerie and pronounced in the soft moonlight. Doc switched on the flashlight.

"Dis ain't good, mon," Easy repeated from the back.

"Settle down, tiger. You'll be fine," Lan said.

"It's a full moon, mon! Don' you watch the movies?"

Doc felt Paradise's hand grip his arm. Toward the back of the ancient graveyard, his flashlight beam came to rest on a small, very worn tombstone.

Lan read aloud, translating the Spanish engraving, "Padre Fernando Salazar – Keeper of the Lost Day."

"Keeper of the Lost Day," Doc said. "No dates, just that."

Lan lit the lantern and set it on the stone. "Shall we, boys?"

Father Salazar's grave lie capped with a large rectangle of stone, offering no markings other than a beveled edge. The three men started in, crowbars chinking against the hard surface.

Doc's mouth felt dry, and sweat ran down his sides. This was it! If only Jake and Paco could be here.

"Dis is all tings unholy rolled into one," Easy mumbled.

"No souls here but ours. Just bones," Lan said.

"Jus' bones, he say. Bones is bad enough, believe me."

Doc wiped a drop of sweat from his nose. "We need to be as careful as possible not to leave any marks. Try to work the bar into the lip."

Lan strained against his bar, biceps bulging. "So we can skip the gym today."

"Everything you've got, on three. Ready?" Doc said.

Lan shifted his feet for better purchase. "Yeah, count it off."

Doc counted. All three men grunted with the effort. A scrape of stone against stone. The heavy lid moved an inch, then a few more.

Lan stuck the end of his bar in and was rewarded with a dull *chunk* sound.

Easy stepped back. "You hear dat, mon? Something under dere for sure. Ain't no six feet down neither."

Doc pushed his own bar in and received the same sound.

"Only about a foot under. Feels like more stone, maybe," Doc said.

Another few minutes of straining, and the three men were able to move the stone lid completely free of the grave. Paradise picked up Doc's flashlight and shone it at the hole. Another flat, stone surface slightly larger than a coffin lid lay at their feet a foot beneath ground level. This one ornately carved.

Easy's eyes shone in the lantern light. "What *is* dat? Two lids? Dis can't be good."

"A monument, maybe? Or some kind of sarcophagus?" Lan said.

"It's all in Spanish. What does it say?" Paradise stood beside Doc.

"*La Dia Perdido*—The Lost Day." Doc worked the words, lips moving. "And underneath, *Holy God the Father, Author of All*, or something close to that. Look at the carving. It's a sun in the sky, and these two round things ... I wonder if they're supposed to be the coins?"

Lan knelt and swept some earth from the lower part of the stone. "*El Hermanos Montejo*. Your brothers, Doc."

Doc remembered the breastplate and bones in the sandy wash behind the baseball field. It seemed like a year ago. All this history tied directly with his home. How many nights had he lain in the old Airstream while the armor wearer's remains rested just a few hundred yards away, waiting to reveal long-kept secrets to the blue sky? Now here he was, very possibly a couple of feet away from the answer to a three-hundred-year-old riddle.

Doc poked around the edge of the second stone with his shovel. "Look. There's a lip. I think this thing is another lid."

"Oh, mon! Here come da bones," Easy said. "Ain't you never heard stories? Dis when da crazy guy come and kills you."

Doc strained, using the bar as a lever. "Get in here. Let's see if we can move this thing."

Easy and Lan mirrored Doc's effort.

Scrape ...

"It moved. Keep going," Lan said.

The slab broke free with a loud creak and slid back, leaving a four-inch gaping crack on one edge.

Doc grabbed a flashlight and shone it into the hole. "I can't see anything." He inserted his bar and lowered it a couple feet without touching anything. Setting down the light, he dropped to his knees and took hold of the lid, straining. Lan and Easy joined in. With effort, the three of them lifted the slab and set it aside.

"It must have had some sort of seal holding it in place." Doc took the flashlight from Paradise and shone its beam into the hole.

This can't be real.

"You've got to be kidding me," Lan said.

In the hole at their feet, a set of stone stairs led down into the earth.

"Very deluxe condo for a dead guy," Doc said. "Even a priest."

"No way, mon. I ain't walkin down no bone yard stairs." Easy crossed himself.

"Why're you crossing yourself, Easy? You're not even Catholic," Lan said.

"Dat's stairs in a bone yard, mon! You can't be too careful! I'll be Catholic, Baptist, whatever I can tink of!"

"We've got to go in," Doc said.

Easy shook his head, held up his hands, and took a few steps back. "Ain't no *we* about it, mon! I'm staying up here with da living people! Least what's left of dem."

"Why don't we wait for daylight, Doc? It *is* creepy," Paradise said.

"We can't. We've come this far. We need to have this thing covered back up by daylight. I'll check it out. You all wait here." Doc knelt and pointed the flashlight down the hole but saw only more stairs.

Oh, well, one step at a time.

The stairs descended at a steep angle, and by the fourth step he had to duck to keep from hitting his head on the edge of the grave—if it was a grave. To his surprise, the narrow stairway didn't stop a few feet beneath the ground. He counted ten steps. Then twenty.

"You all right, Doc?" Lan called.

"Yeah. It's deeper than I expected."

"What's down there?"

The Green Monster ... "Still going!" Doc called back over his shoulder.

At thirty-one steps, the descending corridor ended at a flat stone floor and opened into a cavern roughly the size of his Airstream's interior.

Not what he expected.

A low, limestone table stood against the far wall—maybe an altar of sorts, with three stone arches carved into the wall above. The center arch contained a mosaic—Joshua's Lost Day. Benches, polished smooth from use, were fashioned along the native stone into the sides of the room.

What was this place?

Doc approached the altar, painting it with the beam of his flashlight. A solid block of rock. He scanned up, examining the mosaic. Rusted iron framed the piece. *Why? Why not just build it into the rock?* Doc stepped in for a closer look.

He ran his fingers up the frame's right side and found a hollow spot in the rough metal. A quick exploration of the left side of the frame confirmed his suspicion.

Hinged ... The whole mosaic was a door. He slid his fingers into the hollow spot and tugged.

The mosaic pulled easily, revealing inky blackness beyond.

Chapter Fifty-one

Semantics

Smoke.

The stars shook. The night closed in. Strength fled, and Paradise felt sure she'd crumble to the packed earth beneath her—another body for the bone yard.

Smoke. The unmistakable scent of the thin, Spanish cigarettes ingrained in her memory since childhood.

The tiny orange glow hung suspended in midair just outside the reach of the lantern light. It brightened as he inhaled. Then dimmed again.

Then they stepped out of the undergrowth and into the lantern light. Four of them. Burt, Hollister, Crystal, and a thin Mexican man.

Burt exhaled a long stream of smoke, then smiled. "Nice moon tonight, isn't it? Bright. Didn't even need our flashlights. Long way from Malibu, isn't it, Paradise?"

Paradise opened her mouth to reply, but no words came out.

"You must be Burt," Lan said.

Burt stopped smiling. "Come here, girl. Time to end this nonsense."

Lan shifted, then froze when Burt produced a massive pistol.

"Stay where you are, Willie Nelson," Burt said.

"What you want me to do, boss?" Easy spoke low.

"Just stay back for now," Lan replied.

The thin Mexican man took a step forward. "Señor Simmons, please, I never meant …"

"Shut up, Sammy. Did you think I was just talking? Wanted this gun for shooting cans?"

Paradise forced her fear down. "Burt, please don't hurt anybody! They didn't do anything to you."

"Other than kidnapping my precious little girl, you mean? Hey, I'm not unreasonable. You know me, right? I'm your father! I just want my girl home, safe and sound." Burt dipped the barrel of the pistol toward the opening in the ground. "Plus whatever gold is in that hole. Then you and I can go back to Malibu happy campers, and your pirate pals can go back to sailing the Seven Seas or whatever it is they do."

Deep inside Paradise, anger began to edge out fear. "Are you crazy? You tried to rape me! Then blamed me for it! You had your hands on me my whole life. And not the way a father should. In fact, you *ruined* my life! You should be in jail!"

Burt shrugged, lowering the pistol to half-mast. "Semantics. What's your boyfriend doing down there anyway? Why's he taking so long?"

"You could go down and find out," Lan said.

"Ha! No, thanks. Why do you think we waited till now to join the party? I don't do heavy lifting. And I don't crawl around in graves in the middle of the night. Wouldn't want to get my suit dirty, right? What do you think, Hollister? You want to go down and get the gold?"

Hollister spoke, his voice low gravel. "I want my other forty grand. That's about it."

"What do you mean, your forty grand? I told you I'd pay you when you brought my daughter back."

"There she is."

"Tell you what. I'm feeling generous. Go grab her, and it's yours."

"Nope."

"Nope? I thought you wanted the money."

"You said you'd pay me when I found her. There she is—found."

"Let me get this straight. You won't walk twenty feet to get her, but you want me to pay you?"

"Pretty smart for a wine guy. Bring ... find ... semantics, right? I'll go you one further. You hurt her, or even touch her again, and I'll break your back over my knee."

Simmons shifted the gun toward Hollister. "You're an idiot, you know that?"

Hollister didn't flinch. "And you're a perverted scumbag."

"Scumbag." Crystal burped the word loud into the night.

"What's wrong with you two?" Burt said.

Crystal took Hollister's hand and grinned. "We're gonna have a baby."

"Are you crazy?" Burt said.

A *thunk* sounded from the grave hole.

"Careful, Doc. We have visitors out here," Lan said.

Doc's head emerged from the hole. "So I hear. I wondered if they might show up."

Burt leveled the pistol at Doc's head. "Okay, Romeo, you come on up now."

Doc came up four steps and stepped out of the grave carrying a metal box.

"That's it? The gold?" Burt said.

"Nobody ever said it was gold the brothers had. Maybe they had something else on their mind, other than getting rich," Doc said.

"Ha! And I'm Pancho Villa." Burt lowered the heavy pistol again. "Don't get ideas—it's here if I need it. Geez, Sammy, you people couldn't have fought your revolution with lighter artillery? Now you walk the box over here, Romeo."

"Or?" Doc said.

"I've never killed anybody before. I'll admit I'm more than a little curious. Either way, shoot you or not, I still get the box."

"It's not worth your life, Doc," Lan said.

"I won't argue with you there." Doc took several steps toward Burt.

"That's far enough. Set it down."

Doc knelt and set the box on the ground.

Burt waved the gun barrel. "Now get back over there."

Doc returned, eyes searching Paradise's face. "Are you all right?"

She blinked hard, but tears still threatened. "No."

"I won't let him hurt you. I promised, and I meant it."

"He promised?" Burt said. "Really, Romeo, you've forgotten who has the gun. But, I'll make your promise good for you. I won't hurt her. Even though the little tramp hit me, totaled my car, cost me forty thousand dollars to chase her halfway around the world—"

"Eighty," Hollister said.

"Shut up, Hollister. Please! I swear I'm camping with knuckleheads here! Even after all that, Paradise, you little freak of nature, I'll make my word good to your boyfriend. *I* won't hurt you." Burt glanced back at Crystal. "Crystal? Go ahead and slap her around. And don't take it easy."

Crystal picked a fingernail. "Nah."

Burt's eyes narrowed. "Excuse me? Did you say *no?*"

Crystal didn't bother to look up. "Nah. Negative. No. Not gonna happen. Never. No. Nope." She punctuated her sentence by burping the word "scumbag" again.

"Leave it, Simmons. Open the box, and let's see what's inside," Hollister said. "Don't look like there's a lock."

Burt took a few steps forward and pushed at the object of curiosity with his toe. "Yes, the mystery box. The one thing we all have in common here tonight, isn't it? We all want to know what's in the box. Why not? Everybody wins—unless you're getting shot—which some of you are. What a night, eh? We get to see behind curtain number one. I have my lovely tramp of a daughter back. Hollister and Crystal are looking forward to the birth of their three-eyed bundle-of-joy. And then there's the happy, happy fact that I'm holding the only pistola in Dia Perdido ... Yes! I'm feeling righteously magnanimous." He glanced at Hollister. "That means *generous* to you beer people. Open the box, Hollister. I'd do it, but my hands are tied up with Sammy's grandpa's bazooka."

Hollister shrugged, bent, and worked the lid of the small chest. Getting a grip, he grunted and pulled, biceps bulging through the arms of his T-shirt. It released with a popping sound and Hollister stumbled back, catching himself with an arm. The thin Mexican stepped forward, shining a light into the open cavity.

"What the ...?" Hollister said.

Burt emitted a grunt. "That's not gold, is it?"

"No, it ain't, genius. It's some kind of old book. And it looks trashed. Moldy. Probably got wet sitting down there in the hole for a million and one years." Hollister reached in and lifted the relic out, holding it up in the light.

"It's a Bible. That's what the brothers were hiding. It makes sense," Doc said.

Burt shook his head. "A Bible? Are you kidding me? Why would they go to all that trouble to hide a Bible? Makes sense how?"

"They were spiritual men. It must have had value to them. Historical relevance. The Catholic Church went to all kinds of lengths to protect relics they thought were important. This must have been one of them." Doc took a step forward.

"No, Romeo! No!" Burt raised the pistol. "You stay right where you are! Are you saying this thing might be valuable?"

"I doubt it. Not water-damaged and covered with mold. I think we have to be content with finding the answer to a three-hundred-year-old puzzle. Something worth dying for, to the Montejo brothers."

Burt shifted his arm an inch and fixed the pistol on Paradise. "Then they were idiots, just like all *you* people. Paradise, come on. Time to go. We have a date. I'm going to get *something* out of this trip."

Paradise squeezed her eyes shut. *Please make this stop …*

"*Paradise …*" The voice both foreign and familiar.

"You're not here. You're back on the boat. You're in my head."

"*Forget the doll, daughter. I'm always here. Do you trust me?*"

"I don't know if I can. I'm scared."

"*I know. What do you want?*"

Burt's nasal whine shoved in. "Earth to Paradise. Stop being a freak for five seconds! Move! *Now!*"

"*What do you want, Paradise? Answer me now. No more waiting.*" The voice came from everywhere. The stars, the moon, the night air moving through the jungle trees, the grass below. It rose from the earth and echoed out of the empty hole at her feet. So much comfort and longing.

"I want to be safe!"

"*Done.*"

"I want to be loved …"

"*Done.*"

"I don't want to be alone. I don't want you to leave me."

A gentle laugh on the breeze … "*I never have. I never will. I'm your home—where you've always belonged. Do you trust me?*"

Ice broke. Rivers ran. Old, old water that had forgotten the touch of the warm sun on its surface.

Paradise Jones. Graveyard. Yucatan Peninsula. Balanced on a wire between the Gulf of Mexico and the Caribbean Sea. Planet Earth. Universe …

Paradise Jones … *Loved.*

Paradise Jones … *Home.*

Paradise Jones … *His.*

"Paradise," Burt said. "I'll shoot you between the eyes, so help me. You've got nowhere to go and nothing without me. Look, come home and live with me in Malibu. Make your movies. I'm the only one that can make the charges against you in California go away. I'm it! I'm the lifeline. Without me—no movies, no money, no anything, do you understand?"

"What's wrong with you?" Doc said. "You're married to her mother. Leave her alone."

"You call Eve and I *married?* She's in some rehab somewhere. I don't even know where. And she didn't even have the courtesy to tell me about it herself. Had the lawyer do it."

"She's not going," Doc said.

"Fine, she stays. But she stays *dead*." Burt squinted an eye as he aimed.

"Wrong," Hollister said.

"Wrong," Crystal burped.

"Shut up, hillbillies," Burt said.

Something glowed in Hollister's hand—a phone. A thin, electronic voice sounded in the Yucatan night. Burt's voice … *"Handsy? First of all, she's my stepdaughter, not daughter—so get your mind out of the gutter. Good schools, clothes, vacations—I own her. Get it? Besides, she practically begged for it that night. My wife was stone-cold passed out on the couch as usual. I'd had a few greyhounds myself. Just enough to get myself feeling loose and good. So I went into the pool house and—good timing—she was changing. Sending all the signals with her body but pretending that insipid innocence of hers, just like when she was a kid. So I told her what time it was. She could pony up, or I'd cut her off. Her choice. Then she had the gall to hit me with a lamp, as if we weren't two consenting human beings. If she says I forced myself on her, so what? My property, my money, my way. Besides, she's nuts. And it's her word against the most respected psychiatrist in LA."*

"What is that?" Burt demanded.

"Amazing gadgets, these iPhones," Hollister said. "Even a beer guy like me can figure these little suckers out. So can the LAPD. In fact, they already did, just as soon as I sent this to them. Wanna celebrate over a nice merlot, *Doctor Simmons?*"

"Okay, Hollister. So you're not as stupid as Crystal looks. But I still have the gun, and the last I heard in paper-scissors-rock, gun beats iPhone. Get over there with the rest of them. You too, Sammy. You never did bring that cousin of yours, and I don't trust Mexicans anyway."

"Don't shoot her," Hollister said.

"Get over there or Crystal is bullet number two! Six! I have six! That's one for each of you freaks! Do what I tell you!"

The three did as instructed.

Burt took a step forward and waved the massive barrel. "Now, Paradise, you come with me or, so help me, I'll shoot you in that pretty face!"

"Do you trust me?" the stars whispered.

"Yes. What do you want me to do?"

"Tell him no."

She squared her shoulders. "No, Burt."

"No? Did you say *no*? Do you have any idea how many years I've waited for this night to come?"

"Yes. I know exactly how many."

Burt's knuckles whitened, and his hand shook. His eyes widened, white against the flush of his face. He cocked the pistol, and Paradise's insides turned to water.

"Stop," Doc said. Stepping in front of Paradise, he walked toward Burt with purposeful steps.

"Back off!" Burt shouted.

"You said I could trust you!" Paradise whispered.

"Always."

"Then save Doc? Please?"

"Ah, child. I did that a long, long time ago ..."

The sound of the giant pistol echoed off the moon and rattled birds from their nests. Howler monkeys screamed.

The shot was the loudest thing Paradise had ever heard.

CHAPTER FIFTY-TWO

Jimmy Buffet and Pieces of Junk

A hospital, Sammy called it, but the Centro Medico in Dia Perdido didn't inspire much in the way of comfort or hope to the ailing—or to the waiting. A gray metal reception desk stood sentinel over the minuscule waiting room. The space offered all the comforts of home, providing your home had peeling green walls, dirt-crusted industrial tile floors, and was furnished with a scattering of hard, orange, plastic chairs—one with three legs.

Is this shock? Paradise took a mental and physical survey of her faculties. Only numbness. Totally numb. "He's been in there forever."

"Relax, princess," Crystal said. "It'll be cool. These docs down here in Mexville got all kinds of stuff that's illegal in the States. They can do crazy things. Rebuild him like Frankenstein's monster. Me and the old man might even have our kid down here if I get a bun in the oven. Right, sweetie?" She looked up at Hollister, who sat next to her. He sighed and put an arm around her.

Easy sat at the reception desk, swiveling in the chair and flicking a peso back and forth between his long fingers. "I don' know, mon. It don' look good to me. And I seen a few shot guys before. I tink he gon' die."

Lan leaned against the wall, big arms folded. "That's enough, Easy. Why would you say that?"

A short, thick Mexican man wearing a Jimmy Buffett T-shirt and a police cap banged open the swinging door that led from the inner-sanctum of the hospital. As he limped into the waiting room, he said, "Thank you for waiting. Gun injury, sí? I'll need to get a statement from each of you."

"Chuey? You're a cop, too?" Lan said.

The officer grunted a laugh. "I get that a lot. Chuey's my twin brother. I'm Officer Sanchez. But you can call me Poppy. Everybody does. Chuey's good for nothing but tequila and dominoes. Funny guy, though. Makes me laugh. Did he tell you the one about the nun and the elephant?"

"Uh huh. That *was* funny," Lan said.

Poppy scanned a clipboard. "Which one of you is Doc Morales?"

Paradise squeezed Doc's hand.

Doc returned the squeeze. "I'm Doc."

"You're the guy he tried to shoot?"

"Sort of, I guess. I'm the guy that got in the way."

"Why did he want to shoot you?"

"'Cause he's a scumbag," Crystal said.

"Scumbag?" Poppy echoed.

"I'd say that's about accurate," Doc said.

Poppy stuck his pinky in his ear and scratched. He took it out, glanced at it, and wiped something on his pants. "Then you'll be sorry to hear ... Dr. Ortega says your scumbag will live. The wounds are mostly surface. Lots of blood, though—man! Sammy, what were you thinking, loaning the guy that piece-of-junk pistola?"

"I thought maybe he was gonna shoot cans?" Sammy said.

Poppy wagged a finger at Sammy. "I should arrest you, you know that? Always in trouble. You're lucky you're my cousin."

Sammy's sad eyes fell to the pistol in his hands, the huge barrel blown to shreds. "You think it can be fixed?"

"You're just lucky nobody got killed, amigo. You should throw that thing in the ocean," Poppy said.

"What will happen to Burt now?" Paradise said.

"Ah, yes, Dr. Simmons. I spent the last hour on the telephone with the Los Angeles Police Department. Just like television, eh? NCIS or something. They have a warrant for Dr. Simmons for attempted rape. Not just yours either. Three of his female patients came forward with similar stories when they saw him on the news. We'll send him back eventually, but first I'm going to arrest him for discharging a firearm in a cemetery. Plus making a pass at my sister."

"Your sister?" Hollister said.

"She's a waitress at the cafe over at Viejo Cabra."

"Ha! No kidding? That's your sister?" Hollister said.

Poppy chuckled. "To be honest, who cares about the pistola? But make a pass at my sister, and you spend a nice long vacation in *carcel Mexicana* with the nasty people. Dr. Simmons will be praying to Jesus, Mary, and the saints for a transfer to Folsom Prison the first day. Johnny Cash, yes? Great song! You know what?

Never mind about statements. I'm tired. How does this sound? Dr. Simmons-the-scumbag illegally discharged a piece-of-junk pistola—loaned to him by my *stupido* cousin, Sammy—in the old Spanish cemetery. The pistola blew up in his face because it hasn't been fired since Moses was a baby. Dr. Simmons-the-scumbag is wanted in the United States for attempted rape and will be transferred there at such point of time in the future that I feel like filling out the paperwork, which almost I never do. The end. You like it?"

"Hit the nail on the head," Doc said.

"Amen and pass the salsa," Lan added. "Can we go now?"

"*Excelente*! Sí, adios, you're free to beat it. I'll see you soon, amigos." With a salute, Poppy exited the same door he'd come in.

A bedraggled lot they were, standing in front of the Centro Medico on the empty main drag of Dia Perdido in the early morning glow.

Paradise couldn't help but smile.

"You're all sure?" she said. "The Bible goes to the Mission Dia Perdido?"

Nods and grunts of agreement all around.

"No joke? That thing's actually worth something?" Hollister said.

Doc nodded. "I called my brother. He's an expert on church relics and historical finds. Sent him pics. The Lost Day Bible—cleaned and professionally restored, we could be talking hundreds of thousands of dollars. Even millions."

Hollister gave a low whistle. "Maybe I'm having second thoughts."

"It's for the kids at the mission," Crystal said.

"Yeah, oh well. Eighty grand ain't nothin' to sneeze at. And a free second honeymoon."

"Honeymoon," Crystal burped.

"I thought you only got forty thousand so far. How're you gonna get the rest?" Doc asked.

"Let's just say I know a guy who knows a guy. A guy with long arms. Reach all the way to a Mexican jail. We'll get the money."

"So ... so ... suck your toe ... all the way to Mexico," Crystal sang to the tune of "Jive Talkin'."

The soft, new sun slanted through the buildings, lighting the pastel stucco. The rattle of doors and windows opening floated across the cobbled street as a café owner threw a fresh fleece before the gods of business. He hissed and shooed a skinny dog with his broom.

"I don't know about you all, but I could go for a cup of joe," Lan said. "Breakfast on me?"

"Yah, mon. Maybe Father Salazar show up. Doc says his bones ain't down dere," Easy said.

Lan slapped the deckhand on the back. "You never know, buddy."

The group started across the street, but Paradise grabbed Doc's arm, holding him back. "Doc ..."

"Hey, you don't have to say anything. You're safe now. And free ... Time to make a movie, Miss Scarlett. You know someplace in Hollywood I can park an Airstream trailer?"

"Why, Doc?"

"What do you mean, why? Because I have to live someplace."

"No, why did you walk at Burt like that? He would have killed you if the gun hadn't blown up in his face."

Doc brushed a strand of hair from her cheek. "But it did. You really have to ask? After all this?"

"I would have lost you ... Doc, do you really love me? Really? You don't just feel sorry for me? Or feel like you have to rescue me?"

"I have your back, Paradise Jones. Like it or not."

A bell clanged, wheels rattled, and a donkey cart fashioned from a box mounted to an old car axle rocked past. The hunched driver clucked and coaxed in the universal beast-of-burden language.

Paradise watched him move up the street, heart in her throat. "I'm not going back, Doc."

Doc's mouth opened slightly. "Not ... Why?"

She reached for his hand and traced the scar on his index finger with her own. "Because there's nowhere to park an Airstream in Hollywood, and a girl needs her comforts."

CHAPTER FIFTY-THREE

Three Months Later ...

The sun judiciously retired behind the jungle tree line, but its glow still kissed the sky as patio lights strung through the *Lazarus'* rigging flickered to life.

Paradise watched the show while strains of Sinatra drifted up through the boat's open hatches.

Truck Stop Jesus gave the thumbs up. *"You're beautiful."*

Paradise smoothed the front of the sequined dress. "Is it too much? Sammy's cousin made it. You're sure I look okay?"

"I didn't say you look beautiful. I said you are beautiful."

"Oh."

"And you look beautiful."

"A girl wants to, you know. On her wedding day."

A low wake from a passing fishing boat bumped the hull, and Jesus bobbled. *"Are you nervous?"*

"I wasn't until you said that! Now I have butterflies!"

"I know. Don't you love them?"

"Yes, I kind of do."

Jesus' head slowed. *"So, Paradise Jones, we've had a ride, you and I."*

"Yup, ever since that truck stop. I'm glad I bought you."

"Nope. Since before the foundation of the world, I'm glad I bought you."

"Me too."

"What do you want?"

Paradise reached a finger and gave the Bearded One another wobble. "Everything I already have. I'm so happy."

"You know how long I've waited to hear that?"

"I think I do."

"I think you do, too."

Paradise leaned on the rail, her gaze on the jungle across the harbor. "It's not over, is it?"

"What's not over?"

"The ride."

"No. It's never over, daughter. When these heavens are all a distant memory, it'll still just be starting."

"Good …"

Lan stepped out onto the deck, resplendent in his tux. "You ready, girl?"

"Yes. I'm glad you're walking me, Lan. It means a lot."

"It means a lot to me too, Princess. I'm very honored."

Doc never looked as handsome—or as nervous. They were married in the salon, standing in roughly the same spot Clive Granger and Madaline Lemieux exchanged vows some seventy years prior.

Jake stood as Doc's best man. Hollister as a groomsman.

Tattooed and bouffanted, Ashley smiled from her position as maid of honor.

Crystal insisted on being a bridesmaid. She wore Nike cross-trainers and a purple, spandex sheath dress that showed the slightest baby bump. She and Hollister had rented a tiny casa down the road from the Mission Dia Perdido and volunteered there on a daily basis. Hollister complained constantly about the heat but never quit smiling. Crystal had promised not to burp any words during the wedding but claimed the reception would be a whole different pony-ride.

Sofia dropped flower petals as Paradise crossed the salon.

Others had gathered in the floating chapel. Chuey and Poppy practically identical—both wore clean shirts. Sammy sat ramrod straight, impeccable in his suit and slicked black hair. He didn't flinch when Crystal called him a daisy.

Leena had become a good friend. Even inviting Paradise to room with her at the mission and help with the children.

Eve had arrived in Dia Perdido two weeks earlier. She'd spent long hours on the deck of the *Lazarus* talking with Lan. One day, she'd surprised Paradise with an invitation to visit the Mayan ruins at Tulum. *Surprise* turned to *stunned* when, standing on a pyramid, Eve had hugged her for the first time in her life. After the embrace, Eve broke down crying, and Paradise held her for a long, long time.

Paco, ever the gentleman, performed the wedding ceremony. He claimed he'd known he would all along.

The kiss was long. No one minded, so they kissed again.

A crowd gathered on deck. The mayor of Dia Perdido, a few fishermen—new friends and old. Jake made a speech, then danced with Ashley. Lan clinked a glass, then stood on the rail, hand on a cable stay for balance. "Friends, I'm not much for speeches, but I'd like to say this: Other than Easy, I've never really had a family. Well, I do now. And I couldn't be happier. Doc, Paradise, this is for you." He put his fingers to his lips and gave a shrill whistle. At the sound, every boat in the marina, along with the harbor office, shacks along the shore, the café, and even the jungle at the edge of the beach for a hundred yards in each direction lit up with a million white twinkle lights.

Paradise put a hand over her mouth. "Lan! It's beautiful. The best wedding present of all time!"

"Fit for a star." Lan grinned. "And you are one, on screen or off. I have something else for you, though." He handed her an envelope.

Her fingers trembled though she didn't know why. "What's this?"

Lan waved a hand around. "It's the title, Princess. To the *Lazarus*. She's yours. Yours and Doc's."

"Ours?"

"Why, Lan?" Doc said. "No, we couldn't. This boat's a part of you."

"Sure it is. Always will be. But like I said, we're family now. And I've been at sea a long, long time. I want to stay in one place for a while. Tell you what— consider it a trade. I'm going to head back to Arizona with Paco, and I'm going to need somewhere to land. You know, drink coffee without spilling it. On a floor that doesn't move around. I've always been partial to Airstreams."

"You've got a deal," Doc said.

"With your permission, though, I may come sailing once in a while. And Easy still needs a job."

"He's got one. It wouldn't be the same without him."

Paradise hugged the old man. "I don't know what to say, Lan."

"Just say thanks."

"Okay, thanks."

"You're welcome. Anyway, Doc's been living on this tub with Easy for the last three months while I've been enjoying townie life. He practically owns her already." Lan grabbed a mainstay for support, hoisted himself up on the rail and turned to the crowd. "Now let's dance, everyone!"

And they did. Long into the night.

CHAPTER FIFTY-FOUR

A Shoreless Sea

Much later.

The sun had completed nearly an entire circuit and now lurked beneath the eastern horizon of the Caribbean Sea.

Paradise turned on the bed. Doc lay beside her, his head propped on his hand.

She reached out and touched his nose with the tip of her finger. "We have to change it, you know."

He grabbed her fingers and kissed them. "Change what?"

"Clive plus Madaline equals Our Love is a Shoreless Sea. It should say Doc plus Paradise now."

"We have time."

"Will you miss it, Doc? Baseball? Always?"

"Yes."

"Do you care very much?"

"No. Will you miss acting?"

She sighed and lay back on her pillow. "No. I don't think I will. Actually, not at all."

"Not even being famous?"

"Do you love me?"

"You know I do."

She pushed herself up on her elbow, facing him. "Am I famous to you?"

"I'm your biggest fan."

"Only fan."

"Okay, only fan."

"Well, only *earthly* fan."

"All right ..."

"Then that's enough."

He kissed her. "I have a wedding present for you."

"You mean, other than saving me from my crazy stepdad, smuggling me halfway around the world, and marrying me on a huge sailboat which we now own?"

"Yeah. Other than that." He flipped a coin at her. Gold glinted in the air.

Paradise plucked it off the sheet. "My father's coin? How did you get it?"

"Take a closer look."

"It's different. It doesn't have the Spanish words on the back. Why?"

"Because it's an unaltered eight escudos coin. The real deal."

"Okay ... Where did you get it?"

"In Father Salazar's grave."

"What? But you found the Bible in there ... You never said anything about coins."

"*Gold* coins. And nobody ever asked. We put the grave back together before Poppy got there, remember? Then everyone just forgot about it."

"Except you."

"Uh huh. Except me. A couple weeks later, I took Easy and Lan, and we went back."

She held the coin up. "I'm almost afraid to ask ... Was there more than this one coin?"

"Oh, yeah."

"How much?"

"Enough that it'll completely restore the old mission in Paradise. Enough that the kids at Dia Perdido will never want for anything. And even enough in Lan's old smuggling hole down there that our great-grandchildren will still be spending it when they're old and gray, provided we don't give it all away."

"Will we? Give it away?"

Doc shrugged. "It's just money. I already hit the lottery the day you walked into Shorty's."

Paradise flopped back. "You wouldn't stop looking at me. You were so obvious."

"I still won't."

"We're rich."

"Uh huh."

"I don't mean the gold."

"I know."

The day shone bright and hot by the time they tumbled out onto the deck. Doc shirtless in cargo shorts and Paradise opting for her Esther-dash-Williams-dot-com two-piece.

Doc handed her a cup of coffee and whistled.

"Esther Williams," Paradise said.

"Nope, Paradise Jones," he said.

"I love it when you say that."

"I know."

"That's why I said *Esther Williams*."

"I know."

"But it's Paradise Morales now."

"And I love it when you say *that*."

Paradise sipped her coffee. "So now what, Captain?"

"Did you know there's a little island south of here that has a baseball field right in the middle? They live for it down there. The Majors even scout the place."

"Seriously? The whole world is out there, and you want to go watch baseball?"

"You know what they say …"

"It's like chess on grass and dirt?"

Doc leaned over and kissed her. "Exactly."

"That's the millionth time you've kissed me today."

"I know."

"Don't ever stop."

"I won't"

"Promise?"

He kissed her again. "Cross my heart."

"On that island, is there a Green Monster?"

"There's *always* a Green Monster."

This time she kissed him. "Then let's go sailing, Doc."

58457397R00205

Made in the USA
San Bernardino, CA
29 November 2017